My Warrior's Heart

When Jorund fell, Aaren seized his arms and pinned them to the sides of his head while she straddled his stomach.

"You now have a wolf at your throat, Jorund," she said in a half growl, sliding back on his stomach just enough to lower her face to his. "Beg for mercy . . . and she may not eat you."

She tightened her thighs against his sides, wringing a moan of pleasure from him.

"I've never been eaten by a wolf before," he said thickly. "Is it terrible?"

"You're about to find out." Then she slid lower on him and nuzzled his bare neck. And she bit him.

"One bite?" he demanded with a growl. "That's all I get?"

"If you want more, Jorund . . . you'll have to work for it."

Other Avon Books by
Betina Krahn

BEHIND CLOSED DOORS
CAUGHT IN THE ACT

MY WARRIOR'S HEART

BETINA KRAHN

AVON BOOKS  NEW YORK

For Dors and Regina Maynard
and Marvin and Arline Krahn
With love and gratitude

MY WARRIOR'S HEART is an original publication of Avon Books.
This work has never before appeared in book form. This work
is a novel. Any similarity to actual persons or events is purely
coincidental.

AVON BOOKS
A division of
The Hearst Corporation
1350 Avenue of the Americas
New York, New York 10019

Copyright © 1992 by Betina M. Krahn
Cover illustration by Roger Kastell
Inside cover author photograph by Scott Amundson
Published by arrangement with the author
Library of Congress Catalog Card Number: 91-92449
ISBN: 0-380-76771-6

First Avon Books Printing: August 1992

AVON TRADEMARK REG. U.S. PAT. OFF. AND IN OTHER COUNTRIES,
MARCA REGISTRADA, HECHO EN U.S.A.

Printed in the U.S.A.

RA   10   9   8   7   6   5   4   3   2   1

Author's Note

My *Warrior's Heart* is set in the late Viking era, in southern Sweden. Little is known of the "Swedish" Vikings; they left little record, and few sagas tell of them. But archaeological evidence suggests they were much like their Danish, Norwegian, and Icelandic counterparts. It is believed that much of their raiding and trading carried them "Eastway," up the Dnieper and Volga Rivers, to the Baltic and Caspian Seas, and all the way to what was known as "Byzantium." They are known to have traveled and raided westward, in the Frankish lands, as well.

What *has* been documented of the Swedish Vikings reveals a hardy, robust people who clung stubbornly to their own ways of doing things. They retained their patchwork organization of "jarls" and clans well after the Norwegians and Danes had begun (however reluctantly) to consolidate power under kings. They also retained the old religion of the Asa gods longer than their western counterparts. But for all their resistance to change, they were astonishingly tolerant of the new religion; belief in the Asa gods and burgeoning Christianity coexisted for a long time in many Swedish villages. Many were willing to give the new faith a chance as long as the "White Christ" brought them good harvests, good trapping, and good trading. In times of hardship, the converts were quick to call upon "Red Thor," Odin, Freya and the rest of the Asa gods once more.

In the early days, Christianity had many faces among the northmen; and the tenor and substance of the new faith were dependent on the views of the individual priests and missionaries (sometimes captured in raids) who taught and lived it. As portrayed here, it was often the influence of a converted jarl or clan chieftain that brought about the conversion of a village. The baptism of a jarl into the faith of the White Christ was usually followed by the baptism of his family and his villagers.

Vikings are often portrayed as either great heroes or vile barbarians . . . in truth, they were both and neither. It is my belief that they were simply human, capable of the full range of human experience; cruelty and kindness, boldness and cowardice, brutishness and nobility. It is also my belief that in every age, in nearly every society, there have been those like Jorund, who learned the hard lessons of violence and sought a more humane ethic of living . . . otherwise humankind would have progressed little since its beginnings.

And on a final, personal note, it is my belief that there is both a *warrior* and a *woman-heart* in each human being . . . and that to be fully human we need both in our lives.

Prologue

The night was moon-bright and as chilled as the depths of a frost giant's cave. Four cloaked figures made their way slowly down a treacherous mountain path and paused on a rock ledge overlooking a dark, silent forest. Far below, beyond the forest and extending into the distance, lay a vast silvery expanse of water, the great lake Väner. One of the figures raised a gnarled hand and pointed to distant specks of light on the jagged line where forest and water appeared to meet.

"There it is," came the old man's rasping voice. "The village. Even as I remembered. When we arrive at the hall, I shall go in first . . . alone." He turned to look at the moon-paled faces of his three daughters. The two young ones nodded and he turned to the third.

She stood motionless, staring at those ethereal lights which seemed to move and change with each blink of the eye . . . lights which meant an ending . . . and a beginning, at least for herself and her young sisters.

"Are you ready, daughter?" he said, laying a hand on her arm.

Ready? To take up her life-task and fulfill her destiny? She looked down at her young sisters and for one tumultuous moment wished they could all go back in time; back to their mountains, back to their log hut in the meadow, back to the simple life-ways they had once shared. As soon as she thought it she recoiled from that fleeting longing, naming it weakness, and she focused on the old man's face, nodding.

They started off again, descending into shadows cast by the restless, whispering trees. And with each step, she heard the old man's question drumming in the chambers of her heart.

Ready? Are you ready?

As she moved along the narrow path, her mind filled with old images and sensations, which crowded out the sounds of owls hooting and the rustle of leaves in the autumn-dry forest around her. Suddenly she was in their small log house once more, tussling and giggling with her little sisters before the fire . . . then lying on her back in the summer meadow, filled with the scent of ripe grass, searching the puffy clouds for a glimpse of the gods and goddesses who lived in the heavenly Asgard . . . then, holding the lifeless body of the little forest cat she had raised from a kit, with tears burning down her cheeks. One by one, she began to lock those remembrances away.

With each step she took, she sealed away another part of her old life, and another bit of her softer nature, behind an impenetrable wall. There would be no place in her new world for softness. *And since that was the way of things in the world of men . . . there must be no softness in her.*

Chapter One

There was no leader among the clans of the Norsemen who celebrated victory-luck with more vigor than did jarl Borger Volungson. The ale-feasts in his long hall endured for days, filled with manly contests, hard drinking, and the distribution of the spoils of conquest. But the rout which followed his victory over his neighboring jarl, Gunnar Haraldson, was especially noisy, and the ale flowed especially freely . . . for Borger and Gunnar had long been at odds.

On that blustery autumn night, Borger's long hall was filled with smoky torchlight, the din of raucous voices, and the smells of pungent ale, pork grease, and male sweat. The huge roast boar lay a heap of bones, picked clean and sucked dry, and three barrels of ale lay drained and splintered . . . victims to rapacious thirst and a head-butting contest between two of Borger's men. The sinewy, drink-loosened frames of the jarl's warriors sprawled over the benches and planking tables which ringed the hall, and behind them, along the wall benches, lolled the male villagers who held a place in Borger's hall. Their attention was trained on the center floor, where two warriors wrestled savagely on the hard-packed dirt, their greased bodies heaving and straining.

Old Borger, called Borger Red Beard by many, sat in his great carved chair on the upraised wooden floor at one end of the hall, a drinking horn in each hand and a ruddy glow on his broad face. He lived and ruled his clan as a warrior, shunning the soft trappings of his acquired wealth and clinging to the fierce and simple credo of the warrior: fearlessness, pride in his own strength, and the certainty that might makes right. He dressed as his men did, in a sturdy woolen tunic and breeches, a leather jerkin, wrapped leggings and sandal boots, and he led them by example in the customary manly pursuits: fighting, drinking, and wenching.

As he sat on his great high seat, watching his men wrestling and contending for his favor, his shoulders twitched and his body jerked, responding to their moves, fighting with them in his very heart and sinews. From time to time, he leaned forward to shout encouragement:

"Bite his ear off, man . . . he's got another!" and "Fight hard—I grant spoils to the victor!"

The warriors strained and grunted, fingers gouging, legs flailing . . . until one levered on top of the other, catching his opponent's neck in a crushing hold that soon rendered him motionless. When they were dragged apart by their drunken comrades, both still had their ears, and one had a reward to claim for his prowess. The victor staggered before his jarl and was granted a boon. He wanted a woman . . . a specific woman.

"Dagmar, the thrall woman," he proclaimed loudly, ignoring a feminine squeal of outrage from the back of the hall and the sound of a pitcher crashing against a post.

"The little dark-eyed Dane?" Borger rubbed his ale-soaked beard with a rough hand, contemplating both the request and the stringy young warrior before him. "She'll chew you up and spit you out, boy."

"I plan to take her to wife," Hrolf the Younger declared, then added with a lusty growl, "and do a bit of 'chewing' meself."

Borger gave a hoot of laughter and slapped his thigh, sealing his judgment. "Spoken like a true warrior! Take her then, Hrolf the Younger. And the Red Thor preserve you!"

But as the victor stalked and captured his brown-eyed prize at the back of the hall, and carried her off to her pallet in the thrall house, protest was raised among a group of young warriors seated near Borger's high seat. "Hrolf gets a woman of his own? Why should he get a wife?" and "By Hel's gate, I drew more blood than he did this day—"

Borger turned his craggy head and fixed a hard look on the brash young warriors whose features bore the fierce stamp of his own. "A thrall woman, even one like the Dane, is no fit wife for the son of a jarl. You need women with hearth-skill . . . women who will weave strong sail-cloth and bear strong sons," he declared with an edge to his drink-coarsened voice. "Wait until that toothless old boar, Gunnar Haraldson, pays the ransom for his heir. There will be a hoard of silver to make wife-bargains for you." He raised his drinking horn.

"To Old Gunnar! May he sprout grass on his stubborn arse and be grazed to death by goats"—he flashed a wicked leer about him—"but not before he pays us *ransom!*"

Laughter and shouts of *"Sköl!"* reverberated through the hall as all raised their horns to drink his toast. Soon the hall was filled with noise and revelry once again.

Borger thrust back in his high seat with a drink-sated air of satisfaction and surveyed his domain with pride. His hall was larger than most, built with massive oaken timbers harvested from his own forests and adorned with fine carvings wrought by his own craftsmen. At its center was a great circular stone hearth, large enough to roast a whole ox at a time . . . perhaps the largest in all of Värmland. As his steely eyes scoured the hall, he noted the number of male faces present with features cast in the mold of his own, and felt a stirring in his chest.

It was gratifying to see how tenaciously his manly seed had taken root. Having numerous sons ensured there would be many tales told of him around many hearths after he died in battle and was carried off to Odin's Great Hall, Valhalla. But his pleasure dampened as his gaze fell on the great, strapping warrior he had taken as a prisoner the day before, now chained by the door of his hall . . . old Gunnar's heir. There was but one thing his longtime rival possessed that Borger coveted, yet could never take from him: a worthy heir, a son with true Viking cunning in his heart and a proper Viking battle-lust in his blood.

Though Borger had a goodly number of sons, he did not have, to his way of thinking, a satisfactory heir to his high seat. Jorund Borgerson, his eldest living son and presumed heir, had many of the qualities required to rule as jarl in a Norse clan . . . but ferocity and cunning were not among them. And without a bold lust for fighting and a healthy dose of treachery in his heart, Borger was convinced, a man didn't last long on a Norse high seat.

The celebration continued with dancing, knife-throwing, leg-wrestling, and when the ale-mist in the revelers' senses grew too thick for such skilled pursuits, they took to their benches and heard the savage saga of King Erik Bloodaxe, recounted by an itinerant skald known as Snorri the Loud. Borger was taken with Snorri's tale . . . especially the bloody, heroic sound of the king's name.

"Bloodaxe . . . Bloodaxe . . ." he mused blearily, tilting yet another horn of ale in honor of Snorri's word-skill. He tried that savage epithet with his own name— "Borger Bloodaxe"—anticipating how it would ring around campfires and winter hearths someday when his fame was all that remained of him in earthly realms. "Or maybe Strongaxe . . . or Hardaxe . . ."

The doors to the hall banged open just then, and the chilled north wind blew a cloaked figure into the hall. When those nearest the door turned to protest the icy invasion, they spied a stranger in the long dark cloak and flat, wide-brimmed hat, and their complaints softened, then died upon their lips.

Curiosity rippled through the hall as the stranger came forward into the flickering torchlight, headed straight for Borger's high seat. Those brave enough or deep enough in ale-mist to peer beneath that hat glimpsed a hoary beard and two age-paled eyes that bulged and burned with a strange and haunting light. The visage and stooped shoulders spoke of many years and the slow, deliberate approach to the high seat spoke of bold purpose. By the time the stranger stopped before old Borger, the noise in the hall had begun to quiet and those whose wits were not already drowned by drink watched the jarl and the stranger with interest.

A worn, somewhat raspy voice issued from beneath the hat. "Greetings, Red Beard."

"What manner of man is it that greets me so?" Borger responded with a bleary squint.

"A man who has borne your name in battle," came the voice. "A man who has drunk victory ale in your hall and spilt his blood in your service."

Borger tried to rub the ale-mist from his senses so that he might see the old man more clearly. "You sailed a'viking with me?" he demanded. "Then, by what name did I call you, old man?"

"By the name I was given at birth," came the reply. "Serrick." For a moment, all was silent as Borger scowled with puzzlement, scratched his woolly red beard, and shifted from one meaty buttock to the other on his hard seat. *"Serrick,"* the stranger prompted. "Sword-stealer."

The name rumbled about in Borger's head and dragged across the rusty strings of his memory. He suddenly straightened as if jabbed and jerked forward, eyes widening. "Serrick Sword-stealer? The warrior who captured the sword of Ibn Hassadan . . . when I sailed 'Eastway'—over the world to Byzantium?" Recognition suddenly burst in his mind. "By the Red Thor's Beard! I thought you slain and in Valhalla years ago!"

An odd, crusty sound that passed for a laugh rumbled from old Serrick. "Not in that glorious hall yet, jarl. I was left one viking season to heal of injuries and your village grew too small for a man used to wide-wandering. I took me into the mountains, on the far north range of your lands." His voice grew grave and hushed. "There I lived"—he drew a sweeping arc above him with a gnarled hand—"among the clouds formed by Odin's breath and under stars bright as sparks struck from the forge of the black dwarfs . . . amongst the wild and sacred meadows where the goddess Freya grows her flowers and the groves where the fabled Idun picks her golden apples. There I lived, beneath the earthbound step of the rainbow bridge of heavenly Asgard, and daily glimpsed the Guardian's face."

With each claim, old Borger's jaw loosened more and his shoulder muscles bunched tighter. There was something odd about the eyes beneath that flat, broad-brimmed hat, something which, combined with those bold words, brought Borger's drink-dulled senses to full alert. The Serrick he remembered of old had far less word-skill than this strange, withered hull of a man. He rubbed his head in confusion and squinted at the old fellow from the corner of one eye.

"What brings you from the very portal of the gods to the hall of Borger Red Beard after all these years, old man?"

"A debt," Old Serrick replied hoarsely, shifting his feet, broadening his stance.

There was a rumble of drunken consternation among Borger's men and he lashed an order for silence at them. Drawing a deep breath, he shoved forward in his seat and demanded: "What debt, old man? Do you now come to claim a share of spoils long spent . . . from a voyage long past?"

Again a rusty chuckle came from that hoary head. "*Nej*, jarl. I have not come to collect a debt, but to pay one. Years ago, I had no silver to pay the freeman's tax. And through the years, the debt has mounted. A score of years, jarl Borger . . . still owing."

Borger's combativeness melted instantly, replaced in the same measure by a crafty, wide-growing grin. The old man spoke of paying him! Silver? Gold? Perhaps the old wolf pelt had found riches in the far mountains of his realm. . . . "This is a grave matter, Sword-stealer." He covered his eagerness with a frown. "No man may take sustenance from my land, drink my water, hunt my game, and cut my timber without paying just tribute."

"Ahh . . . but I have done you service, jarl, guarding the north reaches of your realm . . . remembering your name to the north wind in winter and the singing brook in summer," Serrick responded, watching the aging jarl closely.

"The north wind owns no silver and spins no silk . . . nor do mountain brooks run full of Frankish wine," Borger objected, dismissing such poetic service with the wave of a brawny arm. He had always been one to honor the gods and the forces of nature, but never at the expense of profitable human commerce. "If all of Midgard sighed my name, there would still be mouths to feed and backs to clothe, swords to forge and sailcloth to buy."

"You have not changed, Red Beard," old Serrick said, giving the jarl a calculating look. "Except that now there is hoarfrost in your beard . . . and in your welcome. You do not even offer a stranger a horn of ale . . . in hospitality."

Borger stiffened. Lack of hospitality toward a stranger was a most serious charge among the clans of the Norsemen. The hair on the back of his neck began to prickle anew at the strange appearance and manner of the old man who claimed to be his brother in battle. The gods were believed to assume mortal shape, now and then, to walk amongst men, testing the generosity of a jarl or chieftain. Borger fidgeted on his seat as he scrutinized that felt hat and the unusual eyes staring from beneath it. The Allfather, Odin himself, was known to wear a wide-brimmed hat as a disguise among men. . . .

"Ale!" he bellowed, loudly enough to awaken several warriors dozing nearby. "Bring a mead-foaming horn for an old warrior . . . a comrade in battles past."

Serrick's face creased with a gap-toothed smile as he accepted the ale and downed it in the fashion of a true warrior: drinking it all in one breath. Then he lowered the horn and sighed heavily, wiping a trickle of ale from his beard with his sleeve.

"Now of this debt I have come to pay," he said, shoving the empty horn back at the thrall who had served him. "Twenty years of tribute, jarl. And though I have no silver . . . you will be well paid."

Serrick stalked back through the crowd to the open doors of the hall. He beckoned to someone beyond the doorway and soon had two cloaked figures in hand, escorting them through the press of revelers to stand before the high seat. All craned their necks to see as he pulled the hoods from two heads, and sounds of astonishment rippled through the throng.

They were women . . . young and flaxen-haired and fair as summer. When the old man dragged the rest of their cloaks from them, all were stunned by the sight of willowy curves and slender white arms, wrapped in linen tunics with fine, pleated sleeves and soft woolen kirtles that draped gracefully from a carved brooch at each shoulder. Their garments were expertly stitched and bound with colorful red-woven braid that bore testimony to their skill with dye-pot, loom, and needle. But it was their faces that drew the eyes of every man in the hall. Such fresh and comely faces; delicate ovals of pale cream skin, inset with eyes as blue as summer sky and lips the color of ripe berries.

Borger thrust to his feet and slammed his drinking horn to the floor with a flourish. His gaze narrowed on that twin vision of beauty. "What is this, old man? A trick of some kind?"

"No trick, Red Beard. It is your payment . . . in woman-flesh." Old Serrick's tone bore a hint of pleasure and when Borger turned to him, he was smiling. "These are my daughters . . . maidens, untried by men. I bring them in payment of my tribute to you. They will be yours, to do with as you please." He paused, then added with a canny smile: "Upon two conditions."

Borger swallowed hard, sending a hot eye over the lush swell of the maidens' breasts and the promising curves of their hips. His face flamed crimson and his throat was caught hard in the grip of lustful anticipation. He could manage only one half-growled word.

"Mine?"

"Yea, Red Beard . . . if you accept the terms." Serrick watched his old jarl closely as he laid forth the conditions. "Though given in payment, they are to be free women. Will you agree?" Borger nodded, his mouth watering, his hungry gaze fixed on the flush of their fair cheeks and the soft, arousing lines of their nubile young bodies. "And you, Red Beard, will not take them to your own furs . . . nor ever pierce them with the spear of your flesh. Do you agree?"

That stopped Borger short. He sputtered and glowered, while raucous excitement broke out in the hall. If Borger himself could not mate them, all realized, then the maids would be available for his sons and warriors! Around him a drunken howl went up, demanding that he agree. He hitched about and lumbered back to his chair, throwing himself into it with a furious scowl, while his men crowded closer, shouting and ranting at him. He glared and muttered and fumed, knowing that in the end he would have to consent to the old man's terms. His sons needed women . . . and from the fierce looks and words they were hurling at him, there was a good possibility they would slit his throat if he refused. He finally bashed his haranguers aside and rose, glaring at old Serrick.

"These be your daughters, you say? What proof have you?"

All quieted, straining closer to hear. "None but their loyalty to me. And the story of their making. They were sired upon a Valkyr, whose swan plumage I stole as she bathed in a mountain pool. I compelled her to stay with me a while and she gave birth and set them upon my knee."

Muttering raced through the hall at that. It was widely known that Odin's warrior-maidens, Valkyrs, assumed the guise of swans in the sky . . . and that they sometimes cast off their plumage and returned to human form as they bathed in isolated pools. A mortal man who stole that plumage while a Valkyr bathed could compel her to mate with him.

By all Borger remembered, old Serrick was just such a crafty mortal. Hadn't the old warrior stolen the legendary sword of Ibn Hassadan—the very sword he had used himself to barter their freedom from the sea-raiders of Alexandria? A man who could steal such a sword could probably steal a Valkyr's plumes as well, Borger reasoned. But the most convincing proof of the old man's brazen tale was standing before them . . . with flaxen hair and beautiful faces and curves certainly worthy of an immortal mother.

"They are mine to give, Red Beard. Never fear," Serrick assured him. Both maids nodded, verifying the old man's story and casting demure and respectful looks at him.

"Then . . . I agree, old man," Borger snarled, sticking his thumbs into his belt and adopting a bold stance. "I shall accept your two daughters in payment of—"

"Three," Serrick interrupted. "*Three* daughters."

"Three?" Borger frowned. "But I see only—" He jerked his head up as he caught sight of old Serrick making his way through the crowd that had gathered around, then returning with yet another cloaked and hooded figure . . . which towered well above him. Borger exchanged looks of consternation with his men and watched with mounting suspicion.

"My third daughter," Serrick announced, as they came to stand before Borger. "My eldest. Aaren, by name. Sired on a rare, raven-haired Valkyr . . . some years before the others." He had to stretch to reach the hood that cloaked her head.

As the covering slid, all beheld a mass of dark, burnished hair, held in place by a leather headband of the sort worn by most of the men in Borger's hall. And within that sworl of flame-kissed hair was set a face the likes of which had never been seen in Borger's village. Sleek, sun-polished skin stretched tightly over a high forehead, wide prominent cheekbones, and a long straight nose that came to a dramatic point, then flared at the sides into delicate nostrils; each feature set in perfect balance with the others. In the center of that face, two thickly lashed eyes glowed . . . tawny and golden, the color of precious amber. And below those eyes was a broad, sensually carved mouth . . . ripe and silky, the color of red sea coral.

It was a stunning face, smoothly wrought and boldly sculptured, with a hint of the exotic. Beautiful, handsome, comely . . . it was clearly all those things. But no such words could capture the sense of power and light, the force of spirit within that visage which held all eyes entranced upon first glimpse. It was indeed a face that could have been wombed and birthed by a rare raven Valkyr. Or sired by a god.

Borger felt fingers of dread creeping up his spine as he looked on his old comrade at arms and at the bewitching creature who stood taller than most of the men in his hall . . . as high as six freemen's feet, stacked heel to toe. "This is *your* daughter, old man?"

Serrick chuckled and reached for the ties of her cloak. "She is mine." When he dragged away that heavy mantle, Borger sucked in breath unexpectedly and choked on his own juices. Gasps and murmurs of amazement rattled briefly about the hall . . . then all fell deathly silent.

Over her soft linen tunic, Aaren Serricksdotter wore a molded leather breastplate, fitted stunningly to her womanly attributes, and a warrior's breeches, wrapped deerskin leggings, and leather wristbands. It took a moment for their eyes to overcome the shock of her garb . . . to realize that the frame beneath it was just as astonishing. She had long, shapely legs; broad, smooth shoulders which framed high, full breasts; and arms that were sleek, yet visibly muscular beneath her short sleeves. Above her left shoulder rose the polished horn-and-silver handle of a sword, and on her tapered hands were calluses that bore testimony to her use of it. Their eyes burned; their mouths drooped. Aaren Serricksdotter was a battle-maiden . . . a warrior . . . the very essence of a Valkyr, trapped in human flesh.

"My three daughters, Red Beard." Serrick swept his offering with a trembling hand. "Do you accept my payment?"

"Yea, old Sword-stealer," Borger said thickly, unable to tear his eyes from the battle-maiden's provocative breast-plate and what obviously lay beneath it. His conflicting passions choked his voice to a whisper. "I accept."

"Then, by your own word, they are yours." Serrick heaved a sigh of satisfaction and turned away. But after two steps, he stopped and turned back to find Borger's eyes still abulge and his jaw still agape.

"Oh, and did I forget me to say . . . they're under an enchantment?"

A wasp nest stuffed into his breeches couldn't have had more impact on old Borger than those fateful words.

"En-enchantment?" he roared, ripping his gaze from Serrick's daughters to spear the wily warrior with it. "By Hel's gate, old man . . . what have you saddled me with?"

"Nothing too terrible." Old Serrick's withered mouth drew up into a crafty smirk at the sight of Borger's dawning horror. "The enchantment was laid on them by the goddess Freya herself . . . at Odin's command. That I captured and compelled one of his Valkyrs to warm my furs, the Allfather might have understood, for a man should have rightful spoils of conquest. But to capture and plant my seed in *two* . . . Odin was angered mightily that a mere mortal owned such cunning craft. He demanded reparation."

"And?" Borger demanded, jolting forward, his fists clenched, his neck-veins at full swell. The battle-maiden stepped deftly in front of her father, stopping Borger short. He had to tilt his head slightly to meet that fierce golden stare, and the sight of her looming slightly above him sent cold caution through his heated temper.

"By Freya's decree," Serrick continued, "none of Serrick Sword-stealer's daughters can be mounted and bred until the eldest, the warrior-maiden Aaren, is vanquished in honest blade battle *by one lone man.* Until that time, Red Beard, they are given into your hands to enrich your hall with their beauty and their labors. And someday to enrich you with the bride-price they bring . . . if the warrior-maid is ever defeated."

Borger stood eye to eye with old Serrick's Aaren, confounded by her size and the unblinking, unabashed way she confronted him. In all his wide-wandering life, in all the uncommon sights of his voyages . . . he couldn't recall ever seeing a female like this one. Daughter of a Valkyr. A battle-maiden. *An enchanted warrior.*

"Do the women still sleep in the same women's house?" Serrick asked. Borger seemed incapable of answering, so some of his sons nodded mutely in his stead. "Come," he ordered his daughters, "I will show you the way."

The younger ones followed Serrick out, and finally the warrior-maid Aaren disengaged from the jarl's burning stare and stooped to pick up their discarded cloaks. Every eye in the hall fastened on the graceful flexing of her long, tapered legs, on the bend of her sleek shoulders, on the fine curve of her buttocks as the snug breeches pulled tight across them. As she turned and followed her father and sisters from the hall, all eyes fixed on the sway of her bottom and the swing of her thick burnished hair down her back. Every tongue was cloven to the roof of every mouth for a long moment after she was gone.

Borger was the first to recover and he could manage but one word.

"*Ale!*"

Chapter Two

Borger's village had grown since old Serrick's time in it; now there were a number of goodly wooden buildings with sturdy cedar roofs and planking shutters that marked window openings. The hall and houses lay in a circle around a wide clearing, bounded by fields on one side, forest on two others, and the great lake, Väner, on the fourth. Newer huts and houses had been built just outside that main clearing and along the path down to the lake. But the women's house still sat as it always had, directly across the common ground from the long hall.

Serrick led his daughters across the chilled, moon-drenched clearing to the door and paused outside. "The older women and all unmarried freewomen live here," he said in a voice that betrayed the strain of so much talking. "They will show you what needs to be done . . . most of them work in Borger's hall and fields. When you go in, find an empty place on the floor and make your pallets quietly. You have your things?" When his two younger daughters lifted the bundles in their hands and nodded, Serrick sighed heavily.

"Miri . . . Marta . . ." He reached a gnarled hand to each of them.

In the moonlight their eyes glistened and their chins quivered. He placed his hands on their cheeks and stroked tenderly. "Gentle ones, you must be strong. You have learned well the ways of women, for having so poor a teacher. You will have many children about your hearth, someday. You must tell them of Serrick, your father. And of your mother, Fair Leone of the Swans. My heart will be proud when I join Leone in Odin's great Valhalla and tell her that her daughters are fair and good and wise."

"Father—" Marta started to speak, but his fingers on her lips stopped her. Still, he could not stop her from throwing her arms around his neck and hugging him fiercely. Miri did the same, tears rolling down her cheeks. After a long moment, he set them back and whispered, "Go." They opened the door and slipped inside.

"Come, let us speak, daughter." He caught Aaren by the arm and pulled her into the moonshadow of a nearby tree. Removing his wide hat, he looked up into her strong, stunning face. "I have felt the foul goddess, Hel's, cold, dark finger beckoning me," he said, in a dry whisper. "I am not long for mortal realms. That is why I have brought you here . . . why I have given you to old Red Beard."

Aaren had known for some time that he would bring them here . . . and why. She nodded, searching the old man's withered countenance in the dim light. His eyes bulged strangely, and as the night breeze tugged open the neck of his cloak, she glimpsed the large, wattling growth on his neck.

Only two summers ago, he had been a hale and vigorous man, sound of wind and strong of limb. Then last harvest she had seen the lump, and over the months she had watched it grow . . . seen it drawing strength and substance from him while he grew steadily more feeble and wasted. His face was now gaunt, his eyes protruded, and his flesh hung on his bones. Pain was etched in his features and evident in his every movement.

"It is up to you, now, to see the enchantment through in all honor." His gnarled hands fastened fiercely on her wrists. "You are strong and clever, my daughter. You must be valiant as well, for they will test you. But know, Aaren, that you have victory-luck ordained by Odin himself. A warrior can have no finer gift. Be true in your heart, be true to your honor, and you will triumph." He paused and swallowed hard, then released one of her wrists to clasp the upper part of her right arm. It flexed under his touch, becoming hard, smooth, like finely polished birch, and he stroked it with a gentleness she had not experienced from him since she was a little girl.

"Your arm must win for you a seat and a place of honor in Red Beard's hall . . . and must win for your sisters the right to good and honorable marriages. They have no silver, no possessions, no rank in Borger's hall, and their beauty will make them prey to the lusts of men. Your sword-skill must be their protection even as it earns you honor among warriors." He paused and wagged his head. "Old Borger has given his word and he is one to guard it, for the sake of his fame. But beware. He is a lusty old goat, brawling and quarrelsome. He will seek to make some use of you for his own ends."

Aaren nodded, her throat constricting, her fists clenched. These were final words. Hard words. Parting words.

"I will be strong." The huskiness in her voice caused him to look up at her again. Grief surged in her at the pain in his countenance, and she fought a stinging sensation in her eyes. She glanced down at the sword which only that morning had reappeared at Serrick's side. She knew it meant he was going to the wolves, to die with a blade in his hand. Serrick feared nothing on earth . . . except to die quietly on a bed of straw and forfeit Valhalla.

"They will come for you soon and you must be prepared," he said, clasping both her wrists once more in the strength-blessing of one warrior to another. His jaw tightened and his eyes shone with a terrible light. "May Odin fight on your right and Thor on your left. And may I greet you in Valhalla one day."

Aaren couldn't speak. She ached to put her arms around the old man, as her sisters had done, but forced herself to return his tight grip on her wrists instead. When he released her, he donned his hat and with lagging steps turned toward the edge of the village.

"Father!" Aaren jolted two steps after him. He halted, then turned to look at her with the pain of parting visible in his face. "Tell me . . . my mother's name."

For a long moment, Old Serrick stared at his daughter. In all the years since Aaren's birth, he had not once spoken that name to her. It was too painful, even for a warrior. But now she asked. And there would never be another chance to say it. He gazed at her, so tall and strong and proud, a true warrior. But there was still the woman-softness hidden away inside her . . . and she faced a hard path. Would it weaken her to know it? Would she feel more a woman and less a warrior to be connected by the magic of a name to that bold, spirited creature who had given her birth?

Aaren's heart pounded, her hands were cold, her eyes burned as though stung by nettles. "My sisters have Leone," she whispered tautly. "Will you not give me a mother, too?"

Branches swayed overhead, casting wavering shadows over the old warrior so that he seemed to shimmer, as if already losing substance and connection with the mortal world. In that long silence, Aaren felt him withdrawing, and experienced a new and devastating loneliness. He had always been there, as father, master, guide. But from now on, she suddenly understood, there would be just her, alone, against all odds. And she asked to have the name of the woman under whose heart she had lain . . . a name to connect her with another being, with all beings, in the way of birth and life.

"I called her only . . . my Fair Raven. You will see her in Valhalla." Old Serrick dropped his head and turned away, moving with a labored gait toward the beckoning shadows of the forest.

Aaren stood, watching until he disappeared from sight, feeling hollow inside, aching, uncertain in a way that was utterly foreign to her. For one brief moment, she longed to run into the forest with him, to wield her blade beside his against the familiar danger of fang and claw, instead of against the unknown threat of arm and blade. As quickly as that urge welled inside her, she named it—*fear*—and purged it with a sense of horror.

She was a warrior, sired by a warrior, daughter of a Valkyr, she chided herself. It was only the shock of Serrick's leaving that caused her to have such desperate and unworthy thoughts. She had not understood how alone she would feel without the old man beside her. He had not given her the name she asked for . . . but he had given her *Fair Raven.* It would have to be enough. Her gaze flew to the dark blur that even now was disappearing into the gloom of the forest and into the shade of memory, and her eyes closed.

"I will remember you always, Father Serrick." And each time, she realized, it would be with a pain in her heart.

Sometime later, she came to her senses in the blue-silver moonlight and looked around at the dark shapes of the huts and houses, feeling the flow of the night around her and the closing of the past behind her. With that sense of finality came an unexpected sense of beginning . . . the opening of new realms of experience.

She was chosen—destined—by the unusual circumstance of her making to live outside the normal course and flow of mortal life. She had heard the story of the enchantment for as long as she could remember, and had accepted it, prepared to meet it. Now, the time had come for her to live it out, to fulfill her destiny among men. Her warrior's pride and her confidence in her own strength and skill welled in the core of her. She had sisters to protect, a place to win in the society of warriors, a life to claim among the people of this village.

Her gaze settled on the long hall, which loomed large and portentous, across the clearing. The sights and smells of Borger's hall were unlike anything she'd experienced in the isolated mountain vales and meadows where she'd lived with her father and sisters. Her senses flooded once again with the smells of soured ale, grease and ashes, torch smoke, and the sharp, vinegary tang of male sweat.

She thought of the men's faces . . . the coarse features and hot, probing eyes set in rough, sun-leathered skin. She thought of their bodies . . . the sinewy muscularity and latent menace of their sprawled frames. She was not accustomed to men; their great size, their powerful voices, the heat that radiated from them, the force of their manner. She had felt their eyes upon her like hands, probing, testing her. And she knew Serrick was right; they would come for her soon.

Turning back to the women's house, she lifted her cloth bundle and stepped into darkness which bore the familiar and reassuring scent of women.

Across the clearing, the long hall was awash in both ale and speculation. Borger huddled in his great chair, glaring at his brawling and contentious sons and warriors, who were gathered around him, drinking prodigiously and arguing themselves into exhaustion.

"I let so much blood on Gunnar's field, the stream will run red till the twilight of the gods!" young Garth Borgerson proclaimed, smacking his chest. It was an exaggeration, all knew, but in the clans of the Norsemen, a well-crafted boast inspired almost as much admiration as a deed itself. He stalked before his father's high seat and braced his feet apart to steady himself. "I deserve a woman of my own . . . and I claim that little wench garbed in green. By Thor's Right Arm—did you ever see such hair?" He paused and swayed, his eyes losing focus. "Like golden sunlight gathered 'round her face . . . so bright . . . so soft . . ."

"Yea—give Garth her hair," came a drunken rejoinder from Hakon Freeholder, "and give the rest of her to me!" The short, flat-faced warrior made a series of lewd pelvic thrusts and laughter erupted all around.

"Just one night with the blue-eyed nymphs, jarl," came another drink-roughened voice. "I'm not a greedy man . . . I'll leave 'em well-stretched and eager for the rest of you!"

"Yea, jarl, give them the soft, pale ones!" Thorkel the Ever-ready shoved forward and jerked a thumb toward his chest. "And give me the big, fiery one, that battle-maiden. I'll soon have her begging for a taste of my . . . *blade*!"

"Have you ever seen such a woman?" another howled. "Flanks and legs like a high-bred mare . . . beggin' to be ridden! And damn near big enough to ride double!"

Borger felt their laughter buffeting him in great hot waves generated by competitive male pride and roused sexual heat. Never in his long, eventful life had he faced such a dilemma: what to do with three beautiful women, whose pleasures were forbidden to him personally but whose fate had been placed squarely in his hands. Well, mostly in his hands. There was the little matter of an enchantment to deal with. . . .

He scowled and tossed back yet another horn of yeasty new ale, swiping the dribbles from his beard. An enchantment. He'd never encountered such a thing before . . . though the sagas and epics the skalds told were full of such stuff. In earlier days, he might have scoffed at the idea of divine vengeance worked in the affairs of mortals, but he was too far along in life to risk offending the gods of Asgard now. He couldn't overcome the feeling that there had been something otherworldly about the old man ... that wide, floppy hat; those strange, deep-seeing eyes. Whatever lingering skepticism he might have harbored was banished by the appearance of the battle-maiden, Aaren.

The image of the Sword-stealer's eldest daughter—framed and wrought on so magnificent a scale—was scored into his mind. A woman warrior ... a great, strapping handful of female ... a wench with the strength to turn a roll in the furs into a raging, glorious battle of raw power and lust! Hot excitement seared Borger from head to toe, only to be doused moments later when he recalled that he was prohibited from tasting such pleasurable combat himself. He huffed, venting useless steam, and turned his mind to thoughts of breaking the enchantment.

In his mind, he paired each of his battle-tempered warriors with the Valkyr's daughter, one by one. He grimaced and scowled as each fell short of the mark. Slowly, the realization surfaced in his mind: there was but one man in his hall and village who both bested Aaren Serricksdotter in height and outstripped her in sheer mass of muscle and sinew. One lone man.

A cagey spark was struck at the backs of Borger's eyes. It would be interesting to see them together ... this fierce-eyed battle-maiden and his woman-hearted son, Jorund. She was a wench fashioned to fire men's blood and to arouse a desire for conquest in even the most placid of male breasts. ...

"By the Red Thor's Hammer!" Borger came roaring to his feet, his eyes ablaze with determination. "It is time to test this enchantment and see what this battle-maid is made of!" A drunken din of approval raced through the hall and those men still capable of it shoved to their feet.

"I'll soon have her teetering on the tip of my sword!"

"Not if I take her first!"

"I'll have her on her knees with three cuts of my sword . . . then on her back for a few thrusts of my *spear*!"

One after another, Borger's men boasted of their prowess as they scrambled for their blades, each vowing they would be the one to defeat Old Serrick's daughter. The canny old jarl halted in the midst of strapping on his weapon and confronted his half-drunken warriors.

"I alone decide who fights the Sword-stealer's daughter!" he bellowed, planting his fists on his hips. "Be it known that no man may raise a blade to her without my consent." The grumbling and complaints were gradually snuffed by his hard-eyed stare and combative pose. Then he called for his son Garth.

The young warrior bounded forward eagerly, his features glowing with the expectation that he would be given the first chance to fight the Valkyr's daughter. But when Borger spoke, his face reddened and anger swelled visibly in his muscular young frame.

"Go for Jorund. . . . I would have him present."

"Jorund?" Garth exclaimed. "You send for *him*?" There was a ripple of disapproval through the men.

"He won't be any use," came a snarl from the pack.

"There's fighting to be done . . . not flesh-strumming!" came another.

Borger cast a silencing glare around him, then thundered at Garth: "Go!"

The sheer volume spun the young warrior on his heels and set him stalking for the doors and the thrall house, where Jorund Borgerson was most likely to be found. Borger flashed a wicked grin as he stepped down into the midst of his men and waved them along with a brawny arm.

"To the women's house . . . and a test of a Valkyr's daughter!"

Garth ducked through the door of the thrall house and stood searching the pallets and sleeping shelves hanging from the walls for a sign of his elder brother's pale hair and massive frame. Finding none below, he climbed partway up the ladder to the straw-littered loft and spotted him amidst a tangle of female limbs and hair. Garth squinted, muttered a curse under his breath, then began to count. One, two, three . . . Hel's gate, there were at least four women snuggled, pressed, and draped over various parts of his brother's half-naked body. *Four women*, when most of the men had trouble luring one wench—even a thrall—into the furs for a bit of flesh-sport. Garth ground his teeth together and lunged up the short ladder to stand above the infuriating tangle. With one foot he gave Jorund's leg a prod.

"Jorund!" he snapped. "Wake up. Father wants you." His eyes narrowed as the women stirred sensuously, sighed, and nestled even closer to the warmth of their big human brazier. "Jorund!" Garth shouted, propping his foot on Jorund's thickly muscled thigh and giving it a series of jarring thumps.

Jorund struggled up through a jumble of female limbs to find his younger brother half-standing on his thigh, glowering at him. "Wh-what is it, Garth?" he demanded, bracing on his arms and brushing away the hands that sought to pull him back into the wool fleece.

"Father's calling for you," Garth repeated. "An old man came to the hall and brought a woman warrior. I think he wants you to fight her."

Jorund rubbed his face and laughed in husky, sated tones. "Fight a woman? Don't be a thick-wit, Garth. Why would I do that?"

"She's not just a woman, brother," Garth said tauntingly. "She's a battle-maiden, daughter of a Valkyr . . . under an enchantment." He crossed his arms and smirked at the way Jorund sat straighter and shrugged the sleep-shroud from his senses. The promise of a blood-stirring battle held no allure for Jorund, but he could never resist the promise of a tantalizing woman. "She's taller than Father—damned near tall as you—and built sleek as a Frankish mare. She's got a face like a wood nymph"—he lowered his voice—"and eyes like a Persian tiger." Garth wheeled and was halfway down the ladder before Jorund made it to his knees and called after him.

"Wait . . . Garth! Near as tall as *me*?"

* * *

"Aaren?" came a whisper in the darkness.

"Yea, Miri?" Aaren turned on her straw pallet on the floor of the women's house and made out the glow of her sisters' flaxen hair and pale faces in the dimness. They were sitting up, huddled close together, and she pushed up to face them.

"Did you see them? Did you feel their eyes?" Miri whispered, her face luminous with unnamed fears.

"I never imagined there would be so many men," Marta murmured, reaching for Aaren's hand and clasping it tightly. Her eyes widened. "Will you have to fight them all?"

"That depends upon old Red Beard," Aaren answered truthfully. Then, seeing their fears, she slid over on her knees and gave each of them a hug of reassurance. "And on whether I can stand their smell long enough to let them get within skewering range."

When they looked up with alarm, she was smiling and they sagged with relief. "They do smell . . . strange," Miri said, wrinkling her nose with distaste. "Are you sure we have to take one as a husband . . . and sleep with him in his furs and . . . all the rest?"

"You know what Serrick said," Aaren said, her smile fading. "Marriage is a protection for a woman and her children. Either choose to mate with one, or suffer having to mate with them all. You saw their strength, felt the heat of their stares. They will all want you."

"Ughhh." Miri shuddered and wrapped her arms about her waist. Marta stiffened and ran a hand over her waist and down her belly, where it splayed protectively at the top of her legs.

"Until I have won a place in Borger's hall and wrested some respect from Borger and his warriors, the threat of my blade is your only protection. You must promise me you will not be caught alone in the company of men . . . that you will be prudent and watchful," Aaren insisted, drawing solemn nods of agreement from them.

"Do you think you would really *skewer* a man, Aaren?" Marta whispered hoarsely.

"I would if he were about to skewer me." Aaren expelled a controlled breath. For the first time in her years of training and fighting, she truly faced the possibility of killing or being killed. Always before when she fought, she knew that Serrick would not deal her a death-blow. But these men of old Red Beard's had killed in battle and would think nothing of sending their blades biting clear to her bones. "I am a warrior, Marta."

They were silent again as the full significance of that fact settled on each of them in a powerful new way. The honor and respect a warrior owned was bought with a blood-price, and, despite so dear a cost, was as fleeting as breath-mist . . . lasting only until the next challenge of honor, the next meeting of blades. Miri's hands anxiously sought Aaren's again, and Marta spoke in a constricted whisper.

"What if . . . something happens to you?"

"Nothing will happen to me." She shook off their anxiety and produced a confident smile. "I have the victory-luck from Odin himself." She freed one hand and stroked first Miri's fair cheek, then Marta's.

The darkness and the way they looked at her allowed a memory to escape . . . of days long past, when their heads had been topped with downy white and their eyes had seemed big and blue as a robin's eggs. She had been left to care for them for days at a time while Serrick hunted. And whenever the screech of a hunting owl or the scream of a mountain cat frightened them in the night, they had climbed into her pallet and huddled against her with their cold feet and fear-blanched faces. Now they raised those same anxious expressions to her, believing in her, trusting her. Determination surged in her as she tucked that bittersweet memory away again.

"Have I not always taken care of you? Just you wait. By the time I have won a number of blade-meetings, Borger's men will be eager to take you to wife, without a bride-gift. Why, you will have your choice among them."

"Some choice," Marta whispered glumly, shivering as she pulled her cloak up around her shoulders. "A tall, stringy, smelly one . . . or a short, hairy, smelly one." She caught Aaren's arm as she parted to her pallet. "Skewer all the men you want, Aaren . . . we're in no hurry."

Aaren gave a silent, rueful laugh. "A pity I cannot start with old Red Beard himself."

Moments later, noise intruded on the darkness: faint at first, a low rumble punctuated by occasional higher tones. Then the scuffling of feet became recognizable, blended with the unmistakable sound of human voices. Shafts of yellow torchlight pierced the cracks in the planking door of the women's house. Aaren watched those fingers of light intensifying, and she sat up.

Taking slow, even breaths, she conjured the image Serrick had given her to help her prepare for battle. In her mind, bright molten metal appeared in a shining pool above her head. As she relaxed and stilled, it poured over and through her, sliding down her face and neck and throat . . . over her shoulders, breasts, and arms . . . then, her back and thighs and calves . . . steeling her muscles and nerves while encasing her in a hot, impenetrable layer of shining mettle.

When they were close enough for her to make out the sound of the jarl's booming voice above the others, she rose to her feet. The commotion outside and her movement nearby wakened a number of the other women who were sleeping on benches and shelves hung around the walls.

"Aaren?" Marta started up, anxiety in her voice.

"They've come, Marta. It's time." Aaren cast off her cloak and bent to retrieve her sword from the pallet. As she reached for the latch of the door, Marta halted her with a touch.

"Be careful," she said solemnly.

"I'll do better than that." Aaren grinned down at her sisters, her eyes glowing with certainty. "I'll be victorious." And she flung open the door just as a drink-hoarsened male voice from outside assaulted it.

"Come out, Serrick's daughter! Battle-maiden . . . daughter of a Valkyr! Come out and face your test!"

The other women rubbed their eyes in disbelief when they beheld Aaren and saw her duck outside the door. They turned to Miri and Marta. "Who . . . what was that?" one asked.

"That is the jarl's voice . . . What's happening?" said another as she crawled from her shelf, clasping a woolen cover about her.

"She's our sister," Marta answered, spotting the window on the front of the house and hurrying to throw back the wooden shutters. "She's a warrior and she's about to fight."

A woman blade-fighting? The other women stared at each other, slack-jawed, then fled their pallets and scrambled to the window to see for themselves.

Aaren emerged from the women's house into a circle of yellow torchlight and a score of drink-coarsened faces. Planting her feet squarely, she set her fists on her hips and looked around that heaving cordon of maleflesh, assessing them even as they did her. Stocky, stringy, burly, and gaunt . . . slit-eyed, long-nosed, pock-faced, and shaven . . . They did not seem a particularly fearsome lot; carousing, woolly, and battle-scarred . . . with heads fogged by ale-mist and loins weighted with lust.

"Serricksdotter!" Borger hailed her, stepping forward. "The old man named you a warrior. And a warrior must be ever ready to fight." He strode closer, appraising her with a hot, speculative stare. "Will you now defend your honor and Odin's enchantment?"

"Yea, Red Beard. Now and always." She raked his burly form with an equally brazen look and broke into a smile that was both fierce and beguiling. "I will fight your warriors, one after another. Until I am defeated. *If* I am defeated."

The old jarl stiffened visibly at her boast. He was accustomed to such talk from warriors . . . not from women. He stomped closer and shoved his face into hers, testing the steadiness of her nerve with his most threatening regard. But she faced him without quailing, letting her strength of purpose rise into her eyes for him to see.

"Serrick taught me well," she said with a hint of amusement.

He grunted skeptically and turned to his men, but she knew she had just held her own against the wily old chieftain . . . and realized she would hold her own against his men as well. Beneath the preparatory pounding of blood in her veins, that assurance spawned a curious trill of both relief and disappointment in her. She quickly seized the first and purged the second.

Confident now, she laid her scabbard at her feet and spread her legs so that her toes touched both the hilt and blade point of her sword. Bending from the waist, she laid her palms on her blade to stretch the muscles in her legs as Serrick had instructed her. She could feel eyes hot upon her as she executed a series of slow lunges, then straightened and raised each arm straight above her, forcing her muscles taut until she felt the beginning of a pleasurable burn. A slow, drumming excitement invaded her limbs and intensified to a throb of expectation in her veins.

With half an ear, she listened to Borger's men contending for the right to face her. And with a small, knowing smile she made fists and flexed her arms, working the muscles against one another, feeling the blood rushing into them. Then she paused and collected her hip-length hair and began to weave it into a loose braid. It was the last part of her ritual . . . a putting away of softness, a containment of the last bit of her womanliness . . .

Her bold, provocative movements, the lithe power of her long, tapered frame, and the confidence of her warrior's stance had galvanized Borger's men. Their faces burned, their eyes shone like polished obsidian . . . then they began to clamor for the right to win her. Borger drew his blade in warning as he grappled with the decision.

There was a commotion at one edge of the circle and Borger craned his neck to see past the crush of warriors. A crafty grin spread over his broad face and Aaren, senses honed and wary, followed his gaze. At the far edge of the torchlight, the men were being jostled and parted by a muscular young giant with flaxen hair and a tousled, just-wakened look about him. He paused at the sight of her and settled a widening stare on her which even from a distance was startlingly blue.

Aaren found her gaze momentarily held captive on the largest man she'd ever seen. From the way he towered above the men around him, he was even taller than she . . .

and from the breadth of his shoulders and the girth of his thighs, he was massively strong. Her eyes slid up his front-parted tunic, which bared a generous slice of sun-burnished chest, to his face. It was a clean, finely sculptured vision of a face, framed by wide cheekbones, a high forehead, and a sinewy, beardless jaw. Everything about him was eye-stealing . . . eye-pleasuring. She stared, letting the impact of him flood through her senses, until their gazes met in a glancing blow and an odd, sobering chill raced through her shoulders. Of all the men she'd seen in Borger's hall, she sensed that this one alone posed her a threat. With a jerk of her head she ended that unsettling scrutiny and sternly forced her concentration back to the coming fight.

Borger had watched the play of eyes between the battle-maiden and his eldest son with unabashed interest. But he knew better than to look to Jorund for a bid to challenge her, and so turned to his younger sons and warriors. He leveled his blade at young Svein Torkelson. A howl of outrage went up at the selection, but the young warrior bounded from the pack and unsheathed his blade, waving it in exultation at having won the jarl's confidence . . . and in expectation of triumph over the warrior-maid with the long, magnificent legs.

Aaren studied young Svein's form and movements as he came forward. He stood a half span shorter than she, and was lean, energetic, and untempered; a green stripling of a warrior. The small, lingering knot in her gut uncoiled; she could easily take him. She grasped her smooth-edged blade with both hands, widened her stance, and curled into a familiar stalking posture. When a cool, assured smile spread over her tempting features, young Svein took it as a sign of encouragement and charged in with his blade swinging.

The battle was joined . . . almost. Aaren handily side-stepped the lad's overpowered swing, wheeled, and waited for him to recover, all the while wearing that same cool smile. Svein swung heavily again, and again she swayed easily out of reach. The anticipation in his face turned to glowering determination as he felt his blade whirling off, unchecked, into nothingness and found her waiting patiently for him.

"She's afraid of a taste of steel!" he shouted, red-faced. As he came at her again, there were hisses and caws of derision from the warriors.

"Fight . . . unless you have the heart of a woman, as well as the shape!," "She's no warrior, she's a coward!" and "Use your blade, Valkyr's daughter . . . or be prepared to spread yourself for ours!" they taunted. And when she feinted and escaped the lad's third swing without countering his steel, the comments of the onlookers turned uglier still.

Aaren heard little of their jeering, so focused on her opponent was she. When young Svein grew bolder and lunged to hack straight down at her, she poised her blade to deflect his and the force of the impact sent tremors up the young warrior's braced arms. Spurred by the jarring clash, he lunged and hacked again and again, and she met each blow with uncanny precision. She could read the direction of each coming blow in his eyes and in the shifts of his unseasoned frame, and turned them on him, sending him back a pace for every blow he struck. Within moments, he was frantic, panting and crimson-faced, while she breathed hard but evenly and her face was alight with what could only have been called pleasure.

It was like the blade-meetings she'd had with Serrick in the early days of her training, she realized. She had been pure energy, unfocused and easily dissipated. And Serrick had often reined his skill with her, as she did with this lad . . . waiting for her to wear herself down. But as she glanced past her opponent and felt the volatile heat and anger roiling around her, she understood: she was not the young warrior's master . . . she had a point to prove here and a battle to *win*.

She deliberately slipped the bonds of restraint, freeing her power at last. For the first time she swung her blade in attack, and the swiftness of its arc set it singing on the air before it struck . . . dead on target. Around her she heard shocked murmurs, which faded quickly in the rush of blood in her ears and the pounding of her heart. Feinting with her blade-tip, she reversed her swing, catching him completely off guard. He hastily parried and stumbled back, and she swung again, scoring his leather jerkin with the tip of her blade.

Frantically, he lunged and hacked, only to have his blows shunted aside, then returned with relentless precision. Again and again her wrists flexed and her body snapped taut, darted, or swayed as her blade struck home. Then she began to use her feet as Serrick had taught her, twisting, throwing rounding kicks, forcing him to contend with her on two fronts. The strain showed in his face as he grimaced, jerked, and lurched off balance again and again. In desperation, he planted his feet to bolster the power of his blows. As he heaved and reared for a massive strike, she swung a foot forward, sweeping his knee just as her blade connected with his in opposing motion. He stumbled, flailed, then toppled—flinging his arms wide and sending his sword clattering as he crashed onto the hard-packed dirt.

In the space of a single heartbeat she pounced, slamming her foot down on his chest and pressing her blade-tip against his throat. Her chest heaving and body trembling with unvented force, she raised her face to the jarl, demanding he acknowledge her victory and grant her the respect due a warrior. But amidst the grumbling and shocked murmuring of his men, he remained silent, studying her with undisguised calculation in his eyes.

"Which of your warriors do you send to defeat next, jarl?" she declared, lifting her blade and removing her foot from Svein the Unready's chest. She turned a scornful eye on the surly, ale-bitten crew around them. "Are any still clear-headed enough to swing a blade?"

A clamor broke out as Borger's men assailed him, shaking fists and jabbing fingers, each hotly demanding the chance to teach the wench some respect. "Not now—Hel take you!" Borger bashed them aside with a snarl, while keeping his gaze fixed upon her. She could feel his scrutiny like a brawny hand traveling up her legs, measuring her waist, sliding over her breastplate, examining her face.

"The fighting is over this night!" he bellowed. "Go back to your ale horns, your furs, and your women." When they protested, he raised the back of his fist threateningly, daring them to challenge his authority.

Only Aaren spoke up. "I am ready to fight again, jarl," she declared. "Give me an opponent." He turned to her with a lidded look that was some part pleasure, some part warning.

"I said"—he roared at her as he had at his warriors—"there will be no more meeting of blades this night. Go to your rest, Serricksdotter . . . spare your strength for tomorrow." He turned to the others, who watched hawkishly. "Go—all of you!"

Borger's men mumbled and argued amongst themselves as they turned away. Aaren watched them go with a steamy, unreasoning disappointment. She had prepared for a real test of her prowess and had been given only one green stripling to fight. Now her blood still coursed hard in her veins, her skin was aflame with battle-spawned heat, and her muscles and nerves fairly vibrated with the need for a hard, jolting physical release.

She wheeled to retrieve her scabbard and found herself suddenly eye to eye with the great, flaxen-haired giant she had seen earlier. He stood a few paces away, staring intently at her. His light eyes glinted as they moved over her with thorough, assessing strokes that seemed to penetrate her garments . . . then to pierce her skin and sinew to search her very bones. A slow, provocative curl appeared at one corner of his mouth and Aaren felt the pounding in her blood escalate strangely. It seemed to her that he recognized the turmoil inside her, the roiling need to spend the power and heat released in her by battle. And the way his smile broadened made it seem that he saw more . . . much more.

The chilled night breeze swirled over her hot, damp skin and she shivered, wishing she could pull her gaze from him and sensing that to do so would be to retreat. The very thought was abhorrent to her warrior's heart and she stiffened, narrowing her eyes at him. After a pride-saving pause, she turned on her heel and found herself facing the jarl, who stood several feet away in the light of the single remaining torch, watching her reaction to the big warrior. Her cheeks heated inexplicably and her stomach seemed to sink oddly inside her.

She whirled and started for the door of the women's house, but halted at the sound of her name being called and turned to the open window.

"Aaren? Are you all right?" Miri and Marta were crowded into the opening with a number of other women. Their faces glowed with relief as she drew herself up straight and nodded. Embarrassed by her unsettled response to the big warrior and quaking with unspent tension, she stalked to the window and thrust her scabbard and blade into Marta's hands.

"Safe-keep my blade, Marta. I will return soon," she declared.

"Wait—where are you going?" Miri called out to her retreating back.

"To run with the night wind." Without looking back, she sprang into long, fluid strides which carried her to the moonlit path toward the great lake Väner.

Jorund Borgerson tore his eyes from the path where the battle-maid had disappeared and dropped his gaze to his own hands, which were clenched and aching. His chest was heaving and he could feel a thickening in his blood. Never in his life, never in all his travels, had he seen such a spectacle . . . or such a woman. Astonishingly tall, lithe, and graceful . . . with curves that moved like a full-flowing stream and a face stolen from his most exotic night visions. The sight of her fighting was scored into his mind—her strong, fluid movements, her perfect control of the blade, the pure sensual pleasure in her face as she pressed the attack. He was stunned, tantalized, by the potent aura of both "woman" and "warrior" about her.

By the time she ran off in the moonlight, he was all but entranced. He stood staring after her, his heart beating faster, his skin warming, his loins stirring at the sight of her long, muscular legs stretching to cover distance. He would have bolted after her, but a grating chuckle nearby brought him back to his senses . . . and back to the sight of Borger standing a few paces away with an annoyingly pleased look on his face. Jorund frowned. Anything that gave Borger pleasure was usually a plague on the rest of mankind.

"Liked what you saw, eh, whelp?" Borger demanded.

Jorund gave his cagey old father a dark look. "I've a powerful thirst, old man," he declared flatly, striding off to join the other men in the hall.

Soon Jorund was sprawled comfortably across a bench and against a planking table near the high seat, slaking his thirst and ignoring the boasting and contention of the other men. His head filled with the remembered shape of her: long, muscular legs with exquisitely curved calves and powerful, smooth-muscled thighs; taut, nicely rounded buttocks; well-tapered arms hung on broad shoulders above that stunning breastplate . . . which was artfully molded to accommodate full, womanly breasts. His blood filled with the passion and the heat of her as she fought and as she faced him afterward. And his loins began to fill with need of her.

"Who is she, this fighting maid?" he asked, nudging hoary old Oleg Forkbeard, who was seated by him on the bench. Oleg turned blearily to Jorund, but when he opened his mouth it was the jarl's voice that boomed forth.

"She is the daughter of a warrior who sailed with me in the early days . . . and of a Valkyr," Borger declared, drawing Jorund's attention to the high seat. He obviously had been watching Jorund. "She is called Aaren Serricksdotter. She fights under an enchantment cast by the goddess Freya. She must be defeated in a blade-meeting by one lone man before she or her sisters can be mounted and bred . . . or married."

"Let me take a blade to 'er, jarl—" Old Forkbeard said as he reeled drunkenly to his feet. "I'll show her how 'er *mead-horn* gets filled!"

"She'll have your blood s-spilt, old man," came a slurred voice from the back, "long 'ere you'll have a chance to s-spill your *nectar* in her!" There were hoots of laughter all around.

"Since I claim one of the sisters," Garth insisted, "it's only fair that I should be the one to defeat the warrior-maid!" His presumption wrenched a howl of anger from the rest of the men and in the midst of the chaos, Borger turned to his eldest son and spoke in a loud voice.

"And what of you, First-born?" He leaned over the arm of his great chair to regard Jorund with a calculating expression. "Do you also claim the right to fight the battle-maiden . . . for the chance to wrestle with her in your furs?"

Every eye still capable of focusing turned on the eldest son of the jarl. Jorund Borgerson was the largest, strongest man in Borger's village—perhaps in all of Värmland. He could cut timber from sunrise to sunset without stopping, work a ship's oar for whole days and nights without rest, or carry a fallen comrade on his shoulders for a five-day march . . . indeed, had done all of those things. Of all the men in Borger's realm, he was the one best suited by size, skill, and power to defeat the battle-maiden. But for all his strength, he was the man least likely to raise a blade to her.

"I?" Jorund frowned and turned toward his father, detecting the glint in the old man's eye and sensing the purpose in his question. He knew Borger would love nothing more than to see him take up a blade and wreak mayhem with it. "I'll not fight a woman," he said, leaning back, pushing his long, muscular legs out before him and clasping his hands behind his head with a provocative air of sensual pride. "I have better things to do with women."

The wicked, knowing tilt of his grin was the unmistakable heritage of his lusty, quarrelsome father. All laughed; some with true good-humor, some with cloaked derision. Jorund's repute in matters of the flesh was well known. He had woman-luck that old Odin himself must have envied. The women of Borger's hall and village saw to it that he received the finest foods and the clearest ale, saved for him the choicest wool from their looms, and stitched his garments with special care. They laughed at his cleverness and his teasing . . . and at night they welcomed him to their furs with an eagerness that stirred resentment in the rest of Borger's men.

"A warrior . . . and maiden." Jorund turned the unthinkable combination over in his mind.

"Under Odin's enchantment—the Allfather himself ordered it cast upon her," Garth supplied, glaring at his older brother's deepening look of amusement.

"Odin's enchantment, my arse!" Jorund's deep laugh rumbled forth as he sat upright and looked around him at the sullen, drink-bloated faces of his kin and clansmen. "I don't believe in *enchantments* . . . there's no such thing." The way Borger began to puff up like a sweated toad pleased him and he smiled wickedly as he aimed his next verbal thrust with vengeful precision. "Come to think of it . . . I don't believe in *Odin*, either."

"Son of the Troubler!" Borger howled, sending yet another ale horn clattering to the floor before his seat. "You defame the immortals—mock the gods? Better that I had never taken you onto my knee when you were born. Better that I had set you out in the forest as a wolf-offering—"

"I do not mock *God*, old man," Jorund declared through a clamped jaw, "only those cruel and useless images you call gods. There is indeed an Allfather." His usually genial eyes narrowed with determination. "But his name is not *Odin*."

For the second time that night, Borger shoved to his feet, sputtering. It was a moment before he wrung the ale from both his soggy wits and his tongue. "It's that wretched priest what's done this to you—that Brother Godfrey. By the Red Thor's Wrath—I knew I should have tossed him overboard to drown when that storm came upon us. I may yet drown him with my own two hands . . . see if I don't!" Borger stalked back and forth, then stopped and braced his legs to keep from weaving. "Him and his talk of the *White Christ* and *charity* and *turning the other cheek*," he declared, slinging a battle-toughened finger toward the doors. "That foul, deceiving son of Loki . . . that adder with the shape of a man. . . . It's him what's poisoned you against honest fighting and the gods of Asgard!"

"*Nej*, old man." Jorund smacked his palms on the planking and pushed up slowly. His handsome countenance was stony as he stepped over the bench and confronted his sire. "It was not Godfrey who gave me a loathing for the reddening of spears . . ." The scathing heat of his gaze as he scanned Borger's combative frame laid the blame for his battle-loathing at another's feet.

"If you would have the high seat, First-born . . ." But the sparks those words struck in Jorund's eyes halted Borger and for a long moment they faced each other, testing the boundaries of the old bitterness between them. Then Jorund turned and strode out into the frosty night.

Borger sank back into his high seat and into his ale as he stared after his great, strapping, woman-pleasing son and wondered at the way the boy had gone wrong. His favored heir was strong as a bear, quick as a fox, sharp as a blade . . . and appallingly peaceable and good-natured. "What did I do to deserve such a fate?" he lamented to the half-conscious skald, Snorri, who leaned from a nearby bench to give him an ear. "I never asked the gods for much. A bit of victory here or there . . . a bit of fame when I'm ashes and gone . . . and a son and heir with a proper Viking battle-lust in his blood." He huffed, scratched his belly, and made a sour face.

"By the heavens . . . they got the *lust* part right . . . but forgot all about the *battle*!"

As the night air curled through his lungs and cooled his ire, Jorund's mind settled on the sanity and comfort to be had in woman-scented darkness. But after three long strides across the cold, moonlit clearing, he stopped dead, staring at the looming shape of the modest, steep-roofed women's house. *She* was there. He reeled off toward the darkened loft of the thrall house instead, where a jumble of welcoming arms and legs awaited. And again he stopped dead. He was not of a mood for fur-sport. Just now he had more of a yearning for companionship and talk.

He set a course for the thrall house after all, though not for the woman-sweetened loft. He crept through the darkened central chamber of the house, around bodies curled on benches and draped over mounds of straw, making his way to a low, wall-hung shelf from which a deafening snore rumbled forth. He gave the snorer's shoulder a sound shake. "Godfrey!" he shouted in a whisper. "Wake up!"

"Huhhh? Whaaat—" A round, tonsured head and fleshy face came lurching up out of the gloom, eyes wide and confused. "W-who . . . ?"

"It's me. Sit up," Jorund said quietly, nudging the priest to one side and easing onto the creaking planks beside him.

Godfrey pushed up unsteadily on one arm, blinked, and peered around them at the darkness. "It's the middle of the night," he moaned groggily. "What is it? What's happened?"

"You're about to be drowned . . . by Borger's own hands," Jorund informed him.

"Again?" Godfrey's eyes closed and his arm sagged so that he dropped back onto the pallet. "What did I do this time?" he mumbled. "I haven't converted any more of his women, I swear."

"You've corrupted me," Jorund said wryly, sliding his big frame to a comfortable slouch against the rough wall. "Turned me against the gods of Asgard . . . and against fighting."

"I have?" The implications of Jorund's words and the reason for Borger's anger at him slowly seeped through Brother Godfrey's sleep-numbed wits. His eyes flew open and he burrowed out of his patched woolen blanket. "I have? Why, that's wonderful." Beaming at the thought, he rubbed his face and wrested his rotund frame about until his back was planted against the wall and his unshod feet dangled over the edge of the wide shelf, copying Jorund's pose.

"I told him tonight that I don't believe in Odin . . . or Asgard or enchantments," Jorund said with an edge to his tone. "You should have heard him—he howled like a scalded hound."

"I'll wager he did!" Godfrey crowed, grinning before remembering himself and pulling his unholy pleasure beneath a wistful sigh. "I wish I could have seen it."

"And . . . he brought up the high seat again," Jorund said, after a pause. Godfrey opened his mouth, but closed it without speaking as he watched the troubling in Jorund's strong, chiseled face. "He is desperate . . . my brothers and his warriors sometimes grumble about what would happen if he took a wound."

"They wish to know what would happen, who would lead them," Godfrey mused. "Jorund, the high seat carries with it much power and that power could be used well."

"Never on his terms," Jorund said, smacking both fists against his thighs, declaring the subject closed. They sat for several moments in silence, until Jorund's hands uncurled and his body relaxed against the wall once more.

Godfrey suddenly caught a deeper meaning in what he had heard earlier, and turned to Jorund with a hopeful look. "You don't believe in Odin and Thor and the other gods of Asgard. . . . Does this mean you're ready to be a Christian?"

Jorund rubbed his stubbled chin as he studied the sturdy little priest. "Your White Christ has a powerful appeal, my friend. I cannot say I do not believe much of what you've revealed to me. But until your Christ allows a man to have more than one woman, he'll have to be content with my respect . . . not my soul."

Godfrey sighed and wagged his head. "My friend, you have a big and splendid heart. But you are so busy loving all women you can truly love none of them. Perhaps someday you will find one woman, a special woman, who will satisfy you . . . and then you will know the deep and wondrous kind of love my Lord intended and you will glimpse the larger peace that only He can give."

"Only one woman?" Jorund's frown melted into a wry wince. "By the Heavens, Godfrey! For a man who preaches love and goodwill, you have a most unholy cruel streak in you."

Chapter Three

The next morning, the village lay in silence as Aaren stepped from the women's house into the enveloping gray of early dawn. In the stillness, ribbons of mist hung over the commons, and frost rimmed the grass at her feet and silvered the tops of the houses around her. She looked toward the long hall, with its steep-sloping roof bearing serpentine carvings along the peak of the gable, and wondered what lay in store for her that day. Resettling the dagger at her waist with a determined smile, she set off for a morning run down the path toward the lake.

The air was cold and clear, invigorating. As she ran along the cliffs above the water, the shining Sky-Traveler poked his great red eye blearily above the horizon, looking as though he, like Borger's men, had spent the night in hard drinking. She welcomed his light on her face and the brightening glow of the sky above her and the shore below her. By the time she returned to the village, she felt refreshed, ready to resume the task of wresting a place of honor from the hands of men for herself and her younger sisters.

As she strode along the main path, between huts, byres, and animal pens, a number of heads turned and newly wakened villagers who had not been present in the hall the previous night stopped in their tracks and rubbed their eyes at the sight of her. She smiled at their whispers and curious looks; such responses were a measure of her uniqueness and a promise of the respect she was determined to win. But the pleasure died in her face when she rounded the corner of the women's house and spotted Miri and Marta standing before a door blocked by a handful of scowling women. On the ground, between her sisters and the others, lay her cloak, draped over a familiar bundle, and her silver-handled sword.

"Miri? Marta—what's wrong?" But even as she said it, the significance of her things on the ground between the two factions became clear to her. Marta's words only confirmed it.

"These women say they will not have a warrior sleeping in the women's house—" She rushed to Aaren's side with a pale, troubled expression.

"They say it is bad luck for a *battle-maker* to sleep among the *peace-weavers* in the women's house," soft-spoken Miri added.

"They're afraid their looms will foul and their needles break, and that"—Marta's voice caught in her throat—"your blade will make their milk curdle in their breasts."

"Only women belong in the women's house . . . it has always been so. When a woman among us wants to be with a warrior, she must go to his furs for the night. Ask Inga," a thick-featured older woman declared, jerking her thumb at a wraith of a woman peering at them from the doorway. "She once brought a warrior across our threshold, took him to her furs, and her child was born without breath."

"But Aaren is a woman," Marta insisted. "Like us."

"*Not* like us." A graying, fine-featured woman with an air of authority stepped forward, running a wary eye over Aaren's breastplate, male leggings, and wristbands. "She dresses like a warrior and wields a blade like a warrior—"

"Because I am a warrior," Aaren insisted irritably, finding herself caught in an unexpected quandary. She was indeed a warrior, and the shape of her and her sisters' lives among Borger's people depended on the respect and honor she could earn as one. But now they declared that as a warrior she could not stay in the women's house with her sisters. The anxiety in Miri's and Marta's sweet faces struck her to the core . . . as did the thought of being separated from them. "But because I am a warrior-*maid* I have the right to sleep by my sisters in the house of women."

"There are warriors and there are women," the leader proclaimed their common sentiment, drawing nods and murmurs of agreement. "You must be one or the other—"

"Who are you to declare what I must be?" Aaren demanded, advancing on the woman, who drew back a pace before finding her resolve and lifting her chin.

"I am Helga . . . once wife to jarl Borger . . . still keeper of his storehouse." Her work-roughened hand slid to the ring of keys that dangled at her waist, the symbol of her authority and of her right to speak.

"I am not a gleaning from Borger's fields, or a barrel of ale to come under your hand!" The air grew charged, the tension thick as peat smoke, as Aaren confronted their ultimatum with hot eyes and tender pride.

"There's Jorund!" one of the women behind Helga exclaimed, pointing across the clearing. "Ask him, he'll know—" They called and waved, and when Aaren pivoted to see who they summoned, she found herself facing the huge, flaxen-haired warrior she had seen the night before. She watched his smooth, rolling gait and the easy carriage of his massive shoulders as he approached, and felt an odd prickling up the back of her neck. Him? They called him to settle their dispute?

"What say you, Jorund . . . judge between us fairly," Helga said when he stopped nearby and settled back on one leg, scrutinizing the gathering. "You know we do not allow a warrior under our roof. Now this one comes—" She gestured to Aaren with a curt hand and took a step back, toward the safety of the other women. "What say you? Is this a woman or a warrior?"

Aaren watched his wide, sensual mouth slide into a knowing smile as he turned his gaze on her. "A *woman* or a *warrior*?" he mused, in tones as clear as a mountain stream . . . and just as liquid and engulfing. "Hmmm . . . let me see . . ."

Aaren bristled as he leaned first one way, then another, viewing her critically from more than one perspective. Then he stalked slowly around her to view her rear and she wheeled to keep him in her sight.

"What right has he to pass judgment on me?" she demanded, slinging a hot glance over her shoulder at the women, then spearing him with a similar one. The women's only response was a murmur and nervous tittering. He deigned not to answer, either. Instead, he edged closer . . . then closer still, as if testing her, crowding her with his presence, prodding her to react in some way.

Her mind worked frantically, assessing this unprecedented situation. If she stood her ground and didn't move, it would seem she was submitting to his judgment; if she withdrew, it would seem she was retreating from his intense scrutiny, as she had the previous night. Nothing in her battle training or her limited social experience had prepared her for so very personal and disturbing a confrontation.

She saw his eyes wandering over her shoulders, breasts, and waist, and felt them pause speculatively upon her hips. Certain that his hands would soon follow, she braced, making fists, ready to knock him flat if he so much as laid a finger on her.

"Looks like a woman," he murmured, circling her like a forest cat on the prowl. He stopped unexpectedly before her and lowered his head toward her shoulder. He moved his head inward, along the slope of her shoulder to the side of her neck, then her ear, then poised with his nose almost touching the hair at her temple. All along the route he breathed in deeply. He was sniffing her! Her nerves began to quiver with something reassuringly close to outrage and her stomach tightened.

"Smells like a woman," he announced in a husky rumble that poured down the side of her neck like sun-warmed honey. While she was grappling for mental footing against the encroaching wall of his wool-clad chest, she saw his shoulders dip to one side—and felt his hand clamp over her buttock and squeeze!

She brought both fists up and gave his chest a furious punch—but at the very moment he jerked away, so that her move met little resistance and jolted her more than him.

"Feels like a woman, too," he declared, laughing at the anger that flared in her. "She looks, smells, and feels like a woman." He shrugged his massive shoulders. "Then she must *be* a woman. But if you still have doubts, Helga"— he turned his insolent blond head toward the leader of the women and waggled his brows—"I would be pleased to take her to *my* furs to sleep."

The women's tension dissolved in smiles and soft chuckles, and even Miri and Marta were coaxed into a smile at the handsome giant's bold and easy manner. But their laughter, for all its gentleness, struck Aaren like a broadside from a battle axe. Her face caught fire, her body snapped taut, her teeth ground together as her pride weathered a fierce pounding. She scrambled to think of some way to counter it in kind—for something to *say*!—but her tongue felt weighted with stones.

There was a glint in his eye as he turned away that made it seem he had claimed something from her, a small piece of her honor, a bit of her dignity. Suddenly she recognized him as an opponent . . . though an altogether different kind of adversary than old Serrick had outlined for her. This enemy was subtle as a serpent; all knowing smiles and honey-sweet tones and easy, assuming manner. And the threat he posed was far more disturbing than the familiar danger of sinew and blade: he had declared her a woman . . . *not a warrior*.

"You may stay with your sisters in the women's house, battle-maiden," the woman called Helga said, breaking into Aaren's glowering thoughts. When she turned, the woman took a step back and drew in her chin. "But you and your blade must sleep in the alcove at the side . . . where we store things. It is the best we can do."

Aaren took a heavy breath, feeling the persuasive tug of her sister's anxiety. When she nodded agreement, the tension eased all around and the women began to whisper amongst themselves.

"We are short of hands and the work of harvest now weighs hard upon us. And most of the men are busy celebrating Borger's great victory," Helga declared with unmistakable resentment. "Do your sisters have hearth-skill that will earn them their keeping?"

"Miri and Marta are skilled in women's tasks," Aaren said, returning Helga's bold-eyed scrutiny. "They are meant to use their skills in the jarl's service . . . even as I use my blade."

Helga gave Miri and Marta a long, assessing look, then frowned. "This is Sith," she said, gesturing to the coarse-faced woman who had spoken so boldly against Aaren earlier. "She is the head of the dairy. And these are Kara and Gudrun. They tend Borger's hearth and o'ersee the cooking and serving in the hall," she said, waving to two plump, sable-haired women who looked as though they'd sampled more than a bit of their own handiwork. "And that is Bedria, who brews the ale, keeps the bees; and Inga and Moria, who weave and spin . . ." There she stopped and clasped her hands before her as if containing the urge to say more.

"We spend daylight and squander breath," she pronounced disapprovingly, then glanced at Aaren. "Moria will show you where to put your possessions." She led all but a few of the women across the commons and past the long hall toward the fields beyond.

Marta snatched up the bundle of clothes and wrapped her arms around it, and Aaren picked up her sword to carry it back into the women's house. She paused by the door, glancing back over her shoulder toward the far edge of the clearing where the one they called Jorund had disappeared.

"You're wrong, Spawn of a Frost Giant," she muttered under her breath. "I am a *warrior*. And I shall prove it to you."

That morning, Miri and Marta were given small tasks around the women's house and after an awkward bit of just standing and staring, Aaren escaped to explore the village and the surrounding countryside. Most of the wooden houses were deserted; the women and thralls were out in the fields, beginning the cutting and bundling of the barleycorn, rye, and wheat. She walked along the path leading out to the fields and stood watching the waving grain—the precious, wind-ruffled mane-of-the-fields—and the harvesters, women with their kirtles raised and tied and a few thrall men stripped to the waist and covered with sweat.

How well she knew the labor of harvest, the rhythmic swing of the scythe, the scent of dry grasses, the sharp stubble, and the strain of bending. Every autumn she and Serrick and Miri and Marta had reaped their mountain meadows together. A powerful yearning suddenly welled in her and she was tempted to strip off her sword and breastplate and take a place in the row of harvesters. But she recalled Serrick's caution—"a warrior is known by his deeds"—and as she searched the workers she noted that there were no other warriors in the fields just now. She turned away, feeling a disturbing discontent that she understood had to do with the forbidding bar that had fallen over the doors of her old life, separating it irrevocably from the new.

Mid-morning, Aaren sat in the autumn sun, on the top of a great rock overlooking Lake Väner. She had spent some time wielding her blade and working her muscles as Serrick had taught her and now rested. The crunch of stone on stone behind her sent her whirling about with her hand on her dagger. A young lad stood a few paces away, eyeing her warily.

"The jarl . . . he sent me," the boy said. "Come to th' hall." When she picked up her blade and rolled her shoulders, the lad jerked back as if startled by her motion and went scurrying back along the rocky path.

She strode briskly after him, her mind racing ahead to what awaited her in Borger's hall. She had anticipated the call, imagined it, burned for it. She was eager to get on with her next blade-match, to unleash the tension that lay coiled in her against an opponent, and to prove to both the jarl and that great flaxen-haired giant that she possessed a true warrior's strength and weapon-skill. For the hundredth time that morning, Marta's question crept into her mind. How many warriors would she have to defeat before they accorded her a true warrior's place in the hall?

The massive wooden doors of the hall stood open to the early autumn warmth and the hall was filled with dusky light admitted by the smoke hole above the great stone hearth in the center. The long planking tables had not yet been cleared away from the previous night's revel, and atop them and around them on the floor were empty bowls and pitchers and fish bones discarded from the morning's meal. Borger's men were draped over the tables, wearing squints and scowls, their heads banging with the rattle of emptied ale barrels.

Aaren stepped across the sill and paused to let her eyes adjust to the dimmer interior. Her hands clenched at her sides as she surveyed the formidable gathering. A motion to her right caught her eye and she turned her shoulders, bracing; she beheld a man sprawled in the corner, shackled by neck and leg, and secured to the wall with heavy iron chains. A pair of icy gray eyes glared at her through the gloom and a face appeared, strong-featured, muscular, and wearing several days' growth of beard and who-knew-how-many-days' layers of grime.

The sense of his position and plight washed over Aaren in that brief instant of contact: a warrior . . . a prisoner. There was no fate dreaded more by a Norseman than being held captive in the hall of his enemy. Better to die in battle than to live in chains, Serrick had said. She would never allow herself to be held captive, she vowed as she strode through the hall and stood before the high seat.

"You sent for me, jarl?"

"I did." Borger's voice boomed out over a sudden quiet. He leaned forward with his hands braced on his knees and his arms bowed out. As he passed a hard gaze over her, his attention caught on the blade she wore strapped against the front of her left shoulder and slid from it to the molded leather over her breast. A slow smile spread over his features. "What manner of weapon do you wield, Serricksdotter?"

"A blade of the Ulfberhts," she declared, sliding the shoulder strap over her head and slipping the blade from its sheath. The polished blue-silver blade gleamed as she lifted it into the sunlight and turned it slowly, reflecting the light into the grizzled faces around her. A murmur rippled through the men and a number of them shoved to their feet, their eyes fixed on her weapon.

A sword from the Rhineland, from the famous forge of the Ulfberhts, was indeed a treasure. Such blades were widely reputed to be harder, tougher, lighter, and to hold their edge against far weightier weapons. Borger's eyes widened.

"Such a blade should have a name," he said, with undisguised appreciation.

"She has a name. Singer."

"Singer?" Borger snorted and crossed his arms over his chest. "What manner of name is that for a blade?"

"A fitting name . . . for she sings sweetly on the air." With a powerful snap of her arm and swirl of her wrist, she set the blade whirring above her head so that the air hummed with sound. Then she brought it slashing in a downward arc between her and Borger . . . from shoulder to opposite knee and back up the opposite direction . . . so close to the old jarl's arms that it brushed the hair on them as it passed. When she brought it to a halt, tip upraised, Borger jolted back a step, taken aback by her boldness . . . and the display of skill that had shaved the hair from his arm without so much as nicking the skin beneath. A number of the men shoved to their feet, their eyes narrowed to slits, their muscles twitching.

"By the Great Hurler—" Borger bellowed, his face puffing so that his whiskers stood out like a hedgehog's quills. Then he turned to his men and called, "Thorkel Evardson!"

A tall, lanky warrior, well-seasoned by sea salt and blade-battle, rushed forward to accept his jarl's command. Borger looked from Aaren to the formidable warrior, who was exactly her equal in height, and broke into a cool smile. "Draw your blade, Thorkel Ever-ready. And break for us the Allfather's curse."

Aaren gave her new opponent a long look, which he returned in kind, then she strode to a nearby table to set her scabbard aside and prepare for the fight. Her heart beat faster as she tightened her wristbands and braced a foot up on the edge of the table and leaned into it to stretch her legs. In the midst of stretching her other leg, she looked up—straight into the face of the handsome blond giant, the woman-judge.

He stood a few paces away, his chest heaving and his hair wind-tossed, as if he'd just run a long distance. For a few unsettled heartbeats, they stared at each other, bodies taut, faces heating. Then she narrowed her eyes and her lips formed her silent claim: *warrior*.

Behind her, a blood-chilling cry tore from the throat of her opponent. She just had time to clasp the grip of her sword as she pivoted to meet his rush. The suddenness of his attack had caught her off guard, half-prepared; she'd had no time to warm and stretch or even put away her hair.

The first three hacks of his blade forced her back three huge steps, then a sideways slash sent her dodging and feinting. Then something in the familiar ring of steel on steel penetrated her senses and began to resonate deep in her core, calling forth her strength and summoning her nerve and skill. She dug in her heels and met, then countered, his next blow. Around them the men were on their feet, shouting, galvanized by the savage start of the fight and by the battle-maid's struggle to meet Thorkel's attack.

The lean, battle-toughened warrior wore a wild-eyed grin, which dimmed progressively as Aaren's resistance to his blows increased. Aaren wore a smile also, but on the inside. For after the first shock of his lightning-quick strike, she had recovered and assessed his fierce, straightforward style . . . down-hacking and free-swinging that made use of his powerful arms and chest. After two more crashing blows, she understood exactly how to counter him.

She began to divert his powerful blows like a roof did rain, shrugging them off, letting them slide down her blade again and again. Over and over she played her waiting game, giving him the edge, then snatching it from him. Then, growing frustrated by her increasing resistance, he began hurling insults.

"Your father was but a thrall man . . . your mother, a blackened troll!" he snarled, panting. "Your blade does not sing, troll's daughter—it whines for mercy."

With each foam-flecked slur, her shoulders tightened and her grip on her blade grew more sure. Slowly, she pared away sensation—the shaking fists, the shouts of the warriors, the taunts of her opponent—until sight and sound became mere light and vibration. All she saw was her opponent's face, the contorting angles of his body, and the flashing arcs of his blade as it cut through the air around her. And in her racing mind, made fleet by the battle-fever in her blood, his movements seemed to slow and lengthen, became exaggerated and predictable. . . .

Jorund stood rooted to the hard-packed floor, watching the maid battle one of the most renowned bladesmen in his father's band of warriors. He silently cursed old Borger for his prickly pride and his wretched thirst for the dew of wounds. It was sure slaughter, sending a young woman, even a battle-maiden, against a hardened veteran of twelve Viking seasons. But he could not tear his gaze from it, could not keep his shoulders from twitching defensively with every tuck and dart of hers, could not keep his blood from pounding in his veins as he watched.

Then, before his eyes, she suddenly roared to life as she had the previous night. Springing up with her blade braced, she gave Thorkel an upward rip that just missed opening him from groin to chin. As he lurched back, she pressed the attack, using both hands and wielding her blade with such quickness that all heard—or imagined hearing—it sing upon the air.

She moved with fierce, animallike grace, in a swirl of hip-length hair that shone whenever they surged into the dusty shafts of sunlight pouring through the roof. She was both woman and warrior, a living flame bent on engulfing her opponent. Her features were carved by concentration into a taut mask that radiated sensual heat and her eyes glowed like a Persian tiger's—hot and golden—hungry in a way that stirred his loins and ignited his blood. He was riveted to the sight of her long, willowy form, swaying and almost yielding—then suddenly snapping taut and driving forcefully, charging.

Again and again her heels dug into the earthen floor, and the sleek muscles of her legs braced, her buttocks tightened, and her shoulders whipped taut as she swung her blade. She was a raging storm, a nerve-searing bolt of raw fury trapped inside a sleek, steel-thewed frame . . . caged and controlled . . . yet not subdued. Every nerve in Jorund's body was quivering. He began to feel the shock of the blows she received in his own muscles, as if they'd been dealt to him. His arms flexed, his weight shifted, and his gut tightened in response. . . .

Borger stood before his high seat, watching not the fight but his eldest son's reaction to it. Jorund's eyes shimmered like liquid silver, molten with lust, and his face was bronzed and fierce with wanting. Borger read the clenched fists, straining muscles, and involuntary movements of his son's body as signs of arousal, and the old jarl's countenance began to glow. Whether it was the battle or the woman that had inflamed Jorund so, he could not know. But it heartened him to see his son burning so fiercely over anything. For months now, he had been desperate to get his heir's blood up and instill some proper "Viking" ferocity in him.

He turned back to the fight to find Serrick's daughter advancing valiantly on Thorkel and knew she would soon have him worn down. Raw admiration bloomed in him as his eyes slid over her magnificent body and drank in the powerful grace of her movements. Such thighs! Odin's Living Stones! A warrior could reach Valhalla itself while trapped between those thighs! What a creature she was, to inspire such a delicious combination of woman-lust and battle-lust in a man . . . and delivered into his very lap just when he was about to abandon all hope for his eldest son and heir. His crafty eyes almost misted. The battle-wench was the fulfillment of a desperate father's prayers!

Aaren's blood roared in her head, her muscles screamed, and sweat rolled down the back of her neck and between her breasts and shoulder blades. But her concentration was unbroken by the pain and fatigue; her pace continued quick and steady. She could feel Thorkel slowing, could see the strain in his sweat-slicked body and feel the desperation in his blows. It was only a matter of time, she understood without conscious thought. And that knowledge fired both her senses and her caution; the final throes of battle were always the most desperate and therefore the most dangerous.

Drawing on her deepest reserves, she now launched a new offensive, using her feet against him, throwing kicks, connecting with his braced knees and jarring his arms, forcing him back farther and farther. Then she leaped onto the benches along one wall and used the added height to advantage, raining downward blows on his blade. When she bolted down onto the earthen floor again, he bellowed, raised his sword in both hands, and charged her full out.

She felt more than heard his battle cry and her senses focused on a single stark line—a demarcation between life and death. She saw the tilt, the beginning of the swing, and in an instant projected the full circle it would inscribe. Instead of raising her blade to meet it, she whirled to counter with a savage sideways blow, intercepting it at the point of least control.

The hit spun his shoulders to the side, throwing him off balance. He slammed into the hearthstones and wobbled—just as she reversed and brought her blade crashing into the hilt of his. Before he could right either his balance or his weapon, she had struck his sword from his hands and thrust her blade, point-first, at him, sending him sprawling back onto the upraised hearth in a billow of cold ashes. She bounded after him and in the blink of an eye stood astride him, her steel pressed to his heart.

There was dead silence in the hall, except for the sound of Thorkel's choking on the flying ash. Every man in the hall suffered a violent shiver at the sight of her standing on the upraised hearth in the shaft of sunlight, wrapped in the fiery haze of her tangled hair, her long, powerful legs astride their comrade's prone body. In that stunning moment, she was the very essence of a Valkyr . . . the fierce goddess of every warrior's dreams, challenging each man to taste her passion, to drink of her and die a hero's death. Each warrior burned to test both his sword arm and his flesh-blade against her hot, lathered body . . . to find and claim the Valhalla they glimpsed within her.

She fought back crashing waves of dark and light in her senses . . . her lungs were raw and her heart beat as though it would burst from her chest. Then through that inner chaos came the low, sweet trill of understanding—of triumph. She had won! Suddenly the pain and discomfort of her body were swept away in a massive eruption of exultation. She turned to Borger and found him standing with his feet braced wide and his thumbs tucked in his belt.

"I claim victory, jarl," she panted hoarsely. "And with it, I claim a seat in your hall, a place at your board . . . and a warrior's honor in your service." A ripple of angry surprise went through Borger's men at her bold demand.

The jarl narrowed his eyes and raised his chin to answer her.

"This day you have earned a place at my board, Serrick's daughter. But as to the rest . . . you cannot serve both my purposes and Odin's," he declared with a guileful expression. "You will be *my* warrior when you are *his* no longer."

A clamor broke out amongst the men as each demanded the right to snatch her from the Allfather's grasp. Aaren jumped down from the hearth with her blood still roaring in her head and her body still vibrating with battle-fury as she grappled with the jarl's words. He refused to honor her victories? She stood, feeling charred and confused, as he stepped down from his seat and swaggered toward her, his gaze fastened greedily on the damp cling of her tunic beneath the leather breastplate and on the wild tangle of her hair. He stopped two paces away and wheeled to face his men.

"From this day forward," he declared in ringing tones, "there is but one man who may challenge and fight old Serrick's daughter." Not a breath was taken or let in the hall as they waited to learn which warrior had found such favor with the jarl. *"Jorund Borgerson."*

A typhoon hitting the hall couldn't have unleashed more of a storm than that shocking decree. "Jorund?" came outraged shouts from Borger's younger sons and warriors.

"Have you lost your wits, old man?" Garth lurched forward, his fists raised and his face crimson with ire. "He's no fighter!"

"You heard 'im—he's got no stomach for blade-battle!" A burly fellow with sooty hands jabbed a thick, black finger at Borger.

"He'll never defeat her," Hakon the Freeholder snarled, shaking a fist. "He's too soft on women—he'd never raise his hand to one!"

Aaren stood in the center of that storm, buffeted by their anger and stunned by the jarl's vehement proclamation. One man? He was declaring that only one man could fight her? And the others were virulent in their opposition to his choice of this "Jorund" as her sole opponent. Something about the name brushed a cord of memory, but her head was too filled with heat and disbelief to think why it seemed familiar.

Borger stumped back to his high seat and turned a violent glare on the warriors to his left. They looked over their shoulders and drew back to give Borger a clear line of sight. As Aaren followed his compelling stare across the hall, the men parted to give her a clear view of a huge male frame sprawled insolently on a bench.

It was *him*, she realized with a start. Jorund was the great, strapping warrior who had sniffed at her, squeezed her buttock, and declared her a woman instead of a warrior. *Borgerson.* A jolt of recognition went through her at his sire-name. She cast a hot look between the blond giant and the jarl, and perceived the common mold of eye and nose and jaw. He was the old jarl's son!

Objections flew thick and furious around the hall: "He won't lift a blade," "Hasn't gone a'viking for two summer seasons now," "Refused to come wi' us when we raided old Gunnar Haraldson!" and "Whenever there's fightin' to be done, he stays home with the women." Then they summed up their complaints against him with a name: *"Jorund Woman-heart!"*

Aaren watched Jorund's defiantly relaxed pose and unruffled countenance with astonishment that turned slowly to unreasoning anger. What warrior of pride and honor would just sit and listen to himself described so? Soft . . . blade-shy . . . woman-hearted. *Jorund Woman-heart.* They named him a coward and he just sat there, seemingly untroubled by their open derision and unwilling to defend his honor. Her muscles tightened, her jaw clamped, and her tawny eyes narrowed, focusing scornfully on him as well. A warrior with no honor was no warrior at—

It struck her like a fist in the gut: Borger had just declared that no man could challenge and fight her but this Jorund Woman-heart! Horror collected like stoneweights in her stomach as she realized her fate was being linked to that of the coward of the village. How dare the jarl do this to her, when she'd fought valiantly and triumphed over his warriors in her first two tests?

"*Nej!*" she declared hotly, drawing every eye in the hall upon her. She strode to face the high seat, her face ablaze with indignation. "I have no wish to fight a man with no fire in his blood." She leveled a look of fierce contempt on Jorund's insolent frame. He responded by sitting straighter and meeting her gaze full on with a smug, insinuating smile that recalled their earlier encounter and his degrading assessment of her. Bracing her feet apart, she stiffened her spine and impaled him with the spear of her gaze.

"I am a warrior . . . not a coward. And I'll have no dealings with *cowards*."

The taunting pleasure in Jorund's face dimmed as her verbal blow struck . . . then it faded altogether. He glanced around him at the vengeful, expectant looks on the men's faces. Never in all the taunts and teasing, never in all the rough banter directed at him in Borger's hall, had that word been uttered against him. *Coward.* It was a strong word, a *fighting* word. And with it the fiery-eyed maid had willfully crossed the narrow and precarious line between insult and true injury.

The hall grew progressively more hushed and the air grew thick as his big, relaxed body slowly gathered. He fixed a heated look on the battle-maiden and shoved to his feet, every muscle now taut, every feature pared sharper by determination. And he stalked forward.

Aaren watched him come, moving like a great rangy wolf . . . massive muscles working visibly . . . shoulders swaying, long legs flexing . . . feet padding softly. Her heart lurched as he filled, then crowded, her perceptions. He stopped a pace away and closed the remaining distance by small, ever more intimidating increments . . . daring her to retreat, to run from his big, potent body.

Closer . . . closer, he swayed, until his ribs settled against the molded leather that covered her breasts, his thighs nudged hers, and her senses were smothered with his heat. She had to tilt her head back to continue to meet his stare as he loomed above her. He was a full head taller and his huge shoulders were half-again as wide.

She held her ground, refusing to reveal how unnerved she was by his superior size and by the slow, disturbing way he inflicted it on her. She met him eye to eye, determined to face him down, telling herself that if he truly had no battle-fire in his blood then he was not to be feared.

But as her gaze slid into his, her heart pounded harder and her blood surged into her already heated skin. She swayed, feeling as if she was being pushed—or pulled—off balance, teetering on the rim of some bottomless chasm and deathly afraid of falling into it. Suddenly all she could see were the sun-bronzed angles of his face, the wind-tossed jumble of his hair, the bold lightning-blue of his gaze. All she could feel was the heat radiating from his body into hers, melting some nameless part of her and sending it trickling down the curve of her spine and the inner parts of her thighs. It was a reaction to a power in him that had nothing to do with arms and the reddening of spears. It was a power that had to do with the instinctive and long-suppressed "woman" in her.

Her eyes narrowed fiercely to hide her alarm. But a slow, taunting smile spread over his handsome mouth and crinkles of amusement appeared at the corners of his eyes. When he pulled back two steps, she staggered and had to take a step to brace herself, feeling oddly drained and furious at feeling that way.

Jorund turned to Borger and declared in tones that rumbled forth like boulders crashing down a mountainside: "I will defeat her . . . in my own time."

With that, he turned and strode out, leaving Aaren steaming, the hall in turmoil, and old Borger slapping his thigh and crowing:

"Did ye hear that? He'll fight her! *Ale*—this calls for *ale*!"

Aaren didn't wait to hear more. She snatched up her scabbard and shoved through the gawking men to stride furiously for the door. The crackle of her burning pride so filled her head that at first she didn't even see Miri and Marta waiting anxiously, just outside. Their faces were flushed and their eyes were luminous with unshed tears as they hurried to throw their arms around her.

"Aaren! We were so worried," Marta said with a smile of relief, which faded with her next thought. "And now you have yet another warrior to fight . . . that Jorund."

"Aaren . . . he's so big," Miri said, looking fearful.

Aaren heard the angry comments of the men pouring out of the hall behind them, and pulled her sisters toward the women's house.

"Have you not heard it said," she declared with a searing glance over her shoulder, "that the bigger the boar, the bigger the feast he makes?"

Chapter Four

Word that the battle-maiden was about to fight again had spread on swift feet through the village, then beyond. Helga's boy had come running to the fields where the women and thralls were cutting and bundling sheaves of barley. Jorund, who worked with them, dropped his scythe and went running to the hall. Then a short while later, news fanned like wildfire through the line of female harvesters: Aaren Serricksdotter had defeated Thorkel the Ever-ready and Jorund Borgerson would be the next to fight her. The women stared in disbelief at one another, then promptly abandoned their sickles and hurried back to the village themselves, to learn if it was true.

In the hall, they found Thorkel sulking, Jorund missing, and Borger and his men up to their snouts in ale, yet again.

They exchanged horrified looks and ran straight to the women's house. Once inside, the sight of Aaren's angry, sweat-slicked frame and wild, tangled hair caused them to press warily along the wall, as far from her as they could get. Collecting into a tense, silent knot near Inga's stool by the window, they traded prodding looks . . . which somehow elected Gudrun Hearth-tender to speak for them.

"It is true then, Battle-maiden? You will fight Jorund?" The hearth-tender's voice wavered slightly.

"It is true. I will fight the one they call Jorund Woman-heart," Aaren said. "Though there will be little honor in defeating one with no warrior-pride and no battle-fire in his blood. May Borger's bile burn like hot coals in his belly for yoking me to such a one." She ground her teeth at the frowns and harried looks her declaration caused. They were clearly horrified by the thought of her—a female who slept in their house—blade-fighting.

Another movement by the door distracted her, and she found Helga and a number of others crowding through the doorway, pausing at the sight of her, then sliding off along the wall. The far side of the chamber was suddenly filled with women wearing up-tucked skirts and anxious expressions on their flushed and dusty faces. The confirmation was whispered from one to another, and their heads bobbed like grain in the wind as the news was passed. One by one, they turned to her in distress.

"H-have you ever killed a man, Serricksdotter?" one asked in a tortured whisper, while the rest leaned closer to collect her answer.

"*Nej*, I have never slain a man in battle," she declared, flushing hot at the admission. Their tense shoulders sagged and faces smoothed noticeably at her response.

"Then . . . have you ever maimed?" another choked out, shrinking behind the others' shoulders when Aaren turned a simmering look upon her.

"Cut off any parts, she means." Thick-featured Sith took up the question bluntly. "You ever cut off any parts?"

"My share," she proclaimed, telling herself that hanks of hair and an occasional scrape of skin qualified as "parts." Their eyes widened and some reached nervously for another's hands.

"Arms or legs—hands or feet—which?" a woman with frizzed red hair demanded. "Or noses or ears or"—she swallowed hard—"manly parts?"

Aaren stiffened and clenched her hands at her sides. "None of those," she ground out through clenched jaws, adding defensively: "yet." Her confusion mounted when they exchanged wilting looks and murmurs, some pressing moist foreheads, others fanning themselves with their hands. Their pleasure at learning she had wreaked so little havoc with her blade gored her already embattled warrior's pride. "But perhaps Jorund Woman-heart will be the first!"

"Oh, no!" Inga exclaimed above a general intake of air. "Don't start with the Breath-stealer!" There was a clamor of dismay at the prospect.

"Pray not!" the usually dignified Helga cried, her face draining of color. "He needs all his parts, Serricksdotter."

"How would our Honey-hunter swing a scythe or cast a fishing net or carve a comb . . . or help rob my bees . . . without his hands?" Bedria the Bee-woman asked, venturing closer, extending her own hands, palms up, in supplication.

"How could Gentle-rider mount a horse or hunt or wrestle or give the children a ride on his shoulders without his strong legs?" Kara Hearth-tender spoke up next, giving her stout thigh a thump.

"How would Slow-hand lift things for us or train our hawks or shear our sheep?" said a dark-eyed thrall woman with a dark blue swelling about one eye and at the corner of her lip. She lowered her face and voice. "And how would he send angry husbands packing . . . without his big arms?"

"And his face—which pleasures our eyes so—you cannot mar that with a blade," another insisted, stepping closer.

"And his broad back that carries our burdens . . . his big body which warms our furs . . . you must spare them, Battle-maiden! Winters are too long and cold as it is!" another cried.

"And Breath-stealer's eyes, which speak without words . . ."

"And his mouth, which stirs such tempests in a woman's flesh . . ."

Aaren lurched back a step, then another, stunned by the nature of their pleading. They weren't outraged at the thought of her fighting, she realized. They were horrified by the prospect of her fighting Jorund . . . and possibly injuring him! It poured through her like hot pitch: he was such a blade-shy weakling that the village women felt they had to plead for him and protect him! The realization that she was bound to such a man, especially in a matter of honor, set her blood roaring anew and her muscles twitching.

"Odin himself decreed my fate," she snapped, finding herself nearly surrounded and backing toward the door as they pressed closer. "And the jarl has decreed my opponent. I did not choose to fight him." She halted and searched the pained and pleading expressions turned upon her. "But I will be more than pleased to add his name to the role of warriors I have defeated. When I fight, I fight to win, as a true warrior must. Your *Breath-stealer* will have to watch out for his own wretched hide!"

She snatched up her blade and ducked out the door, striding straight for the forest. Desperate to spend the steam pent up in her quaking frame, she spotted a foot-worn path through the trees and began to run along it, driven by her own volatile emotions and a host of women's voices pursuing and entreating her, interceding for their "Breath-stealer." Spurred by their pleas, she stretched out her strain-cramped legs and expelled a blast of tension with each panting breath.

She ran until her legs wobbled, until her lungs felt raw, and until the ringing clash of steel on steel and the voices of the women faded in her head. Then she halted, and walked, retracing her steps, setting one foot before the other until all that was left in her senses was the soft blur of golden light interspersed with vivid greens and browns, and the feel of the autumn breeze caressing her skin.

After a time, she emerged from the trees into a grassy field that ended some distance away in a jagged line of gray-blue. It registered in her mind that this was the meadow near the village, by the cliff overlooking the great Väner. With numbing weariness spreading up her legs, she stumbled toward the edge of the cliff and fell . . .

. . . onto a thick hummock of grasses near the cliff's edge and into a restoring sleep.

Jorund had burst from the side door of the long hall and stretched his long legs along the well-worn path, intending to retrace his steps toward the fields and the harvest work he had abandoned earlier. But he could scarcely mind his course or his feet. His blood and his pride were both aflame, his body throbbed with unspent heat, and his senses were stuffed to overflowing with Aaren Serricksdotter.

She was everything and nothing that he had come to expect in a woman: beautiful yet intimidating, alluring yet fearsome, startlingly warlike yet womanly in a way he'd never experienced before. The size of her was a stunning novelty, the shape of her was sheer enticement, and the raw strength and brazen spirit of her were a pure challenge . . .

especially to a man who knew women well. And no man in the clans of the northmen knew women better than Jorund Borgerson.

By the time he had earned fifteen summers, he had already discovered the secret of womanhood: that there was a unique riddle at the core of every woman which held the key to her deepest passions. Once solved, that puzzle yielded up a woman's responses and loyalties to the man who had dared solve it.

But in this Aaren Serricksdotter he glimpsed not one but a whole maze of tantalizing mysteries. How had she acquired such weapon-skill? How could both "woman" and "blade-fighter" exist together within one tempting skin? What manner of fire burned in her heart of hearts? And what manner of longings lay hidden within her well-shielded breast? The boldness and brilliance of her fighting were undeniable. But twice now, when he pressed close and his probing gaze began to penetrate her, she had wavered, then bristled like a cornered hedgehog. There was a hint of uncertainty in the way she faced him and a trace of surprise in her anger at the provocative, physical way he confronted her. . . .

"Jorund!"

He raised his head and found himself standing with his fists clenched and his chest heaving . . . in the middle of the path which led down to the sandy stretch of shore where the fishing boats were beached and Borger's long ships were moored. He glanced around, surprised to find himself so far from his original destination. Godfrey was barreling down the path after him with his cassock raised about his pudgy knees and his sandaled feet splatting against the packed earth. The portly Saxon priest jolted to a halt, staggered, and sucked in three wheezing breaths before he could speak.

"I heard . . . you're going to fight . . . the maiden . . ." he gasped out, clasping his chest.

Maiden. The word shot through Jorund's mind like a lightning bolt. The first of her mysteries was instantly solved; that odd tenuousness in her . . . it was *virgin.* Battle-*maiden.* He flashed a lusty smile as the thought sent a hot surge through his already aching loins. Despite her size and skill, she was still a young woman . . . one who had never known a man. In any contest between them, he would have that edge.

"Pray, say you will not do so dishonorable a thing—you cannot fight a woman!"

"Have you ever known me to hurt a woman, Godfrey?" Jorund said, propping his large hands at his waist and leveling a penetrating look on the earnest cleric.

"I . . . well . . . n-no." Godfrey's round shoulders sagged. "But I heard that your father decreed that you must fight her, and that you declared you would." He tucked both his chins and gazed at Jorund from beneath a crinkled brow. "And that . . . she called you a *coward.*" Jorund's usually genial face darkened.

"A true injury, my friend. One for which she will pay dearly," he said, narrowing his eyes, "in both *homage* and *honey.* And there is only one blade which can wring such tribute from a woman." He grinned with a wicked tilt as his gaze dropped to the bulge of his swollen male flesh, straining against his breeches.

Godfrey's gaze caught on Jorund's and was dragged downward with it, then rebounded up as he reddened and clapped a hand to his forehead. After seven years as a thrall-slave in Borger's village, the little priest was still sometimes shocked by the Norsemen's casual, often blatant displays of sexuality. "Jorund—I despair of you!"

Jorund laughed. "Despair? I would have thought you would be pleased to hear that the only blood she will shed shall be from that wound peculiar to maids becoming women." Godfrey's mouth thinned and Jorund chuckled. "Such a wound is both a pleasure to inflict and to receive, my god-fearing friend. Tell me now, does that not admirably fulfill your requirement of 'loving one's enemies'?"

The priest flicked a woeful glance heavenward, muttering, "Stop your ears, Lord." He jerked back his chin and gave an annoyed tug at the stout rope that bounded his middle. "You cannot use one of our Lord's commandments as an excuse to break another."

"Then your Lord should be more sensible in his expectations: have people love friends and hate enemies and forget this stuff about turning the other cheek and doing good to those who abuse you. It only confuses people."

"You're not confused!" Godfrey's brow furrowed in accusation.

"Fortunately not . . . at least not when it comes to loving the female half of mankind." His eyes twinkled with mischief as he lowered both his head and his voice. "I'm going to defeat her, my flesh-shy friend, and before the first snow flies. And I'll have her . . . on her back . . . in my furs . . . long, dangerous legs and all."

A flame-hot vision seared through his inner senses . . . long, sleek, exotically tapered legs . . . powerful, agile, exquisitely treacherous legs. Desire flared white-hot through him and he shuddered and expelled a harsh, passion-singed breath. He hadn't experienced such reckless and impulsive arousal since he was a stripling lad who had just discovered the pleasures of taking women to furs. It was unnerving.

A heartbeat later he scowled, wheeled, and strode back up the path toward the fields, intending to quell the ache in his loins and spend the heat in his blood with the physical strain of wielding a scythe. "Come, my well-fed friend," he ordered, waving the priest along after him. "We've grain to harvest. And, as your White Christ would say: the laborers are few."

Godfrey stood a moment studying Jorund's back, considering his unsettled expression and the fierce, rigid set of his big body as he turned away. He'd never seen such a look on his master before. Pleasure had always been an easy thing for Jorund . . . never more than a smile or a wink away . . . far too easy, to the little priest's way of thinking. He pondered the uncharacteristic intensity of Jorund's manner and Jorund's vow to take his pleasure of the fierce maiden who had dared call him a coward. His ruddy face creased with a decidedly impious grin.

"You may indeed have her by snowfall, my big lusty friend. But I believe she already has you."

Some time later, when the sun was beginning to lower in the sky, Aaren started awake and found herself staring into a pair of wide blue eyes beneath a shock of sand-colored hair. She lurched up, unleashing a flurry of squeals and screams that sent her fumbling for her blade in confusion. But before her iron quite cleared the scabbard, she realized that the creatures she'd put to flight were children, and sagged with relief, sliding her blade back into its oiled leather cradle.

The children fled a few paces, then when they realized she wasn't pursuing them, halted a safe distance away and stared at her. All of them had huge, pristine blue eyes, which seemed almost out of place in their rounded, dirt-smudged faces ... and reminded her of other little faces, from long ago. She smiled. Recognizing the tallest one as the young lad who had summoned her to the hall that morning, she addressed him.

"Did you come to fetch me?" The warmth in her middle flowed into her voice, but he drew back a step, chewing his lip, and the others huddled together at his back, looking like frightened goslings. They skittered back as she shoved to her feet and when she made to straighten her tunic, they thought she was reaching for her blade, and squealed and raced off down the path toward the village.

"Wait, don't—" She jogged a few steps after them, then halted, feeling oddly clumsy and chagrined at having frightened them. They were mere children, probably curious about this recent addition to their village and easily frightened by things that were different in their world. Their reaction to her bore an unfortunate similarity to that of the women in the women's house. Her shoulders sagged. It would probably take them all some time to get used to the sight of her and to her unusual place in Borger's hall ... that is, when she finally gained a place in his hall.

The incidents that had followed her morning's victory reared in her thoughts again: Borger's cursed proclamation, her confrontation with that craven-hearted giant, and the unthinkable pleading of the women on his behalf. How had things gotten so tangled in so short a time? If only she could talk with ... Serrick nudged into her mind and she felt a strange, yawning emptiness.

"What shall I do, Father Serrick?" she whispered softly, running her fingertips over the silver knob that formed the pommel of her blade.

When she looked up, she saw the Sky-Traveler lowering toward the rim of distant mountains and wondered if that great golden light was even now steering her father across the rainbow bridge of Asgard to a reunion with Fair Leone in the Allfather's hall . . . and perhaps with his Fair Raven as well. She heard the old man speaking to her out of the burning brightness . . . or perhaps the cooler mists of memory.

Fight, my daughter, he whispered, his rasping voice raising gooseflesh across her shoulders. *You must fight for what you want. And be valiant . . . for they will test you.*

Her senses were suddenly alive and quivering. Was that it? The crafty old jarl was testing her will to fight and her honor in upholding the enchantment by pairing her with a woman-hearted opponent? Then *fight* was exactly what she must do! And the sooner the better.

She took a deep breath and rolled her shoulders, filled with a renewed sense of purpose. Setting off at an easy pace, she soon covered the distance to the center of the village. The women's house was empty except for Inga and Sith, the plain-spoken dairywoman. Miri and Marta, she learned, had been assigned tasks at the jarl's small hearth.

"Cookin'," Sith declared flatly, pointing the way across the commons.

The great raised hearth in the long hall was used primarily for light and heat, and for the celebration of important festivals. Most of the daily cooking was done at another, smaller hearth located in a chamber attached to the long hall by a stone passage. Aaren slipped through the doorway and stood for a moment, searching the hazy chamber. A large smoke hole in the roof admitted light and permitted the thick peat-smoke and the smells of parched grain and roasting meat to escape. One wall was lined with shelves containing crocks, pitchers, and bowls; one was lined with wooden barrels and crocks of salted fish and curing winter-cabbage, and a third was hung with griddle-irons, skimmers, ladles, and tongs used in cooking. In the center, built upon a wheel of low, flat stones, was a fire overhung by iron spits and ringed by large soapstone crocks and iron kettles. Around that fire, swaying and bending in the smoky, dull-glowing heat, she glimpsed two familiar figures.

"Marta? Miri?"

"Aaren!" Marta straightened from turning meat on a spit, and Miri looked up from where she knelt, wrapping meat in cabbage leaves, and scrambled to her feet. "There you are! We were beginning to worry."

"I went for a run . . . to clear my head. You needn't fear for me." As Marta and Miri hurried to greet her, she noted that they wore their old kirtles and had forsaken their fine tunics with the pleated sleeves and carved brooches. "They have you tending hearth?" She scowled and brushed a smudge of ashes from Miri's cheek.

"Kara and Gudrun went to the fields with the others. They needed help and we have good hearth-skill," Miri explained, glancing at Marta, who took it up.

"We must prove our worth, too, Aaren," she whispered softly. Aaren studied their heat-polished faces and luminous eyes, and sighed raggedly. Their need was very like her own.

"So you do," she murmured. Of habit, she tucked a stray wisp of Marta's golden hair back into one of the thick braids tied in coils behind her ears.

Marta smiled and her eyes picked up a spark from the glowing hearth. "There is so much to learn and to try here in the jarl's village! The women speak of new patterns for weaving, dyes we've never seen, and cloth and rich, gold-trimmed garments brought from over the sea in the long ships. And you should see—and taste—the herbs and spicemeats the jarl has brought back from his voyages. Come—" She pulled Aaren toward the heavily laden shelves and craned her neck to peer around the small wood chests and crocks. "There is a spice here like small black balls . . . when it's crushed it burns your tongue and tickles your nose."

As they passed the hearth, two women wearing neck rings which marked them as thralls paused in their labors to stare dully at Aaren. Wiping their hands on the cloths tied about their waists, they mumbled that they had ale to fetch from the cool-house and the day's churning to collect from the dairy. They gave Aaren a pointedly wide berth, skirting the far side of the hearth and slipping out the door with lowered eyes that scarcely masked their resentment.

Aaren watched their escape with a frown. Her left hand tightened on the cradle of her sword. But this was a different kind of battle than she had fought before, this struggle for respect and acceptance, and she knew it could not be won by force or skill of blade.

Marta winced as she glimpsed the frustration in her elder sister's dark expression and she laid a hand on Aaren's arm. "They're frightened of you, Aaren. They've never seen a warrior-maid before. And talk of the enchantment and of your fighting is all over the village."

"And now . . ." Miri gave Marta an inquiring look. When she nodded, Miri swallowed hard and continued. "You're to fight Jorund Borgerson, the jarl's son. And the women are all quite fond of him."

"Fond?" Marta rolled her eyes and made a clucking sound. "A pale way to put it. Their tongues wag like lambs' tails whenever his name is mentioned. After you left us this morning, they had much to say about him. They spoke most freely and—daughters of mischief!—the things they said!" She pulled Aaren to a seat on a bench, then leaned close, and her voice dropped to an awed whisper. "His hair is soft as milkweed silk, they say. His chest is hard as a shield boss . . . his back is strong as a stallion's . . . And he heats furs at night like a slow-burning brazier."

Miri squeezed down beside them on the bench, her voice full of hushed excitement. "They say, he knows ways to make a woman writhe and moan . . . and that when he comes to a woman's furs, he strips the clothes from her body and . . ." She crossed her arms and shivered.

"And?" Aaren demanded, alarm rising in her as she felt her imagination seizing that bit of tongue-fodder.

"And he . . . does things . . . with his mouth." Marta supplied.

Heat stormed Aaren as a sudden, intense vision of Jorund's mouth flared in her mind; broad and sensual . . . bounded by firm, sleek borders . . . lips grandly bowed and expressive as they drew back to reveal straight, even teeth . . .

"He *bites* women? Small wonder they writhe and moan," she snapped, disturbed by the way her entire body tightened with expectation and the way their words tickled her ears and made them itch for more.

"But it must not hurt," Marta said earnestly, "for he's done it to most of them and they all like it a great deal. He is their favorite among the men."

Miri nodded. "And they all have pet names for him. They call him Heart-balm and Gentle-rider, Slow-hand and Honey-hunter, Silk-hair and Flesh-skald . . . but most of all, they call him *Breath-stealer* . . . because of the way he snatches the breath from their lips." Her voice dropped to a choked whisper. "And they say his hands can summon lightning inside a woman's body."

Aaren snorted in disbelief. "What sort of creature could do such things . . . make lightning inside a mortal frame and steal another's breath? It is grist for their tongue-grindings—no more than that."

But her face flushed hot, for she sensed there was more to the women's claims than met the ear . . . more that had to do with the ways of men with women, the ways of *mating*. Despite the numerous skills and the knowledge Serrick had imparted to the three of them, she realized that they still had a great deal to learn about living in a society of men and women. She rose to her feet too fast and swayed, feeling thrown off balance by her own thoughts. Miri and Marta sprang up beside her, searching her reaction even as they examined their own.

"In future, do not listen to such talk. It is the scrape of idle tongues; no more than that." Aaren tugged at the round neck of her tunic as if it was binding her, then slid fingers under her leather wristbands to loosen them, too. "The men have another name for this Jorund Borgerson, remember," she said testily. "*Woman-heart*. He is no warrior if women must defend him. It is a man's task to defend . . . to protect his people, his possessions, and his honor. All men are warriors, deep in their hearts. . . . If he is no warrior, then he is not truly a man."

"Will you still fight him, Aaren?" Marta asked, clasping her arm.

"I have to fight him and defeat him. Red Beard has decreed it," she said irritably. "And the wagging of women's tongues cannot change that."

A drip of melting fat from the meat sent a flame shooting up from the coals, igniting the great side of pork on one of the spits. Marta ran to put it out, and Miri hurried to help. When they turned back, Aaren was brushing dust from her breeches and trying unsuccessfully to drag her fingers through her wildly tangled hair. When she felt their critical gaze roaming her appearance, she straightened and her color deepened.

"Aaren, your poor hair," Miri said, shaking her head.

"You look like a wild thing," Marta declared. "No wonder everyone is terror-struck at the sight of you." She stuck her face close and took a sniff, then wrinkled her nose. "You need a good bath and a sound combing. Come with me . . ." She took Aaren's wrist with an authoritative manner and started for the door.

It was a moment before Aaren could dig in her heels and resist. "What—do you think to bathe me like some helpless babe?" She glared as fiercely as she could and tried to wrest her hand free. "Why, I was bathing your ragged little bottoms—"

"A very long time ago," Marta declared, tugging stubbornly on her arm.

"I am perfectly able to bathe myself," she insisted, jerking free.

"At the very least, you'll need help with your hair . . . it's a cowbird's nest," Marta insisted.

Aaren stared at her, then transferred her gaze to Miri, whose eyes were narrowed in agreement. Her jaw went slack. *A cowbird's nest . . .* she used to call their hair such, when they got it snarled and tatted and she had to spend time untangling it. She stared at them and was struck forcibly by the womanliness of their appearance and the determined set of their faces. They weren't children anymore;

they were young women, who insisted on taking care of her just as she had cared for them. A sudden, powerful wave of loss swept over her, mingled with longing for days gone by . . . for old ways and certainties. Her eyes burned, and to hold the humiliation of an eye-flood at bay, she tossed her head and laughed stridently.

"Oh, no! Not you, Marta Mauler . . . nor you, Miri Mangler. You'll not get within arm's reach of my hair. Too well I remember how you squealed and muttered vows of revenge while I rescued your poor locks. I'll manage well enough on my own!" And with that she darted out the door, into the rosy glow of sunset, and headed for the women's house.

Jorund arched his broad back, bracing on the long oaken handle of his scythe. He looked about the barley field, from the lengthening shadows of the trees at the far end, to the green-gold sea of grain stalks, to the rounded backs and bright kerchiefs of the harvesters bending in a row before him. There was a huge crop this harvest; the fields were groaning, laden with grain. But without more workers, much of it would lay in ruins before it was gathered in. He looked up at the sky, where puffy white clouds drifted like billowed sails across a sea of azure blue, and he prayed the good weather would hold yet a while, so that the harvest could be finished and the village would be spared the ravages of winter-hunger and the necessity of making pine bark bread.

Helga's boy came hurtling from the path and across the field, aimed straight for Jorund. He had run so far and so long that he couldn't seem to stop. Jorund dropped the scythe handle and caught him, lifting and whirling him around with a laugh.

"Whoa, Fleet-footed! What brings you in such a hurry?" He set the boy on his feet and stooped to brush back his tousled hair and peer into his dirt-streaked face.

"You said"—the lad panted—"you wanted to know . . . where the battle-maid could be found."

Jorund seized his shoulders in a gentle, coaxing grip. "Where?"

"In the village! She asked for . . . the bathing house."

Jorund's face broke into a broad smile as he ruffled the boy's hair. "You did well, Little Brother." The boy beamed under the praise, but his eyes nearly popped from his head when Jorund added with a knowing wink: "I'll see you have a honey-cake for this."

Chapter Five

The bathing house was a low stone structure built into the side of a rocky hill overlooking the great lake, some distance from most of the huts, a site chosen because of a spring that flowed from a rock ledge there. When Aaren arrived, with a length of linen, a comb, and a fresh tunic in her hands, she spotted smoky steam already pouring from the hole in the roof and smiled, thinking that she wouldn't have to build a fire.

An old thrall man holding a bundle of birch twigs sat on an upturned log beside the door. His age-faded eyes widened as she approached, and he heaved to his feet and opened the door to stick his head inside. His words were muffled by the thick wooden door and the thick spiral of steam that escaped on the cool air, but it was clear that he was announcing her presence to whoever was inside.

Shortly, the door slammed back and a man Aaren recognized as one of the jarl's warriors emerged; red-flushed, dripping wet, and wearing nothing but a surly look. He stomped in hairy, bandy-legged splendor to the side of the hut, where a number of wooden pegs driven into the wall were hung with tunics and breeches. Behind him, several more male figures materialized from the steam— each as naked as birthing day—and paused to pour buckets of cold water over themselves before exiting with snarls and scowls.

Aaren stiffened, sending her hand beneath the linen and spare tunic she held to the dagger at her waist. But they cast no more than bleary, resentful looks her way as they forced breeches and tunics over dripping bodies and snatched up belts, daggers, and buskins. The message was clear as they and their old thrall strode off down the path to the village: they would not suffer her company, not even in bathing . . . which according to Serrick was by custom both communal and congenial. In bathing, grievances were set aside, differences of place and personal importance were temporarily suspended . . . for it was in nakedness and the ritual of cleansing that all men were recognized as brother warriors, as members of some greater whole.

Now Borger's men, fresh from sweating the ale-poisons from their bodies, denied her even that respect. She stared after their grumbling, swaggering forms . . . and after the old thrall man who had served them but clearly did not intend to serve her. She could probably outfight any of them, but they had just declared by their shunning that it would take more than fighting to make them accept her as an equal into their midst. Her skin burned with humiliation as she watched them go. What would it take to make them accept her as a warrior?

Taking a deep breath and shaking off that pride-blow, she ducked inside the house. She found herself in a surprisingly spacious, stone-walled chamber, lined with benches and raised wooden shelves placed high on the walls. A small pool on the far end was the source of a stream flowing through a stone channel across the floor, and in the center, by the stream, was an upraised stone hearth. Fire still burned under the heat rocks, but she added a small log from a stack just outside the door, to augment it, and dipped a bucket of the cold water and set it on the bench nearest the door. Then she began to loosen the ties at the sides of her breastplate.

Soon her wood-stiffened leather armor lay on a bench along the wall, like the parted halves of a tortoise shell. "Ahhh." She sighed and stretched and curled from side to side, freed for the first time in days from her armor and from the constant tension of confronting hostile and curious faces. She rubbed the soft linen of her tunic over her ribs, soothing her long-imprisoned skin, then propped one foot after the other on the bench to loosen and remove her boots and leggings. Closing her eyes, she savored the feel of her bare toes against the damp stone floor, before untying her breeches and shoving them down her legs. The swirl of warm, moist air against her bared skin was sheer delight.

Just as she collected her garments into her arms, to carry them out to the pegs, there was a scraping sound behind her and the doorway suddenly filled, blocking both the light and her exit. She whirled into a crouch, flinging the garments aside, her body braced for danger. And danger it was, she realized, as she beheld the huge male figure silhouetted against the bright daylight. Her opponent. Jorund Borgerson. Woman-biter . . . Breath-stealer . . . Lightning-maker . . .

"You have quick responses, Battle-maiden." His deep voice vibrated with the same frequency as her fluttering pulse, establishing a low, disturbing resonance between them.

"A warrior must be swift," she declared, dismayed by the thickness in her voice and by the way he seemed to push the air from the chamber as he ducked inside and straightened as much as the roof beams would allow. He stood with his hands propped on his waist, his shoulders jutting forward and his head bent, looking like a great golden eagle ready to swoop. His gaze roamed her with deliberate appraisal, making her fiercely aware that she wore only a short tunic which scarcely covered her buttocks, and that her dagger lay somewhere beneath the pile of garments she'd just dropped.

"And the way you use your feet as you fight . . . most unusual," he said.

"Most effective," she countered, straightening and curling her tingling fingers into fists at her sides.

"That it is." His gaze dropped to her bare legs. "Who taught you to use your long legs so . . . *effectively*?" When she stiffened, the corner of his wide mouth twitched into a half smile that was perversely both fascinating and annoying.

"Serrick taught me." She lifted her chin to eye him down her nose.

"Ummm. Lucky Serrick." He crossed his thickly banded arms over his chest and laid a finger against his lips in thought. "They are such wonderful legs. Long . . . powerful . . . sleek . . . shapely." He dipped his head from side to side, shamelessly admiring her naked limbs. "I've never seen such legs." Dragging his gaze up her thighs, he fastened it on the front of her tunic, which had been molded to her body by her breastplate and still retained much of that revealing shape. Something bright flared briefly in his darkening eyes and his voice became like lapping waves; low, rhythmic, pulsing.

"Nor have I seen such . . . *arms*. Such smooth, slender arms, to wield a blade so forcefully."

She peeled her arms from under her breasts and shoved them behind her, out of his sight, realizing an instant later that her defiance had only stretched the linen taut over her breasts and left the rest of her body unshielded from his brazen scrutiny. Her face flushed and a tide of embarrassed color began to flood through the rest of her as well. He was only an arm's length away and she stiffened and lurched back a few steps.

"You did not come here to praise my arms and legs," she charged, losing the second half of her thought in the realization that he'd done just that . . . praised her parts.

"No, I did not, Serrick's daughter," he said in a deep, rolling purr that caused a strange melting sensation in her middle, just below her stomach. "You are called Aaren, are you not? Unusual." He repeated it like an incantation: "Aaren . . . Aaren . . ."

The chest-deep fullness of his voice held her fixed to the spot as he edged closer. Her heart hammered in her breast and she suddenly found it difficult to draw breath. Her eyes widened and her muscles contracted with alarm as she gasped silently. *Breath-stealer*, they called him. Was he enchanted too, this Jorund Borgerson? For how else could a man steal another's breath, as he seemed to be taking hers?

"I could teach you other ways to use your legs, Aaren Serricksdotter," he said, looming nearer, spinning words like spider silk around her, entrapping her senses, consuming her thoughts. "And I could show your arms a sweeter duty."

Her breathlessness and the strange, fluid heat swirling through her lower body sent her into a mild panic. What was happening to her? She stared at his mouth and then dropped her eyes to his long, muscular hands, suddenly swarmed by the things the women had said about him.

Silk-haired. Stallion-backed. Brazier hot. He could conjure lightning in a woman's frame. . . .

"You have never known such duty, have you?" His golden face bronzed and his blue eyes shimmered with the tantalizing heat which the women had spoken of so longingly. "Never wrapped those long, powerful legs about a man's body," he continued, swaying closer. "Never held a man within those sleek, beautiful arms . . . never cradled a man between those soft breasts."

His gentle voice, his powerful presence, and his openly sensual manner combined to cloak the shocking nature of his words and momentarily circumvent both her distrust and her warrior's pride. She had never encountered such talk before. Legs wrapping . . . arms holding . . . breasts cradling. She was sinking into a deepening thrall . . . until her bare heel sank unexpectedly over the edge of the stream channel. She fell back, but caught her balance with her other foot—plunging it straight into the frigid water.

Cold-shock raced up her leg. The steam swirling through her senses was abruptly dispelled by a blast of icy reason and the sense of his words burst on her mind with horrifying clarity. He was taunting and belittling her, talking to her of—He was treating her like one of the village women!

"You! What are you doing here?" She forced out through a tight throat as she splashed through the water and bristled back into a fists-on-hips stance on the other side. "Have you come to challenge me? Here? Now?"

He chuckled quietly, his eyes glistening, watching her as an eagle watches its prey. "I carry but one blade with me, Battle-maiden. And it is made for pleasure, not for fighting." He spread his arms, inviting her inspection, and let his gaze dip suggestively down his front. She managed to keep her eyes from following his, but the price of that control was a confusing surge of red heat in her face. There was no mistaking his meaning and that taunting reference snapped the last strands of the enthrallment he had woven about her.

"If you are not prepared to fight, why are you here, Borgerson?" she demanded with all the arrogance she could muster.

"Perhaps I came for a bath," he said smoothly. "I have been with the harvesters and it is hard, dusty work." With one long, effortless step he crossed the stream channel and loomed over her again. "A good hot sweat and a cool dousing with water would feel good just now." His bold mouth curled slightly as he lifted the wool tunic from his chest and fanned it . . . just enough to dislodge a dusty scent from the weave.

The smell stormed her defenses . . . a blend of sun-dried grain, dust from the cut stalks, and sweat—male sweat, pungent, musklike, with a tart hint of sweetness. Harvest . . . he smelled like a long-awaited harvest. For one long moment she stood speechless, scrambling to maintain her balance against both him and the remembrance he'd stirred in her. Every nerve in her body began to vibrate with warning. She stalked back a few steps, straight into the dry heat billowing from the hearth in the middle of the floor.

"Or perhaps you came to spy out your opponent," she declared irritably, feeling a trickle of moisture running down her spine.

"Perhaps," he agreed, following her.

"Or perhaps you've come to beg for mercy," she taunted, annoyed by his candor.

"Or perhaps I came to offer it to you, Battle-maiden." A bead of sweat slid from his temple, tracing the square lines of his jaw . . . dragging her wayward gaze with it.

"Mercy . . . to me?" Her face flamed and her hands clenched at her sides. "Mercy is for those who cannot fight. I need no mercy. I need you to pick up a blade and fight me . . . and the sooner the better."

A small, infuriating smile spread over his damp face. "We need not fight at all, Serricksdotter. We are not enemies." His eyes slid over her with undisguised appreciation. "I feel no hatred or malice toward you. Nor, if you be truthful, do you toward me. There is no cause for us to hurl an iron-storm at each other's heads."

"But there is, Borgerson," she insisted, narrowing her eyes at him. "The Allfather's enchantment makes all men my enemies . . . until I am defeated." Fire roared through her blood as he cocked his head and smiled at her.

"Enchantment? You are no more enchanted than I am, Serricksdotter." Her gasp of outrage only seemed to fuel his amusement. He laughed—*laughed*!—at her!

"I *am* enchanted . . . was created a battle-maiden because of the Allfather's curse. And my fighting proves it."

"Your fighting proves nothing. You said yourself, the old man taught you. And that is not so surprising—that a woman could be taught to fight." His grin took on a wicked cant. "After all, falcons can be trained to perch on a hand . . . horses can be taught to obey a man's knee . . . and dogs can learn to dance on hind feet."

"D-dogs can— You slimy spawn of a frost giant's—" She found herself against the bench by the door and when her fist brushed something at her side, she instinctively seized it in self-defense. She gave the half-filled water bucket a surprised glance then an angry heave, splashing him full in the face.

Jorund sucked a shocked breath and staggered back a pace, jaw gaping, sputtering. It took a long, incredulous minute for him to understand that she'd just tossed icy water over him. . . .

"Is that not what you came for, Woman-heart?" she demanded, seizing unexpected advantage. "A good hot sweat . . . and a cold dousing?"

He reacted as instinctively as she had, jolting forward and driving his fists against the wall on either side of her, trapping her between the bench and the door frame. He braced and swelled threateningly around her, glaring into her heat-polished face and defiant eyes . . . which because of her uncommon height were poised disturbingly close to his. Then he paused . . . unsure of his course with a woman for the first time in years.

Just a hand's width from his chest, her breasts rose and fell in hot defiance, their rounded weight and dark, hardened tips outlined with maddening clarity beneath her thin garment. Her long, naked legs—those sleek, erotic weapons—and the womanly softness they guarded were just a heated motion away. She was half naked, and her firm sun-kissed skin bore a sheen and a piquant tang of salt and mysterious, feminine musk. With her tawny eyes glowing and dark-flame hair tangled hopelessly about her shoulders, she seemed feral, female, and exotic . . . tantalizing. A thick, elemental awareness of her surged through his stinging pride and he suffered the infuriating thought that this was probably just what she would look like after a long night of pleasure.

"But perhaps you came to spy me out, instead," she declared when he did not act to avenge the insult straightaway. "Well, then . . . let me show you yet another way Serrick taught me to use my legs. . . ." Her meaning burst on his mind as her gaze dropped, and he arched back just as her knee came crashing up with the kick of a fjord mare. There was scarcely a hair's breadth between his maleflesh and disaster. He jerked back as if punched and she bolted into the doorway with her hands on her waist and her head held high.

"Thrash you, Serricksdotter," he sputtered swiping water from his face with a huge, sinewy hand. "I came here to make peace—to offer you friendship."

"I have no need of the sort of *friendship* you offer." As she stood in the entrance, the lowering sun set her hair ablaze with red and violet fires and cast a golden glow over her skin. "All I want from you, Woman-heart, is a blade-meeting." Light filtered through her tunic, outlining her womanly curves with excruciating clarity, and suddenly his urge to throttle her was intensified by a number of other burning urges.

"A blade-meeting," he echoed, raking her visually, edging closer. Then he unleashed at blunt range the full force of the unique sensual power he possessed. His handsome features took on a visible glow, his eyes shimmered with iridescent lights, and male heat flowed from him in palpable waves. "And nothing else, Long-legs?"

Silence stretched taut between them as she braced against that unnerving onslaught and summoned all her nerve to counter the alarming trickle of excitement in her middle.

"There is one more thing I would have of you," she said, her voice low and resonant. When his shoulders relaxed one degree and his mouth began to curl, she broadened her stance and delivered her final thrust.

"Victory."

He reacted as if she'd smacked him with icy water again. His face went crimson, veins appeared in his temples, and his arms bulged menacingly. The muscles in his great chest seemed to both swell and contract as he did visible battle with his own impulses. Prickles of excitement danced over her shoulders as she watched the urge to respond roiling in him. She held her breath. Would he go for a blade and fight her?

Then, before her disbelieving eyes, he forced his shoulders to deflate, forced his clenched fists open, and lowered his massive arms to his sides. Venting a harsh breath, he set his jaw and leaned back on one leg, scowling at her.

"Heed my advice, Serricksdotter," he growled. "Save both your strength and your pride. Give up this blade-fighting nonsense before you get hurt. Wash yourself." He gestured to her appearance with exaggerated male disdain. "Put on a decent kirtle . . . comb your hair . . . and behave like a woman."

That was it? She'd defied and enraged and offended him . . . and he told her to get a kirtle and a comb and behave herself? His scorn struck her warrior's pride, sparking a blaze in her stomach that erupted upward, igniting her heart and tongue.

"Why don't you fill your hand with iron and make me, Woman-heart?" she hurled angrily. "You think I should behave like a woman? Well, there's only one way to make me: fight and defeat me. Until then, why don't *you* try behaving like a *man*, Skirt-clinger?" She punched a finger at him. "Defend your honor in Red Beard's hall. Defend yourself as a man must, and prove your worth as a warrior." She took a reckless step closer to him, then another, using his own tactic against him—prodding him with her anger. "Take up a blade and defeat me. *If you can.*"

Emotion twitched in his jaw muscle and smoldered deep in his eyes. At the edge of her vision, his fists clenched and unclenched, and her heart seemed to skip beats . . . waiting, anticipating. But he mastered and shunted his anger aside yet a third time, stalking closer and glowering down at her.

"Oh, I'll defeat you, Serricksdotter." His voice rolled like approaching thunder. "Make no mistake about that."

"When?" She braced for a cuff or a shove.

But his only response was a smile that was both fierce and knowing. An instant later, he was striding down the path to the village, his wide shoulders swaying, his long, golden hair ruffled by the breeze. She followed with her eyes, feeling the rhythm of his gait rasping her already frayed self-control.

"When?" she shouted at his broad, absurdly muscular back—though she might as well have been talking to the air, since he was already out of hearing.

Frustration swelled in her veins as she stared after him, feeling thwarted and disappointed in ways she didn't want to examine too closely. "Wretch!" she muttered furiously. "May you outlive your teeth by a score of years . . . water the straw when you sleep . . . sprout boils on your arse and warts on your nose . . ." She cursed him with nine vile plagues, then jerked back into the bathing house and slammed the door behind her. Drawing another bucket of water, she tossed some of it on the glowing rocks, releasing a boiling cloud of steam that matched the one billowing inside her.

If she'd only had her blade! She snatched up her scattered garments, depositing the lot on the bench near the door, then stripped off her tunic and climbed onto the stone ledge nearest the hearth. Pulling her legs up and planting her chin on her knees, she allowed her fury to slowly drain from her with the sweat that beaded and slid along her skin. If she'd *had* her blade, it wouldn't have done any good, she consoled herself. He didn't have one. Not an *iron* one, anyway. She hissed like steam from the hot rocks.

What manner of man was he . . . so huge, so strong, so obviously born to fight . . . yet so reluctant to use those coveted advantages of size and power in battle? He wouldn't lift a blade, wouldn't join a raid or defend his jarl's honor. And he wouldn't raise a hand to a woman—not even one who doused him with water!

He was "soft" on women, they said. At least that made sense; the village women were certainly soft on him.

They apparently found him enjoyable . . . him with his sun-bronzed face, mischief-filled mouth, and bluer-than-summer-sky eyes that seemed to see straight into a woman's very bones. She scowled and shifted uncomfortably as the memory of that bold, caressing gaze bloomed in her mind.

And the way he talked—she'd never imagined that mere words could assault a body so. He obviously claimed his word-skill from the Mischief-maker, Loki, himself. No doubt he spun similar word-webs around the rest of the women in Borger's village and that was why they—

Her eyes widened and her spine snapped straight. He had plied his sly word-skill and his wretched woman-magic with her because in his mind she was a woman, not a warrior. She groaned aloud. As long as he thought of her as a woman, he'd never take a blade to her! And if he didn't, neither could anyone else!

The possibility of being denied the opportunity to fight appalled her. She wanted to fight . . . had to fight! Fighting, all Norsemen understood from birth, was the highest and noblest calling in which a man could spend his allotted seasons on earth. It was a freeman's right to fight and by the might of his arm and blade to win for himself fortune and fame. And for her, it was even more. It was her *destiny*.

Somehow, she had to make Jorund Borgerson acknowledge that she was a warrior and deal with her as one. And there was only one way to manage that, she realized. Provoke him. He could be angered; she had seen the emotion flaring in his eyes. She would just have to goad and challenge and annoy and confront him until he forgot both her sex and his own fear of battle and reached for a blade to silence her.

Determination released a hot tide of relief in her. No more treacherous word-snares, no more bone-melting looks, no more losing herself in his blue-eyed smiles. From now on, when Jorund Borgerson saw her coming, he wouldn't see a woman . . . he'd see *trouble*.

Jorund strode along the path to the village, his blood simmering and his pride aflame. It had been his private plan—a far greater challenge in his estimation—to conquer the battle-maiden's pride and temper with her own desires, then to take her pleasures without the use of force. There was no "Odin" and no "enchantment," he reasoned; thus, no dishonor in charming the wench and in claiming the fierce passion promised in every line and movement of her fascinating body. He hadn't exactly expected her to yield to him on the spot; he had known it would take persistence, cleverness, and perhaps even a rousing tumble along with the wooing. But neither had he expected to be doused with icy water, reviled as a skirt-clinger, and told to behave like a man!

Odin's Living Stones—what was wrong with the wench? She didn't respond to him like any woman he'd ever known. She blustered and growled and boasted, with all the volatile temper and touchy pride of a—He stopped dead in the middle of the path, scowling as the insight struck. *A warrior.* She truly believed she was a warrior and so behaved as she thought a warrior should . . . proud, blade-toughened, eager to fight. The thought astonished him. A woman who honestly believed she was a warrior.

Godfrey's Blessed Heaven—didn't she have eyes in her head? The sight of her as she had stood in the bathing house, unaware she was being watched, rose within him. Those legs . . . no warrior had legs so long and shapely, or a bottom so rounded and firm. His eyes half closed as he searched the memory of her high, defiant cheekbones, and lips so wide and full and colored like ripe apples. No warrior had skin that smooth, eyes that thickly lashed, shoulders that sleek, or breasts that . . . He sucked in a ragged breath. Her breasts. He fastened his inner eyes on them: cool, rounded, hard-tipped, and just a maddening nudge away from his hot ribs. His hands cupped at his sides—imagining, anticipating that delectable weight, that softness—before he curled them into determined fists.

And no warrior shivered when looking into his eyes . . . or blushed . . . or grew warm and breathless.

His jaw set like granite. She was a *woman,* dammit! And he wanted her as a man wanted a woman . . . on her back, in his furs . . . hot and soft-eyed and eager. He was determined to overcome her absurd mannish pride and tame and claim her.

She wanted a battle? Well, he'd give her one. Let her fight both his finely honed pleasure-skill and her own womanly desires, and they'd see who claimed victory. Let her storm and bluster and rage . . . he'd shrug off her anger and "turn the other cheek." Let her show him the might in the back of her hand . . . he'd show her the pleasure in the palm of his. He'd rouse the sensuality he'd glimpsed in the depths of those heated amber eyes and use her own passions to humble and defeat her.

By the time he was through, Aaren Serricksdotter would have learned she was a woman . . . not a warrior. And every time she saw him coming, she would ache for another lesson.

The Sky-Traveler had already settled into the night-cradle of the mountains and drawn his rosy dusk-blanket from the sky after him when Aaren started back to the village. It had taken a long while to sweat the day's tensions from her frame and longer still to wash and tame her hair. By the time she finished, she heartily regretted her refusal to accept Marta's help with the tedious combing. But at last it was done and her clothing, her dagger, and her sense of self-possession were all securely back in place.

She stopped by the women's house to deposit her things, then headed for the small hearth at the side of the long hall to see her sisters. But when she dipped her head through the doorway, she found herself confronting the stares of Kara and Gudrun and a number of other women.

"My sisters," she said, glancing about the chamber. "I came to see how they fare."

"They get on well enough," stout Gudrun answered tersely. "The jarl sent for them to serve ale in the hall."

The news burst on Aaren's mind like an exploding ember: Miri and Marta in old Red Beard's hall, serving ale to Borger's hot-eyed warriors! She bolted for the door.

The tables in the long hall were filled with warriors and select men of the village, continuing their celebration of Borger's triumph over Gunnar Haraldson, though with a bit less vigor than the day before. A great log burning in the hearth and the resin-soaked torches hung on posts around the hall provided plentiful light. Miri and Marta passed along the fronts of the tables bearing large metal pitchers and keeping their eyes lowered to avoid the hot male stares that followed them.

"Here, S-Serricksdotter—my horn is empty," old Oleg Forkbeard called to Miri, waving his drinking vessel.

"Your *horn* has been empty for years, Forkbeard! What would a comely wench want with you?" Hakon Freeholder called out, generating harsh laughter all around him. "Here, wench—" He pushed to his feet near Miri with an ale-spawned leer and a pelvic thrust. "I've a *full* horn and an empty set of furs!"

When he made a grab for her, she jerked back with a cry, dropping her pitcher and sending ale splashing onto her kirtle and onto the sandal-boots of the men nearby. They shoved to their feet, snarling and shaking their wetted buskins, and Miri shrank back, her eyes wide with horror at their glowering faces. In an instant, a muscular blond form vaulted over the table and between them.

"Blame Freeholder," Garth Borgerson snarled, "not the wench—it was not her fault." He turned on flat-faced Hakon with a fierce glare that penetrated his warrior's bravado. The Freeholder's stare retreated and fled . . . only to run into Aaren's. She had arrived just in time to witness the incident and now stood braced near the hearth, her hand on the hilt of her blade.

"I see you like my sister, Freeholder," she said with icy calm that belied the thudding of her heart. All talk at the nearby tables ceased as she stepped forward and swung her gaze to Miri, who melted visibly with relief. She looked back to the surly Freeholder, then down at her own hand on the handle of her blade. Serrick had taught her that to clasp the handle of a blade without drawing it was a sign of indecision in a warrior and that to do so created bad luck in the weapon. Thus committed, she had to draw the blade, but did it slowly, coolly.

"Admire my sisters, Freeholder, look your fill. But never be so foolish as to touch one of them." She rested the point of her blade on the floor between her feet and laid her hands casually across the sides of the blade guard. "The jarl has decreed there is but one man who may challenge me . . . but that does not keep me from challenging one who would take advantage of Miri or Marta."

"We will see what the jarl has to say," Freeholder protested.

"The jarl has no say in this." She raised her chin to stare down at him in warning. "It is Odin's will that I work and not even Borger Volungson can set aside my charge." A movement at the edge of her vision caused her to glance that way, and she found Borger standing with his arms crossed over his chest as he watched them.

"Jarl Borger, she—" Freeholder began, thrusting an accusing finger at her.

But a harsh "Enough!" from Borger halted his complaint before it was fully uttered. Aaren waited tautly, expecting the jarl to support her claim, for it was indeed her right by law and custom, and certainly by enchantment, to defend her family.

"Sheath your blade, Serricksdotter. There's no need for wound-making here . . . nor will there be." The jarl hung his callused hands on his belt and inflated his barrel-broad chest to roar above the din in the hall: "From this time on, the battle-maid's sisters will be as daughters of my own loins . . . under my protection. Harm or insult to them will be the same as harm or insult to me." He speared the Freeholder and his comrades with a piercing stare. "Offenders will answer to my blade, my justice." Then he swung that forbidding glare to Aaren. "And to no other's."

Aaren gasped as the sense of the jarl's decree and commanding look became clear. "It is my right—my charge—to defend my sisters!" she protested.

Borger drew himself up as tall as he could and met her rising anger with a jutting, pugnacious jaw. "My warriors honor my word," he declared flatly. His flint-hard eyes conveyed the rest: if she ever wished to be counted his warrior, then she must honor and obey his word also . . . even in so hard a matter. Every quivering line of her body proclaimed her struggle with defiant urges, but as the moments dragged by, she remained silent. Seeing his will prevail, Borger dragged in a satisfied breath and ambled back to his high seat. He threw himself into his great wooden chair and chuckled as he watched the Valkyr's daughter stow her sword angrily and lead her sister away.

By Odin's All-seeing Eye! he swore. She was a handful, this battle-wench. He licked his lips and stroked his beard, wrestling with a futile stirring in his loins. It was a sacrifice of truly noble proportions . . . pairing such a prize with his woman-hearted son. But it would be worth it, once she got Jorund stoked and fired and primed to fight. She had the battle-itch, Borger mused. The signs were all there—unmistakable—in her impatient hand and shoulder movements, in her flammable eyes, and in the restless flexing of her magnificent legs. And now that he'd taken away the possibility of a blade-fight in defense of her sisters . . . she would turn all that angry, thwarted heat on his lackluster heir.

Borger Hardaxe, he muttered as he treated his belly to a thorough scratching, *they'll compose a saga to your cleverness, someday*.

When they reached the far side of the hall, where the tables were not so crowded, Aaren drew Miri into the shadow of a post and clasped her shoulders, dragging an anxious gaze over her mussed braids and ale-wetted kirtle.

"Are you all right?" she demanded. When Miri nodded, she heaved a great breath and grabbed her hand. "Come, I'm taking you out of here. Borger treats you like a thrall, making you serve—"

"No, Aaren, you cannot," Miri whispered, tugging back and casting a look around them to see how much notice they'd drawn. "Helga said it is an honor he does us, that in the halls of great men, it is the daughters who serve ale and mead. But jarl Borger has no daughters—at least none that are known—so he has ordered us to serve in their stead."

"Some honor," Aaren whispered back. "One that would have you gobbled for a morsel."

"Please, Aaren, no real harm was done. I'll be more careful. And you heard the jarl's decree," Miri pleaded.

"He has declared us under his protection now."

Aaren's blood heated anew at the thought that she had to obey the old boar's commands in order to win a place in his band of warriors. And it would be counted defiance if she hauled her sisters away after Borger had ordered them to serve and extended them his protection. She scowled, shifted her feet, then squeezed Miri's hand. "Then serve if you must. But beware the men. Stay as far from them as you can."

Miri's relieved smile faded into concern. "You must be weak with hunger. Sit, and I'll bring you some ale and some skyr and roasted fish."

As Miri hurried off toward the ale barrels, Aaren spotted an opening on a nearby bench and made for it. One of the men at the table saw her coming and elbowed those around him, who turned sullen faces to her as she approached. They rose and lumbered away, carrying their ale horns with them, and she was left standing by the littered, empty table, gripping her scabbard with whitened fingers as they fled her company.

With a deep, unsettled breath, she swept the debris of their meal onto the floor and sat down at the table, laying her blade conspicuously across the table beside her. Halfway through the motion, she caught sight of the jarl, ensconced on his high seat, watching her with an inscrutable smile. The mangy old badger, she thought, tearing her gaze from his. First he paired her with his woman-hearted son, now he usurped her right to defend her sisters. How dared he?

Apparently old Flea-Beard didn't want her to fight any more than his woman-hearted son did. What was he afraid of . . . that she would prove stronger and fiercer than his male warriors? Was that why he'd paired her with a great, yammering coward who would rather talk an opponent to death than face her in honest blade-battle? She stiffened and glanced about the hall, searching for Jorund, and was both relieved and disappointed to find him absent.

Well, it didn't matter what the jarl or his woman-hearted son wanted, she vowed. She was going to fight anyway, and soon. Tomorrow, if she had anything to do with it.

*   *   *

Across the hall, Garth Borgerson had watched Aaren lead Miri away, then he turned to the Freeholder and those still on their feet around him.

"Count my blade with the jarl's in defense of the wench," he declared, jerking a thumb at his chest. "Whatever bones my father leaves connected, I will cleave asunder."

As he turned away, his foot brushed the pitcher Miri had dropped. He stooped and picked it up, then craned his neck to search the hall, finding his green-clad beauty at the far end of the hall, where the ale barrels stood. He clasped his eager hands around the pitcher and strode after her.

"Your pitcher, Serricksdotter," he declared, startling her so that she whirled to face him with her hand splayed protectively at her throat. He held out the vessel with a hint of a smile.

Miri found his eyes dove gray and filled with an undisguised appreciation that sent hot color into her cheeks. She lowered her lashes and reached for the pitcher, which he relinquished more slowly than she expected. In the transfer, his warm, callused hand brushed hers and her skin tingled as she drew back and cradled the vessel against her breast.

"Miri or Marta . . . which are you?" he asked, his voice deeper and softer than when he'd spoken to the greedy Freeholder.

"Miri," she managed, through the odd tightness in her throat.

"Miri," he repeated, clamping his muscular hands behind him and shifting from one foot to the other. "It is like bird-song. Mi-ri . . . Mi-ri . . ." When she jerked her head up, thinking he was making a jest of her name, she found his mouth curled in an expression that was both mischievous and uncertain, boyish. The intensely personal way he looked at her made her feel suddenly warm and shivery . . . and as though Aaren and the hall full of people around them didn't exist. She could not take her eyes from the weathered strength of his features and his sun-streaked hair, which flowed in sinuous waves to his shoulders. He seemed so handsomely formed and cleanly kept, so warm and solid, so very different from her first impression of men.

"Miri?" The sound of Marta calling her name brought her back to her senses and she blushed at the realization that her sister stood a yard away, frowning at her. She turned back to the ale barrels and made a show of wiping the dirt from the pitcher and dipping it into the frothy brew. A sixth sense told her that the young warrior remained a moment, staring at her, before he moved off. When he was gone, she turned with a full pitcher—straight into Marta's thoughtful scowl. She reddened further, feeling oddly guilty for having been so alone with a man in her own thoughts.

"He—he was just returning the pitcher I dropped," she said, running her trembling fingers around the bottom of the beaten-metal pitcher to wipe away the ale dripping from it. When Marta remained silent, Miri squeezed past her and hurried back to the empty ale horns on the far side of the hall.

For the next hour, as Aaren ate and her sisters served ale in the hall, at least two-score pairs of eyes watched Miri's and Marta's every move. Aaren and Marta were achingly aware of them all, but Miri could feel only one. A dove gray pair that glowed silver whenever she turned their way.

Chapter Six

B y the morning of their third full day in the village, the women had fully accepted Miri and Marta into their midst. Before they departed for the frosty fields, they lingered in the women's house, chatting easily about the village folk and sharing details of village life—including how and where to obtain such things as needles, dried herbals, and materials for bedding—and warning Miri and Marta about which warriors to avoid when serving ale in the hall each night. The women seemed grateful for the extra pairs of hands and for both the skill and willingness with which the younger Serricksdotters applied themselves to whatever tasks they were given. But as soon as Aaren appeared, returning from her morning run and a quick rinse in an icy stream, their talk ground to a halt, their hands fidgeted with kerchiefs and kirtle hems, and their faces became guarded.

In groups of two and three, the women departed for the jarl's small hearth to fill a cloth with hardened curds and flatbread for a midday meal, and set off for the fields. Aaren watched them go, annoyed by the disapproval in their sidelong glances. Was there something about her they truly loathed, or was it just *him*? She huffed disgust. She had yet to raise a hand to their wretched "Breath-stealer" and already they behaved as if she'd dealt him a maiming blow. With a curt word to her sisters, she snatched up her blade and fled the women's house for the jarl's long hall. The atmosphere might prove equally hostile among Borger's band, but at least she understood the pride and competition that generated it.

The hearth in the great hall was cold and the torches had been reduced to charred, smelly stubs. A gloom of exhaustion hung on the air, mingled with the reek of soured ale, stale sweat, and an acrid, wet-fur smell emanating from a number of hungry-eyed hounds prowling amongst the bone-littered tables and the sprawled, unconscious bodies of Borger's warriors. By the household standards Aaren was accustomed to, the place was a foul, stinking disgrace. But then, she hadn't been raised in a hall of fighting men. Perhaps it was just their nature—she mused—to be vile, smelly, and disgusting to womanly senses.

She started, dismayed that she'd classed herself with women, against her fellow warriors. Rolling her shoulders, she shoved away that unsettling insight and strode for the doorway that led to the cooking chamber, bent upon finding something to eat. Moments later, she returned with her hands filled with warm, still pliant flatbread heaped with curds and a wooden tankard of ale . . . and grimaced as she cleared the debris from a table with her elbow to make a place to eat.

It was not long before Borger emerged from his bed closet, rubbing his head and bashing away the beleaguered thrall whose task it was to wrestle him into his leather jerkin and belt and tie the straps of his buskins. "Not now—curse you! My head's ringing like an anvil and my belly's burning like the Black Dwarfs' forge!"

As he stalked blearily for the high seat—tunic askew, sandal-boots flapping—his bellows for food and ale reverberated through the timbers overhead, making it seem as if the carved heads of bears, wolves, and serpents on the posts and rafters had roared to life. The racket brought the hearth-tenders scurrying from the cook chamber with tankards of ale and platters of fresh flatbread, smoked eel, and great steaming bowls of *grautr* and roasted apples.

The combined noise and food smells roused a number of Borger's men, who heaved themselves up stiffly, stretched, scratched, and glowered at each other. Their stomachs howled, their heads rattled like hailstones in a barrel, and their tongues seemed to have sprouted fur . . . none of which predisposed them to sociable behavior. They snarled and shoved one another, snatching at food and dumping their still unconscious comrades onto the floor to make more room for themselves on benches and at tables.

Aaren watched the jarl and her fellow warriors with a scowl, but sternly reminded herself that they were not chosen for their cleanliness and agreeable natures. A warrior was selected and trained according to his courage, and was valued for his ferocity, battle-skill, and unflinching honor. Nothing—not wealth, not rank, not even life itself—was more important to a warrior than the glory of battle in honor of his jarl, his clan, and his family . . .

Suddenly, a bung-eyed fellow at the next table made a racket of clearing his throat and flung a huge wad of spit over his shoulder. Aaren jerked back just in time to escape it. But the fellow staggering behind her was not so lucky; it landed on the laces of his buskins and oozed down his shin. He roared and sprung at the spitter and, in the blink of an eye, the two crashed over the table top and onto the floor, locked in a death-grip. They wrestled and grappled mightily, until the spitter was jabbed in the eye and knocked unconscious as he sucked in breath to howl with pain. Honor satisfied, the victor heaved to his feet, shook his befouled boot, and lurched off toward his place on the far side of the hall. The violence had scarcely drawn notice from the grizzled warriors eating and drinking nearby.

Aaren watched in horrified fascination. Spitting, she surmised, was serious business indeed among warriors; an insult of great magnitude. Serrick hadn't mentioned that. . . .

Suddenly the great doors at the far end of the long hall were thrown back, admitting a flood of light and a blast of cold air. Protest rumbled through Borger's head-sore *hird*, but was soon damped by surprise. Into the hall surged a veritable phalanx of women with hems up-tucked and kerchiefs tied over their hair, pressed defensively shoulder to shoulder. The contingent split as it forged around the great hearth, then re-formed like a determined wedge before Borger's high seat. At their head was Helga, Borger's old-wife. And at their side strode Jorund Borgerson, a glint in his eye.

"Arghhh—what now?" Borger growled, clapping his hands over his eyes and rubbing, as if the sight of them—or their leader—pained him.

Helga drew herself up before the high seat with a nervous determination that bloomed to undisguised disapproval as her gaze slid over the jarl's beltless, ale-stained tunic and sagging boots. "Jarl Borger, I would have a word with you."

"A word? By the gods—that would be a first. Not now, woman," he ordered, waving her off with a rough hand and huddling back in his high seat like a cornered bear. "Can't you see I'm busy . . . celebrating?"

"I have the right to speak, Borger Volungson," she declared, hauling up the ring of iron keys from her side and giving them a shake. He grimaced as if the sound hurt his ears, and glowered savagely . . . which deterred her not at all. "In yonder fields lies our winter fare," she said, flinging a finger toward the side door and the fields beyond. "And with each passing day the stalks grow drier and the groats fall faster through our fingers. We must have help with the harvest . . . strong arms and backs to reap, thresh, and winnow." She cast a narrow eye on the men sprawled around her. "And there are idle arms and backs aplenty in this hall." The women behind her murmured agreement and cast resentful looks at their dissipated menfolk, neighbors, and kin.

"See here, woman," Borger snarled, clearly outraged by his old-wife's attitude. "You should be grateful that I brought my men back from the voyage early this season . . . to stop Gunnar Swine-heart from thieving my flocks and stealing your wretched harvest!"

"You came back because the trading was poor and the raiding was worse," she charged.

"I was here to do the fighting, that's what matters. And my warriors earned a reward. They fought valiantly and they've a right—a duty—to celebrate their great victory over—"

"Great victory?" Helga choked, then took a deep breath. "Well, they've celebrated enough. By the Precious Almighty—look at them!" She stalked toward the nearby tables, pointing at two warriors wearing fresh wound-binding, and in so doing, stumbled over the arm of the felled "spitter," who still lay witless on the sodden floor

"Bites, cuts, and bruises . . . four wounds from knife-fights yesterday alone! They're a drunken, vile-tempered, filthy disgrace—"

"Enough, woman!" Borger thrust to his feet and, once there, swayed from the impact of his own volume. "Your tongue flaps like an untied sail. A man is entitled to a bit of the sacred mead after a triumph of—"

"Sacred?" Helga snorted. "There is nothing *sacred* about sucking half the barrels in the storehouse dry and laying sog-witted for days on end!"

"*Odin's Fury!*" he roared, setting the very roof timbers rattling. He lurched down from his seat, brandishing the back of his fist, and suddenly every victory-soaked head in the hall was up and staring. "You would have us forsake all drink, all sport, all pleasure . . . then shackle and yoke us up, and plow with us for oxen! It's that wretched White Christ of yours again . . . that holy-sickness that sours women's innards and turns their blood to ice. I thank the gods every day, Helga Ice-wife, that you carried your furs from my hall and call me *husband* no longer . . . and I no longer have to suffer the grinding of your jaws!"

Passions were escalating at an alarming rate all over the hall. It was suddenly more than just Helga against Borger; it was woman against warrior. Resentments over the disparity of lot and labor which had roiled beneath the surface had somehow been roused and focused by the antagonism between the cantankerous jarl and his brash former wife. Maids and widows glared resentfully and unwedded warriors grumbled; wives scolded and head-sore husbands groaned and blustered back. The entire hall threatened to erupt into open conflict.

Then, into the volatile heat between Borger and Helga, between warrior and woman, stepped Jorund Borgerson.

"You came seeking help, Helga." His deep voice carried over the noise, causing heads to turn and tongues to halt mid-word. "But perhaps you were wrong to seek it here. Look at them." He turned a taunting look on the men around him. "Bleary-eyed and thatch-headed . . . they swill and stagger and belch like goats. There's not an arm in the place with the strength left to swing a scythe. Of these *mighty warriors*," he declared with a calibrated sneer, "not one is fit to finish an honest day's labor in the fields."

Aaren had watched the confrontation with a mixture of consternation and amusement, until her eyes fell on Jorund Borgerson. He had paused halfway between hearth and high seat, caught in a shaft of light coming through the smoke hole. Against the gray-tinged gloom of the hall, he glowed; his hair shone like fine-spun gold, his sculptured face and corded neck like polished bronze, shaded with silver and blue.

His full, resounding tones jarred her back to the present and she was horrified to find herself staring at her enemy with what could only be called anticipation. She chided herself mentally . . . until it occurred to her that what she was anticipating was their coming fight. Her resolve of the previous evening came back in a blood-heating rush: she intended to provoke him. And there was no better time than when he was being provocative himself.

"Jarl Borger!" Her voice rang out above the contention, and heads turned and necks craned all over the hall, trying to locate the source of that strong, womanly sound. She strode from the shadows at the side of the high seat and claimed a stand between Borger and the delegation of women.

"Have you not heard it said, jarl"—she fixed a derisive stare on Jorund—"that empty barrels make the loudest noise? Methinks I hear the rattle of a very big, very empty barrel in your hall." There was a murmur and a shift of bodies that cleared a path between her and the one she'd just insulted. "Jorund Borgerson blows like the wind— all force and no substance." The muttering became hard grumbling. "He speaks of warriors. But how can he know anything of the lot or the duty of a warrior . . . *not being one himself*?" Feminine gasps and male snickering mingled around them.

"And what would *you* know of warriors, Serricksdotter?" Jorund countered after a notable pause in which his color deepened and his eyes narrowed.

"I know that if a warrior can swing a sword or axe all day in battle, he can certainly swing a scythe." She strode forward and planted her fists on her hips, conscious that she held every eye in the hall. "And he can do it better than a woman . . . or a *woman-heart*."

The tension, so near a flash point a moment ago, suddenly dissolved in hoots, hisses, and caws of laughter. The women glared at Aaren, the men smirked at Jorund, and Borger, who smelled a good fight in the air, stomped back up to his seat and watched the confrontation with unabashed pleasure.

"Well, it seems the jarl has two barrels in his hall . . . one empty . . . and one *full of itself*," Jorund proclaimed with a vengeful smile, drawing a rumble of amusement from the crowd. The sight of her flashing eyes, bold mouth, and provocative stance had momentarily robbed him of words when she appeared. But the sting of her first barb had brought him back to his senses and he was determined not to let her best him or goad him into true anger.

"Since you are so full of *wisdom*, Serricksdotter, answer me this." He cocked his head and looked her up and down. "Can a battle-wench wield a blade as fiercely as she wields her tongue?"

"Pick up your blade and find out, Borgerson. Here. Now," she declared, pouring all the force she could muster into a look so passionate with disdain that he would have to defend himself against it. Her audacity was soon rewarded.

"Very well, Serricksdotter. I shall pick up a blade."

She blinked, scarcely able to believe her ears. He was actually agreeing to fight her? Eager to put him to the test before he could recant, she strode back to her table in the shadows to snatch up her sword. When she returned, he stood with his big arms crossed and one corner of his mouth curled in amusement.

"Not that blade, Battle-maiden. *A scythe blade*. They're heavier and harder to wield than any sword. I'll meet you at the edge of the wheat fields when the sun stands high and we'll see just how fiercely you can swing a blade."

"A scythe?" Her face caught fire as she realized he'd cleverly left himself an out. The cowardly cur! "I am a warrior and I answer all challenges with a sword, Borgerson. I'll not—"

"What's the matter, *Warrior-maiden*?" he crooned, swaggering closer, daring her not to meet his gaze. "Afraid to learn you can't keep up with a *woman-heart*?"

A strangled noise issued from her throat—half frustration, half rage. She was caught in her own trap—her pride snared with the same challenge she'd issued to entrap his! And with a glance at the lurid, prodding expectation in the faces around her, she realized she had no choice but to accept that wretched challenge.

"I will defeat you, Borgerson . . . no matter what blade you wield," she snapped. And on impulse she lowered her eyes pointedly down his front, where she delivered him a savage visual knee.

Borger crowed with wicked delight at her brazen gesture and at the way Jorund's eyes sparked in response. "By the gods—I must see this contest for myself! Thor's Belly-thunder—I'll even count the score. Today . . . midday! They'll meet at the wheat fields and we'll all see who wields a harvest-blade better, a 'warrior-maid' or a 'woman-heart'!"

Laughter broke out all around, and Aaren pivoted and shoved her way through the jostling bodies with her face ablaze. As she reached the doors, she heard Borger and his warriors laying wagers on who would cut the most wheat that afternoon.

She stormed to the edge of the common, then wheeled to stare at the long hall with the warriors' laughter ringing in her ears and the women's vengeful smirks burning in her mind's eye. She had come to Borger's village to fight with all honor and win their respect. Now, because of Jorund Borgerson and his disgusting old father, she was even farther from that goal than when she started! And she knew that if she was bested that afternoon, she'd be the object of derision among both the warriors and the women for the rest of her days.

She thought of Jorund's insufferably smug expression as he goaded her with the weapon she herself had unwittingly handed him. The wretch. She knew exactly what she had to do.

Win.

*   *   *

Despite the urgency of the harvest, there was a festive air among the villagers streaming along the sunny paths leading out to the wheat fields. The women gossiped and laughed as they smoothed their kerchiefs and herded their children along . . . swishing their up-tucked skirts a bit more than usual. Warriors wagered and bragged and preened their freshly combed hair and beards as they strode along . . . vying for the eyes of village maidens and wayward wives. And in the midst of them all strode their burly, ham-fisted jarl, fresh from a sweat-bath and a thorough combing.

When he arrived at the fields, Borger took immediate charge, establishing bounds for the spectators and rules for the contest. His *hird* and the villagers spread along two sides of the great wheat field and watched with mounting excitement as Jorund arrived in a group of women that included a number of the village's ranking females. Anticipation stretched to palpable tension when Aaren appeared with a confident stride, accompanied by her curvy sisters.

Jorund offered Aaren first choice of the six or so scythes lying on the ground, provided by Brun Cinder-hand, the smith, for their use. She hefted first one, then another, checking their blades and wooden grips, then made her selection and produced a whetstone to begin sharpening her choice. Jorund watched her movements with an expression of private amusement . . . until she began to expertly hone her blade to a fine edge. He frowned, reached for the tool with the longest handle, then planted himself beside her and leaned over her so as to interrupt her work. When she looked up, clearly irritated, he slid his blade slowly and suggestively along hers and produced a devilish smile.

"You get what you want of me today, Serricksdotter. A *blade-meeting*."

She was furious at his mocking equation of this contest with an honorable blade-fight . . . and at the way his silky tones flowed like a touch down her neck. But she refused to back away.

"I'll have the rest as well, Borgerson," she answered. "A *victory*."

They stood for a long moment, too close for comfort; intensely aware of each other and of the peculiar tension that tightened their belly muscles, made their skin feel hot and sensitive, and caused their fingers to curl tighter around their blade handles. Neither was willing to retreat, and after a long moment Borger broke the stalemate by seizing each of them by the arm and hauling them to the edge of the field to establish the manner of the contest and the judging.

"It's simple enough," Borger announced. "You start at the corners and work toward the center. When the field is cut and bundled, the sheaves will be tallied and the one who's cut the most will be declared the victor."

Such a contest placed a premium on strength and endurance, for in order to cut more, one would have to cut faster than the other. And scythes, all knew, had a way of growing heavier and swinging slower with every new row. Jorund had a clear advantage here. He glanced at his flexed and bulging arm and when he looked up he found Aaren's eyes fixed on it as well. But instead of apprehension, he saw only deeper determination in the set of her jaw.

Borger ordered them to take positions by the two spears he had stuck into the ground at the corners of the field. When Jorund reached his place, there was a rush of women trying to form a line behind him. They shoved and elbowed for position until Helga asserted her rank to appoint herself and three other women to follow him as gleaners and bundlers.

"And who gleans and bundles for the Valkyr's daughter?" Borger shouted.

Miri and Marta, their fair hair covered with kerchiefs and their kirtles up-tucked, hurried to Aaren's side. But the other women of the village folded their arms and refused to follow; they would not aid her against their Breath-stealer. Aaren's face began to burn as the jarl called twice more for more gleaners to even the odds. Still no one moved.

Miri and Marta looked up at Aaren with wide, hurt-filled eyes and she looked away, her jaw flexing with frustration. She pulled her long hair over one shoulder and began to braid it, as she always did for battle. At length, a thrall man with a half-shaved head, wearing a hooded tunic that reached his ankles, stepped out of the crowd and bustled over to stand with Aaren and her sisters. There was muffled laughter and Hakon Freeholder called out: "Godfrey's used to woman-work—why, he's been wearin' a kirtle fer years!"

The focus of the jest and ensuing laughter reddened, but lifted his portly chin and held his ground. There was still one place to fill behind the Valkyr's daughter.

After a long, heated pause, Garth Borgerson stepped from the small knot of warriors who were staring hotly at Miri and Marta, and awkwardly ambled over to stand with Aaren. Shocked titters and guffaws buffeted him and he reddened. But when Brun Cinder-hand snatched a bright kerchief from the head of a thrall woman and tossed it at him with a braying laugh, Garth picked it up and tied it around his head with a grin.

"The Valkyr's daughter defends the might of warriors," he proclaimed. "It's only right a warrior should lend a hand." A moment later he received the very reward he had hoped for: a warm, irresistible smile from curvy little Miri.

Scythe blades were raised, hovered, then fell in swooshing arcs at the drop of Borger's hand, and the harvest battle had begun. From the start there was a marked difference in the cutting style of the combatants. Aaren swung the long-handled blade from her shoulders, with her back straight and legs flexing, while Jorund cut with long and powerful strokes that originated in his massive back. At first, all watching placed their wagers on Jorund's clearly superior effort. But with each swath of her blade, Aaren's motion lengthened and smoothed, until she settled into an oft-practiced rhythm of cuts that were shorter than Jorund's but more frequent. By the time each had completed the first pass and started a return swath, jeering predictions of the warrior-maid's quick humiliation had dampened considerably.

At the end of the second round, Jorund paused for a drink of water and watched Aaren's sure, fluid motions, appraising the lines of her lithe body. It was so absorbing a task that it took a full minute to realize she was nearly even with him. When she paused for water, too, he was surprised that she pulled out her whetstone and worked the edge of her blade between drinks. He glanced at his own blade, which after two swaths of the long field was showing signs of wear. Annoyance settled on his broad shoulders at the realization that she'd thought to provide for something he hadn't . . . a well-honed blade . . . and that she'd obviously done harvest work before. Irritably, he tossed the wooden dipper back into the bucket and returned to work.

Over and over Aaren braced and swung in rhythmic cadence, until every sinew in her shoulders burned and her legs and back knotted with fatigue. The light calluses on her hands were not enough to protect her from the bite of the wooden handle, wielded so forcefully and relentlessly; her hands began to throb. The sun beat down on her head and sweat rolled down her face and soaked her tunic.

At the end of the third round, when she paused to drink and sharpen her blade, she worked her linen tunic up behind her breastplate, as she always had when harvesting in their mountain meadows, then pulled it out the top and over her head. She wiped her face and shoulders with it and tossed it aside, oblivious to the shocked murmurs of the villagers, as she stepped to the edge of the wheat again.

Jorund had paused when he caught sight of her at the field's edge, and he watched, chest heaving and eyes widening, as she raised and discarded her tunic. Across the shrinking distance, he drank in the stark, sensual contrast of her pale skin and the dark leather of her molded breastplate, and savored every line of her bare shoulders. She was stunning; tapered and womanly, yet with a sleek, underlying muscularity that fascinated him. His eyes traced the rim of her armor and fastened on the flexing of her firm shoulders and the soft jiggle of her breasts, just visible beneath the open leather lacings at the sides. She was both hard and soft . . . a tantalizing combination. And she was also hot and naked beneath that maddening leather shell. His whole body reacted to the thought.

Aaren had nearly caught up with him before he lowered his propped elbow from the scythe handle and put his back into the work again. She concentrated fiercely on the cutting, forcing her mind and will past the searing complaints of her muscles and the disheartening fact that Jorund always seemed to be just a bit ahead of her. The swish of the blades, the rustle of the drying stalks, the familiar, dusty smell . . . all ran together in her senses, blending past and present harvests as row after row fell before her blade.

The afternoon progressed. Shadows appeared and gradually lengthened. With a third of the field yet uncut between them, they now faced each other, slowly working their way toward the center . . . cut by cut, row by row. Both were long past the point of exhaustion and numbed to the pain of relentless exertion. But as they faced each other, coming closer together with each swing of a blade, each fixed on the sight of the other as if spotting the finish line, and the pace picked up.

"You look tired, Serricksdotter!" he called out across the way, his voice gritty with fatigue. "Perhaps you should rest in the shade . . . and leave the finish to me."

"I'll leave you only dust and stubble, Borgerson," she panted, glowering through her pain. He returned her a gritty but genuine smile. And through her work-numbed senses, she felt a small, unsettling pleasure that he was not blood-letting furious with her.

"Hold, Serricksdotter!" His voice burst into her reeling head some time later, and she came crashing back to reality just in time to see him jolting out of the way of her blade. "There's no more wheat . . . we're finished," he declared. She grounded her blade and glanced blankly at the sea of stubble around her feet, scarcely able to believe her eyes. Finished, she thought. She might have stood there, exhausted and dumbstruck, for the rest of the afternoon if Miri and Marta hadn't rushed out to get her.

"They're tallying now . . . the jarl and his scale-tender," Marta said breathlessly. "Are you all right, Aaren?" She nodded mutely and they placed her arms about their shoulders to help her to the edge of the field.

Only after she'd stumbled to her knees in the shade did she realize that her sisters were no longer the ones bundling her cuttings. Somewhere in the blur of those last grinding hours, Brun Cinder-hand, the smith, and Hrolf the Elder had taken their places. She stared at the burly, leather-faced warriors—now be-kerchiefed and bending and bobbing—and would have laughed, if she'd had the energy. Something intervened, blocking her line of sight, and she looked up to find Jorund looming over her with a full water bucket in hand.

"A good hot sweat . . . and a cold dousing," he said, his swollen fingers moving ominously over the rope handle on the wooden pail. She braced to take it full in the face, too exhausted to dodge what she was sure would be an opportune revenge. But instead smiled at her . . . and offered her the handle.

She scowled, suspicious of his generosity. Her face flushed as she accepted the pail with quaking hands and paused, unsure what to do with it. Then it came to her: a cold dousing . . . it had been a suggestion, not a threat. With one eye on him and the other on the people collecting around them, she upended the bucket over her own head and gasped with pleasure at the cold blast.

"Perhaps you should have drunk it instead, Serricksdotter," he said with a teasing edge to his voice. "Since you won't be drinking victory ale in the hall this night." She shoved to her feet and staggered before catching herself and squaring her aching shoulders.

"We shall see who goes thirsty in the hall this night, Borgerson," she declared hoarsely.

Borger's voice carried over the crowd just then, booming and irritable. "Well then—count again, curse your hides. I must be sure!"

Aaren shoved her way through the crowd toward the stacks of sheaves which had been assembled on huge squares of sailcloth. Jorund followed close behind her, and both watched as the counters laboriously re-stacked and re-tallied the product of their labors. For every sheaf laid to Aaren's credit, a corresponding one was assigned to Jorund's. And the reason for the re-count became appallingly clear. They'd finished dead even.

Aaren sank to her knees, watching in horror, and Jorund stumbled back a pace and sat down on the ground with a jarring thud. Arguments broke out between the women who had gleaned for Jorund and the warriors who had gathered Aaren's sheaves.

"It was that Hrolf," declared Gudrun, standing braced with her hands jammed firmly against her aching back. "He added in weeds to fill up the sheaves!"

"Listen to the old kite screech," Hrolf countered, jabbing a finger. "Her what wrapped three straws together and called 'em a bundle!"

But their arguments made no difference; the re-count continued apace until Borger lifted a hand and barked for silence. As the last few sheaves were moved and the numbers mounted steadily higher, Aaren struggled to her feet, her eyes wide and hands clenched, and Jorund lurched up with a groan, looking alarmed. The final tally rang out like a tolling bell over the silent gathering. And even those who couldn't count past their own ten fingers understood the result.

"*Ten-score and twelve . . . and . . . ten-score and twelve!*" the jarl's scale-tender proclaimed.

Their heated pride-bout had ended in a draw.

No one uttered a word at first. Even Borger was shocked speechless. Then, as usual, he recovered his wits and unleashed his tongue.

"So!" he said, heaving about to impale both Jorund and Aaren on a single wicked stare. "It would seem that a 'warrior-maid' and a 'woman-heart' are uncommonly well matched! *Both* wield a wicked scythe-blade . . . and *neither* will drink victory-ale in my hall tonight!"

Borger threw back his head and laughed, joined by titters and snickers that soon grew into full, releasing laughter. Warriors, women, thralls, and children; everyone was quickly caught up in it. Finally, Jorund's broad shoulders began to shake, too, as he surrendered to the awful irony of at last being perfectly matched in size, strength, and skill . . . and by a woman he wanted . . . who wanted nothing from him except the chance to put a few holes in his hide.

Only Aaren stood outside that common mirth. To her, it was too horrible to be amusing: to be so close to victory—one wretched bundle of grain!—yet so far away. As she stared at those fateful piles of sheaves, the villagers' laughter began to buffet her already bruised pride.

She looked around at their reddened cheeks and gaping mouths, and read derision in their coarsened features. Something vulnerable inside her began to shrink, withdrawing behind protective walls of anger and self-sufficiency. From the moment she arrived in Borger's village, the women had resented and shunned her, the men had scorned her skill and her company . . . and even the children shrank from her, as if she was some sort of monster. They'd made it clear: *she didn't belong amongst them . . . any of them.* And out of the darkest corner of her heart there came a devastating whisper: *perhaps she never would.*

An awful emptiness spread through her, a profound loneliness which she had felt only once before . . . the night Serrick left her. She stiffened and looked for an opening in the crowd, an escape, and ran straight into Jorund's blue-eyed stare. It was humiliating, feeling naked, inside and out, before her sworn enemy. But she couldn't seem to pull away. She just stood, feeling alone and exposed, an oddity ordained by a divine whim . . . not a man and not a woman either . . . except in Jorund Borgerson's eyes.

Not a woman? Pride blazed to life inside her, pouring desperate heat into her stiff limbs and empty middle. What did that matter? She was a *warrior*! It was only the extreme fatigue that allowed such weak, unworthy thoughts to plague her.

"I'm not through with you, Jorund Borgerson," she declared hotly. And when she thought he'd been properly scorched by her flaming look, she pivoted with as much agility as her wooden legs could manage and struck off for the village. But her stride faltered briefly when his husky voice pursued her.

"I would hope not, Long-legs."

Two pairs of eyes had taken in Aaren's deep and unsettled reaction to the draw and to the villagers' mirth afterward: Jorund's and Brother Godfrey's.

Jorund had watched her blanched face and eyes darkened with a hint of pain, and was roused and confused by what he saw. She hated losing, he knew. But was she really so thin-skinned that she could not see any cause for laughter in what had happened? As he stood watching her stalk away, watching the almost girlish twitch of her braid as it bounced against her buttocks, he thought harder on her expression and realized there was more to her reaction than bruised warrior's pride. He had glimpsed something softer . . . something vulnerable.

That thought hung in his mind as he felt himself being moved bodily and started back to his senses. Helga and Kara had him by the arms and Sith was shoving him from behind, intent on trundling him back to the village, with or without his consent. "You need a hot sweat and a good, thorough rub," Helga insisted, "else you'll be sore as the Devil's head tomorrow."

As Jorund surrendered to their motherly bullying, he shot a look far ahead, to Aaren's lone form, and wondered fleetingly who was going to rub Aaren Serricksdotter.

Brother Godfrey had also watched Aaren's face moments earlier, and with rare insight discerned the tumultuous state of the heart behind the proud, stoic mask she wore. He had been a stranger himself once, in Borger's village. He recognized the loneliness and the pain of not belonging, because he had also felt it in his early days here. That shared feeling moved him to follow her when she fled the gathering.

He trailed her along the paths, then through the commons and the village, to the path that led along the cliffs above the lake. When she stumbled and fell on a grassy knoll and didn't rise, he ran to see if she was hurt. Falling to his knees beside her, he muttered a prayer and rolled her over. Her breathing was slow and steady, and there was no evidence she'd struck her head.

"Sleeping," Godfrey pronounced with relief. "She must be half dead." And he sank onto a weedy hummock beside her, to keep watch.

Chapter Seven

Aren awakened to a seeping chill through her body and the prickling of grass-straws alongside her face. She turned her head and a sharp pain shot along her shoulder, up her neck, and exploded like a hot ember in the back of her head. She squeezed her eyes tight as she conquered that pain, then pried them open, one at a time. She appeared to be lying on the ground, near the cliffs overlooking the shore. She blinked and tried to sit up, but at the first movement, her entire body erupted with pain.

"Here—I'll help," came a voice she didn't recognize. She turned just as a thick pair of hands clasped her shoulders and propelled her upward, and she found herself nearly nose-to-nose with a ruddy, broad-faced fellow with a cropped fringe of hair ringing his otherwise bald head. "Thank the Almighty, you're awake," he said. "I was worried."

"Who are you?" she demanded, shrinking back and squinting at him through the pain in her head. The very next instant, she recognized him. "You're the one who gleaned behind me . . . that strange fellow . . ."

"I am Brother Godfrey," he said as he sat back on his heels and smiled, shrugging off her unflattering evaluation. After seven years in a Norse village, he was used to being thought odd.

"You're a thrall," she declared, glancing down at the iron ring he wore around his neck and thinking that his speech sounded strange to her ear. "And you're a foreigner . . . a captive." He nodded.

"And a priest of the White Christ," he informed her with a broad, gap-toothed smile. "I saw you come this way after you left the fields and feared . . . I thought you might need help."

"I need no help," she answered, with an involuntary creak in her voice. Cold air brushed her bare shoulders and tugged at the cover she was clutching. She glanced quizzically at the woolen cover in her hands, then peered beneath it, seeming a bit shocked to find herself in just her breeches and breastplate. She recalled stripping off her tunic during the cutting of the wheat . . . but after that . . . and after the counting . . .

"You did seem to need a bit of help last night, however," he chided gently. "I could not wake you and could not carry you . . . so I covered you as best I could and stayed with you." He glanced down at his thin, short-sleeved tunic and breeches, and Aaren's face heated as she realized the cover she was holding was his outer garment. When she thrust it back into his lap, he seemed dismayed. "No—I am not cold, Serricksdotter. You should keep it until—" He tried to hand it back to her, but she scowled and struggled to pull her legs beneath her and stand.

"Ohhh—" She bit her lip hard and squeezed her eyes shut. There wasn't a spot on her entire body that wasn't being hammered with pain.

"I feared this," he declared, heaving up and spreading his heavy cassock about her shoulders, despite her attempt to wave him off. "The cold and damp have set your muscles stiff. Here, let me rub your legs." He waddled over on his knees, pulled her legs out straight, and began to massage some blood back into them.

"*Nej*—I'm good enough," she declared through her teeth, trying to jerk her legs out of his hands. It was like trying to juggle logs; they felt huge, wooden, and awkward. "Give me a little time and I'll work out the soreness," she insisted, trying gruffly to hide her shame at feeling so helpless.

But Brother Godfrey, she quickly discovered, was not easily deterred. He kept a gentle but controlling grip on her foot. "Rest yourself, Serricksdotter. All warriors need such tending from time to time." As he worked, briskly rubbing and kneading her ankles and calves, he glanced up with a smile and she realized that he had credited her with that coveted title: warrior.

Her gaze fell to the flattened grass nearby which bore mute testimony to his presence there during the night. "You stayed here all night?"

His pudgy hands stilled for a moment and he reddened slightly. "I was afraid to leave you. This time of year, the wolves come down out of the hills, sometimes right to the village. So I sat with you."

"Why?" She scowled, realizing she made a faint breath-plume when she spoke. He had stayed with her and given her his garment, even though he must have been quite frozen himself. The accusation in her tone faded to confusion. "Why would you watch for me? And give me your tunic?"

"I wanted to help. I'm a priest, after all." His cold polished cheeks glowed as he said it and she noticed that his brown eyes warmed and brightened, as if a flame had begun to burn inside him.

"A priest?" She recalled that Serrick had spoken of priests once, in connection with the gods, but she couldn't remember much of what he'd said. Serrick was one to honor nature more than the gods of Asgard, whom he said dealt cruelly with mere mortals . . . including himself. "Then who do you belong to?"

Brother Godfrey paused in the midst of rubbing her calves. "Do you mean as a thrall or a priest?" he said with a chuckle. "As a bond slave, a thrall, I am bound to Jorund. But my true master is the One Great God called Jehovah. The Almighty. And his son, the Christ."

Aaren narrowed one eye in concentration. "I think I have heard of this Christ somewhere. What color is he?"

"Color?" Godfrey looked puzzled at the question.

"The great Thor is red . . . Odin abides in blue. Does this Christ not have a color?"

"Ahhh." His hands stilled and he settled an intent look on her. "He is called the *White Christ*."

"And what is his weapon?" She frowned at the odd look on his face, and prompted: "He must have something to fight with . . . all the gods do. Thor has his hammer, Mjollnir . . . Odin, his great spear, Gungnir. What is your Christ's weapon?"

Godfrey sat back on his heels with his hands in his ample lap and looked bemused. But after a moment, a great, beaming grin burst across his fleshy face. "My Lord's weapon is Love."

"Love?" Aaren laughed, surprised and intrigued by the little thrall man's answer and by his pride in his colorless god. She felt drawn to the warmth and openness of his portly face and his easy acceptance of her. He was the first person in Borger's village who hadn't scowled at, or shunned, or run from her . . . besides Jorund.

"Love is an exceedingly strange name for a weapon. What sort of weapon is it?"

"A most powerful one." Godfrey's voice softened and his eyes fairly sparkled. "It is a weapon of the heart, Serricksdotter. It has the strength to change people's lives . . . to heal their troubled souls . . . and to bring peace and salvation to the world."

Brother Godfrey wasn't speaking of a weapon wrought in a forge, she realized. He was indeed speaking of the same *love* that Serrick had spoken of when teaching his daughters about the world, and in recounting tales of the heroes and women of great fame. Love was heart-softness, a marrow-deep yearning, a longing of the kind that Serrick had held inside him for the Fair Leone both before and after she left them. Aaren leaned forward and rubbed her thighs, feeling confused and a little disturbed.

"But love has no substance—it cannot dent a shield boss or notch an arrow or swing a blade . . . or defend against one. What would your god and his son want with such a weapon?"

"With such a weapon, they can melt men's hard hearts and move their hands to mercy and kind deeds. With such a weapon, they can begin to make people free, can feed the hungry and help the poor, and can end fighting and bring peace between nations and peoples."

Aaren crossed her arms over her chest and cocked a skeptical look at him. "If your god can use this 'love' to make people free, then why are you still a slave?" She didn't mean to shame him with her challenge, but she could scarcely credit his claims for his god or his god's bizarre weapon. Whoever heard of fighting with a heart? How could a heart stand and defend against a savage battle-wave of iron and sinew . . . much less claim victory?

Godfrey surprised her with a very pleased expression. "Oh, Jorund offered me freedom. More than once. I have no need of it. I remain a thrall to honor my Lord, the Christ, who was himself a servant . . . and to be a symbol, an example among Borger's people. You see, those who follow Christ, priests especially, are called to love all people and to help and to serve others."

She didn't see at all. Love of freedom was deeply ingrained in Norsemen's hearts and minds . . . cherished above life itself. To be made a thrall was the ultimate degradation and the goal of each thrall's life was to win freedom. Only free men and women had rights before the jarl and before the law of the Thing, when the clans gathered. It was unthinkable to her that anyone would reject a precious offer of freedom. Prickles of caution crept up her spine.

"We are to do good works," he continued, "to share whatever we have with others, and to forgive when we are injured. I can do all that I am required to do by my god while still being Jorund's thrall . . . and his friend."

It was the priest's second mention of Jorund. For some reason, the way he had given her the bucket of water yesterday came to mind. *Sharing.* Her eyes widened.

"Does Jorund Borgerson follow your White Christ, too?"

Godfrey sighed and made a curious series of hand motions touching his head, chest, and shoulders . . . a magical sign connected with his god, she guessed. "He believes in the one Almighty God and in God's son, the Christ, and he has learned to 'turn the other cheek,' which is a difficult thing for him—for any Norseman—to do. But he is not yet ready to be Christian in all things. He still has . . . one too many heathen ways."

Aaren sat up rod straight, her interest piqued by mention of Jorund finding something difficult. It was wise, Serrick had taught her, to learn all you can about your enemy and his weaknesses before engaging in battle.

"What do you mean . . . 'turn the other cheek'?" she asked.

"Our Lord has said that we must not return evil for evil . . . wrong for wrong," he explained. "For if good people work violence, even in the name of blood-vengeance, where will the fighting end? So, He has instructed us that if our enemy strikes us on the cheek, we are to turn our heads and give him our other cheek as well." He searched her reaction and nodded wistfully, as if he had expected the horror dawning in her handsome features. "We are commanded to love our enemies . . . and to do good to those around us, even to those who hate or misuse us."

"Love your enemies?" she choked out. "Instead of fighting them? That makes no sense at all. Small wonder Jorund—" She stopped, staring at the round-cheeked cleric with widening insight.

Was this what had made Jorund Borgerson a *woman-heart*? This Brother Godfrey with his helpfulness, his irresistible grin, and his easy, accepting manner . . . had he befriended Jorund Borgerson, then filled his heart with this 'loving enemies' nonsense, and turned him against fighting? If so—and if this heart-weapon was even half as powerful as the priest believed—then it was indeed dangerous to be around!

"I must go," she declared, rising painfully to her feet. Her shoulders and the backs of her legs ached, but she was relieved to be on her own two feet, and eager to be away from him.

"Move slowly and I'll help you." Godfrey heaved to his feet beside her and, despite the disparity in their heights, braced an arm around her for support. She shrugged him off with a scowl and backed away.

"You've helped . . . enough." She could see that her rebuff confused him and felt a twinge of guilt for her seeming ingratitude. But she knew with a warrior's unfailing instinct for danger that Godfrey was a potential threat. She could not allow herself to be tainted and weakened, as Jorund probably had, by the priest's notions of "loving enemies" and "turning cheeks."

"You have my gratitude, Priest Godfrey." She thrust his

cassock into his hands without looking directly at him and turned on her heel to begin the trek back to the village, feeling both enlightened and disturbed by her encounter with him. She recalled Jorund's actions at the bathing house. He had been angry with her, but had 'turned the other cheek' more than once. Was it a belief in this strange god . . . or was it that he was soft on women . . . or was it pure cowardice that kept him from taking a blade to her? Moments later, she caught herself standing on the path, scowling, staring into the memory of his face as he handed her the water bucket. There had been a horde of unspoken words in his eyes.

"What does it matter why he won't fight?" she said aloud. "It makes no difference to me."

But as she rolled her aching shoulders and struck off again for the village, she knew in her deepest heart that it wasn't true. It was coming to make a great deal of difference to her. And she refused to think why.

The frost had already been trodden from the grasses on the path leading from the outlying dwellings to the commons, and the houses along her way sat strangely silent. The haze of peat-smoke which morning fires usually cast over the village was absent and hounds nosed around the remnants of a fresh meal in the hall. Only the cook chamber at the side of the long hall showed the gray plume of activity and Aaren headed for it, hoping to locate her sisters. Relief poured through her at the sight of them, bending over the great iron kettles set on the hearth. They seemed just as relieved to see her.

"Where is everyone?" she asked, wincing at the vigor of their hugs.

"They're all out in the fields, harvesting," Marta declared, feeling Aaren's arms and scowling at her bare shoulders. "You're half frozen! Where have you been? We worried ourselves into knots last night!" She turned on Miri. "I told you we should have gone out to search for her."

"I can take care of myself." Aaren crossed her arms and leaned over Marta, asserting her authority through size. But that old tactic didn't work this time . . . not with her standing there half naked and frozen. "Besides, I was not alone. I had a thrall with me . . . that little round priest."

"Oh, Brother Godfrey!" Miri said, spearing Marta with a look of vindication.

"You know him?" Aaren asked. When they nodded, she expelled a long, slow breath, realizing that since they'd begun to spend their days separately, her sisters might have a number of acquaintances she knew nothing about. The idea settled heavily on her fatigue-weighted spirits.

"He's an odd man . . . always so cheer-filled and eager to help," Miri said earnestly, pulling Aaren to a bench and hurrying back to the hearth to dip a bowl of meat-flavored porridge for her. "All the women like him. A number of them have taken up his beliefs and become Christians."

"They have?" Aaren scowled as she began to spoon the warm, flavorful *grautr* into her mouth. Marta hurried back with a tankard of ale and perched on the bench with her.

"Helga, Sith, and Kara and Gudrun . . . they are all believers. In truth"—she leaned closer and her voice lowered—"that is why Helga is no longer the jarl's wife. She began to believe and insisted the jarl be as a Christian husband to her." When Aaren looked blankly at her, she sighed and explained: "You see, Christians are allowed only one wife. And they must not go to the furs with other women while they are married. It is the White Christ's law."

"Most of the women like the teachings and ways of the Christians . . . they do not like all the maiming and dying of the fighting, and they dislike sharing a husband," Miri continued. "But the jarl and his men . . . most will not agree. So, Helga carried her furs from the jarl's hall and calls him husband no longer. They have a son in common, but can hardly bear the sight of each other. So when Helga challenged the jarl a second time, he was furious, but he could not decline."

"Helga challenged the jarl *again*? To what?" Aaren paused with her spoon in mid-air.

"To a harvest contest . . . threshing grain," Marta informed her. "And Gudrun challenged that nasty Hakon Freeholder, and Dagmar the dark-eyed Dane challenged her new husband, Hrolf the Younger . . . and Sith even challenged old Oleg Forkbeard!"

"Imagine the two of them . . . waddling and squatting and swinging sickles." Miri giggled, her eyes twinkling. "After you and Jorund Borgerson left the fields last evening, the men and women started to argue and began to dare each other to contests like yours and Jorund's. Now, even the children compete, to see who can carry water the fastest to the harvesters! If the weather holds—and Sith says by the cows' tails it will—then the entire grain harvest will be cut and threshed by tomorrow's sunset!"

Aaren bolted down the rest of her porridge, fat-pork, and ale, and strode out along the cart path to the fields with Miri to see for herself. Helga and Borger . . . Gudrun and the lusty Freeholder . . . Sith and wizened old Forkbeard. It was just as her sisters had described it. And beneath all the commotion, the harvest was proceeding at a promising pace.

The cutting of late hay, and the bundling of barleycorn and rye and the precious hops, was going on in fields as far as the eye could see. Near at hand, on the great sailcloths where the stacks of wheat sheaves from her contest with Jorund had lain, there were now large piles of grain. Around them worked ham-fisted warriors, flailing sheaves and beating out grain with the same ferocity they would have used in swinging swords and axes in battle. Their faces were dusty and their grins were broad as they teased the women who worked beside them.

Aaren stared at the results of the competition she and Jorund had generated. Perhaps it hadn't been for naught after all, she thought. With a bemused smile, she turned back to the village. When Miri caught up with her and asked where she was going, she declared, "I've already done my part. My whole body hurts. I need a good hot sweat . . . and a good hard rub."

Not long after Aaren and Miri had left the cook chamber, Marta heard a scream coming from the long hall and went running to investigate. Near the great doors, she spotted the two thrall women whose task it was to clear away the refuse from the morning meal in the hall and to feed the prisoner. They were huddled together, staring at the huge, manacled form of Borger's captive, who was up on his feet in a crouch, growling at them like a wild animal. When Marta called out to them, they scrambled toward her with wild eyes and ashen faces.

"He's mad as a dog," Una cried, clutching Marta's arm.

"Threw his food all over me!" the other wailed, holding up her begrimed kirtle in a trembling fist. "And lunged straight for my throat, he did!"

Marta scowled at the overturned bucket on the floor nearby and the foul-smelling slurry that had splattered from it. That was his food? "What was in that bucket?"

"Th' same food he always gets . . . the hall scraps. Th' jarl said if he wouldn't eat it one day, he would have to the next," thick-featured Una declared with a glower.

It took Marta a moment to realize they meant the *very same food* . . . mere scraps and swill to begin with, now slimy and rancid after days of sitting uneaten. She pulled free of the women's hands and edged warily to where the bucket lay—just beyond the prisoner's reach. She bent to pick it up, but the smell was so bad she snapped back up and kicked it away instead.

"Careful!" Una whined. "He'll bite a hunk out of you if you get too close."

"Just like his old sire!" Olga choked out. "They say old Gunnar Haraldson eats babies—"

The prisoner roared and lunged against his chains, setting the thrall women running, squealing, from the hall. Marta, who stood much closer, was too stunned to scramble out of the way and found herself face to face with the crouching hulk. He bared his teeth at her and growled from low in his throat. Her blood stood still in her veins as she faced his battered, filthy form and realized that his light eyes burned as they raked her.

But it was those fierce gray eyes that also made him seem human. She willed herself to ignore the dirt and dried blood and bruises on his face, forcing herself to see that he was just a man . . . and a warrior, like Aaren. Her gaze fell to the heavy iron shackles that had scraped his wrists and ankles raw. She winced at the sight. He was treated worse than the hall hounds.

After a long moment, she summoned the courage to breathe and move, and headed for the cook chamber. She dished up a huge bowl of the mutton stew she'd been tending since dawn, and snatched up a pitcher of ale and the rest of the morning's flatbread to carry it back to the hall. The prisoner was slumped against the wall, in the shadows, but when she returned he stirred and glared at her. She judged where the length of his chains would allow him to reach, then slowly placed the bowl on the floor, stacked the bread on top of it, and nudged it toward him with her foot.

He snarled and she gasped and stumbled back a step— but only one step—and there she stayed. After a long silence, he slid over on his knees to investigate the food, then glared at her, then at the door, as if demanding that she leave. When she didn't move, he picked up a piece of the flatbread and threw it at her. She flinched, then straightened, irritated.

"You'd best save your food for eating, Gunnar's son . . . unless it is your wish to die like a cow in the straw." He lunged at her, but this time she knew the limits of his bonds and did not flinch or wince. Burning with frustration, he fell back into a stoop, then his long, muscular frame knotted into a cramped ball. He was half starved and exhausted after five days of captivity, but the look on his face said that no matter how depleted his body was, his spirit would never surrender.

"You'd better run, wench . . . or I might decide to eat you up," he ground out, his deep, menacing tones setting her fingertips vibrating.

She watched the guarded hunger and fatigue in his eyes and felt an odd fullness in her chest. "The stew tastes much better than I would." She tucked her arms about her waist, feeling bolder, sensing that his threat was a response to Una's and Olga's prattle. "And warriors, whatever their clan, do not eat babies . . . or young maids."

"Do they not?" he said, his eyes glittering as they roamed over her. "And how would you know about warriors, Tasty Maiden?"

"My father was a warrior. And my sister is one."

"Your *sister*?" He frowned and sank to his knees again, eyeing her strangely. "Your sister is the battle-maiden . . . the one they call a Valkyr's daughter?" Marta nodded and saw his eyes darken and drop from her to the stew. "Then I won't eat you up, Little Morsel. Now, get out of here . . . before I change my mind."

Marta felt his eyes return to her as she walked away, and she felt a tumbling in the pit of her stomach. Behind those fiery gray eyes, inside that hunger-weakened form, was a powerful warrior, a jarl's son, a man of obvious strength and pride. She couldn't help but wonder what he would look like beneath the dried blood and grime. But it was the remembrance of what Brother Godfrey had said to the small gathering of women in the women's house last evening—about helping those in need: the poor, the sick, and *the prisoner*—that set her on a brave and compassionate course.

After a short time, she returned to the hall with a bucket of water, some linen strips, a pot of clean goose grease, and herbs. The stew, bread, and ale were gone, and the prisoner was seated against the wall with his head lying on his arms, across his upraised knees. At the sound of her footfall, he jerked his head up, his eyes gleaming with feral threat. The sight of her and the things she held made him stiffen.

"I gave you your chance, Valkyr's daughter. Come no closer," he warned. "You remind me too well of how tasty little maids are."

"I *will* come closer." Marta raised her delicate chin and squared her shoulders with a bravado borrowed from her elder sister. "And you will not eat me up." She glanced at the empty bowl. "You have no room in your belly for me, after all that. And if you did eat me, who would bandage your wrists and bring you food tomorrow?"

She took a step, then another, and started like a frightened doe when he lunged at her. She was too fear-frozen to avoid him, but after a long, shocked moment, she realized he had not actually attacked her, at least not with his hands. He stood crouched, because of his chains, and raked her with eyes molten with heat. But looks alone, Father Serrick had always said, never killed anyone. When she swallowed her heart back into place, she lowered the bucket to the floor and reached with trembling fingers for one of his big, battered hands.

To her great relief, he did not resist, and soon she was kneeling warily near his sprawled form, washing the grime from his bleeding wrists and ankles. As she mixed the herbs and grease and applied it, she felt his eyes wandering over her hair and face and breasts, and her face heated.

"Are you really enchanted, Little One?" His voice was much softer and when she looked up nervously, she saw that his eyes were also softer. The tumbling in her middle settled into a slow, sensuous eddy of warmth.

"My sisters and I are under Odin's curse, it is true," she said, wrapping his wrist with a strip of linen. "But I fear it is my sister Aaren who is cursed most of all. She must fight and fight . . . again and again."

"Nej," he said, raising his fettered hand to touch her sun-bright hair, then stopping it just short of its goal and lowering it. "It is the men of old Red Beard's hall who are cursed most . . . to see you and to have you walk among them, knowing that they cannot have you." His laugh was harsh. "Curse their filthy eyes, they deserve such torture."

She was both confused and disturbed by his words. Their gazes met and held, and his grim smile faded. She glimpsed the naked jumble of pain, frustration, and longing churning in him before he jerked his face away. She finished bandaging his wrists and ankles in breathless silence, then warily thrust the linen rag into his hands and gave the bucket a nudge in his direction.

"You can do the rest." She got to her feet and backed away a step, where she paused, feeling suddenly awkward. "W-what is your birth name, son of Gunnar?" Her heart would not beat again until he spoke.

"It does not matter," he said, scowling. But after a moment of being pinned squarely beneath her disappointed gaze, he answered. "Leif." Then he struggled with something inside him and finally said, "And you, little Valkyr's daughter. What do they call you?"

"Marta," she said, smiling and willing him to smile back. He did not. She turned and started for the cook chamber, but stopped as his voice rumbled behind her.

"Marta."

"Yea, Leif Gunnarson?" she said, turning back, her heart feeling as if it was winging from her breast at the sound of her name on his lips. But his face and eyes were dark and fierce once more.

"Do not come near me again."

Marta colored hotly, lowered her head, and hurried out. But once in the cook chamber, she curled her hands into fists and spread her feet in unconscious imitation of Aaren's most determined stance.

"I'll come near whoever I please, Leif Gunnarson. And there is not a thing you can do to stop me."

Jorund had spent the first half of a sleepless night in the loft of the thrall house, having his aching frame warmed and massaged by several nubile young wenches whose busy hands and generous body heat should have pleased him. Instead, their coy ministrations had annoyed him and he was hard-pressed to show enough enthusiasm to keep from hurting the wenches' feelings. When they finally slept, he extricated himself from their sundry embraces and crawled from the loft to spend the second half of the night in his own little-used sleeping closet, in the long hall. The small, curtained chamber was dark and cold, and his handsome pallet furs were musty from disuse. As he lay there, wide-eyed, his body on edge, he understood too well the reason for his discontent.

Aaren Serricksdotter rose from the troubled pool of his thoughts like a water-nymph; as exquisite and tempting, and as impossible to catch. Her tawny eyes and flame-kissed hair, her hard thighs and soft, jiggling breasts filled his senses and tortured his breathing. Muscle by muscle his body contracted until he was aching all over again, swollen with wanting. He could have slaked his flesh-need in any number of pallets, even in the middle of the night, yet that possibility held no allure for him. He was past taking a woman's body just to vent a troublesome urge. His real need, he knew, was to conquer Aaren Serricksdotter with pleasure. And he would be truly satisfied with nothing less.

By morning, he had gone over and over their last encounter, that wretched harvest-battle and its aftermath, and realized two important things: there was something soft and vulnerable inside Aaren Serricksdotter . . . and to reach it, he must have her to himself. With others around, she would always swagger and bluster and play at being the warrior. But alone, without her pride to defend, she could soften to his touch, to his word-skill. And he could reach inside her to ignite the womanly passions that lay imprisoned in her warlike shell.

Alone, he decided firmly. He had to get her alone, somehow.

The women's house was quiet that morning when Jorund stuck his head inside the half-open door. In the dim interior, he could make out two feminine forms . . . one lying on a bench in the far corner, the other sitting on the bench beside. It was his battle-nymph and one of her young sisters—the one Garth was forever laying claim to—who was rubbing oil into her bare back and shoulders. He lifted wistful eyes skyward and murmured a silent thank-you, then slipped inside.

Chapter Eight

Just as the battle-maiden's sister turned to pour more oil on her hands, Jorund clamped a hand over her mouth, startling her, and put a finger to his lips, commanding silence. The flaxen-haired maid stared at him while he gestured that he would take her place, then she glanced between her sister and him uneasily. He poured on his most irresistible smile and a pleading look . . . and she reluctantly yielded her place and duty to him.

He settled on the bench beside Aaren, aware that her sister was hovering anxiously by the door to see what he would do. He poured some of the oil into his big hands while his eyes roamed the exotic taper of her back and the tantalizing bulges of the sides of her breasts, where they were pressed against the swath of linen beneath her. She was completely bare from the waist up, and from the waist down was covered only by a pair of deerskin breeches that were noticeably loose . . . probably not tied.

She wriggled her shoulders drowsily, entreating, "More. Do more."

More. The word sent a blast of dry heat through his lungs. He took a deep, calming breath and sent his fingers gliding over the smooth surface of her body, just as he had in his mind the day before. Godfrey's Blessed Heaven! Her skin was silky and soft; pale where the backplate of her armor had lain against her skin, and reddened where her upper shoulders had been exposed to the sun. With light pressure from his big hands, he traced the firm, neatly defined muscles beneath her skin, starting at the small of her back and flaring gently outward to the caps of her shoulders. She was indeed hard and soft to the same touch . . . all latent power and unexplored sensuality, at his very fingertips.

When he pressed his thumbs together and dragged them up the sides of her spine, a pleasure-filled groan slid from her half-conscious form. He grinned. When he gently kneaded the muscles of her upper back and the tops of her broad shoulders, she mewed, half in pain, half in pleasure. His eyes began to glow. He ran his hands in a long, leisurely caress up her sleek sides, where his fingertips stroked the compressed roundness of her breasts . . . and the rhythm of her breathing changed.

A tiny shiver proceeded from her shoulders downward and his eyes narrowed. She was becoming alert. With his gaze hot on the lashes lying just above her elegant cheekbones, he slid his hands slowly down her sides . . . and straight under her breeches. Then, with only a slight turn of his wrists, he cupped her buttocks and massaged firmly and sinuously.

This was *not* a sisterly bit of massage! Aaren realized, surfacing from the netherland of physical release. She tensed and blood flooded into her face and breasts at the outrage being inflicted on her bottom. She wasn't being rubbed down—she was being *touched*!

Her eyes flew open and she pushed up and around . . . to find Jorund Borgerson grinning at her, while he—

"You!" she choked, bashing his hands from her and curling around in a flash to face him on her knees. "H-how did you . . ." She fumbled to raise her breeches and jerked at the ties, then suddenly realized she was also bare from the waist up—"Ohhh!"—and scrambled to pull the linen from beneath her knees to clutch against her breasts. By the time she scrambled off the bench and backed away, her face was hot and that humiliated heat was sinking all the way down into the tightening tips of her breasts.

"What are you doing here?" she forced out, past the humiliation collected in her throat.

"I was just helping to rub the soreness from your . . . *body* . . . Serricksdotter." He advanced a step.

"In a sow's eye, you were," she charged, jolting back. "You—you were *touching* me—" The sight of him, so big and warm—his eyes darkening with some private pleasure as they skimmed her exposed body—knocked her wits end over end and set her responses in turmoil. She was embarrassed and confused, and—she cast a panicky glance around the main chamber—she was completely alone with him. Where on earth was Miri?

"Of course I touched you, Serricksdotter. That is the only way to rub soreness from a . . . *body*," he said smoothly, knowing full well it was the intimacy of his touch that had offended her and that she couldn't think clearly enough to separate the two. He smiled, guessing what was interfering with her formidable wits just now. He pressed his advantage, advancing again with his slow, stalking sway. "Can it be that you are afraid of being touched, Battle-maiden?"

"No," she said vehemently, clutching the linen tighter against her breasts.

"Then perhaps it is me you fear. *My* presence. *My* touch."

"No!" she said, grasping at the merest wisp of ire. "I do not fear anything or anyone, Jorund Borgerson. Least of all, you."

"Shall we test your truthfulness, Serricksdotter? Shall we see what you fear?" It was the perfect taunt, the perfect challenge . . . her pride would force her to prove him wrong. He had managed through the subtle shifts of his shoulders to back her toward the wall beside the bedshelves . . . straight into a corner. When her bare back smacked against the wall, her eyes flew wide and she tightened her grip on her delectably inadequate cover. He planted himself a foot away and slowly raised his hands toward her shoulders.

She had watched him stalk her, knowing she should punch him or knee him and run for her blade. But she couldn't make herself do it. There was something potent and enticing stirring in her blood . . . something that seemed more in his control than hers, something that he called forth in her. And—Freya help her!—she wanted to know what it was. There was no other man in the village who made her feel this peculiar swirling in her senses and set her entire body on edge the way he did. He knew about women. And just this once, she wanted to learn about women . . . about her own body, about this thing that was rising up hot and formless and powerful within her.

She saw his hands reaching for her and made no move to stop him. She wasn't afraid of him . . . or anyone . . . or anything. She wasn't afraid—

His hands closed gently on the taut muscles along her shoulders, and her knees went weak. The warmth, the tenderness of his fingers sent pleasure trickling downward, like a warm spring shower. As he began to massage those aching muscles, she felt her resistance melting and her whole body heating. Wonder wound through her body and coiled in her mind as his fingers curled behind her head, kneaded the tense column up the back of her neck, then threaded through her damp hair to stroke her tingling head in slow, expert circles. *Slow-hand*, the women called him. Now she knew why.

"Does this frighten you, Serricksdotter?" he said with a ragged edge.

"No." She whispered the half-lie with her eyes half closed. On one level it was entrancing, on another it truly was terrifying. Control of the situation was clearly in those big, firm hands that were making butter of her muscles and mush of her will. And not being in control frightened her. It went against everything she'd been taught.

"And what of this?" he murmured, moving his hands down her back, so that she was forced slightly forward, against his body. With his arms fully around her, but not quite embracing her, he traced her spine and caressed every muscle in her back. "Does this make you want to run from me?"

"No," she breathed, lifting her eyes to his. Those great, shaded pools of sky, filled with equal measures of pleasure and hunger. It was a mild surprise for her to realize that what he was doing to her seemed to give him pleasure as well.

"Or this?" He raised his hands to her shoulders, then slid them down her naked sides, where they clasped her waist tightly and pulled her forcefully against him.

She could scarcely shake her head. The size of him, the sudden impact of their bodies, and the feel of his lean musculature against her own tautly molded frame overwhelmed her senses. She felt the ridge of his hardened flesh against her belly and was mildly shocked to realize that it was meant for her . . . that she had caused it and that her body responded to it. Blood-heat settled into her loins, as if drawn to the swollen heat of his manflesh.

Thigh to thigh they stood, hardness to hardness. And there was suddenly a new ache deep inside her, one that could not be assuaged by a simple massage.

"You spoke truthfully, Long-legs. I believe you do not fear my touch."

She watched his generous lips as he spoke and longing surged so powerfully in her that it took her breath. It was a magic peculiar to him, his own unique enchantment, that allowed him to draw the life-breath from another mortal being without even touching her.

"Breath-stealer," she said in a whisper. "When you steal a woman's breath, what do you do with it?"

"I'm no thief. I always give it back," he vowed, his voice thick and sultry, enveloping her like the steam of a sweat-bath. He lowered his head and ran his hands up her sides, to the sides of her breasts, driving all the air from her lungs in a soft rush.

"Have I stolen your breath, Fearless Maiden?"

She could only answer with her eyes, for he had just stolen her voice as well. "Then I will be pleased to give it back to you." He lowered his mouth to hers by agonizing increments, then paused a hair's width away and blew ever so gently on her lips. That hot, moist stream of breath drowned her mouth in swirling, liquid sensation. Pleasure surged and eddied through her lips, engorging and weighting them so that they parted. But his restitution was a sham, for instead of giving back her breath, he dangled it between them, allowing her use of it only in short, shuddery gasps that bordered on whimpers. Then he covered her mouth with his, flexing his lips softly over hers, moving in slow, lazy circles that both coaxed and compelled her to return that shockingly intimate contact.

Mouth to mouth, they stood, softness to softness. Her arms went slack and her knees buckled. As she clung to the remnants of her sanity, the thought surfaced in her head: this was what he did with his mouth that pleasured the women so! It shocked her enough that she pulled back, breaking that hypnotic contact.

"You don't bite," she murmured wonderingly.

"Not unless I'm bitten first," he whispered over a soft chuckle, pulling her back to him.

The force of his mouth on hers deepened and his tongue traced the edges of her lips and the lush crevice between them. She had never imagined two people doing such a thing; pressing their mouths together, opening to each other, feeling the soft, liquid slide of tongues over lips and of teeth gently raking. It was like being devoured . . . but oh, so pleasurably.

His arms tightened steadily around her, leaving no room between them for the defensiveness that held a scrap of linen in place. She withdrew her arms and wrapped them around him, where they began to trace the bold contours of his back. He was like a marvelous broad plain beneath his soft woolens, solid and rolling. How enthralling it was to be joined to a man in this way . . . to yield her mouth to his slow, shocking plunder, to fill her arms with his strength and warmth, to have her senses drenched with his musky male scent and the subtle lapping motions of his male body against hers.

A scraping noise and a muffled gasp burst on the quiet around them. But it was the sound of Aaren's name that penetrated the pleasure-fog in her senses and made her drag her lips from his. The sound of feet thudding on a packed floor and more gasps and murmurs sent her shoving back blindly in Jorund's arms. But his embrace tightened around her and held her to him as he swung them around partway, to face the intruder.

Miri and Marta stood just inside the door, panting, and behind them, eyes wide and jaws slack, stood Helga, Sith, and wraithlike Inga. They had come at a run, expecting to find bloody mayhem committed in their women's sanctuary . . . and found the battle-maiden and their Breath-stealer locked in heated embrace instead of heated combat!

"Aaren?" Miri squeaked out, her face crimson. "Aaren?" Marta echoed, blushing.

Aaren was struck speechless as she glimpsed their shocked faces and the horror of her situation dawned. She was caught in her enemy's arms . . . weaponless . . . half naked . . . and worst of all, *half surrendered*! What in the twisted roots of the great tree Yggdrasil had come over her, to let herself be drawn into such a disgrace? She shoved furiously against his ribs and freed herself, only to face further humiliation when her linen cover stuck to his shirt and her breasts came away bare. She snatched the cloth back and covered herself . . . then found her untied breeches sliding precariously down her hips. She caught them with the other hand and hauled them up . . . burning with mortification.

"I-I was afraid of what would h-happen when I left you," Miri stammered in explanation, her innocent gaze riveted to the sight of Aaren's flushed skin, passion-darkened eyes, and swollen lips. "I told Marta and then Helga . . . and w-we were afraid you'd be . . . you would be . . ."

"Cuttin' each other up," Sith finished for her, eyeing the pair of them as if committing every detail to memory. "Well, they ain't doin' no cuttin'," she declared to the others, "and we ain't gettin' th' churnin' done by standin' here. Come on." She gave Inga and Helga a shove and snagged Miri's and Marta's arms to drag them out the door. But the look the old dairywoman cast over her shoulder as she departed said that the only thing getting churned that morning would be her tongue. Her story of finding the battle-maiden half-naked in Jorund Borgerson's arms would soon be all over the village!

The instant they cleared the doorway, Jorund reached for Aaren with a grin, undeterred by the interruption and apparently intending to take up where they had left off. She came abruptly out of her humiliated daze and smacked his hands away.

"Don't you dare touch me, Borgerson," she said, furious, as she struggled to hold her cover in place and fumble with the ties of her breeches. "Not if you wish to keep your wretched hands."

He blinked and jerked his chin back, then retreated a step. She'd gone from flaming ember to frozen clinker in the bat of an eye! Watching her quaking hands grapple with simple ties, he realized she was embarrassed at being caught half-naked in his arms, and guessed that she resisted and protested now to salve her pride. Well, he was not about to let her touchy pride interfere with the sweet savor of the prize he sensed within reach.

"You wouldn't hurt my hands, Long-legs," he said, coming closer, wearing his most cock-sure and irresistible grin. "You like how they feel on your skin too much."

She backed away, looking frantic. "Don't wager your blood on it, Borgerson."

"You like the way I touch you, Serricksdotter. The way I caress and stroke you ever so gently . . . the way I soothe and excite your skin. No one has ever touched you like that before, have they? No one has ever stolen your breath as I did. Well, there's more, Long-legs. Much more. We've just started to make pleasure."

"We have not. We've just ended it." The low, sultry rumble of his voice crowded her senses and sent her wits hurtling into action. This time she knew what to expect, and she wouldn't let herself be trapped by his big, insolent frame or his tantalizing word-webs . . . or her own wretched curiosity. "If you ever touch me again"—she leveled a scathing look at him—"you'll pay for it."

She crossed the chamber to the bench by the opening to her sleeping quarters and snatched up her tunic, determined to put something between her bare, susceptible skin and his all-too-tactile gaze. To don the garment, she had to drop her cover and bare herself, but to turn away would display timidity in her enemy's presence. . . . Dragging in a harsh breath, she tossed her cover aside with a defiant flourish and lifted the tunic over her head.

When she thrust her head and arms through the openings and looked up, he was standing half a pace away, his eyes fastened hotly on the bumps visible on the front of her garment. His nearness was unnerving, as he clearly meant it to be, but she held her ground and lifted a warning glare to him.

"You have lovely breasts, Serricksdotter. Ummm . . . as soft as the rest of you is hard."

Before she could protest, he ran his forefinger up the underside of one breast and dragged his knuckle sensuously back and forth over one tightly budded nipple. Sparks shot along her nerves and she reacted with both hands, giving him a fierce shove that caught him off guard and knocked him back a full pace.

"That is the end of my mercy, Borgerson. Touch me again and you'll pay." She truly meant it as a warning, but the instant she uttered it she realized he would only take it as a challenge.

His look of surprise at the strength of her rebuff quickly melted into a wickedly sensual, self-possessed grin. Never in his life had he been physically opposed by a woman; her powerful shove came as a genuine shock to him. But under his surprise rode a white-hot current of excitement that he'd never experienced with a woman before. Her tall, broad-shouldered body was as strong as it was beautiful, and she wasn't afraid to use that strength. Persuading her, he realized, could get intensely physical. The idea galvanized him.

"If I have to pay, Serricksdotter," he said in husky tones, "be sure I'll make it worth the cost." He engaged her eyes with his and made a smooth grab for her shoulders. She stepped into his grasp with her knee swinging, and he just managed to twist his pelvis aside so that she struck his groin instead.

"Whoa!" He reacted instinctively, using his tight grip on her shoulders to spin her forcibly, then lashing an arm about her bucking waist to pull her against him sideways and avoid her dangerous legs. But he no sooner had her heaving form trapped against him than she stomped on his foot.

"Aghh! Dammit!" The second he opened his mouth to groan, her thrashing head smacked him in the mouth and he got a mouthful of hair. Through his pain, he grappled with her wildly tussling form and managed to seize one of her flailing hands. But she turned even that against him, raising her wrist and sinking her teeth into the hand gripping it.

"*Owww!*" He released her with a shove and lurched backward, staring at the red teeth marks on the back of his hand in complete astonishment. "Odin's Bones—she bit me!" he exclaimed. When he snapped his head up, she was crouched nearby, feet spread and arms and hands braced, ready to take him on again. Her long hair was a wild jumble about her shoulders, and there was a fierce glint in her tawny eyes. She looked feral and untamed . . . as dangerous as a cornered she-wolf.

"I warned you, Borgerson," she ground out between gasps.

He glanced down at the red oozing up into his pores, then fingered his throbbing lip, and fell back a step, looking at her in pure disbelief. She acted as if he was trying to beat her instead of pleasure her! That a woman he wanted would resist his much-practiced wooing was absurd enough, but that one would actually hurt him—*him*, the friend and lover and defender of women!—was unthinkable!

"I meant to enjoy you, wench—to make pleasure with you!" he bellowed. "And you—*you bit me!*"

"I'm a warrior, not a *wench*. And I'll not be cozened or bullied or manhandled by anyone . . . especially not a *woman-heart*," she snapped, watching anger inflate his massive shoulders and carve his features into a formidable mask. She'd wounded his vanity as much as his hand, and she knew that such a pride-blow hurt far more than a few teeth marks . . . especially to a man used to having his way with every female he encountered.

But as she watched the dark turbulence welling in his handsome and usually genial countenance, she felt in her chest an aching swell of confusing regret which tainted the anticipation she felt for their coming fight. For surely now he was angry enough to take a blade to her troublesome hide. . . .

"A warrior?" He stalked closer and halted abruptly, as if observing some invisible line of contention between them. "You're no warrior, wench. You play at being one, but have you ever wielded a blade in full blood-battle? Ever felt your iron bite so deep into flesh that it splinters bone? Ever heard the cries of your own fallen kin and comrades, or watched—" He clamped his jaw shut and the heat of the words he did not speak leaped into his pale eyes, setting them ablaze. "You're no warrior, Serricksdotter, until you have done all that and more." He paced two angry steps aside, then back.

"But you're no woman either"—he jabbed a finger at her—"for there is no womanly softness in you at all."

"No weakness, you mean," she countered fiercely.

"Softness and weakness are not the same thing, wench. And you're surely no woman, Serricksdotter, if you don't know that." He stopped dead and pinned her with a stare that seemed to pierce her to her very marrow.

"But if you're no warrior and no woman . . . then what are you?" he sneered, making her darkening amber eyes his targets. "You're all hair and fangs and claws . . ." The impression he'd had of her earlier flooded into his mind again: coiled and sinewy, tawny-eyed and dangerous.

"You're a she-wolf," he declared. *"Odin's She-wolf."*

The taunt lay burning on the air between them for a long, heated moment. Then before she could respond, he strode to the door and ducked outside, leaving her red-faced and quivering, and feeling strangely wounded by his verbal slash.

A she-wolf, he had called her. All hair and fangs and claws.

She stumbled to the bench and sat down hard, her limbs aching with the unspent energy of confrontation. Beneath that miserable slow burn of thwarted battle-need, a yawning emptiness opened in the middle of her, a feeling of loss . . . very like that which she felt on the night Serrick left her. As she examined it, she realized that only part of it was the disappointment of her failure to make him take up a blade and fight her. The other part had to do with the way Jorund Borgerson had looked at her . . . as if she were a loathsome thing . . . as if he didn't want to touch her, to hold her against his body, or to press her mouth with his, ever again.

She sprang to her feet and furiously began to shove the hem of her tunic into her breeches. Her hands couldn't work the lacings of her breastplate and buskins fast enough to suit her. She growled from between clenched teeth but, startled by the wolfish sound of it, choked off that noise a moment later. In the blink of an eye, she was out the door and striding for the foot-worn path down to the lake shore.

But no matter how hard she ran or how far she walked that morning, it was always there the moment she stopped: the awful realization that she wanted Jorund Borgerson to want her almost as much as she wanted him to fight her.

She had just lost a precious, heart-felt connection with Father Serrick, and with each day that passed she could feel Miri and Marta slipping further away from her as they made their own lives and did new, womanly things that she could not share. Jorund Borgerson had begun to invade the void created by those losses, filling her senses with undreamed-of pleasures, and her mind and heart with untold confusion.

When he stroked her skin, she found herself growing gentle to match his touch. When he looked at her with eyes filled with wanting, she felt a helpless flush of pleasure that he found her soft breasts and long legs eye-pleasing. And when his body had settled against hers and his lips poured over her mouth, she went all weak-kneed and breathless . . . and she yielded, molding herself to the power of his larger, stronger frame.

Finding herself near the fishing boats along the sandy part of the shore, she climbed up on the grassy bank above them and propped her chin on her fists. Now Jorund Borgerson was furious with her, she thought dismally. Would he ever try to touch her again? Would he ever want that delicious mouth-meeting with her again? Would he ever look at her again with that breath-stealing blend of sky-blue teasing and molten silver need?

She felt an odd sense of connection to him that went beyond the closeness of bodies and the meeting of mouths. Her intuition said it was a womanly feeling . . . and that it came straight from the soft, inner part of her that she had thought was sealed safely away.

The moment she thought it, her stomach contracted and her throat began to constrict around a hard lump of anxiety. *Softness.* There was no room for softness—not in the fierce, uncompromising world she was fated to inhabit and not within her! A trickle of panic ran down her spine as she realized that the wall she had constructed to separate the woman from the warrior in her had weaknesses . . . and that Jorund had managed to locate and penetrate those weak spots with his special woman-skill.

She began frantically stuffing all of those treacherously soft and womanly impulses toward him back behind her wall, then fortified it with dire images of the other warriors' fierce faces and of the women's scornful appraisal of her. She had to be strong . . . had to uphold her honor and that of her sisters, or all was lost!

What did it matter if Jorund Borgerson looked at her as if she was honey to be tasted? she admonished herself. *It changed nothing.* He was still her adversary, her sworn opponent. And she was still bound by the enchantment, her honor, and the jarl's decree to take a blade to his insufferably conceited and despicably craven hide!

She shoved to her feet to start back, but after only a few strides she halted in her tracks, feeling unsettled, feeling that something was wrong. Her senses sprang to life and she scoured the area around her, ready for action. But there was only sand and swaying boats and lapping water and . . . a wind. A full wind, heavy with moisture. She looked up and found the sky half-filled with flat, dark clouds. Alarm bolted down her spine and through her legs. Storm clouds. And on the heels of that thought came another . . .

Harvest!

When Jorund left the women's house, he ran along the path that led through the forest, desperate to put that humiliating confrontation with Aaren Serricksdotter behind him. He had failed to seduce her, failed to convince her to abandon her absurd notions of blade-fighting him . . . and even failed to keep his own cursed temper in check. After all his smug determination to turn the other cheek and turn her bluster into whimpers of pleasure . . . he'd hurled insult after insult at her!

He lurched to a halt on the narrow trail and bent over with his arms braced on his legs, panting. He could have sworn he'd almost had her . . . holding her lithe, fascinating frame against him, running his hands unhindered over her body, toying with her mouth in that delectable ravishment of a kiss. He groaned and straightened, running his fingers through his wind-whipped hair. What in Godfrey's Heaven had possessed him to call her a *she-wolf*?

She had possessed him, he understood; her with her long, dangerous legs and defiant chin . . . and her soft lips and vulnerable eyes. Never in his life had a woman gotten under his skin as she had . . . made him lose control. He couldn't stand having her tell him to keep his hands to himself; couldn't bear stopping, once he'd tasted her; and couldn't believe she preferred her touchy, mannish pride to a hot bout of passion with him! He glanced down at the ring of red teeth marks on the back of his hand. He'd been damned close to giving her the full-out blade-fight she was asking for! That realization sent him into complete turmoil: imagine taking a blade to a woman!

In both his experience and his pragmatic ethic, *blades* were the implements of pain and destruction, and *women* were the means of healing and creation. The two were utterly and irrevocably opposed. And despite the hard evidence of his own senses—he flexed his bitten hand—he could not reconcile them.

Trust his contentious old father to somehow find and pair him with a beautiful, blade-fighting female . . . an unthinkable combination of danger and desire. He'd known from that first night what Borger intended, and he was adamant that the old boar wouldn't have his way. He was through with blade-fighting . . . that was the end of it.

He started back along the path, grumbling to himself. There was a woman in Aaren Serricksdotter, somewhere beneath that fierce exterior. He'd tasted her and felt her. He wanted her. And he intended to find her again . . . no matter how long it took.

When he emerged from the trees some time later, he felt a swirling blast of cold, moisture-laden wind and halted. The trees at the edge of the woods were swaying and the sky was half filled with a blanket of dense clouds. It took a moment to register, then he lurched into a run, headed straight for the fields.

The harvest!

Chapter Nine

The old dairywoman's cow tails had been wrong. Late that very morning, the weather turned and the North Wind came riding down out of his mountain lair to darken the sky with his great cloud-cloak and chill the land with his breath. All the folk of Borger's village saw him come and they read in his fierce bluster the portent of crop-stripping gales and driving rain. Those villagers not already in the fields emptied their hands of tools and kettles and half-washed clothes and went running to help bring in the grain.

Aaren arrived at a run, alongside a number of others who dispersed into the fields to quicken the pace of cutting and bundling. She paused on the cart path, chest heaving, and scoured the patchwork of fields, looking for a place to start. Several workers were just standing at the edge of a nearby rye field, staring balefully at the sky and at each other.

"Here—you! Give me that and take one of the women's sickles!" She wrested a scythe from an old thrall man's hands, then turned to the women and young boys. "The rest of you with sickles start on the other side . . . cut and bundle as you go. Those without blades fall in behind me to gather and bundle." Then without a wasted moment, she laid to and began to cut.

Jorund found his way to the fields blocked by a muddle of carts, panicky horses, and a number of villagers staring at the sky and bemoaning the calamity about to befall them. He seized reins and calmed several of the sturdy fjord mares which were used to transport threshed grain and hay to the barns, sending them on their way. Then he turned to the trouble in his people's faces and seized their situation just as firmly as he had the horses.

"The North Wind is a coward," he declared, lifting his face into the wind and pointing skyward toward the last bit of blue. "And he has not even fully defeated the Sky. It will be some time before he can turn his full fury on us . . . and by the time he does, we will have already taken our grain from the fields!" He shook a fist skyward.

The anxious villagers looked at Jorund's great fist, raised against their common enemy, and their faces thawed and their shoulders set with determination. They turned back to join the others in the fields, shouting encouragement to one another. Then, seeing them heading back to work, Jorund looked for a place to work himself.

He strode into a rye field and wrested a sickle from the hands of a harried young woman with a small babe tied on her back, sending her to the edge of the field. Pouncing to his knees at the head of the row, he began to swing the curved blade with determination. Halfway through the row, he felt a tapping on his back and turned to find Helga's boy holding out a long-handled scythe.

"My mother says you'll cut faster with this," he said, panting.

"Your mother is a wise woman, Little Brother." Jorund grinned, shoving to his feet, and traded blades with the boy. He arched his back and raised his elbows, swinging each in a circle to work the stiffness out of his shoulders . . . and found himself looking straight into Aaren Serricksdotter's steady gaze. She was cutting in the field across the way and had paused when she caught sight of him. When he searched her expression, she looked away and went back to cutting. He studied her wide shoulders and thick, swaying braid and his mouth turned up in a wry curl at the thought that she was just as sore and miserable as he was.

They worked at a frantic but steady pace. From field to field the villagers moved, like swarming bees, changing tools and places, spelling each other and stepping in to take up whatever task was required. Now and then, one would pause and lift a defiant fist to the old North Wind.

Aaren lost track of where her sisters were, of who gleaned and bundled behind her, even of which field she worked in. She was lost once again in a haze of numbed pain and determination . . . until someone clasped her by the shoulder and forced her around. She found herself facing a yellow-haired fellow whose features were a cleaner, more handsome version of old Borger's.

"Hold, Serricksdotter!" Garth Borgerson jerked his hand from her when he saw the glare on her face. "Leave something for the rest of us to cut," he said with a nervous laugh. When she blinked and looked at him in confusion, he grinned and began to peel her cramped fingers from the scythe handle. "Even a Valkyr's daughter must rest sometime."

Aaren staggered aside, then trudged to the edge of the field with the vision of his smile hanging in her mind. It was the first time anyone in Borger's village or his band of warriors had looked at her with anything other than mistrust or resentment. She collapsed in the dried weeds and closed her eyes, trying not to listen to her body's groanings, but a movement in the grass nearby made her pop her eyes open.

Looming above her was a thick-framed warrior with carrot-red hair and features coarser than old Borger's. Another of the old goat's offspring, she realized. But before she could scuttle back, the fellow thrust a bucket at her and declared in a gravelly voice, "You can't work if you don't drink, Serricksdotter." When she looked dumbly at the bucket, trying to decipher his meaning, his raspy voice rumbled forth again. "Go on . . . you earned it."

His broad mouth twisted into what looked like a wry smile. Rattled by the unexpected offer, she took the dipper and drank deeply of the foaming ale. The drink's warmth seeped quickly through her middle and spread along her limbs to deaden the ache. She watched the fellow stride back to his own work with a sense of bewilderment. Two acknowledgments of her existence in the same day . . . she must be out of her head with fatigue and seeing things!

The rains started just at dark; wind-driven sheets of huge, cold drops that flattened stalks and battered both humans and animals. But the harvest frenzy had already snatched most of the grain from the jaws of the storm, and the horses and carts lurched into motion and quickly trundled the last of their precious cargo toward the barns, byres, and hay sheds. The workers, cold, fatigued, and now soaked to the bone, were left to slog their way back to shelter on their own. Once in the village, they scattered to their huts and houses, to warm and dry themselves and line their bellies with cold fare and sour ale.

Jorund dragged himself into the hall and headed for his sleeping closet, to change his sodden clothes and crawl into his furs for some rest. Borger entered the hall behind Jorund, heading toward his own sleeping quarters, and he caught sight of his son's destination.

"First-born!" the old boar called out. Jorund paused, then turned, his shoulders sagging with fatigue and irritation. Borger swaggered even with Jorund and stopped, wiping water from his ruddy face and rain-slicked beard.

"I see you slept in your own furs last night, boy." He smirked. "Have the wenches in the thrall house lost their savor?"

Jorund met the crafty gleam in his father's eye and felt his blood heating precipitously. The old badger knew what had driven him back to his solitary pallet, curse his eyes! He had always had an extra sense for detecting smoldering lusts. And from the unholy pleasure in his face, Jorund guessed he'd already heard about the encounter with Aaren Serricksdotter in the women's house that morning.

"You sample the wenches often enough . . . you tell me," Jorund ground out, turning away to push aside the heavy curtain.

"Jorund!"

He halted, but turned only his head, looking over his shoulder at his sire. As always, tension rose between them. After a moment, Borger relaxed his braced stance and his cagey eyes took on a lewd glint.

"They said you had her naked." Borger narrowed one eye and licked his lower lip. "Are her breasts as full and toothsome as they seem, behind that armor?" Jorund was stung by the ill-concealed lust in the old man's face. The thought of the ranting old cur slavering over Aaren Serricksdotter brought Jorund's blood up. He made fists of his aching hands and leveled a vengeful look at Borger. Let the old hound stew in his own imaginings. . . .

"More so."

"I knew it! Curse me, if I don't know a prime bit of arse-sport when I see it!" Borger crowed, slapping his sodden thigh, then sobering as Jorund turned away to his closet. "Hold, boy! I've not finished with you."

"What now, old man?" Jorund demanded, staring straight ahead. He could feel his father's eyes measuring him in the long silence, and knew he was being compared once more to the old man's cursed standard of *the warrior*.

"You did well this day in the fields." Borger's voice came low and earnest, surprising Jorund. Fine praise and thank-words were not Borger's way; he was always one to bully more than persuade. "The folk saw the Harvest Stealer riding down on them and lost heart . . . until you came. You and the Valkyr's daughter. They saw you look straight into the jaws of the Cold Reaper and take up harvest blades to do battle. And they did the same."

Jorund felt a familiar heat swelling his veins and setting fire to his belly. He made fists of his hands and clamped his jaw tight. It was true. But even the truth could seem tainted and misshapen when bent to Borger's purpose.

"You could lead them, First-born." Borger stepped closer and the hushed urgency in his tone overwhelmed Jorund's resolve not to look at his father. Borger's face was grave and his eyes glowed with a fierce, compelling light.

"Yea, I could lead them," Jorund declared, his voice like the knell of iron striking stone. "But never into *battle*." He turned away.

"Jorund!" Borger's voice stopped him halfway through the curtain. The jarl stalked forward, his body tensed, his tone fraught with both command and dark persuasion. "Take a blade to the battle-wench, boy, and break her curse." He edged closer. "Then with her at your side, take up your arms and lead your clan . . . claim the respect and loyalty of my warriors, and seize the high seat for your own, once and for all. My seat carries much power, First-born . . ."

The words hissed and slithered along Jorund's nerves, seductively joining his two deepest desires: his longing to lead his people and his desire to conquer the battle-maiden and take her for his own. Borger was cunningly tempting him to take up the sword . . . to conform to the violent code of the warrior once more. Conflict rose in him like a sea squall, dark and tumid, heavy with unslaked desires and unvented angers. His body quivered, his throat tightened with need, and his eyes burned dryly.

To have all he wanted, all he had to do was pick up a blade. And draw blood. Starting with Aaren Serricksdotter.

"Go to Hell, old man," he gritted out. Then he stalked into his private closet and jerked the curtain shut behind him.

Borger stood for a moment, staring furiously at that heavy fabric. His cramped frame eased and his expression grew crafty once more as he recalled Jorund's trembling silence . . . and recognized that the rebellious whelp had actually been lured by his words.

"I may indeed go to Hel's cold, dark realm, instead of the glorious Valhalla," he said with a grin. "But not before I see you fight once more, First-born."

If the village had been attacked that night by any of Borger's several enemies, it would have been taken without so much as a murmur of resistance . . . the exhaustion of the warriors and village folk was so great. They fell on their pallets and crawled into their furs and slept until the next afternoon, and even then were loathe to venture out into the cold, lashing rain and raw North Wind. By nightfall, most were recovered enough to resume their chores and duties. But it took word from the long hall that Borger would burn a sacred ash log and open his ale barrels in honor of their harvest victory to revive them completely.

They crowded into the hall carrying their wooden bowls and drinking horns, talking and laughing and jostling. The great trunk of an ash tree burned brightly in the hearth, spreading warmth and cheer, and several barrels of ale and the juicy meat of two roasted boars filled them with more tangible goodwill. Extra benches had been set on the hearth side of the tables, but many villagers still had to eat standing up, and didn't seem to mind at all.

Aaren wound her way among the revelers, drawing many eyes. She was garbed in her breastplate and best tunic, made of fine woolen dyed blue with woad and trimmed in red cording. She had abandoned her headband, but her hair was tautly braided from the crown of her head to her buttocks . . . as if, in clothing herself for the celebration, she had also prepared for battle.

And indeed, she had. For she intended to take up her challenge of Jorund again at the first opportunity, and to provoke him all the way to a blade-fight. In the time since their miserable confrontation in the women's house, she'd found her thoughts alarmingly divided between *blade-meetings* and *mouth-meetings* with him—wanting both . . . dreading both. And she feared that such a division in her desires could spread confusion through the rest of her. The only way to forestall such a wretched development was to get him to pick up a blade as soon as possible . . . tonight, while he was still furious with her.

The warriors sat at their tables and milled about the great hearth with drinking horns in their hands and their voices booming. As she passed, many stared at her, some in speculation, some in dull resentment, most in visible hunger. She stopped near the high seat and surveyed the tables, looking for Jorund and for a place to sit. Finding neither, she tried the other side and found it just as crowded. Then she spotted the young warrior who had spelled her in the field the day before, sitting on a hearth-side bench, staring at her with a grin. When he was sure he had caught her eye, he nodded, then slid to one side and smacked the seat beside him.

It was clearly an invitation. She glanced warily about, finding no one directly behind her. It must have been meant for her. She took a steadying breath, then accepted, easing onto the bench in taut silence. Two stringy, leather-faced warriors across the planking gave her surly looks and carried their food and drink elsewhere. Her brash young host snorted a laugh.

"Pay them no mind, Serricksdotter. They're pride-sore that you left them so little grain to cut yesterday. They each lost a wager with a wench, which cost them a long-awaited wrestle in the furs." Aaren felt her face heating with

unwarriorlike embarrassment. She was relieved to have
Miri arrive just then with a bowl of roast pork and cabbage
and a horn of new ale; she buried her nose in the foaming drink . . . missing the flirtatious exchange of glances
between her sister and her new comrade at arms.

"What are you called, Borgerson?" she asked minutes
later, having come to the bottom of her bowl.

"I am called Garth," he answered. "And this great, ugly
toad is Erik, my half brother." He slapped the fellow next to
him on the shoulder and Aaren recognized the flame-haired
fellow who had given her ale during the harvest. Garth
leaned closer to divulge: "His mother was attacked by a
carrot before he was born, and it marked him." He laughed
at her startled look and Erik groaned good-naturedly at
what was apparently an old joke. "And that is Hrolf the
Elder"—he pointed to fellows farther down the table—
"and that handsome devil is Brun Cinder-hand, our smith."
Sooty, thick-fisted Brun was anything but handsome, but he
managed a red-faced nod. "And that is Hakon, called the
Freeholder, and of course you've already met . . . Thorkel
the Ever-ready."

Amidst raucous laughter, Hakon and Thorkel and two
others glared at Garth and picked up their drinking horns,
shoving up from the planking and shouldering their way
through the crowd. Garth laughed again, elbowed Aaren's
ribs, and called at Thorkel's back: "Perhaps he should have
a new name . . . Thorkel Sore Loser!"

Aaren had begun to relax, returning Garth's grin, when
the warriors around her fell silent and she looked up to
find Jorund Borgerson taking one of the seats Hakon and
Thorkel had just vacated at the far end of the table. Those
seated on the bench between her and Jorund leaned back,
one by one, to give them a clear line of sight to each other.
The level of heat in the hall seemed to rise precipitously as
they confronted each other.

She was unprepared for his impact on her senses. He
wore a blue-black tunic that hugged his broad shoulders
and fell casually open at the tie placket to reveal a wedge
of his bronzed chest. His chin was freshly shaved and his
shoulder-length hair was neatly combed. But it was his

intense blue eyes and boldly curved lips that captured and
held her gaze for longer than was prudent . . . long enough
to interfere with her heartbeat, but not long enough for her
to discern how angry he was with her or what he intended
by seeking out her table.

She lifted her chin and tore her gaze away in what she
hoped was a convincing show of disdain. But underneath
she was struggling to subdue the frantic drumming of her
heart and the tumbling sensation in her stomach. There
was nothing to be alarmed about, she told herself. She
was in a hall full of people and thus in no danger from
his silken word-snares and treacherous pleasure-skill . . . or
her unthinkable weakness for them.

After the eating was done, Borger looked out over the
gathering and called for wrestling. His warriors shouted out
names of combatants they wished to see matched. The jarl
squinted and stroked his beard, and finally selected two
of those nominated for battle: Garth Borgerson and Harald
White Leg.

Garth bounded up eagerly and stripped off his jerkin and
tunic, while his opponent did the same. The other warriors
formed a ring in front of the high seat, pushing back the
villagers, then brought out a bucket of grease and proceeded
to smear it over the wrestlers' bare backs and chests. In the
midst of being prepared for battle, Garth looked up to find
Miri clutching her ale pitcher to her breast and staring at his
neat, muscular body with adorably wide eyes. He inflated
his chest and flexed his muscles for her and her mouth
formed a helpless "O" that made him beam with brash
male pride.

With the added incentive of the maid he had marked as
his future bride looking on, Garth wrestled with the ferocity
of a rogue bear, and soon gained a victory from the bigger,
but slower, Harald. Borger proudly awarded him a new dagger and the warriors began to shout out other names. More
matches were made and more bouts fought; some bitterly,
some jovially, and some with a notable lack of emotion. Ale
and wagers flowed freely and voices grew steadily louder
and more heated. After half a dozen matches, someone
shouted out the name *Jorund Borgerson*.

It was picked up and chanted by a number of voices, until old Borger lowered his ale horn and lifted his hand to quiet them. He wiped his mouth thoughtfully, then scanned the tables, looking for his eldest son. He found Jorund seated not far away, at a table with a number of his younger sons . . . and the Valkyr's daughter.

"What say you, First-born? Will you wrestle?"

Jorund leaned back against the table, propping his arms out like mighty branches along the tabletop. He appeared to consider it, then shook his head. "*Nej*. Not this night."

Borger grunted and jerked about in his chair, clearly irritated by Jorund's refusal. But the noise in the hall resumed as he turned his attention elsewhere for the next match.

Aaren looked at Jorund through lowered lashes, feeling a burning disappointment that he hadn't agreed to wrestle. He was bigger and stronger than any man present . . . was he really so much of a coward . . . or a cheek-turner . . . that he couldn't even engage in a manly bit of sport? Then it struck her: this was her chance to challenge him! Here, in front of Borger's warriors and all the village women, he'd have to respond to a challenge. Drawing confidence like a deep breath, she assumed a casual pose against the tabletop and turned her head his way.

"Why will you not wrestle, Borgerson?" she said in a loud, clear voice.

Noise in the immediate area dropped precipitously, and heads turned and necks craned to see how he would respond. He turned toward her and gathered his great body; drawing his arms in, tightening his belly, sitting straighter. Garth and Erik abandoned their seats and pulled the others along with them, to clear the plank between Jorund and Aaren and watch what would happen from a safe distance. Their sudden motion drew Borger's attention, and when the jarl's head snapped in their direction, many others did as well.

"Well, Serricksdotter . . ." Jorund looked her over appraisingly. "Perhaps I don't wish to wrestle tonight."

"Or perhaps you're afraid to," she countered, casually but with a taunting loudness. The quiet spread a bit wider around them.

"Or perhaps I don't have a proper opponent," he said, matching her tone and volume, acknowledging her provocative game and announcing that he intended to play as well. "I have always been particular about who I *wrestle*, Serricksdotter. Ask anyone." He cast a wicked grin around him, drawing suggestive laughter from the men.

She straightened, annoyed, sensing that he and the other men had more than one sort of grappling-sport in mind. She tried to think of what else she had intended to say and of a way to get her challenge back on course. "You make excuses. Given a chance, a true warrior is always eager to fight and prove his strength. There are a number of worthy opponents here, Borgerson," she declared firmly.

"Who?" he demanded. *"You?"* His body tautened, instantly primed and ready for action. "Are you challenging me to wrestle, Serricksdotter? Because if you are, I accept." He leaned toward her like a falcon eyeing its prey, his eyes glowing, his face bronzed with anticipation. His voice dropped to the bottom of its register.

"I would love nothing better than to wrestle with you, Long-legs."

She was momentarily disarmed; she hadn't expected him to offer to wrestle *her*. She met his threatening eagerness with a rigid spine and molten amber eyes, frantically calculating her chances against him in a wrestling match.

"Of course, to be fair, the breastplate would have to go," he said, fixing a stare on her armor that penetrated to the soft flesh behind it . . . and set it tingling. A wave of shocked muttering and muffled snickers rolled through the men nearby, and was relayed on a wave of whispers through the rest of the hall.

"We strip to the waist to wrestle, Serricksdotter," he continued. "And we grease down." He ran a hot, speculative gaze over her most prominent female attributes. "I would be willing to grease you down myself, Battle-wench . . . if you would return the favor and . . . *grease me*."

Lewd chuckles grew to desultory laughter around them. Her own blood betrayed her, rushing into her face, and her tongue turned traitor too, refusing to move. He was both taunting and seducing her publicly . . . and she couldn't utter a single word in her own defense!

"Think of it, Serricksdotter," he went on, his voice sensual and hypnotic. "Naked to the waist . . . skin to skin . . . loins to loins . . . flexing and straining . . . hot and writhing . . ." The laughter gradually damped and all breath was baited in expectation as the seduction in his tone deepened. "I could teach you a few of my special holds, Long-legs. There is one where I wedge myself between my opponent's thighs . . . hard and tight . . . and then slowly—"

"*Nej!*" she choked out, shooting to her feet. "*Nej*, I'll not wrestle the likes of you. I do all my fighting with a *blade*. When you're ready to use one like a man, come and see me, and perhaps I'll teach *you* a few lessons!" She snatched up her drinking horn and strode off toward the ale barrels.

It was a reasonable recoup of dignity; what it lacked in originality, it made up for in vehemence. But she was still humiliated to the core at the way he'd turned her own challenge back on her *again*. And what was that disgusting excitement she had felt? Apparently he had some wretched, unearthly power to excite her, and it didn't seem to matter a whit to her reckless responses that the entire hall and village were looking on.

Miri and Marta came hurrying toward the ale barrels after her, their widened eyes full of questions that Aaren didn't want to answer. She nodded to them to allay their fears and turned away, intending to leave the hall. But as she skirted the crowd, looking for a passage through to the doors, she heard the jarl's voice booming . . . and felt his words striking like a spear, dead on center, in the middle of her back. She froze.

"First-born! How came you by that mark on your hand?" Borger demanded. He had watched Aaren avidly as she stalked away from Jorund, then made to leave. And he timed his question so that she would be directly opposite Jorund when it struck them both.

"Bitten," Jorund declared, without stirring his big, relaxed body. "By a wolf."

A murmur of excitement—"Wolves!"—snaked through the crowd and Aaren whirled, red-faced and caught between disbelief and outrage. So this was to be his revenge: tongue-lashing her in public. There was no telling what humiliation he planned to heap upon her now!

"Wolves raiding my village?" Borger roared, sitting forward and glancing between Jorund and Aaren, his eyes alight. "How can that be? My herdsmen have said nothing to me of lamb-takings!"

"Ah, this was no ordinary wolf." Jorund sat forward as well, leveling a knowing look on Aaren that made her heart pound faster and her throat constrict. "This was a *special* wolf . . . a *she-wolf* . . . an enchanted creature." The warriors and folk around her caught his meaning and turned their drink-reddened faces on her in lurid fascination.

She wheeled, determined to make her way through the crowd, but she was confronted by a sea of half-drunken faces which seemed to crowd closer together and bar her way. Casting a frantic look around for another exit, she suddenly realized she was running, retreating from a mere word-battle, before it had begun. She turned back to find Jorund watching her with a sly expression. She had to stand her ground!

"It was a big wolf . . . so sleek and shapely . . . tawny-eyed . . . and silky-moving . . ." he continued, drawing muffled snickers from the warriors seated around him, especially Garth and Erik Borgerson. *"Wait!"* He stuck his nose up and sniffed the air. "I think I just caught her scent again. Ummm . . ." He made a show of closing his eyes and savoring her imaginary smell, leading a few of the more gullible thatch-heads to earnestly whiff in Aaren's direction as well. "That's her. I'd know her scent anywhere. Where is she . . . the *she-wolf*?" He scanned the crowd, deliberately overlooking her.

Before her widening eyes, he slid from the bench into a crouch and sniffed again. He began to stalk this way and that, like a prowling beast, sniffing the air and nosing those people standing nearest the hearth and high seat. When he came to women, he sniffed and shook his head, and they giggled and batted him away. When he came to the men, he gasped and shuddered or waved his hand before his face and rolled his eyes as if overcome by foul fumes. But even the gruffest warriors among them laughed, no matter how red-eared and reluctant. Slowly, Jorund made his way back and forth across the hall, tracking her, closing in on her.

Aaren watched his mimicry in mingled horror and amazement. He was playing at being a wolf . . . making a perfect fool of himself. Yet the warriors' and villagers' laughter didn't seem at all scornful or ridiculing. It was as if they shared the jest with him . . . enjoying the spectacle he was making of the conflict between him and her!

Every inch of her skin seemed to catch fire. She couldn't just stand there, being stalked like some cursed animal. But she couldn't exactly take a blade to him for a mere bit of foolery, and she certainly couldn't run from him. It struck her—too clearly and too late—that she didn't know how to handle Jorund Borgerson at all! He wasn't anything like a man was supposed to be. He didn't do the things men were wont to do, and he didn't seem to value or want the things men were supposed to want . . . like dignity, acclaim, honor, and power. She was totally unprepared to deal with the likes of him!

Suddenly he stopped nearby and froze, sniffing in her direction and creeping closer. He stopped by her feet and went down on one knee, casting a knowing leer at the drink-merry faces around him.

"By Godfrey's Heaven—I think I've found her!" he cried, running his nose up the side of her, a mere foot-length away, inhaling. The crowd quieted to nervous chuckles and suggestive murmurings as he dipped his head again and sniffed his way up the front of her thighs, pausing tauntingly over the spot at the top of her legs before moving up her belly. By the time he reached her breasts and raised his gaze to hers, his face was dusky and his eyes were glowing with dark, earnest fires. With her eyes captive in his, he dropped back onto one knee, threw back his shaggy blond head, and howled like a wolf.

"Aaooooooo—"

The hall erupted with laughter.

Aaren gasped as if she'd been smacked. Her whole being was in turmoil and she reacted out of sheer desperation, giving his shoulders a fierce shove that knocked him back on his rear. He sputtered in surprise that melted to wicked delight as he sank back on one elbow.

"There she is." He waved his free hand at her. *"My she-wolf."*

Aaren stood looking down at him, furious at his unstinting good humor, his blatantly sexual taunting . . . and at her own inability to stop his humiliating public use of her. She was shamed beyond all bearing to have been stalked and prowled and sniffed like a bitch in heat!

"Who is the one acting like a wolf, Borgerson? Not me!" she declared, bursting out of her paralyzing chagrin to stalk around his prone body with her fists at her waist and a disgusted look on her face. There were guffaws and hoots of laughter from the warriors nearby as she took up his wretched game.

"Look at him." She gestured contemptuously to his sprawled body. It was gratifying to see the smile fading on his mischievous mouth. "He prowls like a wolf . . ." She continued her stroll around him, pausing to stoop above him, sniff, and make a sour face. "And he smells like a wolf." She ambled on. "And he makes a *noise* like a wolf."

"Then he must be a wolf." She paused, heartened by the way his face seemed a bit redder than before. "And from the way he stalks . . . I would say he's hungry. Very hungry indeed." She tossed a vengeful smile at the warriors hovering close by. "You had better throw him a pork butt before you go to your pallets for the night . . . if you would sleep safely."

The men's laughter was like a warm tide, lapping at her back, as she turned and strode from the hall.

The great lake shimmered darkly under the waning moon as she ran along the shore, dispelling the heat and confusion in her. By the time she entered the deserted women's house and sank onto a bench near the dull-glowing hearth, she had cooled enough to think. She sighed raggedly and rubbed her aching thighs, overcome by the memory of his handsome blond head poised so near . . . breathing her in.

She didn't know how to deal with him on any level. The more she tried to provoke and annoy him, the more he teased and charmed her. The more proud and combative she behaved, the more outrageous and seductive he became. And the most worrisome part was that tonight some wayward part of her had actually been relieved by his brazen pursuit.

He'd made it appallingly clear—to her and to everyone else in the village—that he still wanted her. And like almost everything else about him, why he still wanted her baffled her. Any other warrior in Borger's band would have been angered enough to take a blade to her days ago. Yet, there he was, holding his temper and somehow ignoring or dismissing—or forgiving—the fact that she couldn't hold hers.

To divert herself from such thoughts, she rose to her feet and paced, then laid a few more logs on the fire to warm the house for when Miri and Marta returned. As she watched the hungry yellow flames licking up the sides of the wood, she recalled that Brother Godfrey had said Jorund found it difficult to "turn the other cheek." She recalled the struggle visible in his eyes when he mastered his anger at the bathing house . . . then again when she had bit him on the hand.

It must take a great deal of will-strength, both to resist the casual violence common among his fellow warriors and to subdue his own natural impulses. There was no lack of power or strength in Jorund Borgerson, she thought, her hard-set shoulders melting. Perhaps what he needed was something . . . or someone . . . to unleash it.

Chapter Ten

Across the commons, the celebration had continued with more contests, and finally with tales and beastepics recounted by the skald Snorri. After a while, the din of rowdy, drunken voices gave way to the sounds of shuffling feet as the villagers drifted back to their homes. The sounds of leave-taking slowly gave way to the growls of warriors competing for comfortable spots on the benches, then to vigorous snoring. After a while, Borger staggered off toward his furs, leaving a small number of his sons and warriors still lifting horns around a table by the light of the dying fire.

Jorund stared blearily into his brew, feeling frustrated and annoyed. He had tried to drown the fire in his blood with ale, but all he got for his efforts was a thick pall of steam in his senses. For the balance of the night, after Aaren left the hall, he'd been the recipient of invitations ranging from flirtatious looks to sensual caresses, and despite the troublesome weight in his loins, he'd declined the lot of them, sending Alys, Brway. His excuses were feeble and he knew it. But he could scarcely tell them the truth: that he somehow felt it was wrong to take them and their pleasures when it clearly wasn't *them* he wanted.

A handful of the younger warriors came slamming back into the hall and steered straight for Jorund. Garth was at their head, looking hot-eyed and irritable as a bear roused in winter. He planted himself before Jorund with his arms flexing.

"Challenge the wench, Jorund," he demanded, jabbing a finger at his elder brother. "Break this cursed enchantment once and for all." Erik and the others at his back nodded.

Hrolf the Elder, seated across from Jorund, flicked a bleary look up at Garth, then laughed and glanced at Jorund. "He's been with that little Serricksdotter, he has . . . and he's got an ache in his flesh-bone."

"By Hel's gate—I've gotten no closer than an arm's length to her. And I'll get no further until *he* honors his word." Garth clenched his jaw and smacked a fist onto the table in front of Jorund. "You vowed you'd defeat the battle-maid, brother. Well, get on with it!"

"Yea, Jorund," Erik growled at his elder half brother. "The battle-wench makes a fool of you . . . and shames all manhood in the bargain."

"Yea—quit bein' a cursed cheek-turner and take a fist to the wench!" another demanded.

"*Nej*—he has to use a blade," spoke a clearer-reasoning head. The speaker turned and thrust the hilt of a sword at Jorund. "Use my blade, First-born, and shave a bit of fur from that *she-wolf's* hide!"

"Or have you forgot how to swing a blade . . . Woman-heart?" This last came from Hakon Freeholder, who had just risen from a bench across the way and now sidled closer.

Jorund looked at the tight, irritable faces of the warriors collected around him and shoved to his feet. "You know what is wrong with you . . . you need a bit of fur-burn on your arse, the lot of you." He raked them with a narrow look. "And you haven't a chance in Godfrey's Hell of getting it, because you don't know the first thing about women . . . not how to make love to one . . . or how to *defeat* one." Stepping over the bench, he strode back through the hall toward his sleeping closet.

"Listen to him," Hakon snarled, jabbing a contemptuous finger at Jorund's back. "Him and his talk of *loving* women. Even if he does pick up a blade, he'll never defeat the Valkyr's daughter."

"Do not be too sure of that."

The warriors squinted around them, searching for the owner of that unfamiliar voice. Brother Godfrey rose from the bench against the wall and stepped out of the shadows.

"What are you doing here, thrall man?" Hakon demanded. "If the jarl finds you in his hall—"

"He will drown me with his own bare hands. I know," Godfrey supplied with an undaunted look at Hakon, who scowled at the little priest's boldness. "Have you no eyes to see? Or is it that you have no wits to understand? Jorund is indeed fighting the battle-maiden . . . each time they meet."

"He's never taken a hand to her, much less a blade," Garth declared.

"He is fighting her with kindness." Godfrey leveled a searching look on their hardened faces, one by one. "It is the truest, surest weapon to use against a woman's heart. You would do well to learn a thing or two from Jorund." After a moment's silence, he trudged from the hall.

"That *love* nonsense again." Hakon snorted, as he looked around him and found a number of his fellow warriors staring at the door where the priest had disappeared. "*Loving* women . . . making *love*. Next thing you know he'll be demandin' we all take up that *kissing*." He shuddered and a number of others scowled at the prospect.

Hrolf the Elder spoke up. "You ever kiss a woman, Hakon? I did once . . . just to see what it was like. That little wench, Alys, fair to ate me up afterward." He grinned and shook his head at the memory. "There's something about it women like. Gets 'em all heated up. Maybe Jorund and them old Franks he learned it from are on to something."

The men sat in silence after that, sinking into their ale with expressions of bleary concentration. And a number of them fingered their lips speculatively . . . behind their ale horns.

Halfway across the muddy commons Godfrey paused and crossed himself, rolling his eyes toward the dark blanket of the night sky. "All I can do is plant the seed, Lord. You must make it grow."

The harvesting was completed, but the work of harvest continued at a frantic pace over the next few days. There was threshing, herd-culling, drying fish, and curing meat; gathering, salting, smoking, and shelling to be done. Along with the preparations for winter food went the gathering of winter fuel: the cutting of peat, the felling of moderate-sized trees for wood, and the rendering of tallow for lamps to dispel the coming winter gloom. Added to it all was the work of repair to roofs and shutters, and barns and sheds.

Borger strode back and forth between animal pens and granary, slaughter-yard and smithy, lending an occasional hand, but mostly growing itchy and short-tempered at being so confined. He had already spent a full moon more than he was accustomed to in his village. After three days, he declared it was time to make another harvest, a deer-taking, and decreed a hunt for himself and his warriors.

"What of you, Serricksdotter?" Garth called to Aaren across the jumble of wooden staves and half-worked iron pieces that lay around the smithy. "Will you try your hunt-luck with us?"

Aaren paused, eyeing the small gathering of warriors before the open shed at the side of the forge. They were drawing spear and arrow tips from the smith in preparation for their foray into the wooded hills. Her throat tightened as she watched the lot of them turn eyes upon her . . . some muttering, clearly outraged by even the suggestion that she might accompany them.

"I enjoy a good hunt," she observed, seeming more casual than she felt. This was the first time she had been included with the warriors! Her heart thumped wildly in her breast. "But I had to leave my bow in the mountains and have not yet fashioned another."

"Well, that is no difficulty. Brun here has a number of prime birch-staves, already carved . . . and I'll lend you some of the best gut ever strung on a bow." Garth cast a prodding look at Brun; anything that helped the Valkyr's daughter secure a fight with Jorund, that look said, improved their chances with her sisters. The smith nodded, red-faced. But a number of the others grumbled at Garth's back and Aaren paused, torn between the inviting prospect of spending head-clearing days in the forest and the unpleasant idea of having to bear with the surly lot of them for hours on end. Garth watched her with a Borgerlike expression in his eyes and smiled.

"Jorund will be coming," he observed. His steady, conspiratorial gaze said the rest: in the fury of the chase,

Jorund's blood would be high. Aaren lifted her chin
and turned a taut look on the burly smith.

"Let us see these staves of yours, Cinder-hand."

The Sky-Traveler had reappeared in uncloaked splendor
that afternoon as they rode through the gold-dappled forest.
The leaves were half fallen, which admitted plentiful light,
and the air was redolent with the scents of leaf-must, fir,
and pine. The familiar autumn feel of the woods would
have been a release to Aaren if she hadn't been mounted
on a large and willful fjord mare and hadn't felt Jorund's
eyes boring into her back.

It had been years since Serrick's only horse had died and
since then they had traveled afoot . . . which had effectively
isolated them from the few farmers and herders they had
traded with in earlier days. Her anxiety was translated to
her mount, which pranced and shied and generally regarded
her with mistrust. It was a small ordeal just making it to the
warriors' base camp in the high valley wedged between the
foothills and mountains. And she had the annoying feeling
that Jorund had enjoyed every bit of her discomfort.

Once in camp, her irritation mounted, for the warriors
grew rowdy as they shed the constraints of village life;
jesting coarsely, contending, shouting, and wrestling with
each other. As they selected sleeping spots and cut pine
boughs for bedding, they turned their crude banter on her.

"You'll be cold over there all by yourself, Serricksdotter."

"If you get too cold, you can come to my furs,
Serricksdotter. I'll warm you up!"

"Better watch for animals that stalk by night, Serricksdotter."

Jorund watched her face redden as she ignored their
taunts and made her solitary pallet apart from the fire.
He sensed that their words made her uneasy and was filled
with an unexpected and somewhat irrational urge to protect
her. If there was any female in the world who needed no
protection, it was Aaren Serricksdotter. But he could not
dismiss that powerful, compelling urge and finally stepped
forward.

"Perhaps it is you who should beware, Hakon Freeholder," he called out. "Have you forgotten? *She-wolves*

can be dangerous. And this one might decide to do a bit of night-stalking herself." He raised his healing hand in evidence and the others laughed. She paused in stowing her sleeping fleece and glared at him. He grinned back and made a show of dragging his bedding between her pallet and the others' sleeping places. "And if she decides she's hungry . . . I want to be her first victim."

Borger and his men howled with laughter and Aaren flushed crimson . . . snatched up her bow and quiver, and headed for the deep forest.

She was the last of the hunters to return to the camp that night. She ate quickly of the roasted meat and parched grain, then wrapped herself tightly in her blanket and sank onto her pallet of boughs. Borger and his men began to exchange stories of the afternoon's sightings and of the glories of past hunts, and she lay listening, feeling acutely alone. When their voices lowered, she turned to see what was happening around the fire . . . and immediately encountered Jorund's light-eyed stare.

He was lying on his pallet across the way from hers, his big frame casually sprawled. Heat radiated from him, as visible as breath-mist in the cold air. In her mind she heard Marta's words: "slow-burning brazier." She shivered and squeezed her eyes shut, listening to the sounds of the men seeking their pallets . . . and to the erratic thudding of her own heart.

The next day she went off on her own again and didn't return until dusk. The noise from the camp could be heard leagues away, as she approached. When she entered the clearing, she found the men ale-warmed and boisterous. A few of them had taken bucks, one or two foxes, and one had a dramatic tale to tell of an encounter with a bear. But by far the prize of the day was a massive boar, taken single-handedly by Jorund. She joined them, seating herself on a log to eat, and the talk slowly quieted. The jarl turned to her.

"And what did you take today, Serricksdotter?" he demanded.

"Besides a long walk!" Hakon Freeholder crowed, causing the others to laugh. Aaren looked casually around her and stuffed another bite of fresh-roasted boar in her mouth, chewing thoughtfully. In the silence, all eyes turned on her.

"A buck," she said simply.

"Well, where is this great stag, Serricksdotter?" Free-holder taunted, rising up from his seat and craning his neck to look for her kill. "I see no carcass."

"It was too large for me to carry. I had to leave it in a tree. I will need help fetching it in the morning."

There were snickers and mutters of derision until Borger raised his hand for silence and cocked his head toward the upstrung carcass of the massive boar Jorund had taken. "Bigger than yon boar, Serricksdotter?" She glanced up at Jorund's prize, then at Jorund himself.

"Bigger," she said matter-of-factly.

Jorund narrowed his eyes at her.

"This I must see for myself," he declared, annoyed by her subtle challenge . . . when he had been feeling protective toward her. "I will go with her to this great 'kill' tomorrow morning. And *if* it is still there . . . and *if* it is bigger than my boar . . . then I will carry it all the way back to camp on my own two shoulders."

"I'll come, too! This I have to see!" Garth declared. A number of others joined him, insisting on going as well.

Thus, the next morning there were at least eight witnesses to Jorund's unpleasant shock when he looked up between the branches of the great oak tree to behold a massive stag wedged securely. Those same warriors laughed at his glower when Garth climbed up in the tree and measured the heavily racked stag's length with a marked strip of leather . . . and called down the fateful finding. Those same warriors threw back their heads and let loose great wolf howls . . . which made Jorund's face red as madder dye . . . and made Aaren laugh for the first time in a fortnight.

Just at dusk, as the light was turning golden and the forest was settling into stillness, Aaren left the camp for the nearby stream, to wash. She did not see Jorund take note of her departure, or see him set out after her. She caught sight of him only after she had cleaned herself and turned back toward camp. The pace of her heart picked up. He was walking ahead of her, to her right, thus was the first to enter the trees nearest the stream. She found herself searching the trees for sight of him as she walked. She froze, mid-step, hearing the low, blood-chilling growl of a wolf.

Jorund's cry pierced her senses an instant later and she bolted through the woods, her heart pounding in her throat and battle-fire erupting in her blood. Jorund—a wolf had *Jorund*!

She jolted into a break in the trees and spotted him on the ground, tussling wildly with a great, twisting ball of gray and brown fur. She reached for her knife and found only an empty loop at her waist—she had left her blade back where they had been carving up meat for drying, in camp! She faltered for one heartbeat and panic welled in her chest— *Jorund!* Then, in the grip of a feral, protective instinct, she charged the heaving beast, seized the fur and flesh on the back of its neck, and planted her legs to haul up and back with all her might. The animal yelped in surprise and let go of Jorund to turn on her, but she managed to brace and thrust the wolf away before it could sink its fangs in her.

Curling and tensing, she set her body to deflect the animal's charge. But the wolf scrambled to a halt in the dry leaves, crouched, and laid its ears back, showing its teeth. She moved back slowly, scanning the ground for a branch or rock to use as a weapon, and stumbled on a root— smacking straight into a massive tree. She sucked in breath and braced for the animal's impact.

"Don't move, Serricksdotter." It was Jorund's voice. Aaren pulled her eyes from the beast just long enough to see him rising and brushing himself off. The sound registered in her ears, but the sight of him was incomprehensible to her. He'd almost been eaten by a wolf and she was in imminent danger of it—he couldn't possibly be *smiling*.

"Easy, old girl . . . this is a friend." It took her a moment to realize—he wasn't talking to her, he was talking to the wolf! "Easy, Rika." The animal's growling eased only slightly. "Stand still, Serricksdotter. The way you charged in to do battle . . . she thinks you're an enemy." There was a trace of amusement in his voice as he crossed his arms over his chest and watched the beast sniff at Aaren and prowl closer.

"*I'm* an enemy?" she rasped out. "The way *I* charged in?" She looked from man to beast and back, her eyes widening. "I was s-saving your miserable hide, Borgerson—that beast was about to tear your throat out!"

Her mind's eye was suddenly filled with the vivid, terrifying images of Jorund, lying bent and savaged and bloodied—images she hadn't had time even to conjure, but which had propelled her mad race to rescue him. Her knees went weak. He might have been mauled and killed . . . or maimed. Her stomach turned over at the thought of it. As she shoved that disturbing inner vision aside, she focused on an equally disturbing outer one: Jorund, standing with his hands on his hips, *laughing.* Cold confusion drenched her from head to toe.

"I know this wolf, Serricksdotter. She would never tear anybody's throat out. Her lunge surprised me a moment ago, but we were merely having a bit of a wrestle in greeting." What he absorbed from the anxiety in her face and the concern her words betrayed brought a glint of insight to his eyes. "And you thought you were rescuing me from a wild beast?"

The teasing tone of his voice aroused something unexpectedly vulnerable in her. How dare the wretch make sport of her when she'd been defending him . . . and was almost physically sick at the thought of what could have happened to him?

"I expected you would need some help defending yourself," she declared, her throat tight. Then the sense of his words struck her. "You *know* this wolf?"

"Of course. I raised her from a pup. She runs in the mountains during the summer, and comes down into the village to winter with me every year. Her name is Rika."

Aaren watched the big, tawny-eyed beast approach, sniffing, eyeing her warily. Her heart was beating so loudly in her ears she could scarcely hear him say in a firm, soothing voice: "Rika, behave. This is a friend." The animal paused, glanced at Jorund, and gave her tail a wag. But when Aaren moved, she snapped to attention and growled from low in her throat, causing Aaren to freeze against the tree again.

"She is not convinced you're friendly," Jorund said with a twitch at the corner of his mouth. "*She-wolves* can be so stubborn." He laughed at the sparks that struck in her eyes. "I suppose I'll just have to show her you're not dangerous." As he moved slowly across the clearing toward her, Aaren felt the air being crowded from her lungs. "And you'll have to help me, Long-legs. No fighting . . . and no biting."

Soon he stood before her, gazing down at her. The fear and confusion she felt were all driven from her mind as he filled her senses . . .

"See, Rika?" he said without taking his eyes from Aaren. "She won't hurt me . . . or you. She's a female . . . like you. And a huntress . . . like you. But she can be gentle, too. Come, girl. See for yourself." As the wolf lowered its head and ambled closer, he patted the side of his thigh to encourage her. Aaren stiffened as the wolf nudged between them, brushing both of their legs. The wolf's head bumped against her as it nuzzled Jorund's hand.

"Now, you pet her too, Long-legs. And she will take your scent and think of you as a friend."

Aaren wasn't sure she wanted to be thought of as a wolf's friend, but there was something compelling about his voice, and she reached out to give Rika a tentative stroke, then another. She froze as she felt the beast's wet nose against her hand. She glanced down in amazement to find the wolf alternately sniffing and licking her.

"Go on, Serricksdotter . . . pet her," he coaxed, backing up a step to give them room.

Aaren bent slightly and extended first one, then both hands, giving the wolf's head a pat, which gradually enlarged to become a thorough ear-scratching rub. When she straightened, Rika leaned into her knees and trampled her feet, insisting the treatment continue. Aaren could have sworn there was a grin on the beast's maw. It was strangely pleasurable, running her fingers through the animal's thick, warm fur. Jorund's chuckle made her look up.

"You have a soft touch, Long-legs." His eyes were lit with that warm teasing she knew was more dangerous to her than any wolf. He bent and picked up a piece of dried branch and waggled it over Rika's nose. "Here, girl—make yourself useful and fetch this back to me." He sent it sailing off across the break and into the trees. Rika bounded after it and Jorund turned to Aaren with his mouth curled in that boyish, irresistible way of his.

"Rika is not my first wolf. I have another by name in the village, you know," he said, his voice low and caressing as he closed the distance between them. *"Wolf-tamer."* He made no move to touch her with his hands . . . there was no need to, with his words gliding over her like warm honey. His blue eyes tugged at hers until she surrendered them to him, holding her breath. "And do you know how I tame a wolf, Serricksdotter?" She could make no sound; her throat was caught in the hard grip of desire.

"First I hobble it . . . gently, so it won't hurt itself." He flexed and pressed the lower part of his body into hers, pinning her to the tree. The impact of his hardening flesh against her poured heat into her loins and sent it spilling down the insides of her thighs.

"Then I feed it well, from my own hand, until it is full and sleek." He ran a finger around her lips, setting them afire. Her stomach yawned with sudden hunger and her knees buckled.

"Then I pet it. Firmly. Gently. And often." That beguiling hand slid from her mouth and along her shoulder, massaging with slow, sure movements. It moved up the side of her neck to caress her cheek. It was all she could do to keep from curling around that hand, from arching her suddenly heavy and sensitive breasts into him.

"And if it gets out of hand . . . I give it a good smack." His hand dropped to give the side of her buttock a playful bounce. The jolt made her gasp—both from surprise and from the sensual reaction it set off in her. A smoldering ember of desire exploded in her core, blowing its burning fragments along her nerves, setting them afire.

Neither of them had noticed Rika's return, or the way her ears stood on end, or the way she stalked closer, every sinew taut with anxiety as she watched them. Aaren arched and surged against Jorund, meeting his mouth with hers, and the wolf barked and lunged at them, pouncing on

Jorund's shoulder and knocking them both sideways.

"Wha-at—" He caught his balance and shoved the furry menace aside. "*Nej*—Rika!" he commanded furiously, seizing the animal by the neck and wrestling her to a halt. "I was only kissing her!" he declared. "Go lie down—here!" He picked up the stick Rika had dropped at his feet and threw it again. "Go chew on that."

He turned back to Aaren and pulled her into his arms again. "She doesn't understand kissing. It must look to her like we're biting each other."

"Kis-sing? What is kis-sing?" she whispered, letting the soft sibilant sound roll over her tongue.

"This." He demonstrated, clasping her against him and gliding his mouth over hers in lazy, silken circles.

"A mouth-meeting is called a kiss?" she whispered breathlessly.

He laughed, staring down into her liquid amber eyes. "The Franks name it that. I learned it on one of the first raids. . . . You like it, this mouth-meeting with me?" When her tongue flicked over her bottom lip, he lowered his head and fulfilled that wordless and irresistible request for more.

Their bodies blended, curve to hollow, mound to valley, plane to plane. He swirled her tongue with his, taking the kiss deeper, drinking in the lush heat of her response. After a long, bone-melting minute, he slid his mouth from hers and whispered softly.

"Now, isn't this better than fighting me?"

His throaty words lodged in her mind, refusing to be swept away in the tide of passion he was drawing from her. Better than fighting him? Ummm. Much better. This was warm and tender and so achingly soft. She much preferred a mouth-meeting with him to a blade—

Her drowning wits suddenly broke the surface of that treacherous, engulfing stream of thought. She preferred kissing him to fighting him? The idea shocked her. What was happening to her? What was she doing . . . in his arms, her mouth opened to him, reveling in the way his body undulated against hers? She was *surrendering* again, that's what—both to him and to her own volatile desire for pleasure!

She shoved him back forcefully, breaking his embrace, and he staggered, his passion-weighted eyes flying open. She saw no more as she bolted for the camp, but behind her she heard his shock turning to anger.

"Aaren—come back! Dammit, Serricksdotter—come back here!"

He ran after her, dodging snags and forest undergrowth, his face bronzed with anger and his blood hot with need. But at the edge of the camp, he jolted to a stop. She was already striding into the fire circle, being greeted by Garth and several others, who cast glances toward him and smirked, as if intuiting that something had happened between them. He turned to his pallet to give the visible evidence of his passions time to subside, and busied himself with cleaning his boning knife. He was furious. He had an overwhelming urge to treat her like the warrior she claimed to be and trounce her bodily . . . or take a blade to her!

His hands trembled as he drew an oiled cloth over the edge of his knife and, once raised, the temptation to take up a blade rose inside him like a dark, shapeless specter . . . formed of his thwarted longings for her woman's body and the long-denied habit of violence that his early life had imbedded in his very sinew. The clamor of old battles echoed in his hungry core, and the dim, surflike roar of battle-lust surged in his blood . . . seductive sounds, growing louder, calling to him out of memory, like a siren song. *Power . . . satisfaction . . . honor . . . fame. . . . Just take up a blade—be your father's son.*

Fight. All you have to do is fight.

He raked a look toward the fire, where she was settling on a log next to Garth and Erik, feeling deeply disturbed by those old, resurgent impulses . . . and by new impulses he had never associated with a woman before. She somehow brought out the aggressive-male side of him, conjured in him the desire to best and subdue and possess her. Worse yet, he seemed to enjoy those feelings and the edge they lent to his carnal desires: the possibility of total abandon in sensuality, instead of his long-practiced self-control . . .

As he sat watching Aaren, a familiar four-legged form lumbered out of the trees nearby. Rika sniffed, then lowered her head and started toward him. But as she passed Aaren's sleeping place, she halted in her tracks and trotted over to nose around Aaren's rolled fleece. Jorund called softly to her and she broke off her investigation to trot toward him. Again she stopped halfway and swung her head toward Aaren. Despite Jorund's gentle coaxing and repeated calls, the wolf lowered her head and followed her nose to where Aaren was seated on a log near the fire.

Jorund growled and unrolled his sleeping fleece with a furious jerk. It wasn't enough that Aaren stole his peace of mind and his love of pleasure . . . now she was taking his wolf as well!

The knowledge that she preferred kissing to fighting weighted Aaren's spirits as she sat by the fire, staring into the flames. What kind of attitude was that for a warrior to have? And adding to her burden was the unholy panic she had felt earlier when she thought Jorund was being hurt. There was no use denying it further; the truth was so painfully obvious. She wanted Jorund Borgerson . . . wanted the magic in his hands and his mouth . . . wanted his touches, his kisses, his silky, enthralling word-webs. She wanted to experience with him the pleasures of her woman's body, wanted to learn what it was to wrap her legs around him . . . to have him wedge himself between her thighs . . .

But for her to experience such things, she realized, she would have to get him to fight her. The full reality of what she was seeking began to seep through to her. To have the victory she had vowed to claim from him, she would have to swing her lethally honed blade at him; at his handsome head, strong shoulders, and pleasurable hands. She would have to fill his lightning-blue eyes with rage and anger, directed at her, and she would have to try with all her might to deal him a wound.

Her heart stopped. *Wounding Jorund.*

For the first time in her life, her enchantment felt like a curse.

She had always borne a fierce pride in her special status . . . Valkyr's daughter and enchanted warrior. She had felt favored, gifted with things not granted to ordinary women. But now she began to see her enchantment as the divine vengeance it was meant to be. How cruel of the gods to make Aaren and her sisters pay for their father's offense. There seemed no justice in that. But then, she thought bitterly, one didn't look to the gods of Asgard for justice. They only involved themselves in the affairs of mortals when they wanted something; to relieve boredom, to play a trick on one of their fellow gods, or to slake their lusts.

She thought of little round Godfrey, who spoke of his strange, colorless god with affection and talked openly of things like sharing and peace and kindness. And she began to wonder . . . about the grinding lot of the warrior, with its constant wear of competition and fighting . . . about the softer parts of her nature that she had locked away . . . and about the quiet joys she had forfeited when she was forced to join the world of men. Suddenly, a god who valued kindness and loving and wanted peace among mortals seemed much more reasonable than the volatile, capricious gods who gloried in conflict and valued fighting and ferocity and hard vengeance.

Moments later her thoughts were in turmoil again. These dangerous musings . . . was this how Jorund had become a cheek-turner? She rubbed her temples and scowled as she stared into the yellow-gold flames.

A booming voice from across the campfire penetrated her thoughts and she looked up.

"Look what's come into camp," Hakon Freeholder declared, slinging a sneer across the fire toward Aaren. Her muscles contracted defensively, but before she could respond, a great shaggy form jumped across the log beside her and stood panting, gazing at her. "It's that toothless old she-wolf of Jorund's," he declared, heaving a pork bone at Rika, who dodged.

"Worthless piece of worm-fodder," another growled, picking up a small rock and hitting her on the haunch. She skittered back, lowered her head, and growled. "Go on, you flea-bait! You got no fangs left to bite anybody. 'orund pulled 'em all out."

Aaren shoved to her feet and stepped in front of the wolf. "Leave the animal alone, Freeholder. She's done nothing to you."

She gave the wolf's fur a determined ruffling that was as much for the Freeholder's benefit as Rika's, then turned away toward her pallet. As she collapsed onto her bed of pine boughs, scowling, she heard the words over and over in her head: " . . . *got no fangs left* . . ."

Rika suddenly loomed above her in the dimness, tawny eyes glowing, tongue lolling. She had followed her new source of affection and now nosed Aaren's leg, then licked her arm, insisting on more attention. Aaren swallowed her trepidation and pushed up onto one elbow, giving the she-wolf's ears a good scratching. Face to face with Rika, staring into her gaping jaws, Aaren saw that she did indeed have fangs . . . very large, very wicked-looking fangs. It was a moment before she understood what Borger's men had meant: to them, a wolf that wouldn't use its fangs was the same as toothless. Rika had been tamed . . . and they had nothing but contempt for that which had lost the will to fight. Aaren shivered. It was a hard standard. But then, they were hard men.

She wrapped up in her blanket and turned on her side, away from the sight of Jorund rising from his pallet and moving toward the fire, his movements short and irritable and his handsome face as dark as the night-forest around them. When Rika nudged and wriggled and trampled a place onto the pine boughs beside her, claiming a share of the pallet, Aaren was grateful for the warmth and company.

The next morning Aaren found the contents of her leather hunting bag strewn over the ground near her pallet, and Rika lying nearby still chewing on the tasty leather of the bag's strap.

"Get out of here, you worthless piece of flea-bait!"

The other warriors looked over to find the wolf cowering with her ears back and Aaren looming over her, red-faced and glowering. They laughed as Aaren made a lunge for her and she went scrambling for the trees.

"Still eager to defend that bag of bones, Serricksdotter?" the Freeholder called out.

Rika followed her everywhere she went that day, sidling closer and closer, looking as dejected as it was possible for a wolf to look. Bit by bit, the sight of her flattened ears and the white moons around her drooping eyes worked on Aaren's anger. By evening, when Rika crawled toward her pallet, Aaren sighed and grudgingly gave her a pat.

"I suppose we she-wolves ought to stick together."

Chapter Eleven

The hunting party arrived back in Borger's village the next day, and their good hunt-luck became an excuse for celebration . . . among the men. The women watched the ale being trundled out in the hall yet again and called an immediate halt to their own labors for the rest of the day. But instead of sitting in a dank, gloomy hall, drinking themselves into oblivion, they chose to pack up their food and their children, and trek out to the nearby nut grove, to enjoy what might prove to be the last of the Autumn Month sun.

Aaren watched the men swaggering off to the hall, relieved to be rid of their rough company for a while, and scowled at that unsettling thought. When Miri and Marta insisted she come with them, she agreed and soon found herself trailing a noisy throng, carrying a woven birch basket filled with sour apples, curds, and a sample of the bee-woman's finest mead.

After eating, they lay propped on their elbows on a cloth spread on the dried grasses between the mostly bare hazel trees. Miri glanced at Marta over Aaren's head, scowled, and bobbed her head insistently, prodding her sister to speak.

"Aaren, when do you think . . . you will fight Jorund?" Marta asked in a timid voice.

"Only the gods know." She sighed, staring up at the clouds over head. "And they're not saying."

"Well . . ." Miri halted and Aaren looked at her. Miri was biting her upper lip the way she always did when she was unsure of herself. "What do you think would happen if one of us . . . if we happened to . . ."

"If one of us . . . tried to go to the furs with a man before you were defeated?" Marta finished for her in a rush. Aaren sat bolt upright, her eyes widening on Miri's and Marta's reddening faces.

"It would be a disaster!" she declared, horrified. "How could you even think of such a thing—defying the gods, shaming Father Serrick, dishonoring yourselves and our enchantment in the eyes of old Red Beard's entire clan? Look what Odin did to our father just for claiming something that was rightfully his. Imagine what he would do to someone who defied his enchantment!"

"Oh, we would never do such a thing," Marta insisted frantically, scowling at Miri, who nodded. "We just . . . wondered." After a moment's uneasy silence, Miri spoke.

"And we wondered . . ." She swallowed hard and made herself say it. "What it would be like to . . . Aaren, you were with Jorund Borgerson once . . . naked, with his mouth on yours. What did it feel like? Was it as nice as the women say?"

Aaren felt her face catch fire. Torn between stalking off and staying to scold them for speaking of such things . . . she hesitated just long enough for both urges to pass. Her sisters were young women now, and they were comely enough to catch the eyes and the interest of men. And as she searched their expectant faces, she realized that they were eager to learn the ways of women with men and anxious to get on with their lives. Her shoulders sagged. They probably *wanted* Jorund Borgerson to defeat her.

She grasped her knees with whitened fingers and her heart began to hammer in her breast as it struck her: *she wanted Jorund Borgerson to defeat her, too!*

Defeat. She had always understood, in a dim way, that sooner or later she would be defeated. Serrick had always spoken to Miri and Marta of husbands and children and home-hearths, and for them to be mated and to bear children, she would have to be overcome in battle. But Serrick had never once spoke to her of when it might occur, or of what life would be like for her when she was defeated. How strange that she understood full well what her defeat would mean for her little sisters . . . but had no idea what it would mean for herself.

After she was defeated, what sort of place would she

have in Borger's band and in the village? Would defeat at a woman-heart's hands demean her in the jarl's and his warriors' eyes? Would finding woman-pleasure mean losing some of the warrior-heart in her? What would she be? A warrior still? A woman?

She had no answers. All she had was a growing tangle of desires that were harder to suppress with each tantalizing, infuriating encounter she had with Jorund Borgerson.

"Yes," she said softly, staring into a vision that only she could see. "It is nice. A mouth-meeting is called a 'kiss.' And if it's done properly, the feeling reaches down into your body and makes you want to . . ." She halted, shocked by the sound of her own words, and came back to the present to find Miri and Marta staring eagerly at her. "Is there someone who makes your thoughts wander into such pleasure-paths?" she asked, scowling. Miri flushed and lowered her eyes.

"Garth Borgerson . . . speaks to me often and he smiles at me."

Aaren turned to Marta, who shrugged as if to deny there was anyone special in her thoughts.

"I see." Aaren got to her feet and let out a disgusted sigh. "Well, you will just have to pray that Jorund Woman-heart becomes Jorund *Warrior-heart* someday soon. And that he's as good with a blade as he is with a—" She had almost said *kiss*. Blushing violently, she turned on her heel and strode off, over a carpet of fallen yellow leaves.

The nut grove meandered along a stream bed and as Aaren followed it she came to a small meadow, rimmed by trees and covered with the dried stubble of harvested clover. Several children were playing a ring game, laughing and repeating a singsong chant as they weaved in and out of each others' hands. As she stood watching, a dim memory slipped out through a crack in her inner fortress . . . a similar game she had played with her sisters in the days when she was still just a little girl. The past and present began to mingle in her thoughts and for a moment she relaxed her guard and let them wash through her.

The wind ruffling her hair . . . bare toes sliding through

cool grass . . . the sound of girlish laughter, hers and her sisters . . . movement in wide-swinging circles and free, galloping loops . . . instead of the intensely focused lines and constricted, explosive points of battle training . . .

Moments later, something startled the children. They broke their circles and squealed and clustered together like frightened ducklings. Aaren's battle-honed senses searched the far side of the meadow. A wolf! Scouring the nearby trees for signs of others and spotting none, she ran out into the clearing to face the lone beast, praying it was the one she'd recently come to know.

"Rika! Rika!" When the wolf halted, sniffed in her direction, then raced toward her, most of the children ran from the meadow screaming. But two girls were caught between her and the wolf, and they turned in blind panic and ran straight into her. She scooped them up in her arms and braced . . . as the animal slowed to a trot and threw itself joyfully against her legs, nearly knocking her down in a forceful bid for affection. She expelled the breath she was holding and shoved her chin above the little arms clamped around her neck.

"Go away, Rika. Shame on you—frightening little children." She gave the wolf a shove with her foot. "See there, it is only old Rika, Jorund's wolf. Nothing to be afraid of. I have you, now . . . you are safe." They were all but strangling her, and she just managed to get out: "Come now . . . let me see your faces."

It took some coaxing, but they finally released her neck and sat back in her arms. Their faces were tear-streaked and their noses needed wiping. She gave them a reassuring smile and sank to her knees, lowering them to her lap. When Rika trotted over to investigate, the children squealed and threw themselves on Aaren's neck again and she had to scold poor Rika and send her away once more. The wolf padded off with her tail dragging and flopped down in some tall grass across the way.

"Here now." She settled the warm little bodies onto her lap and wiped their tears away. "It is good to be careful of wolves. They are not usually friendly. But you mustn't be afraid, either. A wolf can tell when you're afraid and he'll

chase you, even if his belly is full—just to watch you run.
So when you are older, you must move slowly and find a
tall tree and climb it. But for now . . . you're safest with
your mothers and the other children . . . or with me."

"Safe with you?" one asked, wide-eyed at finding herself
in the renowned and feared battle-maiden's arms. Aaren
laughed and gave her hair a reassuring stroke.

"Yes, with me. You are always safe with me. I will
protect you."

Their little faces filled with relief and wonder, and she
felt an odd pricking at the backs of her eyes. It was a
warrior's task to protect and a woman's task to cradle and
reassure. And she suddenly found herself overwhelmed by
powerful, confusing urges to do both. . . .

Jorund stood in the trees at the edge of the meadow
watching Aaren with the children. He had quit the raucous
merriment of the hall for the quieter pleasures of the company of the women and children. He needed relief from the
constant strain of wanting and the growing resentment he
felt toward Aaren. Day by day he grew more hot-blooded
and irritable, watching her unholy pride rising between
them like a wall, while he ached for the pleasures he
knew they both wanted. Rika had loped along before him
as he wandered past the cultivated fields to the nut grove,
then had left him behind. He arrived just in time to hear
children screaming and see them hurtling down the path
toward him, crying that a wolf had tried to get them in the
bee meadow.

When he rushed to the clearing, he discovered both of his
she-wolves . . . one cuddling and reassuring two frightened
children and the other sulking in the grass. He smiled,
relieved, and leaned a shoulder against a tree trunk at the
edge of the clearing, moved by the sight of Aaren's glowing face and the dulcet tones she used with the children.
When she laughed, his heart gave an odd lurch and his
throat tightened. Her long, tapered hands gently brushed
the children's hair . . . her eyes twinkled as she set them
on their feet, then got to hers . . . and she led them around
and around in a ring game.

When they all fell down laughing, he watched her tumble

with the children and absorbed the easy grace, the girlishness of her movements. He had never imagined seeing her like this. Or perhaps in his deepest heart, he had.

Noise from the path caused her to sit up and the children huddled close to her. Several harried women and a number of panting children ran into the meadow and stopped at the sight of her, sitting on the ground with their little ones. The mothers hurried to take them from her and she explained awkwardly that it was Jorund's wolf . . . it had only given the children a fright.

The women nodded wary thanks and scooped the little girls up in their arms. Aaren stood shifting from one foot to the other as they hurried away. The longing in her face was difficult for Jorund to watch. In those unguarded moments, as she turned away and dug at the clover stubble with her toe, he glimpsed a yearning he had not expected in her and a warmth, a softness in the heart of Aaren Serricksdotter. Together, they melted the ire he had been fighting for the last several days.

This was the woman he had glimpsed inside that tough warrior's shell. This was the tenderness he craved. It was no longer just pleasure he wanted, or even conquest. He would not be satisfied until he had all of her: her fierce passion, her gentleness, her vulnerability, her strength. He wanted her body, her heart, her presence . . . he wanted her entire life, mingled with his.

One woman, Godfrey had said. And he had laughed. But now, one woman embodied everything he desired, the puzzle of a lifetime. And he was determined to have her.

He shoved off from the tree trunk and stepped out of the shadows.

Aaren heard the rustle of the grass behind her and whirled, bracing. The sight of him coming toward her with his golden hair shining in the sun, his shoulders swaying, his eyes alight with both promise and desire, took her breath. She wasn't prepared to confront him just now. Her defenses were down . . . she had just allowed too many memories out, had just suffered a heart-tugging breach of her inner wall.

Scrambling to regain control, she backed away. When he stopped several feet from her, she paused and drew a calming breath. "What are you doing here, Borgerson?"

"I came to enjoy the afternoon . . . the sun. And I came to find you."

"Me?" She swallowed hard. "B-but you don't have your blade with you," was all she could think to say.

"You are the most constant and predictable female I have ever known," he said in a tone filled with good-humored reproach. "Most women change their minds at least a dozen times a day. But you always have just one thing—the same thing—on your mind."

"As do you," she said, feeling the irresistible pull of his gaze. He laughed with a deep, rolling sound that vibrated her fingertips.

"Fighting," he charged, bending toward her from the waist.

"Pleasure," she accused, copying his posture with a half smile. He was teasing her . . . she was teasing him. It seemed the most easy and natural thing in the world, almost as if they were old friends. He strode past her and gestured to the meadow around them.

"You know what this is?" When she shook her head, he looked around with a broadening grin. "This is the bee meadow. In the Spring Month it is covered with clover up to your knees. And those trees over there"—he pointed to a section of woods—"are where the bees have their hives. Bedria is our bee-woman and the brewer of the best mead in all the southern clans. Have you ever robbed bees, Aaren Serricksdotter?"

"*Nej*," she said, shaking her head. "Once, Father Serrick found and robbed a honey-tree in our low thicket. I went along to help, and I watched them light on him until they almost covered him." She shuddered. "He got only a sting or two, but it was a terrifying sight."

"You? Terrified?"

"I confess . . . I am afraid of bees." She reddened. "Of nothing else in all Midgard," she protested quickly, then muttered, "only bees." Then she frowned, recalling something she had heard. "They call you *Honey-hunter*. Then you must help Bedria with robbing her bees."

He laughed wickedly and strolled closer. "Women do

talk," he said with an enigmatic smile. He paused before her with his hands on his waist, and rocked back on one leg. "It seems strange to me that you should fear bees, Long-legs. Do you not know that bees and women are close kin?" His eyes were beginning to glow. Her breath came faster as she caught the first waft of heat radiating from his body.

"Kin?" she said, feeling that odd breathlessness that she knew to be the effect of his special woman-magic. When he nodded, not taking his gaze from hers, she had to jerk in a breath.

"There are but two kinds of creatures in all the world that make honey," he said softly.

"Two?" The separate strands of her reason and feeling were melting together.

"Bees. And women."

"Don't be daft," she said with a soft, distracted laugh. "Women don't make honey."

"Oh, but they do, Long-legs." His eyes caressed her slowly and his big, languid body seemed to uncoil before her eyes, coming to life . . . reaching for her. "Shall I show you how?"

She couldn't swallow, could scarcely breathe. She knew what he was going to do to her, had known it from the moment she saw him. And she wanted it, wanted to taste him, to feel his hard body against and around her. When he raised a hand to cup her chin and tilt her mouth up to him, she let her eyes drift closed, trapping the sight of his bronzed face, the sensuous fullness of his mouth in her mind. And suddenly he was cradling her against his body and laving her lips with his tongue.

He tasted like grain, salt, and honey—the things that sustained, seasoned, and sweetened life. And she opened to him, allowing him into her depths, yielding the tender, inner surfaces of her mouth to his slow, ravishing strokes. He swirled her tongue and coaxed it, teased it . . . tempting it to venture on its own. And she slowly began to fulfill the haunting wish-dream she had lived with day and night . . . exploring his firm, masterful lips and delving past them into the sweet, silken source of that potent word-stream that always engulfed her will and drowned her senses.

Torrents of warmth swirled through her, melting her sinews, softening her bones. Her knees went weak and she sagged against him, uttering a sound that was part sigh, part gasp. He swayed, then braced and lifted his head. She could scarcely focus her eyes, but when she did, she saw that he was blinking, trying to gain control of his vision, too. He turned his head toward the trees, then suddenly released her and bent to sweep her legs from under her.

"What are you doing?" she squealed, flailing, then frantically clamping both arms around his neck as he cradled her in his arms.

"Carrying you," he said, his breath labored, his eyes fierce. He struck off for the shelter of a nearby tree.

"Put me down—you can't lift me—"

"I already have." He laughed, though the strain in his face told the effort it required.

She flushed and her jaw worked, but no sound came out. He *was* carrying her. He was probably the only man in the village who would attempt it . . . much less do it. It was a demonstration of his physical power, she realized dizzily, and of his sensual determination. He was treating her like a woman. And she liked it.

He set her back on her feet at the base of a tall birch, which had shed half of its leaves, and drew her into his arms. His breath came fast, his skin was hot . . . and his eyes had the intensity of lightning bolts.

"Do you know even a small part of how beautiful you are?" He took her face between his hands and poured a kiss over her mouth that was so gentle it made her ache. Behind that control, she could feel his power coiled, his desire reined and straining. "Perhaps it is better you don't know." He pushed her down to her knees, then to a seat on the leaf-blanket at the base of the tree and sank with her, beside her . . . connecting their mouths, pressing her onto her back, sliding his chest over hers.

"I have never made love to someone in armor before." He paused, with a throaty chuckle. "I think this will have to go, Long-legs, before we can meet properly." His hand slid to her side and when she didn't protest, his fingers quickly untied the lacings of her breastplate and pulled them completely out. She arched to allow him to draw the molded leather from beneath her, then sucked in breath as he settled his chest over her breasts once more. "So much better . . ." He ground against her sensitive nipples and massaged her soft mounds with his chest, then his fingers. And his mouth captured hers once again, trapping her helpless moan inside.

The dull ache of wanting she had lived with since he kissed her in the woods was now a fierce, driving hunger for the feel of him, for the weight of him on her . . . for the gentle, swirling pleasures he was working in the hardened tips of her breasts . . . and for the deeper, stronger claiming she sensed would follow. She filled her hands with his hard shoulders, his heavily layered back, his silky spun-gold hair, reveling in the textures of him and committing each sensation to the deepest well of her heart.

His mouth drifted across her face, down the side of her neck, caressing, teasing, nipping. Then her tunic slid up and he lowered his head to her aching breasts, nuzzling and then swirling their tips with his tongue. She gasped and went taut beneath him. The wet heat of his mouth flooded into her, and the gentle tugs of his suckles and nibbles reached all the way into her woman's mound, exciting her so that she wanted to squirm, to press her warm, aching flesh against his hardness.

"Ummm." He raised his mouth to her ear, setting it atingle with that sultry vibration. "You're magnificent, Long-legs. So hard. So soft." And she realized his hand was working the ties of her breeches . . . then peeling them back. She quivered as his hand glided down her belly and paused over her woman's mound. For a moment, he kissed her deeply, letting his big hand rest on her, radiating heat into her most sensitive flesh, drawing her desire into her loins to meet his touch. She grew turgid with expectation, and when the kiss and the caress lengthened without deepening, she moved restlessly, a small but telling motion beneath his hand. He lifted his head and smiled into her half-focused eyes.

"Now, Long-legs." His voice came like gently lapping waves. "Make honey for me."

His fingers slid along the groove of her womanflesh and gently invaded those tender folds. She gasped and held her breath, concentrating on the shattering sensations of his fingers stroking her most sensitive parts. It was as if he reached into the core of her woman's body with his very hands, caressing and stirring her. Then the whole world began to whirl softly, sensuously, as if directed by and in rhythm with his hand. Warmth surged, her body contracted . . . and she felt a liquid flow beginning in her womanflesh.

Hot and sweet. *Honey.*

She could scarcely breathe, her whole body was aflame, throbbing with a rising tension . . . simmering with a hot, mounting need for something she didn't understand. She writhed, feeling unable to absorb another sensation and yet drinking in more . . . lost in the need in her blood and sinew . . . aching for release.

"Don't fight it, Long-legs," he murmured raggedly into her ear. "Let it take you. Let it wash through you . . . let it carry you."

Don't fight. His words lodged in her mind even as they rumbled through her tortured frame, freeing her responses. The storm in her blood was like the mounting rage of battle-fury: hot, wild, scintillant. Like living fire, it engulfed and consumed her, burning the dross of old anxieties and frustrations from her heart . . . purging the tensions that days of confrontations and denial of battle had accumulated in her blood. She arched into his hand, feeling her blood swelling in her veins, her muscles contracting, her nerves quivering . . . and suddenly the tension burst in her loins, exploding white-hot, like a pleasurable lightning blast through her senses . . . discharging them, making way for the pure, sweeping flood of release. She soared, clinging to his shoulders, shuddering as storm wave after storm wave of pleasure broke over her.

Don't fight . . . lingered in her head as the maelstrom in her blood subsided. She raised her eyes to his, finding them heated to molten silver. "There is more, Aaren. Much more."

More, she thought. Heat still swirled in her blood and desire eddied in her body, but the charge in her senses was dissipated enough for her wits to reassemble. In the comparative calm, that one word—*more*—began a chain of thinking. How much more? A heart-stopping thought burst through her mind. Had she crossed the boundary set by her enchantment? The very possibility sent an icy, sobering draft through her heated core. Not an hour ago, she had been scolding Miri and Marta . . .

As he bent to claim her mouth and gently slid the lower part of his body onto hers, she felt a violent contraction of fear in her stomach. Coldness seeped through her as she scrambled to recall what Serrick had said of the limits of their freedom. Mating, a man's flesh-spear . . . a woman's body absorbing it. Not yet, she thought frantically.

The sudden stiffness in her response made him look down at her. Seeing the tumult in her eyes, he made to reassure her with a kiss. It was a long, breath-stealing interval before she managed to drag her mouth from his.

"Fight me," she whispered urgently. "It is not too late— you have not yet pierced me with your flesh-blade." Her eyes were dark, luminous, like liquid amber, compelling. "Fight me, Jorund. So we can finish it."

Her words cut through the steam in his senses, and he shifted them back and forth in his head, like hot coals he couldn't bear to hold yet couldn't seem to drop. *Fight her . . . finish it.* He didn't want to think, but couldn't keep his thoughts at bay.

"Don't be daft, Long-legs." He forced a sensual smile and undulated against her so that she quivered with involuntary pleasure. "You don't want to fight me. You want to wrap your long, silky legs around me—"

"But I *do* want to fight you," she said in a desperate hush. "And I *need* you to fight me. I cannot be with you until you defeat me in honorable battle."

"Honorable?" He laughed harshly, grappling with the realization that she was serious . . . the fear and desperation mingled in her beautiful features were real.

"I have to fulfill the terms of the enchantment, Jorund. I have to be defeated in battle before I can be . . . mated." She abruptly wriggled and pushed at his ribs to escape the wit-numbing impact of his body against her still throbbing flesh. He started as if she had slapped him, and shifted his weight to the ground beside her.

"That cursed enchantment of yours. It has nothing to do with honor," he declared, his face darkening as he watched her withdrawing from him. "It is but an old man's dream . . . or his half-mad scheme. You have nothing to uphold, Aaren, for there was never an enchantment . . . or an Odin or a Freya to pronounce it on you!" She gasped and shoved him away from her as she struggled to sit up. He rolled back and thrust up on his powerful arms.

"You're wrong, Jorund. It has *everything* to do with honor. There is an enchantment . . . and I am duty-bound, by blood and by my warrior's oath, to uphold it. And whether *you* believe it or not, your father and his warriors and the rest of the village believe it." Her eyes widened. "If I let you take me . . . if I go to your furs without fulfilling my duty, without upholding my sisters' honor . . . they will despise me as weak and revile me, and Miri and Marta will have no rank, no future, no right to marry. And those would be just the first of the calamities to befall us if I defied the gods and the enchantment."

Even as she spoke, the image of Hakon Freeholder's cruel, narrow eyes and surly expression rose in her mind: " . . . *got no fangs left* . . ." She heard it again in her head and suddenly realized why it had haunted her so since that night by the campfire. Jorund had named her a *she-wolf* before the entire village. And she had seen, too well, the fate of she-wolves who allowed themselves to be tamed . . . who lost their will to fight . . . who lost the honor their fierceness inspired among warring men. She knew that Rika's fate—derision and contempt—would be her own if she surrendered without an honorable fight.

"I care nothing for what they think—I've never cared!" he declared hotly, rising to his knees above her. "I do what I know to be right and true. There is no damned enchantment and nothing bad will happen to me or to you when we make love." Anger raced like a lightning fork through his blood. "You and your wretched code of honor. You go about—playing at being a warrior—Well, I have a code, too, Serricksdotter, and it does not allow taking a blade to the woman I want to make love with . . . to the woman I want to live with and make children on."

Aaren could hear only one word in three. *No enchantment*, he declared, *no warrior* and *no honor*. The impact of his scornful denials, after what they'd just shared, was crushing. She blanched and pushed to her knees, staring at him as if she'd never truly seen him before. His expression was bitter, his eyes burned with defiance and resentment.

"Fight me, Jorund." It was half demand, half plea, born of desperation.

"Nej." His taut features, his swollen shoulders, and his clenched fists echoed it.

With sobering clarity, she suddenly understood that he also meant *never*. He did not intend to take up a blade and fight her . . . ever.

The enormity of their conflict was wrenchingly clear. He expected her to abandon all honor, all pride, all duty and respect—everything a warrior held dear—for a bit of pleasure with him, because he honestly didn't believe she was a warrior. And even if she could convince him, it still wouldn't matter. He didn't care about his own honor as a warrior, she realized with a half-choked sob. Why should he care about hers?

She scrambled up, jerking at the ties of her breeches, panicked by the tears welling in her eyes and the crushing sensation in her chest. Jorund lurched up, calling her name and reaching for her, but she stumbled back, out of reach. She managed one last look as she turned away, and found him standing with his eyes dark and hollow.

It was some time later that she came to her senses and found herself on the cliffs overlooking the lake Väner. Her lungs were raw, her face burned, and her eyes felt grainy. She was crying, for the first time in years. She wiped her cheeks with the heels of her palms and drew a great, shuddering breath, trying to regain some control.

The emptiness she had felt inside when Serrick left, and when she'd faced the villagers after her harvest battle, was nothing compared with the cavernous loss she felt now. She wanted Jorund Borgerson and he wanted her. He was the only one who could challenge her and break her wretched enchantment. But he didn't intend to fight her. Not now. Not ever. And that meant this wretched battle of wills between them would rage on . . . each encounter lowering her defenses against him, until, sooner or later, he would batter down her inner walls entirely and she would surrender.

It would be disaster all around. She would be dishonored, her sisters would be disgraced . . . and the gods—wherever they happened to be—would be outraged and vindictive. . . .

As she sat, watching the cold, wind-whipped waves of the water below, a surviving spark of spirit deep within her began to grow, countering the darkness that threatened her heart. She still had her pride, her sense of honor, and the strength of will that had sustained her through training and battles and adversity. She was a warrior . . . used to taking things in hand and demanding her due . . . and it was high time she began to assert herself as one. She couldn't—wouldn't—dishonor herself or allow him to dishonor her by taking her without a proper fight.

She had to try one last time to make him angry enough to pick up a blade and fight her to a standstill.

When she got to her feet, her breeches slid down and she stared at herself in horror. Her tunic was untucked, her breeches were half tied, and—worst—her breastplate was missing! How had she allowed things to go so far? Well, never again, she vowed. He wouldn't take her armor from her breasts . . . until he'd taken her blade from her hand.

Glancing at the lowering sun, she struck off across the field and forest, headed for the bee meadow to retrieve her breastplate. At the entrance to the now deserted nut grove, she spotted movement in the tall grasses near the trees and her senses sprang to alert. A moment later Rika emerged from the thicket, carrying Aaren's breastplate in her mouth, the backplate dragging beside her. Aaren stopped, horror-struck, then lunged at the beast and wrestled her battle garment away from it. One bottom corner of the padded leather frontpiece was thoroughly chewed.

She leveled a fierce glare on the beast, who was panting and watching her eagerly.

"Worthless beast," she chided softly. "Why is it that you remember you have teeth only around me?"

The noise of revelry, ale-spirit, and contention drifted out over the quiet commons that evening, penetrating the darkness, echoing through the shadows. Aaren approached the half-open doors of the long hall and paused, listening, steeling herself for the coming confrontation. She had donned her best tunic and her breastplate, plaited her hair into a taut battle-braid, and given her sword a new edge and a bath of oil. Each preparation had salved her stinging pride and bolstered her determination to try one last, desperate gambit to force Jorund's temper to a blade-wielding explosion.

When she spotted Garth Borgerson striding toward the smithy, she called to him and he steered in her direction with a genial greeting. But when she spoke, his face blanked with surprise.

"Does Jorund Borgerson have a long-blade?" she demanded, letting the battle-heat in her blood rise into her gaze.

"Yea, he has a sword. I know it," Garth answered, his eyes widening as he glimpsed the significance of her question. "It sleeps in his bed closet, with him."

"Then go and get it, Borger's son, and bring it to the hall," she said with quiet intensity. "Tonight he will have need of it."

Chapter Twelve

T he warriors and village men ignored Aaren when she entered the hall and halted before the great hearth, searching the raucous, fire-lit gathering for her quarry. She spotted him at a table near the high seat and went to the table directly across the hall from him, staring heatedly at the young warriors seated there until they abandoned the table to her.

Something in her manner was different tonight, they realized; something in the rigid carriage of her shoulders, the defiant angle of her chin, and the determined sway of her hips that charged the air around her. They mumbled to each other and shook their heads as they watched her remove her sword and scabbard from her shoulder and lay them conspicuously across the table before her. The intensity and deliberateness of her movements aroused a sense of expectation. When she emptied her ale horn and leveled a searing look on Jorund, across the way, tension mounted throughout the hall.

The noise of clattering tongues and shuffling feet burst on the thickening quiet. Women and thralls and freemen of the village hurried into the hall, red-faced and panting, craning their necks to locate the principles in the coming conflict. Within the space of a few heartbeats, word had been passed through the hall that the battle-maiden had sent Garth Borgerson to fetch Jorund Borgerson's sword. And when Garth strode from the shadows carrying Jorund Borgerson's memorable blade, expectation escalated to excitement.

Garth paused between Jorund and the high seat, holding up the great weapon and raising an eyebrow to Aaren as if asking what he should do with it. Her eyes traveled over the pommel of the handle, which was made of silver and shaped like a snarling wolf's head. It was heavily tarnished, but it was clearly a formidable weapon. She felt a prickle across her shoulders that was some part anticipation and some part dread. Suddenly her mind and heart filled with the fearsome image of Jorund Borgerson, white-eyed and bronzed with blood-fever—in the full grip of battle-fury—swinging that massive blade in great, savage arcs.

She rubbed her damp palms up and down her thighs beneath the table top, and her heart beat faster as she shifted her eyes to where Jorund sat, staring at her with a tightly controlled expression. At her curt nod, Garth carried the blade to Jorund, laid it on the planking before him, then stepped back to the group of assembled warriors.

"What is the meaning of this, Serricksdotter?" old Borger demanded, shoving to the edge of his chair and staring down at her with glowing eyes, like a hawk assessing his prey.

"It is a reminder to the Woman-heart that he has a vow not yet fulfilled," she declared, rising. She stepped around the table into the clearing before the high seat, then paused and set her fists on her hips. "In this very place, almost this very spot"—she pointed to the floor at her feet—"he swore he would defeat me." She leveled a fierce look on Jorund. "And I am weary of waiting for the gods to move his sorry arse to fight me."

"Ho-ho!" Borger hooted at her insult, and a wave of eager laughter spread through the warriors. As her brazen insult was relayed through the crowd, a gasp of outrage wafted through the women.

Jorund felt his ears growing hot and a tide of red surging up his neck into his face. He had been furious with her that afternoon in the meadow, and in the intervening hours his ire had not cooled. Instead, it had fermented into a thick and volatile brew of stinging male pride and sexual hunger . . . which now poured like potent Frankish wine through his veins, dulling his judgment and loosening his control.

As he gazed at that lush, petulant mouth, at the alluring angle of her shoulders and the provocative tilt of her hips, he suffered a disastrously intense recall of the feel and the taste of her. Beneath that hot surge of wanting came anger that she had enjoyed his deft pleasuring yet still clung to her demand that he fight her . . . and to her wretched delusions of being a warrior.

"But I see now why he dreads raising that sword." Aaren swaggered closer to him, transferring her disdainful gaze to the tarnished sword before him. "It is so foul and corrupted a blade that it would likely snap with the first good blow from mine!"

Gasps and howls of both protest and laughter swirled around them and Jorund's hands gripped the edge of the table. A warrior's blade was counted a part of his very being—dearer and closer to his heart than a woman. A muscle in Jorund's jaw flexed and all watched his gaze lower to the great sword and glide along its tooled leather cradle . . . a look fraught with both protectiveness and loathing.

"And even if his foul blade did not break," she declared boldly, "I doubt he would have the courage to wield it against me." She pinned him with half-narrowed eyes. "He flinches whenever that toothless wolf of his yawns!"

Coarse male laughter buffeted Jorund and his arms began to quake, his shoulder muscles knotted, and his legs ached from the tension rising in him. He glared furiously at her, torn between feeling wounded and outraged. He made love to her with his words . . . she made war on him with hers!

She stalked the table where he sat, her fists at her waist, her shoulders back, her long legs weaving their lithe, seductive movements through his senses. He suffered a frantic, fleeting urge to shove to his feet and walk away from her provocations, but could not seem to move. The anger swelling in his veins would not be denied any longer; he could feel it expanding, throbbing, taking him over.

"And even if his nerve didn't fail him," she declared, pausing before the table, brazenly sinking her gaze like talons into his, "he would never be quick enough to defeat me. There is a reason he is called *Slow-hand*." She raked visual claws down his broad chest, penetrating to his most proud and sensitive parts. "The more wrought up he gets, the slower he moves." Her eyes glowed with challenge and her voice dropped to a husky growl.

"And around me, he gets wrought up very easily."

His eyes went molten at her thinly cloaked scorn of his lovemaking. How dare the witch taunt him publicly with his desire for her! He came to life before their eyes, thrusting to his feet so forcefully that the bench beneath him overturned. His shoulders inflated, his features sharpened, his great fists clenched at his sides. He had literally risen to her baiting. Now, scarcely a breath was taken or let in the hall as all waited to see what he would do.

"There is an ear-rending noise in this hall," he proclaimed. "Worse than the screech of owls . . . more grating than the caw of crows . . . as piercing as the scream of kites and eagles." He moved deliberately around the table, his head up, his eyes weighted with warning. "It is the howl of a *she-wolf* . . . in heat . . . but unmated, unmounted, and unbred!"

A wild clamor broke loose in the hall. He had returned her insult in kind—turning the confrontation into a full-blown *flyting*! It had been a long time since anyone had been challenged to that precarious ritual exchange of insults in Borger's village.

"Tell her, First-born!" old Borger crowed and burst to his feet. "You there—back away! Give them some room!" He swung one brawny hand in a wild arc and suddenly everyone in the hall was on his or her feet, pressing forward, watching the combatants stalking each other . . . waiting for the next volley in that verbal battle.

"Unmounted and unbred by *choice,* Borgerson," she declared, circling, curling her shoulders slightly forward. "Not from lack of opportunity."

"Nor from lack of interest," he retorted. "You crave a mating, she-wolf—I've seen your pantings and writhings—but you wouldn't have the slightest idea what to do with a mate if you got one." He punched a finger at her. "You cannot love for fighting!"

"And you cannot fight for loving!" she snapped, stung by his vengeful public appraisal of her most tender and private responses. *Pantings* and *writhings*! She jolted forward. "It is a man's duty to take up a blade in all honor and defend himself and his people. But you hide behind the women's skirts—let them defend you whilst you 'chew charcoal' by the cook hearths and take on women's work—"

"Yea, I help the women—someone must," he declared, sweeping the men in the crowd with a contemptuous look. "Their lot is hard and thankless in our northern clans. They do the work of *living* . . . the planting and harvesting, the spinning and weaving, the chopping and hauling, the shearing and threshing. They see to the food and raiment and fuel . . . and even shelter. They defy death to bear children and suffer their children's perils and ills as they raise them up. And they teach the young ones to revere and obey their wide-wandering fathers and far-grasping jarls . . . who do naught but the work of *dying*. They wrench mere babes from their mothers' arms and lead them out into an iron-storm, to feed the ravens upon some foreign shore. And for what? For the empty glory of some fat old jarl's deed-fame! Yea, I prefer to live among the women . . . even as I prefer life to death . . . and pleasure to pain!"

As he spoke the women had rushed from all over the hall to collect at his back, murmuring ever louder, echoing his words and complaints. He understood them, he helped them, and now he spoke for them and their difficult lot. Their faces reddened and their eyes flashed with long-leashed resentments as they lent him the support he had so often extended to them.

"You would not have to be told of a woman's plight, *She-wolf*," he declared above the rising din, "if you were more of a woman yourself!"

"*Nej!*" she choked out past the fury collected in her throat. "I am no woman . . . I am a warrior! And if you were a real warrior—*Woman-heart*—you would not have to be told that a warrior's lot is equally hard! A warrior forsakes the comfort of his home and family, never knowing whether he will return or pour the river of his life-blood upon some strange and foreign shore. A warrior lives with pain and hunger and scarcity—sleeping on the cold ground, slogging through swamps, fighting for every morsel of food he gets . . . then sating the eagles with his own flesh when he falls in battle."

There was a clamor of shouting as the warriors of Borger's *hird* lurched to their feet and hurried to array themselves at her back . . . a display of solidarity with the one who defended them and their difficult lot. They stuck out their grizzled chins and jabbed angry fingers at the women across the way, grumbling and snarling as their male pride was unleashed by her fiery words.

"A warrior protects and defends . . . subdues and claims," she declared, bolstered by the long-sought support of her fellow warriors. "It is a warrior's daring and might which win honor and substance for his family. The right to good land, a share of raid-spoils, the right to speak and be heard— all are bought with the dew of his wounds!"

Tumult broke out behind her as the warriors gyrated angrily and taunted and hurled long-nursed complaints against the women. Their grievances were answered in kind by the women's high, strident voices. And suddenly it seemed as if a lightning bolt had streaked through the hall, leaving the entire village charged, polarized—male against female; Christian against pagan; battle-maker against peace-weaver.

"Quit your godless warring," one woman shouted, "and stay at home to plant and reap your own crops—instead of stealing someone else's!" There was a howl of support from the other women.

"You'll take no more of my sons to die far from home on a heathen sword!" declared another.

"You'll not warm my furs again—fill my belly with yet another babe to lose and rue!"

"That will be no loss!" an angry husband countered. "There's scarce one night in a month I can pry those scrawny thighs apart now!"

"You with your holy-words and prattle of love and kindness—where is this *kindness* when your weary warriors return home in desperate need of rest and pleasure?" another charged. "All we hear is the nagging din of old crows."

"You enjoy the spoils of the raids well enough—silk-grabbers, wine-swillers, silver-snatchers! Where would you get your new brooches, your silk kirtle trims, your green and amber beads—if we did not go a'viking?"

Old Borger was wild with delight. He stood before his great chair with an ale horn clenched in his fingers, his body quivering, his eyes glistening. He loved nothing better than a good brawl, and one was certainly brewing here . . . The whole blessed village was about to erupt!

"See what you've started, Daughter of Mischief?" Jorund snarled at Aaren, flinging an arm toward the angry faces aligned in factions behind the two of them. The noise and confusion of the flying insults only heightened their conflict. "Are you so thirsty for the dew of wounds? Will nothing less than blood-letting satisfy you?"

"It is not blood I seek, it is honor . . . another thing you know nothing about!" She stalked closer to him, reading in his face his struggle to contain his mounting fury. "You with your shameless word-spinnings and slaverings and pawings—you tried to dishonor me, Woman-heart. You defamed my enchantment and my blade-skill, you abased me before my fellow warriors . . . then slunk about in secret to coax and cozen me with your pleasure-skill. No more, Woman-heart. Fight me! Fulfill your vow this night, or your people will know—as I do—that you never intend to fulfill it!"

"*Nej—nej!*" A ball of patched brown woolen came hurtling from the edge of the crowd. Brother Godfrey scrambled to a halt between Aaren and Jorund, his rotund form twisting frantically between them. "*Nej*— do not do this—I pray you! You must not fight!" He clasped his hands in desperate supplication to Aaren, then to Jorund. "It is not for men to fight with women—and the letting of blood in rage is wrong! It is a grave sin!"

"Who let him in here?" Borger bellowed, smashing his ale horn on the floor and lurching down from his high seat. "Out of the way, Christ-lover!" he roared, bashing a fist through the air. He'd never seen his son so wrought up— so perfectly and terrifyingly furious! And he wasn't about to let that cursed little Christian interfere with his pleasure. "Get out of my hall—out of my sight!"

But Godfrey defied Borger's wrath to seize Jorund's arm. The priest felt the tremors in Jorund's flexed and bulging muscles and stared up at his molten blue eyes. He flew into full panic; Jorund was fast slipping past the realm of self-control. "My friend, I beg you! Remember

what our Lord says—seventy times seven you must forgive—"

Aaren had never seen Jorund so roused, so angry—like
a terrifying storm about to break. Her legs went strangely
weak. The tumult in her—anger, regret, anticipation, and
dread—wadded itself into her throat as she watched the
priest trying to reason with Jorund, to dissuade him. Jorund
tore his gaze from her to look at Brother Godfrey with
his jaw clenched and his chest heaving. And she knew
that unless she did something—gave him one last push—
he might yet slip away from her.

"Wolf-tamer!" she called to him, measuring the distance
to her blade as she strode to the side of the hearth. Her fists
clenched and her face burned. The noise in the hall dropped
precipitously as her voice claimed everyone's attention,
even Jorund's. The rage in his eyes took her breath away.
She braced defiantly and raised her chin.

"They say you pulled the she-wolf's fangs." She planted
her fists at her waist and sneered: "Well, I say this little
priest and his White Christ have pulled yours! They've
turned you into a cursed Christian *cheek-turner!*"

He was so near the edge, his control so precarious—of
all the insults she might have dealt him, that particular
one hit dead-on, in the center of his heart. His control
snapped.

Shock exploded through the hall like a lightning strike as
he bashed Godfrey aside and launched himself at her. She
saw him coming but only had time to take a step or two
before he slammed into her, engulfing and carrying her to
the hard-packed floor with him. Their fall sent some women
and warriors scrambling out of the way, some straining
closer.

She was knocked breathless for a moment, but as she
felt Jorund's weight bearing down on her, she began to
struggle. She writhed and grappled beneath him, but he
quickly snagged her wrists and pinned them to the floor
by her head. Then he trapped her dangerous legs with
his and managed to contain their powerful lashing. He
lay on top of her, his great muscles straining as he
struggled with her. His face loomed over hers, looking

savage and foreign, burning with both hunger and retribution.

"You'll pay for this, Woman-heart—"

"Silence, witch!" he snarled. "I pleasure you with my tongue, and you flay me with yours! Well, no more! It is time to end this madness."

"Yea," she panted, twisting and jerking beneath him, "finish it! Take up your blade and fight me!"

"There's but one blade I'll ever take to you, She-wolf." He ground his pelvis hard against hers. "And I'll do it here and now—and disprove your cursed enchantment once and for all!"

The weight of his body, the heat of his breath on her face—harsh parodies of tenderer pleasures—sent pain through her heart even as his words sent panic through her mind.

"Yea, Woman-heart," she choked out with the last bit of defiance she could muster. "Wield your flesh-blade against me if you dare—for in truth it is the only blade you know how to wield!"

His mouth came down on hers, crushing, commanding, and no matter how she arched her back and jerked her head she could not dislodge it, or dispel the bitter taste of panic rising up her throat. She had pushed too hard, too far . . . it was going all wrong!

"*Nej*, Jorund!" Godfrey rushed to them and began to pull at Jorund's tunic, then at his arm, which held Aaren's wrist in a punishing grip. "For the Almighty's sake," the little priest choked out, "do not do this thing—I pray you! Do not disgrace her or yourself with this sin born of anger! Please, Jorund—no!"

"Get him!" Borger bellowed. "Get that sniveling holy-worm away from my son!" When there was a stunned pause, he charged in to pull Godfrey from Jorund's shoulder himself. The violent motion thawed some of his frozen warriors and they rushed to his aid. But it took Borger and three of his battle-seasoned men to pry away the tenacious priest. And when they did break Godfrey free, he struggled with the strength of four ordinary men, grappling and shouting to Jorund as they dragged him away.

"Haul his holy arse out of my hall—lock him in the storehouse!" Borger ordered, spitting in disgust, then turning in lusty expectation to the heaving, tussling pair at his feet.

But the damage had already been done. Godfrey's frenzied pleas had somehow penetrated the pounding of blood in Jorund's head. The force of his mouth on hers, the harsh pressure of his body against hers, the churning, violent heat in his stomach and limbs felt foreign, unnatural to him. And as soon as that feeling lodged securely, the full impact of what he intended finally righted itself in his mind. He was set to take her—there—on the spot! Deeply shaken, he dragged his mouth from hers and stared down into her face . . . as if awakening in a strange place . . . in a stranger's body.

Beneath him, Aaren's eyes were defiant yet oddly luminous, haunting. In their depths he caught a glimpse of deep emotion—regret, perhaps, or sorrow, or even a twinge of fear. It was so fleeting he could not capture or name it, but it did its work on him all the same. As the harsh dominance of his body over hers eased, her resistance eased as well, and her straining slowed, then ceased.

They lay together in that taut, volatile pose, panting, painfully aware of the heat and passion coiled between them. For a long moment they searched each other, both realizing how close they had come. But only Jorund understood how far they had yet to go. And he knew instinctively that they would never close the distance between them here, while Borger and the rest of the village looked on.

When he levered up onto his arms above her, there were gasps—which turned to groans of disappointment and disgust as he shoved to his feet. Somewhere in the distance he heard old Borger's wail of disappointment: "What's wrong with you, boy? Get back down there and finish it!" A hue and cry went up as he stood astride her, his chest heaving, his eyes narrowed with determination. But the howls of protest changed abruptly to puzzled muttering as he bent and hauled her up with him.

While she scrambled for both dignity and footing, he snatched up her heavy braid and pulled it over his shoulder, shoving his way through the parting crowd toward the door. Outraged, she squealed and struggled and stumbled at his back. But reeling along behind him, being dangled and dragged by her own hair, allowed her no chance to plant her feet or strike a blow at him, much less free herself.

He hauled her by the hair of her head through the hall and outside into the cold night air, bellowing: "Rope—I need rope—and plenty of it!"

The stunned villagers joined their jarl in charging out the doors after Jorund and Aaren, and in a flash, Garth and Brun were running for the smithy and lengths of rope stored there. The rest of the crowd gathered close to watch, some shocked, some titillated, others bewildered by the twists and turns of events.

"And horses!" Jorund bellowed above her furious screeches. Several young warriors went running toward the stable. "And food—provisions to last a month or more—quickly!" Helga led a knot of women scurrying to the jarl's small hearth and storehouse. Borger seized the sense of his son's orders and wheeled on Hrolf the Elder, who stood closest to him.

"And swords—fetch both his and hers from the hall— quickly!" he bellowed.

When the rope appeared, Jorund swung Aaren around by her braid, catching her feet with his and toppling her. She fell smack on her rear, and he was astride her in a flash, corralling her wrists and binding them while she writhed and bucked and called down every foul and hideous fate she could imagine onto his head.

"Curse your eyes—you'll regret this, Woman-heart!" she ground out, knifing her legs up beneath him.

"No doubt I will!" he agreed, dodging one of her lethal knees, then dropping his full weight on her legs to flatten them while he coiled the rope around her shoulders and bound her arms securely to her sides.

"I'll have your blood on my blade by morning—I swear it!" she shouted, trying desperately to kick as he slid back on her legs and slipped a second rope beneath her knees.

"Take a lesson from my fate, Serricksdotter," he muttered, panting as he subdued her thrashing feet. "What you vow in haste . . . you always rue at leisure."

The villagers' gasps and murmurs turned to snickers and bemused laughter at the battle-maid's predicament. By sheer overpowering might of muscle, Jorund had managed to bind her arms and legs securely, and when the horses were brought, he hoisted her and dropped her face down across one saddle, securing her with a rope and delivering a smack on her buttocks. *"Owww!"* Her angry wail trailed off into threats and growls of protest which made the horse dance skittishly and show white around its eyes. Jorund climbed on his own massive mount and donned his fleece-lined jerkin as the women tied the bags of provisions and rolled blankets on behind him. His mount pranced nervously as he reined it in and cast a determined glare at Aaren, then at his people.

"I am taking her to my *shieling* . . . up in the mountains," he declared over Aaren's frantic gasps and growls. "And I swear by Godfrey's Heaven that neither of us will be seen in this village again . . . *until I have tamed and mated Odin's She-wolf!*"

A cheer went up as he gave his mount the heel and rode off into the woods with Aaren jostling along behind. Borger whooped and bellowed with pride at the promising display of raw male power he had just witnessed in his offspring. "Did you see that, Forkbeard?" he demanded, all but felling the old warrior with a forceful clap on the back. "He'll have her defeated and on her back before the month is out—mark my word!"

He was so busy crowing about his cleverness that at first he didn't notice the ring of men gathering around Miri and Marta. With the battle-maiden out of the way, his warriors were anxious to get on with the disposition of her toothsome sisters.

"I've had a loin-ache since the night I first laid eyes on the pair of them," the Freeholder announced, leering hotly at Miri and sending her shrinking back against Marta.

"Hold, Freeholder—that maid is mine!" Garth jolted forward, his chin jutting and his fists drawn back. Shoving and grappling ensued until the fracas finally drew Borger's attention.

"What is this?" Borger bashed his way through the crowd to insert himself into the fray. His burly strength sent both Garth and the Freeholder hurtling back into the hands of their fellows.

"Freeholder thinks to take himself a *bride*, now that the battle-maid is gone!" Garth snarled, lunging against Brun's and Erik's restraint.

It was all Borger needed to hear. He cast a nasty glare around the circle of his sons and warriors, reading in their dusky faces the lingering blood-heat roused by the *flyting* and by Jorund's near taking of the Valkyr's daughter before their very eyes.

"Hear me well, you slavering pack of hounds!" He swaggered toward Miri and Marta, then pivoted and spread himself between them and his men. "There will be no more talk of brides or marriage, or even of sharing furs with these maids until Jorund or the battle-maid—or the pair of them—returns. Then and only then can I be sure the enchantment is well broken and that the gods will not take vengeance on me for defying them! And if I catch any man touching them before that day—I'll geld him with my own two hands! I swear it!"

The men lowered their eyes resentfully and grumbled, but none challenged the old jarl's will. After a long, tense moment, they began to disperse, heading back into the hall to drown themselves in ale. The women withdrew as well, dragging their shawls and mantles closer about them as they hurried off to their solitary pallets.

Soon only Miri and Marta and Garth and Brun Cinderhand remained in the cold moonlight. Brun looked to Marta with a hungry-calf sort of look on his broad, square features, but she lowered her eyes, squeezed her sister's hand, and turned away toward the women's house. Brun let out a heavy breath, then turned back toward the hall, leaving Garth and Miri alone on the broad, frosty plain.

"I . . . I would know, little Miri . . ." Garth shifted feet and swallowed against the tightening in his throat. "Would you . . . do you mind that I . . . claim you?"

Miri's heart fluttered and her eyes warmed, becoming like balmy summer sky. "It is bold of you to speak so,

Garth Borgerson. And I admire boldness." The relief in his face was short-lived. "But I do not know whether I would like sharing furs with a man I have never touched."

He stiffened, searching her sweet face with mounting turmoil. Then she reached through the stillness, extended her hand, and he quickly enveloped it with his bigger, warmer one. At the contact, the tension in her shoulders melted and a smile of wonder crept over her countenance. He felt reassuringly solid and smooth and warm . . . so very warm in the chilled night air. A powerful new longing rose within her.

"How bold are you, Garth Borgerson?" she whispered. "Bold enough to hold me with more than a hand?" Heat flared in his eyes at her unexpected challenge and he pulled her to him . . . wrapping her with his strong arms, folding her to his hardened warrior's frame.

It was like sinking into a mountain hot-spring . . . feeling his presence lapping around her, his warmth invading her garments, and his strength claiming her. She melted against him, nuzzling her cheek against the coarse woolen of his tunic and the smooth leather of his jerkin, and sliding her arms around his waist. It was wonderful, having Garth's body pressed tautly to hers . . . all she had hoped . . . and so much more.

They stood embracing, silent. Then Miri raised her face to his in helpless wonder, and ran her tongue along the groove of her lips, staring at his. The sight galvanized Garth and for the first time in his manly life, he was seized with the desire to merge his mouth with a woman's. He held his breath and lowered his mouth onto hers.

It was soft and moist and sweet—so incredibly sweet. It was like honey-cakes . . . like sips of Frankish wine. The pleasure-shock radiated along his nerves and rattled his very sinews. By the time he raised his head, he could scarcely see. He was drunk with the taste and feel of her. It took a full minute to realize she was slipping from his arms. He staggered, then planted his feet and focused on her.

Her eyes were shining and she had caught her reddened lower lip between her teeth. When he made a move toward her, she jerked back a step and whirled—running for the women's house. He stood, roused and wanting, in the cold night. But after that first blast of disappointment faded, he began to grin. She wanted him. He drew a deep breath and turned back to the hall, fingering his newly sensitive lips, his heart soaring like a nighthawk on the wind. On the wings of his thoughts, he sent Jorund all the help the gods of Asgard might be willing to spare. Halfway to the hall, he paused and cast a glance up at the night sky.

"And you, White Christ—wherever you are. Your friend Jorund could use your help, too."

Much later, deep into the night, Marta crept from her pallet in the darkened women's house and donned her thick woolen cloak. Slipping out the door, she hurried toward the long hall, pausing in the moon-shadows to search the commons and the buildings around her for signs of others who might be abroad at such a late hour. The quiet extended, unbroken, and she hurried on to tug open the massive door of the hall and dart inside. The great iron hinge creaked and she froze, scarcely breathing as she lowered her hood and glanced about at the limp and snoring forms of the warriors and villagers that littered the benches and floor.

Most of the torches had sputtered out, but there was still enough light to see Leif Gunnarson propped against the wall on his mat of straw, beneath the ragged fleece she had found for him. His shaggy head was leaned back against the wall and his eyes were closed, but as she stole closer, his eyes opened and fixed on her as if he had heard and tracked her movements from the moment she entered the hall. He did not move a muscle.

"What are you doing here?" he said quietly.

"I . . . I don't . . ." Her throat tightened as she looked into those clear gray eyes that seemed to see into her very heart. She didn't know why she had come . . . except that there was an ache in her heart and she felt a compelling urge to be near him and to have him look at her the way he was now.

"Go away, little Marta," he said with an odd huskiness to his voice.

"But I . . ." She couldn't swallow, could scarcely speak. Tears welled in her eyes, turning them into shimmering pools in the dim light. For days now, he had demanded she leave him alone, had rebuffed her kindnesses, and met her brave mien and even temper with unrelenting disdain. But there was always something in the way he looked at her—an ill-hidden longing, a tender edge to his gruffness—that tugged at her heart. And it was to that hint of protectiveness, to that suggestion of wanting, that she instinctively turned tonight, as her fears overcame her.

"Did you see what happened to my sister Aaren?" she whispered, her voice clogged with unshed tears.

"I saw." His eyes traveled gently over her pale face and silky hair.

"I am afraid for her." Tears spilled down her cheeks and her chin quivered. She suddenly felt empty, standing there, needing something she didn't understand from a man who seemingly had nothing to give her.

Leif watched his curvy and courageous little keeper—the solace and the torment of his captivity—struggling to control her tears, and his whole being was thrown into turmoil. He was torn between his desire to comfort her and his desire to protect her, between his raging need for her gentle strength and his dread certainty that he would only cause her heartache. It took all of his self-possession to force his body to remain still; he had no strength left to guard his tongue.

"If your sister has but a small part of your courage, Little One, she is in no danger."

Marta held her breath as she searched his taut features, sensing how fiercely he held himself in check. She shook her head slowly, her eyes luminous and haunting. "I am not brave, Leif Gunnarson. I must not be—for I am afraid of what will happen to us all."

The sight of her standing there, overcome by tears, struck the final blow in his battle against his own desires. He flung the fleece aside. Two crouching steps were all his chains would allow—but they were enough. He hovered over her, straining at the ends of his bonds, and raised one huge, battle-hardened hand to wipe away her tears. His touch only seemed to produce more tears, and he groaned and cupped her face between his hands.

"Little Marta, do not cry," he said hoarsely, running his callused thumbs back and forth over her soft cheeks. When she looked up at him with that awful blend of misery and maiden-hunger in her eyes, he felt as if he'd taken a battle-blow to the chest . . . he could scarcely draw breath. When she leaned toward him, he just managed to grab her shoulders and push her back to arm's length. His heart pounded and his gut churned.

"Do not come any closer," he said. When she raised her quivering chin and pressed against his restraining hands, opening her arms to him, he groaned and gave her a shake. There were pride-battles and blood-feuds and long-nursed hatreds between their people . . . there would be only pain and dishonor for her if she was caught with him. He stared at her, wanting yet fearing to want her . . . unable to send her away yet unable to draw her close.

"I am a captive in your jarl's hall," he said in a tortured voice. "Who knows when the ransom may come . . . my father is not so rich as Borger."

She answered with her eyes. They shone defiantly through her tears.

"Do you not see, Little Maid?" He gave the chain weighting his arm an agonized shake. "I cannot even stand straight before you."

"You stand taller in your chains than most men do in their freedom," she whispered. And the longing that filled her sweet face battered the last of his will to resist. His voice was choked as he uttered one last, feeble objection.

"I . . . have fleas."

Marta smiled through her tears as she slipped through his hands and pressed close, invading his arms and capturing his warrior's heart.

"Then I will soon have them, too."

By moonlight, Jorund guided his great Norman horse along the familiar trails leading up into the high reaches of the densely forested hills. The rhythmic, muffled thud of hooves kept the passage of time as they left the village far behind and entered a frost-kissed realm of stark moon-silver and night-shadows. The barren trees rustled as they passed, like the old Sisters of Fate, the Norns, gossiping over their time-spinning and fate-weaving . . . trading whispers of portent on the night breeze.

Again and again, he turned in his saddle to search Aaren's bobbing, silent form, welcoming the cold night air into his lungs and overheated thoughts. He had acted on pure instinct, overpowering and carrying her away, and now was somewhat unnerved by his violent response to her challenge and by the potent male pleasure he felt at having conquered her. It had never been his way to force a woman, but Aaren Serricksdotter pulled passions from him he had never experienced before . . . some exhilarating, some tantalizing . . . and some disturbing.

As they rode along, he considered what lay ahead for them and realized that his brash demonstration of power would have consequences . . . probably volatile ones. If the past was any guide, she would be bruised and pride-sore and blood-letting furious by the time they reached his lodge in the mountains . . . just itching for another confrontation. She would snap and snarl like a cornered she-wolf, and he would have to begin the taming process all over again. He let his eyes roam the provocative curve of her upturned buttocks, recalling her helplessly sensual responses, reliving the way she had responded to his gentling touch. And he expelled his lingering tension on a long breath, and began to smile.

When they were well into the forest, he stopped the horses and dismounted, untying her from the saddle and hoisting her onto his shoulder, then lowering her to the ground. She moaned, rousing as he laid her in a pile of leaves at the side of the trail and untied her legs.

"Hold still, Serricksdotter," he said, grappling with her wriggling feet. "I'm only rubbing some of the feeling back into your legs." He paused at her strangled gasp of disbelief and gazed down at her. "Unless you'd rather I did more . . ."

When she glared at him, he smiled.

"Not speaking to me, are you?" He made a "tsk-ing" sound. "You were not so word-scanty a while ago, my haughty she-wolf."

She levered up onto one elbow as he exchanged one foot for the other and gave it a thorough rubbing, which soothed the throbbing. But her relief evaporated when he dragged her to her feet and hoisted her over his shoulder again. An instant later she found herself plopped upright onto her horse, then repositioned astride it.

"Behave yourself," he ordered, seizing her foot and wrestling it back down when she tried to swing it up and over the saddle. "Or you go right back over the saddle." Then he picked up the reins and led the horse to his own, where he seized his own reins and began to lead them at a walk.

"Are you not curious about where I'm taking you?"

She refused to answer.

"Since you asked so sweetly," he declared, with a nod to her narrowed eyes and stony countenance. "To my *shieling*—in the mountains. It is a small summer lodge I built with my own two hands. I've never taken a woman there before."

"You're not taking one now," she gritted out, furious that he'd overpowered and shamed her—hauled her about like a bag of turnips before the entire village! "You're taking a *she-wolf*, remember?"

He paused, flashed her an infuriating smile that claimed her response as a victory, and continued, both walking and talking. "It's a tight little log hut—built into the side of a cliff overlooking a small meadow. In summer there are berries everywhere . . . and there's a rock spring for fresh water . . . and plenty of wood nearby . . . a winter's worth, if it comes to that." He glanced up at her with a questioning look and she returned a snarl.

"You may have pulled Rika's fangs, Wolf-lover," she warned, "but I still have mine. And if you come near me, I'll use them—I swear it!"

He smiled and strode on. "I have plenty of warm furs for sleeping . . . including some beautiful blue-silver fox pelts that I took on a journey into the far north country. Think of it, Long-legs . . . my warm, silky furs beneath your bare buttocks on a snowy winter's night . . ." She stiffened, feeling an ominous trickle of excitement from her stomach down toward those parts of her she dreaded awakening.

"You'll not strip my buttocks bare," she snapped. "Not without a loss of blood."

"There will be long nights ahead." He glanced up at her. "Long quiet nights . . . with only you and me beside a hot, crackling fire. I know how to set you ablaze, too, Long-legs. I'll start with kisses . . . long, slow, patient kisses . . . on your lips . . . your ears . . . your throat . . ."

"Come near my throat at the risk of your own, Borgerson," she threatened, outraged at his battle tactics and not a little aroused.

"A whole winter of long, sweet nights . . . lying side by side . . . and breast to breast, thigh to thigh. I'll feast on your skin and drink from your lips . . . rest in the valley of your breasts . . . wrap myself in the warmth of your thighs." His voice grew thick and sultry as he described the sensual tortures he had in mind for her. "And I'll make magic for you . . . conjure lightning and thunder inside your very body. Then after the pleasure-storm passes, I'll spin rainbows through your senses. Think of it, *Honey-maker*," he said with an irresistible grin.

This was a new and disturbing *flyting*—one in which her dire blood-threats were met with beguiling sensual promises. Alarming heat crept up her throat and into her cheeks as she found her ire softening, found herself sinking into his cunning word-snares. She lashed out in a near panic.

"Perhaps you do not know that bees and women have something in common besides *honey*, Woman-heart. We both have *stingers*," she declared fiercely. "And I am itching to use mine."

"Ummm . . ." He rubbed his chin and frowned. "I don't believe I've ever seen a woman's *stinger*, Long-legs." Brightening, he waggled his brows at her. "I can see this will be a most instructive winter. Let me guess . . ." He scratched his temple thoughtfully. "I know that bees bear their stingers in their *tails* . . ."

"Oh, you—" She groaned, struggling about on her seat, wrenching one leg up and over the saddle before he could stop her. But instead of the successful dismount and flight she expected, she found herself falling, and without the use of her arms to steady and balance herself, smacked the ground with her side. *"Aghhh!"* The horse shied and lurched forward, and Jorund grabbed the reins to halt it, then raced back to her and lifted her to her feet. Jamming his shoulder into her midsection, he hoisted her and carried her back to her mount.

"What's it to be, Long-legs?" he demanded, seemingly undaunted by her growls and struggles. "Fight and you ride on your belly. Cease fighting and you can ride on your buttocks." When her struggles slowed but did not cease, he added with a taunting pat: "Such handsome buttocks. It would be a shame to waste them."

She had no choice, she realized through the resurgent roar of blood in her head. He had the advantage and further resistance would only tax her strength and weaken her ability to fight later, when conditions were more in her favor. She surrendered and stilled, and soon found herself planted back in the saddle and being secured to it by a rope tether looped through her wrist bonds.

Chagrin doubled the angry heat under her skin and she jerked away from his grip, staring sullenly at the path ahead and refusing even to look at him.

Jorund's determined smile cooled a bit, but he would not be daunted by her angry withdrawal. He had expected her to be furious, had steeled himself to take her worst . . . and return only his seductive best. Sooner or later she would succumb to the pleasure he would make for her . . . and to her fate as a woman . . . *his* woman.

The night stretched on and the cold deepened. As the tension drained from her weary body, Aaren began to shiver. Jorund removed his fleece jerkin and draped it about her shoulders. When she shrugged it off, he grabbed her bound hands and held them with gentle force.

"Do not be foolish, Serricksdotter. It will be a long night. Take the warmth I offer."

For one long moment their gazes met and something in his compelling words sent a frisson of anxiety through her heart. She jerked her hands and her eyes away, but not in time to forestall a painful crush of longing in her chest.

After a while, she felt his warm fleece settling around her shoulders and she could not bring herself to reject it again, no matter how dangerous that warmth was to her warrior's heart.

Chapter Thirteen

The Sky-Traveler stood cold and bright above them the next day, when they reached the small mountain meadow where Jorund's *shieling* lay. The high country frosts and winds had already stripped the flat-leafed trees to spread a golden blanket over the ground. The short-grazed grasses in the meadow were brown, but all around were tall, stately spears of vivid green, the needle-leaf spruce and soft-limbed firs which soared to pierce the sky-vault itself. The sound of water rushing over rocks filled the silence.

Jorund rolled his aching shoulders and dismounted to lead both horses up a slope toward a steep cliff that rose high above the great firs. At the base of that smooth rock face nestled a modest log structure with a hewn cedar roof. As they approached, Aaren could see another, smaller hut tucked into the rocks, farther away. But before she could examine it or the brisk stream that wound down the rocks between the two structures, Jorund stopped the horses and pulled her from her horse to set her on her feet.

When she swayed, weak-kneed, he caught her against him and the contact with his warm, hard frame sent a shiver of alarm through her. She stiffened and pulled away, and he scowled.

"We're away from the village, Serricksdotter. Here there are no prying eyes or ears . . . no one to brandish your pride for. You can cease playing the warrior."

Aaren drew on her deepest reserves, sensing that whatever ground she surrendered to him now—even from fatigue—would be forever forfeit. "I am not *playing* the warrior, Borgerson," she said tersely. "I *am* a warrior."

After a long moment, he seized her shoulders and thrust her toward the small summer lodge. Swinging the low door open, he pushed her inside. When she straightened, she found that her head brushed the bottom of the roof beams, but the interior was considerably larger than it had seemed outside. By the light coming through the door, she could make out a wall formed by the cliff face, along the far side, and saw that a vertical channel had been hewn in the stone, leading upward to a smoke hole that admitted additional light. At the foot of that wall, a low, flat ledge ran the length of the lodge and in the middle of the ledge was a hollowed, blackened spot, directly beneath the channel—apparently a hearth. From the two side walls hung sleeping shelves and there was a rough cedar storage box built against the wall near the door.

"Over here." He pushed her toward the stone wall. "Sit." When she didn't comply, he seized her shoulders and forced her onto the ledge beside the hearth. She jerked her shoulders defiantly as she landed and she saw that his eyes narrowed and a muscle in his jaw flexed. He uncoiled the rope from her arms and shoulders, using it to tether her still tied hands to an iron ring imbedded in the stone beside the hearth. Then he stood over her with his hands on his hips, considering the ring, her bound hands, and the hostile look on her face.

"Still the warrior, Long-legs?"

"Yea, always a warrior, Woman-heart," she answered, testing her stiff arms and bracing for whatever the glint in his eye promised.

"Very well. Then I will treat you like a warrior." He abruptly dropped to his knees beside her and seized her legs, banding and dragging them against his side as he worked the lacings of her buskins. With her hands tied to the ring, she could only writhe and kick, uttering dire threats. But with a few deft movements he had ripped the laces from her sandal-boots and had her footgear wrenched from her wriggling feet. Next, he seized her leggings, unwrapped them, and tossed them onto the floor. Then, to her horror, he shifted and pulled on her legs so that she was stretched out along the stone shelf, lying with her hands bound by ropes above her head and her knees caught hard in his grip.

"No! Curse you, Borgerson! If Odin doesn't have your blood for this—I will!" she snapped, bucking and heaving with all her might as he attacked the ties of her breeches. He had her pinned on her back and was apparently bent on stripping her buttocks as well as her legs!

Curling his fingers over the waist of her breeches, he pulled and succeeded in baring one hip. Then he leaned his body across her knees, trapping her legs with his ribs, and used both hands to peel her breeches down her thighs. He paused and grinned when they reached her knees, letting his eyes roam her sleek, naked thighs and applying force with his body to roll her over so that he could scrutinize her bare buttocks. As she choked on her outrage, his grin broadened and he sought her gaze.

"No stinger," he pronounced solemnly.

"Ohhh! Wretch!" she exploded, arching violently—which only allowed him better access. In one coolly executed movement, he shoved to his feet and ripped her breeches from her, dangling them before her with a triumphant smile. She rolled onto her side and scrambled back on the cold, abrasive rock, pulling herself upright and dragging her legs beneath her, trying to shield herself with the meager tail of her tunic. "Give me back my clothes and boots, curse you!"

"You want to be treated like a warrior, Serricksdotter," he said with satisfaction. "Well, one of the perils of being a warrior—of which you spoke so knowledgeably—is being held captive in your enemy's camp. And one of the hazards of being a prisoner is being stripped to keep you from escaping, especially in cold weather." He bent to gather up her sandal-boots and leggings, wrapping them together with her breeches into a ball, which he stuffed under his arm. Then he ran a hot, appraising eye over her bare feet and up her long, naked legs.

"I need not tell you that without boots and breeches you would not last long in these cold forests. I have things to do—tend the horses, gather wood, find meat. These"—he held up her clothing—"will assure that you are here when I return." He turned away, then back, with a most reasonable and accommodating tone. "Any time you wish to be treated like a woman, instead of a warrior, I will gladly return your clothes and boots, Long-legs." He waited a moment for that to register and when he saw her face redden and her chest swell, he ducked outside.

"This is just like you, Woman-heart!" she shouted. "Low and cowardly . . . and despicable . . . and cruel . . ." The door slammed shut on her tirade and she heard the scrape of something being lodged against the door, trapping her in the chilled, darkened lodge.

She stared around the cabin in the dimness, then at the door, feeling angry and confused and oddly bereft that he'd stripped her and then just left her there. Chiding herself for her divided feelings, she seized her hotter emotions and used them to purge the others while she huddled close to the iron ring and drew her knees up, banding them with her arms. If he thought a little cold and nakedness would humble her . . . he was badly mistaken!

It was just past dark when Jorund returned. With only the heat of her burning pride for warmth, Aaren had steadily grown more chilled and miserable. Her muscles were drawn into hard knots, she seemed to have lost most of the feeling in her lower half, and her teeth chattered uncontrollably. During the long wait, she had seized each bit of discomfort to bolster her anger against Jorund, constructing flaming word-spears to hurl at him the moment he returned. But when the door opened, she jerked her head up from her knees and her burning arsenal of denouncements was drenched by a wave of relief. His arms were full of wood and provisions, and he seemed big and warm; the mere sight of him made her go limp inside. He paused inside the door, calling her name, but she couldn't seem to answer; the muscles in her throat suddenly seemed as frozen as the rest of her.

"Aaren? Come now . . . don't be so stubborn . . ." He stopped dead—staring at her balled, quaking form—and dumped everything in his arms onto the floor. In two strides he was beside her, kneeling on one knee by the stone ledge, feeling her chilled face and arms, running his hands down her lower legs to her icy feet.

"You're half frozen," he said grimly.

"I'm f-f-fine, B-Borgerson," she croaked, trying to jerk away from his hands, and failing.

He scowled and ripped his fleece jerkin from his shoulders and wrapped it around her legs. Without another word, he hurried across the lodge to rummage in the cedar box for oil and a wick to fill the hanging lamp . . . then carried the wood and tinder back to the stone hearth beside her and began to build a fire.

After the first shock of his return, she tried desperately to resurrect her ire and to pretend that her legs weren't cramping and her bare bottom wasn't numb and that she didn't feel small and wretched and humiliated. But all her efforts were increasingly undercut by the warmth that lingered in his garment and the fledgling heat of the fire he was nursing to flame, both of which only seemed to make her quake more. She clamped her teeth together, praying that she wouldn't make a complete fool of herself.

When the fire was well caught and crackling, he freed her from the iron ring and began to lift her onto the floor by the hearth. She insisted on moving on her own, but stumbled and slid to her knees before the fire. As his warm hands untied the knots and gently massaged her bruised wrists and cold hands, she searched for a bit of protest inside her and found none. He worked his hands up her arms, then along her shoulders, rubbing warmth back into them with smooth, circular motions. And as his touch restored warmth and feeling to her icy frame, it also worked a broadening charm on her senses. Her shivering slowed to small, lingering tremors that had less and less to do with cold.

"I did not intend to leave you alone so long. I would have been back earlier," he said, sliding his hands up the sides of her neck, "but I had to unload, then repair the pole shed for the horses. And it took a while to set a snare and take a rabbit . . ."

The golden glow of the fire set warm lights in his eyes as he caressed his way down her shoulders and sides, until he reached her hips. His hands paused, holding her, as he sought her eyes. "I did not mean to hurt you." He shifted back onto his knees and pulled her feet onto his lap, holding them for a moment before massaging her toes, the arches of her feet, then her ankles. "Just like a woman." He grinned. "Women always have cold feet."

Her very senses began to melt beneath his warm ministrations. He raised a quizzical brow to her and his handsome lips moved. It took a moment for her to right the sounds in her head.

"And do you know why?" he had asked.

"W-why what?" she mumbled, losing her flow of thought in the shimmering pools of his eyes.

"Why women always have cold feet," he prompted.

She blinked, then shook her head, bewildered by the question, since she hadn't been minding his words.

"It's because all the warmth in a woman goes to her heart," he said quietly. His hands stilled, splayed on her bare thighs and pouring heat into them, as his tone wrapped around her senses like a blanket. "You have a warm heart, too, Long-legs. I've seen it in your eyes. I've felt it beating next to mine." He slid one hand up her thigh, then lifted it to her chest as he sought her wide, wondering eyes. When she did not move, he pressed his hand over her heart and slid his fingers downward, between the stiff edge of her breastplate and the yielding softness of her breast.

"Such stout armor"—his whisper caressed her—"must protect something very soft."

She wrapped a hand around his wrist, but in truth, she was not sure whether it was meant as a rejection or a claiming. It was only when his hand moved to deepen that possession that she came out of her trance and used her grip to thrust him away. That movement broke the spell and brought her vulnerable position crashing back to her.

She scrambled back shakily and summoned a glare. "Keep your hands to yourself, Borgerson," she said hoarsely. "I've warned you."

He studied the spark in her eyes and the burst of color under her cheekbones and smiled, seeming perversely pleased by her revived spirits.

"Yes, you did. Now what was it you promised me?" A wicked glint came into his eyes as he leaned toward her on one arm. "Oh, yes. Something about my throat . . ."

He tugged at the ties at the top of his tunic and lay his corded neck and the top of his shoulder bare . . . offering her the sleek, bronzed skin of his throat and his visibly throbbing pulse.

"It's yours, She-wolf," he said huskily. "Anytime you want it."

The temptation to seize him and bury her mouth in that seductive curve hit her like a rogue sea wave, staggering her. She panicked and hit him back with her palms, sending him rolling onto his rear. "Stay away from me, Woman-heart!" she demanded.

He sat for a moment in his graceful sprawl before a knowing grin spread over his face, then he rolled to his feet and began to unpack the provisions, placing them on shelves above the great cedar box built into the wall.

Aaren pushed stiffly to her feet, tugging her tunic down over her hips and eyeing the door. Even if she made it outside and managed to find the horses, it was dark and she still had no boots, no breeches, and no idea where they were or how to get back to the village. She was trapped here. Captive in her enemy's camp. Prisoner to a man who wouldn't fight . . . but had just managed to storm and conquer both her body and her senses.

She sank down onto the stone ledge near the fire, shaken by his demonstration of power over her. Her obligations to her sisters' welfare, to their enchantment, and to her own warrior's honor were sacred to her. But all he had to do was look at her with those soft blue eyes, extend his hand to her, spin a few silken words . . . and she forgot both her honor and her enchantment. She held her cold, stiff hands out to the fire. For all his gentleness, Jorund Borgerson was the most dangerous man she knew.

"Here you are, Serricksdotter." She raised her gaze to find him presenting her with the carcass of a skinned hare and an iron rod on which to spit it. "A prime, fat one. I caught it . . . you can cook it."

"In a sow's eye, Borgerson," she declared, huddling back on her seat. "I'll not work over the hearth like a *woman* for you." He studied her angry pose, then shrugged and proceeded to prepare their meal himself.

*   *   *

After eating, he reached into the storage chest for a great bundle of furs, which he unrolled with a flourish. She eyed that warm, inviting stack—some so lush and silvery that they looked blue in the firelight—and felt the rise of temptation in her loins once more. To counter it, she expelled a harsh breath and glowered at him.

"Only one set of furs, Long-legs. But it is plenty big enough for two," he said, raising an eyebrow suggestively.

"Share your furs like a woman? Like one of your *many* women?" she announced with exaggerated disdain. "I'd rather freeze."

His eyes narrowed briefly, but then he snuffed the wick in the hanging bowl lamp. He dragged the pallet in front of the door and crawled into his furs alone, propping his arms behind his head. As the fire settled into red-glowing coals and the light lowered, his breathing slowed to a steady rhythm and she guessed he was quickly asleep.

Sliding back up onto the ledge by the fire, she tucked her knees under her chin and snuggled her toes as close to the coals as she could. She dropped her head against the cool stone at her shoulder, fighting the emotion rising in her chest and crowding into her throat. His words echoed in her ears: *such stout armor must protect something very soft.* She understood now, he had not been speaking of her body alone. He had sensed her struggle to both contain and shield her softer self behind that inner wall inside her. And he had devised the perfect strategy for breaching it . . . letting his tenderness call to hers, rousing her gentler feelings against her, using them to storm the fortifications of her heart from inside as well as out.

A pricking began in the corners of her eyes and she squeezed them shut. But as she wrestled with her stubborn feelings, the tears surged and began to slide down her cheeks.

She was at war with herself. One moment she snapped in anger, the next she sighed with longing; one minute she was vengeful, the next she was sick with regret. With one breath she blew hot; the next, cold—it was like chills and fevers in her very soul.

She swiped at her tears and settled her gaze on him, feeling a deep, painful stirring within her. For the first time in her memory she was truly afraid. What would happen to her at this man's hands? Each time he touched her, or stroked her with his words, she could feel her warrior's heart fraying a bit more at the edges, unraveling inside her. What would she be if it came completely undone? What good was a warrior with a heart that had come unstrung?

The crackle of flame brought Jorund wide awake the next morning and he started up . . . to find Aaren perched on the edge of the hearth with his fleece jerkin over her knees, feeding small twigs and bark to a fragile flame. He smiled and dropped back on his elbows, relishing the sight of her and studying the care with which she nurtured that developing heat. When the first small log was securely caught, she glanced up and found him watching her. Their gazes locked and she tensed, coming visibly to the edge of her nerves again.

"That was helpful of you . . . starting the morning fire," he said, stretching his long legs and arms, then arching his back.

"I was cold," she responded, tearing her eyes from the display he was making of his muscular male frame.

"Then perhaps if you grow hungry enough, you'll tend a cook-pot as well," he teased. She was not amused.

"I want my clothes," she declared flatly. "You have no right to keep me here like this."

"I have every right, Serricksdotter," he countered, sitting up. "According to your code, my might gives me the right. Unless you are strong enough to defeat me, I have the right to do whatever I want with you." His mouth took on a wry cant. "Is that not the way of the warrior?"

"The way of the warrior is to honor a worthy opponent, to respect him," she answered, her voice strained. "To respect *her*." Tiny flames at the backs of her eyes flared. "You dishonor me, Borgerson . . . whether you think me a warrior or a woman."

"And just how have I dishonored you, Serricksdotter?" he demanded, shoving to his feet and towering over her.

His features lost their just-wakened softness. "Do I dishonor you with my teasing words . . . with the way I fondle and adore your body . . . with the way I hold my temper when you swagger and boast and goad me with your warrior nonsense? Do I dishonor you with my desire to hold you, or with the pleasure I stir in your loins, or with the joy I take in simply watching you move?" He stalked closer, his eyes hot and his tone fraying with frustration.

"Why is it honorable of me to fight you with a blade and possibly kill you . . . but dishonorable of me to try to love you with my body?"

He stared down into her face, sorting through the jumble of emotions he glimpsed in her and willing her to understand the destructiveness of her warrior illusions. But as the pull of wanting deepened within him, he watched her confusion being replaced by pained determination.

"Why can you not see that in mocking my warrior-hood and my enchantment . . . you mock my honor, my very heart?" she said with a tremor in her voice. "And as long as you refuse to defend your honor and respect mine, I cannot prize being joined to you. There would be no honor and thus no pleasure in our mating . . . not as long as I am a *she-wolf* and you are a *woman-heart*."

The muscles in his face worked visibly, then he drew a deep, irritable breath and wheeled to retrieve her garments and boots from the storage box. He tossed them at her feet, lifted the bar at the door, and strode out into the frigid morning air.

She sagged to a seat by the fire, staring after him, feeling drained and shamed by her own impulses, and confused. She had lied just now, she realized . . . or at least part of her had. Part of her didn't want to mate with a man who had no pride or honor, but part of her desperately wanted the tenderness and passion he stirred in her. Honor and dishonor, fighting and loving . . . wretched Odin must be delirious over the success of his revenge.

Pushing those plaguing thoughts to the back of her mind, she dressed hurriedly, then slipped out the door. Before she had taken two steps, his hand clamped on her arm.

"Where do you think you are going?"

"Women and warriors alike have morning needs, Borgerson."

He looked a bit chastened, then nodded and led her to the shelter of the trees. When she was finished, he took her by the arm and led her across the stream and up the slope to the other hut. It was a bathing hut, built over a rock spring that trickled slowly from the side of the cliff on its way to join the larger stream. There was a wide wooden bench, a small oven for heating rocks, and a clear pool hollowed out of natural stone. He allowed her to wash, as he had done, then escorted her back to the lodge. When they were safely inside, he released her arm, but did not move away at once. She felt his gaze on her and stiffened.

"Let me go," she said calmly. "Let me return to my sisters . . . to the village."

"I cannot." He searched the tension in her face. "There is much to settle between us. And I have sworn that neither of us will return until it is done."

"It can be quickly settled," she insisted. "Just pick up a blade and prepare to fight."

"Do you not see that what we must settle requires far more than just the spilling of blood?"

His words sent a slither of anxiety through her. She couldn't listen to such talk.

"You—you're just afraid to raise a blade against me," she charged, scrambling to find a footing in outraged pride. But the minute her barb struck, she wished to recall it. He blanched and his jaw clamped and the muscles worked tautly beneath his skin.

"Yes, I am afraid!" he declared fiercely. "Afraid of hurting you." Her heart hovered and quivered strangely in her breast, as if uncertain how fast to beat. He was afraid *for* her? That was the one thing she hadn't expected to hear.

"I don't want to hurt you, Aaren." His features tightened and his eyes grew strangely luminous. Suddenly she could read them the way she always felt he read her own. She glimpsed the need, the wanting, and the pain within him. And she saw there was more . . . so much more that she did not understand in the depths of his matchless eyes. It took her breath. He was summoning forth the woman in her;

tenderness seeking tenderness, need calling to need. For a brief moment, her confusion, her own woman's longings, were visible in her face.

"Fight me, Jorund," she whispered, entreating him with all her heart. And he answered from the depths of his.

"I am fighting you."

His penetrating gaze drove his meaning into her very bones. He was indeed fighting her . . . with kindness and pleasure, gentleness and promise . . . all the things a woman's heart must desire and a warrior's heart must scorn. And the success of his chosen arms—his *weapons of the heart*—was evident in her growing desire for him and in her waning desire to fight him. Panic collected in her stomach as she felt another of her heart-strings unraveling. She lurched back, her look of longing turning visibly to contempt.

He watched the change of her expression and felt the woman he had touched so fleetingly sliding out of his grasp. The pain of her withdrawal was so sharp that it set off a defensive explosion in him . . . full, gut-roiling, limb-quaking fury. With his last bit of reason, he realized he had to get out of there, away from her, before he did exactly what she wanted . . . what he dreaded with all his being. He snatched up his fleece jerkin and slammed out into the frigid sunshine.

But the contempt he had seen in her face had not been for him; it had been for her own weakening.

She stared at the door, still seeing his swollen shoulders and the pained anger in his face. It was a long moment before she realized that she was seeing the meadow as well, and the trees around it. The door was open—he had forgotten to bolt her inside!

Her heart skipped a beat as she rushed to the door and peered outside. She was frantic to flee both him and the sense of shame temptation created in her, and after a moment's indecision, she rushed to the storage bin and rummaged through it until she located an extra tunic and a small eating knife that had been stowed in the bag of provisions. She quickly donned the garment for added warmth and tucked the small knife in the empty loop at her waist. Then with a last, quick glance around, she darted out the door and made a run for the trees.

Jorund climbed quickly up the steep slope at the side of the cliff, using the exertion to spend the anger in his body. Each jabbing foothold, each fierce grasp of a rock or root vented a small part of the frustration coursing in his blood. He gritted his teeth and snarled wordless curses as he stumbled on loose rocks and felt dried branches clutching at his arms and shoulders. When he stumbled onto the top of the cliff overlooking the meadow, he set his hands at his waist and threw his head back as if to inhale some of the blue from the sky.

Then he closed his eyes and saw her face as it had been: soft with longing and hard with contempt. She roused and angered and entranced and tempted him as no other woman in his life had been able to do. Each time he confronted her, he felt himself losing ground to his own volatile impulses. It frightened him . . . this raw, animal spirit prowling his insides . . . watchful, waiting for his control to slip . . . straining to unleash his strongest and most destructive urges.

He shuddered and drew breath after cold breath, until he felt the fever in his blood subside. Then he opened his eyes and raised his head, searching the great mountain tops around him for perspective. There was more than just pleasure or control, or even a clash of beliefs involved here; he had to be patient and slow to anger. He dipped his gaze just then and caught a movement in the meadow below. His senses came alert, focusing on a blur of white with a dark ribbon whipping around it. Suddenly there were shoulders and arms and a braid . . . legs working. Aaren! But the very moment he recognized her, she was swallowed up by the trees.

He exploded to life, racing for the steep slope. "I must have left the damned door open!" He slid and stumbled down the rocky mountainside, whipping scratchy limbs aside and jumping over boulders. He swore quietly, berating himself for not keeping her tied or hobbled a while longer.

The moment his feet hit level ground, he bolted for the trees where she had disappeared. Several yards into the woods, he jerked to a halt, realizing that he couldn't go plowing through the forest like a bull elk in rut. She would hear him coming and there were a thousand places to hide in these craggy woods. He would have to go slower, using his knowledge of the surrounding forest to outwit her. Striking off in the direction he'd seen her go, he searched the downed twigs and leaf litter for signs of her footprints.

"Wait till I catch up with you, *She-wolf*," he muttered. "By Godfrey's Heaven, I'll show you who has fangs and who doesn't!"

He tracked and listened, finding little evidence of her passage and growing doubtful of his strategy, until he came to a ridge overlooking the main pass into the high valley. He paused, shading his eyes, and searched the trees and the narrow, rocky passage below. And as he expelled a hard breath and turned to move along, he spotted a flash of white and quickly flattened against a tree, searching the darkened trunks and branches below for another glimpse, then finding her.

She moved silently and skillfully, alert to every sound around her, sure of every footfall. She was no stranger to the mountains, he knew, but her effortless, forest-wise movement still surprised him. She was strong and graceful, magnificent—very like the she-wolf he had declared her to be. He began to follow her, moving with all the stealth he possessed in order to close the distance between them before she detected his presence.

In and out of the trees he stalked her, pausing when she paused, listening when she listened. And as he gained ground, he began to think of how he would surprise and subdue her. Without rope it was going to be hard. . .

Aaren strode beneath a canopy of towering evergreens and tall, white-barked trees which were hoarding their golden leaves. One hand was on the small knife at her waist, beneath her tunic, and the other steadied her passage through the undergrowth. She knew that Jorund would have found her gone by now and was probably tracking her. But her greatest concern was finding the proper course back to the village. Once she found that narrow mountain pass they had traversed the morning before, she hoped she would only have to locate a stream and follow it down out of the mountains.

A noise from the distance caught her ear and she slowed, searching the tangle of dried fir limbs and dormant branches around her. There was a small clearing not far ahead, where a huge old fir had recently fallen. The great old trunk lay among the shadows cast by its encroaching neighbors and the undergrowth had not yet filled in the newly opened forest floor. She approached with her senses piqued and her step wary. Leaves rustled and small twigs snapped, then all was silent for a moment. She paused at the edge of the clearing, clinging to the cover of morning shadows. And she saw it.

The wolf was poised across the clearing, staring at her, ears up, eyes wide . . . as if she had surprised it. Long years of living in the wild high country whispered caution . . . but more recent experience had diluted her natural distrust. Her encounter with Rika in the bee meadow sprang to mind. The muzzle was tan, the mask dark gray . . . in just the right proportions. It was possible that the beast had followed her and Jorund into the forest, but there was only one way to be sure. She took a deep breath and called quietly.

"Rika?" She moved out of the tree's shadow. "Is that you, girl?"

The animal reacted immediately to Aaren's voice, springing up and racing toward Aaren at full speed. When it reached the great log, it gathered and leaped . . . with a vicious snarl.

Jorund was a mere thirty paces away, behind and to Aaren's right, when he saw her stop and search the far side of the small break in the trees. He stopped as well and his eyes lighted on the wolf at the same moment hers did. But a half-instant later, he saw another movement off to his right: low, skulking motions. He realized there was a second wolf just as he heard Aaren calling to the other animal, thinking it was Rika. Without even time for the conscious thought to form, he knew it could not be Rika, since it traveled with a pack. The danger seized him: where there were two wolves, there were likely to be more!

Alarm shot through his body like a lightning bolt and he snapped his head in her direction just as the wolf launched itself over the tree trunk—straight at Aaren's throat. Jorund exploded through the underbrush, running into the ragged clearing just as the wolf reached her.

She cried out as the beast knocked her to the ground. The impact stunned and knocked the wind from her, and the beast scrambled to press the attack, its ears back and its fangs bared. She raised her arms and rolled as it lunged for her face and throat, slashing with its huge jaws. Suddenly a new force burst in from the side, knocking the wolf from her.

Jorund had hurled himself at the wolf bodily, using his broad shoulders and powerful arms to ram it broadside and dislodge it from Aaren. But the next instant, he found himself on the ground with the animal lunging at him, biting and snarling. He grappled with the beast at his throat and succeeded in thrusting the gaping jaws away—just long enough to grope for his knife. He rolled and thrashed, working to get his arm and blade up from his side—and finally ripped into the wolf's belly. He shoved the huge carcass aside, pulling himself from beneath it and pushing up onto his arms.

Staggering to his feet, he turned to Aaren, who was only now regaining her wits. She had struck her head on a rock when she fell and now she sat up, shaking her head and blinking to recover her vision. A low, blood-chilling snarl from the far side of the clearing caused them both to freeze.

Jorund whirled and found himself facing not one wolf but *two*. He barely had time to brace before the first wolf reached him with its claws raking, its teeth bared and flashing.

The clearing erupted in a storm of twisting, writhing sinew and slashing teeth. Jorund fought desperately to keep his feet, knowing that to go down before two wolves would mean certain death. His powerful thighs contracted and released in explosive jolts, while his arms lashed and his massive chest strained and heaved. He managed to wound and throw off the first wolf just as the second moved in to attack his legs from behind. He wheeled and bent and nearly buckled under its clawing charge.

The wolf sprang up at him and they wrestled, locked in a deadly combat, slashing at each other—one with teeth, one with steel. Again and again Jorund's arms broke free to drive his blade into the wolf's pain-maddened form. When his blade finally pierced the wolf's ribs and found its heart, the beast made a last convulsive lash with its jaws, then fell with a sickening thud. Jorund staggered, panting, air-starved, but before he could draw breath, the animal he had wounded earlier charged him again.

The clearing filled a third time with blood and sound and fury . . . spattering red, the thuds of fist smacking flesh, and the rasps of lungs struggling for air. Aaren scrambled to her feet, staring in horror. Still half dazed, she groped for her small knife and found it gone. Casting frantically about for something—anything—to help, she seized a rock and lurched toward the battle, taking aim . . . and slamming the rock into the wolf's head—just as Jorund plunged his knife deep into its belly, striking something vital. The animal jerked and made a gurgling yelp, and Jorund thrust it away, where it fell to the ground in a heap.

Jorund weaved and fought to keep his feet. His bloodied fists were still clenched and his arms still vibrated with unvented rage. He turned dazedly about, raking the silent trees with his gaze, making pained, growling sounds that seemed to come from deep within his chest. Aaren called his name, but when she tried to take hold of his arm, he knocked her away with a sidelong slash of his fist. She stumbled back and landed with a jarring thud on her rear, and he wheeled on her with a look that set her blood contracting in her veins and caused gooseflesh to rise across her shoulders.

His features were pared lean and bronzed with violence. His nostrils were flared, his facial muscles tight, and his generous lips drawn into a snarl that bared his teeth. But it was his eyes that truly jolted her. They were pale—

blue-white with rage, their usually dark, luminous centers mere pinpoints. He stared at her unseeingly, tensed and trembling . . . still hard in the grip of battle-fury. Once past the first shock of seeing him so changed, she made it to her knees and called his name again and again.

"Jorund, it's over. You've killed them all . . . it's finished. Jorund, look at me. It's Aaren . . . Jorund, look at me!"

She crept closer as she talked, wary of the knife still clenched in his other fist. Slowly, his eyes began to darken and to focus meaningfully on her. His coiled stance eased and his braced arms and fists lowered. "Thank the gods!" she breathed, edging closer, allowing him to adjust to her presence a little at a time. When she was near enough, she reached for his hands and when he did not resist, she inspected them for wounds.

"There is so much blood—I cannot tell how badly you are hurt," she said, staring up into his face. His expression was more normal now, but she still had the eerie feeling that she was looking into the eyes of a stranger. "Can you walk? Can you make it back to the *shieling*?" He dropped his gaze to his own bleeding hands and nodded. She pulled the spare tunic she was wearing up and over her head and took a steadying breath as she reached for his knife. He allowed her to pry it from his fingers, and in short order she had cut and torn strips from the tunic and wrapped his hands. When she took hold of his arm, he gave her a strange look.

"I saw you," he muttered, his expression dark, glazed. "Then I saw wolves . . . pack wolves . . . not Rika . . ."

"And there may be still others who will run to the smell of blood. Come, Jorund—we must leave here."

She urged him along as quickly as she dared, and was relieved when twice he corrected their course. Each time she looked at him, she saw a bit more of the Jorund she knew and her anxiety eased. When they reached the *shieling*, she led him straight to the bathing hut and bade him sit on the wide wooden bench while she stripped his blood-spattered jerkin and tunic from him, then bathed and examined his hands.

"Small gashes and a number of scratches—they bleed much, but are not deep," she pronounced with genuine relief. "There is nothing that will not heal quickly." Then she investigated the sources of the blood on his chest and face. More scratches, nothing worse. "Your victory-luck, Jorund Borgerson, is truly a gift from the gods."

As she washed and tended his wounds, she discovered a number of garish white marks on the sun-bronzed skin of his back and shoulders. They were like Father Serrick's body marks . . . battle-scars. Her fingers drifted wonderingly over them, tracing the lingering paths of the blades that had cut him. Then she feathered a touch along the fiery new tracks in his skin, wounds he had taken in defense of her. And she felt as if everything in her middle was melting and sliding toward her knees.

He had come after her and had seen the wolves stalking her. And when he saw she was in danger, he had taken their full fury upon himself.

He had just killed three full-grown wolves with his bare hands. It was an act of courage that left her speechless. Jorund Borgerson had proved beyond all doubt that he was no coward. And from the old blade-marks on his body, it was clear that he had seen battle and been wounded more than once. *He was no woman-heart!* The certainty sang through her veins.

Then why was he so loathe to fight?

She knelt by his feet, trembling as she tore strips of linen from the spare tunic and wrapped his bleeding hands. As she worked, she felt him watching her and looked up to find his face troubled, his eyes dark and turbulent. When the last knot was tied, she let her hands rest gently on his and lifted her face to him.

"There are few men alive who could do what you just did." Her voice was warm, but her words melted none of the tension in his countenance. "And you have fought . . . have been wounded before. Then why do you let your brothers and the others call you a woman-heart?"

The instant she said it, she bit her tongue, wishing to take it back. His face reddened and he flung her hands from his with a low throat-sound that was some part growl and some part groan. Shoving to his feet, he towered above her. Then he lurched for the open door and stormed out.

When his senses finally cleared he found himself in the place where he always sought solace: the clifftop overlooking his meadow and stream. The cold air slowly purged the angry heat from his body, and time and distance from the wolf-battle restored a semblance of control in his mind and emotions. He collapsed in the tall grasses and lay staring up at the wispy mares' tails fanned across the sky, trying not to think.

He didn't want to relive the look on her face as she stared at his body and didn't want to hear again the awed hush in her voice as she spoke of his scars. She had truly believed him a coward and for some reason that realization was fresh and wounding to him. She had honestly meant every blustering insult she had hurled at him.

Why do you let them call you a woman-heart? It echoed in his head and in the deepest hollows of his heart. *Why?* How could he tell her—she who had never known the horrors of battle, she who spoke so glowingly of honor and battle-glory?

He closed his eyes and tried not to let the old images invade his mind. Desperately, he fastened his mind on other inner sights—an image strong enough to counter those haunting visions. He conjured a memory, a woman.

The bee meadow . . . tawny eyes . . . soft breasts beneath his chest . . . hard thighs against his loins . . . Aaren rose up inside him, lush and sensual, seeping through his beleaguered mind and ravaged senses. The feel of her skin recurred in his fingertips, the sweetness of her mouth materialized on his tongue, and the depth of her erotic response surged through his blood. As he dwelled on those sensations, his anxiety was slowly channeled into the more familiar, more productive tension of desire. Finally, the strain of wanting also faded and he was left with a poignant sense of release.

It was some time before he began to feel the scratchiness of the dried grasses beneath his bare back and the chill of the cold breeze on his naked chest. He sat up and looked at the linen bindings on his hands, then at the angry red scratches on his shoulders. It was not so bad, considering there had been three of them, he thought, pushing to his feet.

He stood for a while gazing off into the blue-shrouded mountains beyond his little valley. There was no reason to hurry back to what he was certain would be an empty lodge. If he had thought clearly enough, he would have given her her blade for protection on her journey back to the village. His thoughts focused on the possibility of spending the winter in these high, forbidding reaches . . . of what work it would involve and what solace it would provide . . . he descended the rocky slope to his lodge.

Chapter Fourteen

Jorund was so intent on his dark musings that he did not notice the small plume of smoke curling from the smoke hole in his lodge, or that both horses were grazing in the meadow, or that the door was standing partway open.

When he ducked inside and straightened, he stopped dead, staring at a crackling fire on the hearth. His gaze drifted to his wet tunic, thrown across a makeshift line of rope strung between the rafters, near the blaze. A movement by the storage box in the corner startled him and he jerked around to find Aaren clutching a drinking horn and a full ale skin to her breast. He stared at the things in her hands and worked his way up to her face, which was reddening.

She was still here!

His lungs swelled unexpectedly in his chest, crowding his heart. He glanced back at the fire and his freshly washed tunic . . . and saw that his furs had been moved to the sleeping shelf nearest the hearth. Each was a sign that she intended to stay. Relief poured through his chilled frame like trickles of warm, sweet ale and he turned to her with a searching look.

"You washed my tunic." It was half statement, half question.

"It was all bloody, Borgerson," she said with a wince. "And you wear your only other garment on your hands." She glanced at the wound-bindings she had fashioned from his spare tunic. "It was either burn the thing and watch you go naked . . . or wash it and spare myself the constant sight of your—" She pursed her lips, scowling. But she didn't need to finish for him to know that she found the sight of his bare body disturbing or for him to guess the reason why. When she looked up, he was grinning.

"That was most helpful of you, Long-legs." He rubbed his chest slowly and watched as her widening eyes followed his bandaged hand, then darted away.

She shifted the things she was holding and flushed. "I . . . owed you a debt, Borgerson," she said, avoiding his gaze. "You may have saved my life." When he said nothing, but continued to stare at her, her color deepened. "You probably saved my life." When he still said nothing, she frowned and cast a wary glance at him. "Very well—you *did* save my life. And I am . . . grateful."

He broke into an irresistibly mischievous smile.

"Just how grateful are you, Long-legs? Thank-filled enough to prepare something to eat? I am ravenous." He held up his hand-bindings. "I will have trouble doing hearth-work with these."

She raised her chin and studied him through narrowed eyes, deciding. "I suppose I could do the hearth-work." When she saw the pleasure her offer produced in him, she jammed her fists on her hips and glowered, admonishing: "But—it is only what one warrior would do for another who was injured."

Setting the ale skin and drinking horn on the side of the hearth, she set about preparing something to eat. Jorund ambled over to his sleeping shelf and lowered his aching body stiffly onto his furs, watching her movements, bemused by her new tractability. She wouldn't cook for him as a woman . . . but she would as a fellow warrior. He wasn't sure, but he thought it was probably progress.

How much progress, he would have been delighted to know. In the terrifying fury of a few violent moments, Aaren's whole notion of Jorund Borgerson was changed. He was a fighter, she had learned . . . a man of courage and strength, a man whose heart did not quail at personal danger, a man who would spend his own blood protecting others. And that new vision had inflicted grave damage on her inner defenses. It had taken her desire for him from the realm of the impossible to the possible, and had freed the hope and the longings she tried to isolate within her.

She located a soapstone crock in the storage box and set it into the coals, then stood chewing the inner corner of her mouth.

"There is salt pork and dried beans and barley in the box," he said, smiling wryly. "If you put a bit of water in the crock and add the beans and a bit of salt . . . then cut up the pork . . ."

"I know what to do, Borgerson." She bristled as she turned back to the storage box, and her curt motions said she was both aware and annoyed that he was watching her every movement.

When the crock was bubbling, she returned to the provisions for flour and oil and the flat stone griddle. She carried them to the hearth, setting the griddle into the edge of the coals, and knelt beside them, trying not to reveal her indecision.

"For the bread, you take a double handful of the flour to a single handful of water . . . put it into the bowl . . ." His voice sallied forth from the shelf again.

"I can make flatbread, Borgerson," she declared tautly, without looking at him. She poured oil onto the bowl, then onto the heating stone. "I'm not a thick-wit." But for some reason she was behaving like one, she realized. Preparing food was a simple life-task and the meal would be hers as well as his. But in the villages hearth-tending was known to be woman-work and her desire for the food to be tasty and pleasing seemed to be a particularly womanly sort of feeling. Despite her bluster about doing it as one warrior for another . . . it had the curious feel of a woman doing it for a man . . . of *her* doing it for *her man*. It was yet more evidence of her growing feeling for him and of the changes in her innermost heart.

The softening of her resolve was devastating to her, but she could not shrink from him again and live with herself. She understood all too clearly that it took more courage to stay and face him and the unknown, unexplored part of her than it took to leave.

When the food was prepared, Jorund ate with relish and rolled his eyes appreciatively. Later that night, when he insisted on giving her part of his furs for warmth, she did not refuse. They passed the night on opposite sides of the fire . . . but no longer on opposite sides of understanding.

The next day, Aaren threw herself into the tasks of providing food and care for him while the scratches on his hands and arms healed. She cut wood with an axe, carried out the old ashes, and laid a new fire. She hunted for meat and took a young buck, which she cleaned and dressed, and hung to cure. Then she prepared a stew of meat, leeks, and dried peas in the soapstone crock, and she ground barley and precious wheat together to make flour. And it seemed that whenever she looked up from her tasks, Jorund's eyes were on her.

"You make fine bread," he teased, soaking up the last of his stew with bread. "Where does a battle-maiden learn to do woman-work so well?"

She felt the red rising into her cheeks, as it often did of late, and leaned back against the stones near the hearth, shifting her bowl awkwardly in her hands. "From Father Serrick. He knew many things." She sighed and glanced across the fire at him, feeling a need to tell him more and unsure if it was wise to do so. In the end, she surrendered to the combined force of his irresistible interest and her own need to reach out to him.

"We lived high in the mountains and had only each other. When there are only four of you there is no such thing as men's work and women's work . . . there is only *work*, which is needed to survive. I had no choice but to learn ways which belong to both men and women."

Jorund felt a sweet ache spreading in his chest as he studied her solemn face. Those few words had explained more about her than she knew.

"You were *forced* to learn both. And I *chose* to learn both," he said quietly. When her eyes met his across the fire, they were filled with wonder at his observation. "What a curious pair we make."

They sat for a long moment, looking into each other's eyes. His words somehow gave substance to the bond that had grown between them from that first moment in the circle of torchlight, outside the women's house. Their size, their passions, their single-mindedness . . . they did indeed make a pair. But such an odd pair: one fierce and one gentle; one proud and fiery, and the other even-tempered to a fault; one with a warrior's view of life and the other with a woman's. Longing, uncertainty, pleasure, pain . . . each read a tangle of feelings in the other's eyes. And long-checked desire threatened to erupt between them.

Aaren broke that disturbing visual connection and set her bowl aside, starting for the door. The sound of her name made her pause and look back. He was smiling, back to his old, teasing self as he raised his bandaged hands.

"Give me a few more days and I'll make bread for you."

She ducked outside and when the door was shut behind her, her eyes began to sting. She knew she had to get away for a while.

When Jorund went to look for her later, he found her gone . . . along with his bow and quiver of arrows and one of the horses. His first reaction was that she had left him again, but on second thought, he wasn't so sure. He groaned, staring at his battered hands, then jolted into the shed for his horse, determined to ride out after her no matter how difficult it might prove. But before he got a halter over his horse's head, he glimpsed her emerging from the trees, leading her mount. As he ran down the slope from the shed, he recognized the cargo slung across her horse: three fresh wolf skins. He stared at her wind-blushed cheeks, then at the savage bounty she carried, and his jaw went slack.

"You went back after them?" he said. "After the pelts?"

"Of course," she answered with a wary look. "I guessed that the cold would have kept them well, if the kites and great mountain cats had not yet found them. And there they were, just waiting to be skinned and cured. I decided you should have a prize to show for your effort, Borgerson." Her eyes twinkled. "Think how the children's eyes will widen when they see the pelts and hear the tale of your great wolf-slaying."

"And just how would they hear such a tale?" he said, crossing his bandaged arms over his chest and looking bewildered as she led the horse past him and untied the skins, dumping them onto the wood pile at the side of the lodge.

"Well, I thought *I* would do the telling . . . unless you insist on doing it yourself." She cocked a teasing look at him as she spread them out. "After all, you got to kill all three of the wolves." She sniffed with a mock injured air. "A bit greedy of you, I thought . . . snatching all the glory for yourself. You might have saved that last one for me. I would have done the same for you." She laughed at his astonishment and set about stretching the first pelt upon the side of the lodge, to prepare it for scraping.

He stood watching her, speechless. She had almost been savaged and eaten by wolves, he had risked life and limb to save her . . . now she was already calculating how to make the most of such a harrowing adventure around the winter hearths once they returned to the village!

She baffled him. She hunted and blade-fought and brandished her pride like a warrior. She valued fighting and honor, the protecting of womenfolk and children, and the sacredness of a vow . . . just like a warrior. Her words struck him square between the eyes: *she would have done the same for him.* And he knew in the depths of his marrow, it was no boast. She would have withstood a wolf attack, would have risked her life to save his. In fact she had *tried* to do it . . . that day in the forest with Rika!

She *was* a warrior! It poured through him like molten iron: a warrior with all the courage and skill, all the honor and pride a warrior could possess.

The realization stunned him, as did the fact that it was so obvious . . . and had been from the beginning, if he had but opened his stubborn male mind to it. A flush of chagrin rose up his neck, then into his ears and face. Every crass, demeaning remark, each low, sexual taunt he had ever flung at her now came stinging back to him, piercing his inflated male pride. He had seen her as a desirable body, a curiosity, a conquest, then finally as a person. But until this moment, he had not seen all of her. Nor, he realized, had he wanted to.

She was a *warrior* and a *woman*. Was it possible for her to have two hearts within her breast? He strolled toward the pole shed, then turned back to watch her with a massive ache in his chest which was spreading into his loins. He wanted them both, woman and warrior. And deep in his heart he sensed that in some way he needed them both, as well.

At the front of one stall in the shed, he fished the hay out of the stone manger and felt clumsily around in the bottom for a hand-hold in the stone. A moment later he replaced the stone slab and carried two swords out into the cold sun and around the slope to the spot where Aaren worked at scraping the wolf pelts.

"Aaren." He waited for her to turn to him, then held out her blade to her, across his bandaged hands. She started at the sight, then looked up at him and wiped her hands on a skin before reaching for it. "I thought perhaps you should have it . . . for protection." He smiled with a bittersweet edge as he indicated his wounds. "I will not be ready to fight wolves again for a while. You may have to do it next time."

Aaren folded her blade to her breast and smiled up at him with shining eyes. She wasn't entirely sure what the return of her blade signified between them, but it seemed that he was acknowledging her skill with a blade . . . and her right to wield one. As she turned back to her work, she felt a new sense of hope.

It was only much later, after dark, in the firelit lodge that night, that she glimpsed his own sword resting on its point in the far corner, and recalled that he had been carrying it when he gave her back her blade. The sight of it, with its great, snarling wolf head, sent an inexplicable chill through her and she glanced at the shelf where her own blade lay sleeping among the blue-silver fox furs. Her heart slowed, then lurched to beat much faster.

She had her sword; he had his. The presence of both blades within the same lodge now seemed an unsettling portent.

For the next two days, Aaren provided food and care for Jorund, tending the hearth and changing the bindings on his wounds, which were healing quickly. He was openly warm and teasing with her, complimenting her hearth-skill and her tanning-craft, and admiring her resourcefulness in augmenting their supplies with gatherings of roots and pine nuts and a few dried berries she located in an old briar patch near the meadow. Her customary response to his praise, which he heard so often he began to repeat with her, was: "It is only what one warrior would do for another." But even as she answered with warriorlike bluster, she blushed in a decidedly girlish fashion and could scarcely meet his gaze.

The new pleasure she took in doing "womanly things" for him and the delight she took in his teasing admiration preyed on her pride. But she could not resist exploring this tantalizing new side of herself. She found herself watching his movements, looking for a chance to be his hands, seeking a way to place her body near his so that she might explore the contrast in their shapes and discover more of what it was like to be a woman in relation to a man. And she privately savored those quiet moments in the mornings and evenings when she unwrapped his hands and cleaned and inspected his wounds, or helped him tie on his boots or strap on his belt. Each small task deepened the intimacy between them and made it all the harder for her to lie in her chilled, solitary furs at night, knowing that his generous, pleasurable heat lay only a few steps away.

On the fourth morning after the wolf-slaying, Jorund was restive and eager to reclaim his mobility. He insisted Aaren remove the bindings on his hands and he flexed them and pronounced them healed enough to withstand a climb up to the cliffs overlooking the valley.

"I am not so sure, Jorund," she said, shaking her head. "There has been no festering—you were lucky there. But if you reopen one of them . . ."

He grinned and leaned close to her ear with a tempting rumble. "Then you must come with me . . . and make sure I behave."

Thus, he led her on a climb up the steep slopes that led to the top of the cliffs far above the meadow. They moved slowly, testing each foothold, pausing frequently to catch their breaths. Once they reached the top, Aaren knew why he had been so eager to come. The view was breathtaking. Mountaintops, some craggy and some worn smooth, stretched around them into a blue-shrouded distance which seemed to blend with the sky-vault itself. Below them spread a richly textured cloak of dark green, fawn brown, and birch gold. And above them, seeming close enough to snatch from the deep sky-pool, were wispy clouds shaped like the tails of the mares the Valkyrs were known to ride.

"It is beautiful," she breathed, turning from one vista to another, drinking it in with all her senses.

"Yea, it is that," he said, delighted by the wonder in her eyes. "This is the place I come when I want to set my mind at sea . . . to voyage through dreams and memories."

She looked at him with puzzlement and he laughed, turning her shoulders and pointing her toward the golden Sky-Traveler, who had only just begun his day's journey. "Look there . . . where Norsemen have 'traveled Eastway.' Such lands lie there—a distance of many months of sailing—which would dazzle your eyes with riches, tickle your tongue with new tastes, and delight your skin with strange textures. After sailing up rivers and carrying the long ships over a number of great falls, you come to Byzantium . . . a land of swarthy people with dark eyes and unending summer. The men know the secrets of gold-working and silk-weaving, and live in great, soaring halls covered inside and out with brightly colored glass and beads and stones. They ride swift horses and worship one god and fight like demons . . . and they have many wives, who all wear rings in their ears, chains of golden coins at their throats, and jewels in their bellies."

Aaren's eyes widened as his words conjured pictures in her mind and she clasped his arm, insisting, "You have seen such things?"

"I have," he said, smiling, glancing at her hand on his arm. "I have sailed on a number of . . . voyages."

"The women truly have jewels in their bellies?" She slid her other hand speculatively down her abdomen and searched his face for some sign he was teasing her.

"I saw them." He nodded. "Their scribes write in strange runes and their traders deal in spices—Borger brought a number of their spicemeats back with him, though they are seldom used. The women wear silk and dance wildly to the music of drums and harps and pipes. And they—" He halted and grew a wicked grin. "They are fascinated by men with light hair and eyes."

She released his arm with a good-natured shove. "No doubt you speak from experience."

He laughed and wrapped an arm around her shoulder, turning her a quarter turn so that she faced another distant vista. "And this is the Southway for trading and raiding. After a dozen sailing days, you come first to the lands of the Danes." He made a face. "More quarrelsome than Borger, they are. Short of stature and dark-eyed and treacherous. But they make a special wheel of curds which is a delight to the tongue." He bent closer to her face and extended a hand to sweep the distance away and bring images closer to her mind.

"Then with more sailing you come to the land of the Franks. Christians, mostly. The sun lingers long in their land and in the warmth they grow berries called 'grapes' and make the juice into wine. And they grow much wheat and barley and have whole fields full of apples and plums." Their noses were almost touching. "Have you ever tasted a plum?" When she shook her head, tantalized by his nearness, he explained: "They are round and sweet, like honey-soaked apples. Have you ever tasted wine?" She answered with another shake of the head and a sigh. "When we get back to the village, I will see that you do. Old Borger has a taste for wine and often strikes bargains with the coastal traders for it."

"Where was I?" he murmured, brushing her hair with his nose and pouring warm breath into her ear. "Ahhh. The Franks trade and weave all manner of cloth, and they dye silk and make tapestries—great cloths woven with pictures that tell stories. And the colors they produce would make the rainbow bridge of Asgard quake with envy." He grinned at her shock. "And the women . . . they like men with light hair, too. It was from them that I learned how to kiss."

Her eyes flew to his mouth and her lips parted, feeling thicker and warmer. For a moment they stood half embraced, his head near hers, their cheeks almost touching. Need that sank through her core like a stone-weight, dragging her stomach with it, made her stiffen. He considered her sudden tension and drew back, turning his face toward the horizon.

"I come here to think . . . and to see to the ends of the earth . . . to visit again in dreams and visions," he said, rubbing her shoulder gently with his fingertips. "Eastway, Southway . . . there is a way west as well, into the greatest sea of all . . ."

"And which whale's pathway did you travel, when you left your blood upon an enemy's blade?" she asked quietly, praying he would not hate her for asking. The need to know more about his past burned inside her, for she sensed that it was in the fields of his past that the seeds of their future had been sown. He stilled, then straightened, but did not move away. She summoned the courage and raised her gaze to him. His expression was grave and his look was searching. Heartened by the fact that he had not denounced her or pushed her away, she ventured more.

"Will you not tell me how you took the battle-scars you bear?" she whispered.

She asked about his scars, but he knew, in truth, that she asked much more. And he looked down into those warm amber eyes and knew that someday he would have to tell her. Perhaps if she knew the truth, she would understand why he did not fight . . . why he could never fight her.

"You have been on raiding voyages," she prompted in low, solemn tones. "You have gone a'viking, have you not?"

He expelled a ragged breath and nodded. Then he urged her toward an outcropping of rock nearby and bade her sit. He sank to his knees in the dried grass before her, resting his battered hands on his thighs and staring off toward the distant azure realms of the Southway.

"I sailed with Borger and his men for seven years," he began. "And in that time I left the dew of my wounds on several shores. From the time I was old enough to lift a blade, Borger saw that I was taught the ways of the warrior: weapon-skill, strategies of battle, and how to survive in the wilderness. I learned well . . ." His voice lowered as his thoughts fled back in time. "I was but ten and three when I killed my first man on a raid. He had only a knife to defend his home and I . . . I had a long-blade. Borger celebrated." He looked away. "I emptied my stomach."

He paused and his hands curled painfully. "After a time, I learned not to see their faces . . . not to hear their cries . . . not to see their blood. And I learned to talk of it afterward as all warriors talk: words of glory that painted images of courage and cunning and honor. The raiding grew less profitable; again and again we came to settlements of other Norsemen, and then to fortified towns where our usual lightning-quick raids would not succeed. We had to rely more on trading furs and sea-ivory, and we profited less, for Borger was not half so cunning a trader as he was a fighter. Then came one season when the trading failed completely. We had spent the entire winter in the Southway, seeking profits and finding none. With empty bellies and nothing left to trade, we sold our sword arms to a king of the southern Franks."

His voice and his eyes grew distant as sights and sounds boiled up out of memory, filling his senses again. "The fighting was hard . . . we were greatly outnumbered. Every way we looked, defeat bore down on us. I saw my kinsmen falling . . . I felt death's chilled breath upon my neck." His fists clenched, his jaw muscles worked tautly, and his eyes began to glow with that same fierce light which had shone in them as he fought the wolves.

"I raised my wolf-blade one last time and began to swing it with every burst of battle-strength and hatred I could summon. I felt death itself invading my arms . . . pouring itself out through the edge of my steel. They came at me and I set my feet and slashed and hacked through that storm of iron and flesh. My senses clogged with the blood and the screams and the strain of fighting, until I heard nothing more, saw nothing more, and felt nothing at all. I just went on wielding my blade and drawing blood . . . killing . . . and maiming."

Aaren's stomach knotted as she watched him and realized he was speaking of the battle-fury that came over him . . .

242   *Betina Krahn*

the state he had been in after he killed the wolves. Sliding onto her knees beside him, she laid her hand on his bulging arm.

"It is the battle-fury, the berserker rage, Jorund. It happens to the mightiest of warriors in the throes of fighting. It is naught to be ashamed of. Most warriors are proud—"

"Proud?" His eyes were fierce, his shoulders trembling. "Behind me and all around me lay a swath of death and destruction. Everywhere I trod, blood was knee deep, bodies lay twisted and mangled . . . They lost count of how many I killed that day. I was so blood-maddened I could not stop. I swung at everything, everyone that came near . . . killed some of the king's men along with the enemy, and even wounded one of my own kinsmen. Then, when there was no one left to slay, I staggered into the woods, slashing at trees—at the air itself—until I collapsed."

She listened with her heart as well as her ears. In her mind, she saw him again as he had been with the wolves: white-eyed, snarling . . . deadly. And she saw him as he had been years ago.

She understood that strange narrowing of the senses during combat; she had experienced it herself. And she had felt the burn of battle-fire in her blood which was a foretaste of the consuming blood-rage that had roared in his. Suddenly she shared with him a compelling oneness of feeling, which let her experience some of the pain he was reliving. Then in the silence the tension and anxiety began to fade and she was left with a knot in her throat and an ache in her heart.

"Afterward, I slept for three days. Then I awoke, not to sleep again for months. When we returned home, I put away my blade and haunted the night, wandering like a death-spirit." Some of the savage light in his eyes dimmed and he looked at her. "It was the women who saved me. I had always loved the women and spent much time among them . . . and they gave me the healing solace of their company, their hearts, and their bodies. And Godfrey came to me, speaking his words of forgiveness, talking of love and peace and salvation. And I began to see—there was a way to live besides fighting and killing."

"But what you did, Jorund . . . it was in battle." She tried to reason with him and with her own rising anxiety. "Battle is fighting for a purpose, to an end."

"That makes the killing-madness that comes over me useful . . . to bloated jarls and greedy kings," Jorund said bitterly. "But it is still madness. And it is still wrong. You have never been in battle, Aaren . . . never seen the faces of men as your blade batters and rasps through their ribs . . . never felt your garments grow heavy, wet with blood . . . never heard valiant men screaming, pleading with you to end their death agony. There is no glory in battle."

He seized her shoulders and poured his conviction into his voice. "There is only glory in living, Aaren . . . in loving . . . in building and creating. It goes against much that I was taught and once believed, but I have experienced much and searched my deepest mind and talked many times on it with Godfrey." Jorund released one of her shoulders and slid a fresh-scarred knuckle gently down the side of her face. He paused to feather his fingertips gently across her lips.

"You must see . . . the wolf-fight was the second time I have fought since that long-ago battle. Both times, the madness has come over me. Aaren, I will not be a mindless beast. Fighting, the violent code of the warrior . . . that can no longer be my way. And if Borger's men call me a *woman-heart*, then let them. Words will not change what I am or what I must do. I would rather be thought a coward than become a man-butcher."

He would not fight, she realized, because he believed he could not fight and still be a man. That pain-spawned conviction made his refusal easier to understand and more difficult to bear. She understood, as she looked deep into his eyes and felt the aching tenderness of his touch, that he was indeed afraid to fight her . . . afraid of raging out of control and killing her.

It was in that moment that she understood what love truly was . . . a heart-softness, a marrow-deep yearning, a desire to do anything and everything necessary to protect another . . . even at great cost. And she recognized those longings in his eyes. Jorund Borgerson loved her.

The joy that exploded in her middle was so full, so poignant, that it approached pain. She didn't know whether to throw her arms around his neck or to grab him and shake him . . . whether to laugh at the irony of it, or to weep for the heartache of it. She had decried his lack of pride, not understanding that the strength she glimpsed in him came from a hard-won and uncommon sense of honor . . . and never suspecting that it would be the depth and power of that honor that would raise the final and most devastating barriers between them.

"Jorund—" she said, her eyes filling with moisture, becoming luminous windows on the tempest in her soul. She raised her hands to his face and traced his cheeks, his lips, and his stubborn, noble chin. "There must be some way—"

But he stopped her words with his fingers against her lips. The pain in his face was terrible to witness.

"Aaren, there is nothing to be said. No way to change it. I am what I am."

He led her down from the clifftop in silence. Her face was stiff, her eyes dark. Her every movement bespoke a warrior's finely honed control. Throughout the day and into the evening, as she went about her tasks, she was unfailingly calm and restrained . . . even helpful. But there was an unsettling air about her . . . like that of a yawning wolf, a creaking bough, or a patch of new ice . . . all was not as it seemed. Inside she was tightly coiled and growing slowly tighter.

Jorund watched. He read the tension within her and felt his own building by slow, agonizing degrees. He jested and smiled and teased . . . coaxing her help with preparations for his bathing, and once in the bathing house, cozening her help with removing his garments. But instead of rising to his gambit, she steeled herself visibly and performed each service he asked with brisk efficiency. Then she withdrew, leaving him feeling hollow and hungry in a way he'd never imagined he could be . . . and a bit angrier at the fate the old Norns had chosen to weave for him.

A week after Jorund abducted Aaren and carried her to his mountain lair, Borger sat on his high seat, deep in ale-mist, his spirits sagging like his untied boots. He had just received word from Gunnar Haraldson that the silver for the ransom of his son would take another month or more to raise.

"Spit and roast you . . . you old Son of a Troll," he snarled, though without much heat. "Making me feed your whelp yet another month while you keep me waiting for my silver." He looked back through the hall toward the doors where Leif Gunnarson awaited his freedom. Old Gunnar's heir was near as big as Jorund and every bit as strong. But Leif had a true warrior's pride and temperament, had a proper Norse battle-lust in his heart.

He turned to Snorri the Loud, who dozed precariously on a stool by the high seat, and flung a hand to the far end of the hall and Leif Gunnarson. "Just look how the old eel's spawning has fared in captivity—strong-hearted, sound-limbed, and hot-eyed as ever! If only my Jorund was such a one . . ." He tossed back the dregs of his horn and let out a huge sigh as he propped his head on his fist. His optimism for his son's reformation as a warrior had begun to wane in direct proportion to the amount of ale he consumed this night.

"I wonder if she's killed him yet." He sighed blearily.

Miri stood nearby, clutching her ale pitcher to her breast, listening to the jarl's dismal ponderings. She fled the hall to the cook-hearth, where Marta and Brother Godfrey intercepted her. When she repeated the jarl's words, Marta paled and hugged her, and Brother Godfrey reddened angrily and made a sign upon his portly breast.

"Think nothing of the old boar's grunting," he insisted, lifting Miri's chin. "Your sister is not a man-slayer . . . and Jorund would never raise a blade to her. They will find some way to settle things between them without blood-letting and killing." Miri and Marta managed nods and brave smiles as he gave them each a reassuring pat. Moments later, as he hurried across the commons, he paused with a glance up at the night sky.

"I am depending on you, Lord . . . not to make a liar out of me."

*   *   *

That same blustery night, leagues away, Gunnar Haraldson also sat by the blazing hearth in his long hall. His tall, graying form, which had once filled the great, carved high seat with masterful presence, now looked gaunt and pain-wasted as he curled around the burning throb in his belly and bound leg . . . injuries from Borger's raid. He scowled from beneath whitened brows, deepening the lines that pain and trouble had etched into his once strong face.

"I would have you know my course," he declared to his captains and chief warriors, watching them glance at one another, then at his wounded leg. He could read their thoughts; his days as jarl among them were numbered . . . and his heir lay captive in the hall of his hated rival, the treacherous Borger Volungson. "I have sent word to old Red Beard that it will take a while yet to raise the silver for Leif's ransom."

There was a murmur of discontent and one of the burly captains spoke, summing up their thoughts. "Why should you pay in silver, jarl, when it was old Red Beard who attacked us? By rights, it is he who should pay *wergeld* . . . for his bloody treachery."

"Borger will pay," Gunnar declared, his countenance glowering. "Blood for blood, pain for pain. He will hurt as I have. But it may ease Leif's lot in Borger's hall if old Red Beard believes we will redeem him with silver. With such words I have bought us time . . . to heal and to prepare."

"Let us mount a raid—use our ships for a water-borne attack—and steal Leif back," a stringy sea captain declared. "We'll burn Borger's village to the ground!"

Gunnar studied his men, knowing their anger, feeling it himself. "*Nej* . . . I intend to let the greedy old cur deliver Leif into our hands himself. There will come a time for raiding and burning," he said grimly, "but not until Leif is back. It will be his vengeance as much as mine."

The first snow came the next afternoon, falling from a gray, leaden sky like bits of down pulled from a fatted goose. Jorund stood just outside the lodge doorway,

watching the flakes falling and recalling his boastful determination to have Aaren on her back, in his furs, by the first
snowfall. She was indeed in his furs, every night . . . but
on the far side of the lodge, and alone. So much for his
much practiced woman-skill and his vaunted male pride,
he thought grimly. For all his pleasuring and patience and
caring, he seemed farther from his goal than when he'd
started.

This new coolness of hers, this utter lack of feeling,
was worse than her fiery blasts of pride and temper, and
for some reason it stirred the still waters at the bottom of
his soul the way little had in recent years. She wanted him,
cared for him . . . there had to be some way to penetrate
the wall his revelations seemed to have re-built around
her heart.

He strode out to the horse shed. She was not there. He
tried the wood pile. No Aaren. With mounting anxiety,
he scoured the nearby woods, then checked the bathing
house. There he found her, the door barred against him.
He pounded furiously on it.

"Aaren Serricksdotter . . . come out or let me come in."
When she made no response, his temper quickly frayed.
"I'll tear down the door if I must!" And he pounded some
more, so that his half-healed hand throbbed.

There was a scrape and a hinge groan, and her face
appeared in a small opening. When he pushed on the door,
she countered the force and glowered at him. "Go away,
Borgerson."

"In a sow's eye, She-wolf. We have things to settle—"

"Not for six days, we don't," she declared testily. "Take
it up with me then."

"Six days? What makes you think—" He halted, staring
at her pale face, clouded with irritation and discomfort. As
well as he knew women, it still took a moment for the sense
of it to strike him. "Six days? You mean to say . . . it is your
woman's time?"

Her eyes flashed and her face reddened. "How dare you
say such a thing to me!" she snapped, trying to slam the
door and finding it blocked by his big foot and shoulder.
Her fury mounted precipitously. "Go away . . . get out . . .

leave me alone! Give me just six wretched days of peace and quiet—that's all I need!"

Jorund stared down at her with a huge grin spreading over his face . . . which he quickly stifled. "I see," he said in a solicitous tone. "Are you hurting, Long-legs?"

"Oooh—" she groaned. "No! I'm not hurting!" She tried to shut the door, but again he prevented it.

"Would you like me to rub your shoulders or back? That often helps."

"No."

"Then is there something special you'd like to eat? We don't have any honey, but—"

"No!"

"I could heat some rocks and wrap them in a blanket for you."

"Curse you, Borgerson! I don't want any rocks—I've got plenty of rocks!" she shouted, on the brink of tears. Then her voice shrank and became oddly choked. "I don't want *anything*. Except for you to just . . . go away."

Jorund stepped back and the door slammed in his face. But when he turned away, he was grinning again. He strolled toward the lodge, feeling delighted. Just when his spirits had been at low ebb, he was given a dramatic reminder that inside his proud, self-contained warrior was a tender and vulnerable woman. He paused and looked up at the snow showering around him and thought to himself that the first snow was always the most eagerly awaited, but the shortest lived. Lasting things were worth waiting for.

Jorund's hands had healed enough for him to carry out the hearth-tasks and do some fishing. He discovered a shed elk antler while passing through the woods toward the fishing hole in the stream, and he spent his spare time whittling and carving a comb from it. She would want something to groom her hair when her time was over, he thought, and he would give it to her as a gift. And someday, he thought with a grin, he would use it on her hair himself.

Each morning and each evening, he carried food and drink and offers of wood and assistance to her in the bathing house. At first, she refused them all. But by the second day, she hesitantly accepted the food he brought, and by the fourth day she sat on the wooden bench in the bathing house, surrounded by food-gifts, fragrant pine boughs, a pallet made of woven blankets stuffed with dried grasses, and small bunches of dried flowers he'd found at the edge of the meadow. She looked around her at the visible evidence of his caring and felt tears rolling down her cheeks again.

What in Godfrey's Heaven was she going to do?

It was no longer just a matter of her honor and enchantment, it was a matter of their loving, and of the cruel bonds which the fear of his own strength and his own deeply held beliefs had placed on him. She had to uphold her enchantment, had to find a way to overcome the obstacles to their loving, and—hardest of all—had to free Jorund from the beast he carried inside him. It sounded hopeless. It was unreasonable to expect a mere mortal to cope with all of that. Her woman's heart was twisting in her breast, weighted with despair.

But her warrior's heart, accustomed to finding opportunity in adversity, rose up to buoy her sinking spirits. And as she sat staring into the hearth flame, a familiar voice spoke out of the depths of her memory . . . a voice of wisdom and caring. Father Serrick.

"Fight, my daughter," he said to her again through time and distance. *"Fight and be valiant . . . and if you are true in your heart and true to your honor, you will triumph."*

"Fight?" she murmured, her gaze raking the roof beams, the hearth, and the stone pool, as if trying to find a route of escape. "How can I do that, Father Serrick? It is the fighting which has brought all this trouble upon me. Please, I don't want to fight—not this time—not any more!"

But again the voice echoed in her mind and she could not say whether it whispered from the past or the present. *"Fight, my daughter. You have the victory-luck . . . A warrior can have no finer gift."*

"Victory-luck"—she groaned—"when what I want is to be defeated honorably."

"Victory-luck," Old Serrick whispered yet again.

"But the only victory I want is to be finished with this cursed enchantment . . . to have Jorund fight and free me . . . and then love me."

"Be true in your heart . . . you will triumph." Again and again she heard it in her head, until her father's raspy voice merged with her own and began to work a kind of charm on her.

The words struck a deep, new chord of resonance in her innermost mind. Victory-luck, triumph . . . if she truly had luck, if she was meant to triumph, then Jorund *would* fight her and defeat her. And she *would* have his loving and she *would* learn the joys and pleasures of her woman's heart and frame.

"Fight. It is the only way. Oh, Jorund," she said with all the longing and desperation in her, "you must fight me . . . and trust that my victory-luck will see us through."

Chapter Fifteen

On the seventh day of Aaren's selfimposed confinement, the Sky-Traveler threw off his cloud-cloak and smiled brightly, melting the land's thin garment of snow to a tattered lace work of white. Jorund stepped outside the lodge and greeted the morning with relief, stretching his back and arms . . . and awakening his awareness of his male need, which he had forced into cramped submission for the last several days.

Today was the day, he had decided. The long hours of solitude, punctuated by brief, tantalizing glimpses of Aaren's womanliness, had both sharpened his desires and deepened his determination. The scratches and cuts on his hands were completely healed, and now her time was through . . . in more ways than one. No more sparring, no more evasion. He wanted her; she wanted him. And he intended to see that they had each other before another day passed.

He ducked back into the lodge and set about moving the furs he had given her back to his sleeping shelf. In the process, he uncovered her blade and paused with a fierce glint in his eye. "She won't be needing you again, Bone-biter." He seized it and leaned it in the far corner with his own blade, then began to prepare *grautr* and venison for their morning meal.

When the food was ready, he went to the bathing hut to fetch her. "A fine morning, Aaren," he said, smiling his best when her face appeared in the crack of the door opening.

"So it is," she answered evenly.

"It has been six days," he said, testing the waters.

"So it has." Her expression remained carefully neutral.

He shifted feet and felt his gut tightening. "I have prepared a morning meal."

"I have already eaten, thank you," she said, avoiding his gaze. "And I have yet to bathe. Later, perhaps . . ." She closed the door and he was left staring at the rough cedar planks, embarrassed by his own eagerness.

He returned to the lodge and ate his meal alone. Then after seeing to the horses, splitting more wood, and checking the snares he had set the evening before, he stalked toward that stolid, forbidding door with a scowl. What in Godfrey's Hell was taking her so long? He narrowed his eyes and produced a fierce grin, realizing he had the perfect gambit to open the door and coax her out.

He hurried back up the slope to the bathing house with the elk-horn comb he had spent his every spare moment carving. When she opened the door, he put on his most winning smile and held it out to her.

"I thought you might need a comb for your hair." He was gratified by the way her whole countenance softened and her eyes took on a luminous, heartfelt glow as she reached for it.

"A comb? Jorund, how wonderful of you. And it is beautifully made. I thank you."

She clasped it to her breast, then quickly closed the door, leaving him standing there in bewilderment. He stalked back down the hill, his expression and thoughts growing dark as storm clouds. He pacified his more drastic impulses with the thought that he would give her just one more hour to finish . . . then either she was coming out or he was going in!

Aaren stood with her back against the door, hugging the comb he had carved with his battered hands and feeling as if her heart was coming completely undone. All morning she had been in turmoil, dreading facing him again, hoping against hope that the separation might have diluted the longing in his eyes or caused her desire for him to wane. But when she had looked into his face just now, it was all still there . . . the desire, the promise, the determination. And she felt an answering swell of tenderness in her chest which crowded her lungs and sent her heart into an erratic rhythm.

She made her way on weakened knees to the wooden shelf where she had passed recent nights on the stuffed pallet he had made to comfort her. She sat running her fingers over the smooth, even teeth of the comb. He had whittled away her defenses just as surely as he had cut away those bits of horn. And what had he made her into? Tears welled in her eyes as she answered: a warrior who dreaded the most important battle of her life.

Some time later—she wasn't sure how long—there came another round of pounding on the door. It startled her and she thrust to her feet, gazing around her and feeling trapped and panicky. After a pause, the pounding resumed and she heard him calling her name. When she lifted the small bar and opened the door, he planted a shoulder in the planks and exerted pressure, forcing the door back.

"It's been seven days for me, too, Aaren," he declared irritably. "You've had the bathing hut to yourself long enough. It's time for me to bathe, now."

She swallowed hard and swung the door wide to admit him, knowing as she did so that she was admitting her fate and future as well.

"Of course. I was just finishing my hair," she said calmly, moving back to the wooden shelf as he entered. She perched on the edge and leaned her head to the side, dragging his comb through her hair several times, feeling his stormy eyes on her.

Jorund's woman-starved senses fastened on the sight of those pale fingers of bone sliding through that burnished, erotic softness. The sight ignited the volatile vapors seeping through his blood. He hadn't counted on just how womanly and desirable she would look or on how the smell of dried flowers, the sweet clover he had used to stuff her pallet, and her own musky-sweet scent would invade his lungs and fill his head. He had honestly planned to bathe . . . later to share a meal and perhaps a walk with her . . . then to take her into his arms by the fire and let the heat between them have its way.

But suddenly he couldn't move. His belt and tunic seemed heavy and abrasive against the sensitive skin of his belly and his lips began to burn. He watched her rise and tie on her breastplate and it seemed that her every movement was slowed and magnified in his senses; the deep breath that thrust her taut nipples against her tunic, the slow slide of the molded leather onto her breasts, the twist of her body as she threaded and tightened the laces, the sideways toss of that soft hair when it tumbled in the way. By the time she turned to him, his arms felt empty, his blood drummed urgently in his veins, and his loins felt weighted and hot.

"Is something wrong?" Her gaze dropped to avoid his and her heartbeat quickened. When he stepped closer, looming above her, she fought the urge to run. The silence heated between them. She understood: he knew, as she did, that their time had come.

"I need your help," he murmured, raising his hands and holding them as if they were still injured, "with my garments." She lifted a turbulent look to him.

"Your hands are well enough to wield a carving knife . . . you do not need me to remove your garments again."

"But I do, Long-legs." His voice softened and came as smooth as honey. "I have never needed anything more." Her breath caught in her throat and as she struggled to free it, he added the persuasion of his fingers feathering along her cheek. She closed her eyes, feeling that touch gliding across her very heart. Her hands curled into fists at her sides.

"I . . . I don't want to touch you," she whispered, knowing it was half truth, half lie.

"Yes, you do, Long-legs," he countered with compelling certainty. "And it is useless to deny it. Help me."

It was useless to deny . . . and impossible to resist. Perhaps it was weakness, she thought. Or perhaps it was fate. Every nerve in her body tingled when she touched the bronze buckle of his belt. The heat of his body had invaded that bit of metal and the leather that girded his waist felt hot and supple in her hands as she unhooked it and drew it slowly from his body. Taking a deep, steadying breath, she dropped it on the wooden shelf and paused, preparing herself. Then, with trembling hands, she seized the bottom of his tunic and pulled it up and over his head. She stumbled back a step and stood, frozen, as he closed the door and added another log to the stone oven.

"Come, help me wash," Jorund said softly, lowering himself to the edge of the shelf.

She hesitated, studying him, and her eyes flicked nervously toward the door again. The need for him whispered in her blood—irresistible, inevitable—as she struggled to find solid mental footing, balancing precariously between determination and desire. She let out a ragged sigh and her rigid posture softened. It was no good trying to escape again; their problems would still be there and as difficult to solve. She dipped a pail of water and carried it to him, pausing, still uncertain. He smiled and reached for her, drawing her between his knees.

"You've mended well," she said in a soft, thick voice, wetting a small square of cloth and dragging it gently over his features. Her fingers left the cloth to trace a muted red line which began at the edge of his jaw and spilled down his neck and onto his shoulder. "Your scratches are completely grown over." The sultry combination of tone and touch sent desire boiling up in him, hot and sweet and potent.

"So they are," he said, running his eyes over her breastplate, her shoulders, and her face, poised just above his. "But they still itch like old Loki's nose. Soothe them for me, Long-legs." He reached for her hand and pressed her fingertips to his lips.

His silken persuasion swirled through her will like the haze of warmth and wood smoke curled through her senses. She raked her fingernails gently over the marks on his shoulders and down the streaks on his chest. Somewhere in that intimate service, her desires slipped past her control and her fingers continued down where no injury had occurred . . . over his nipples, then downward still, ruffling the golden hair that trickled down the middle of his chest and belly. His stomach muscles contracted, then his whole body flexed like a supple birch bow.

"Is that better?"

"Ummm." His hands came up to clasp her waist and their warmth unleashed a towering need in her. She lowered her head and pressed her lips against his new scars, wanting to banish them and the pain that had caused them, to replace them with pleasure. Then her mouth slid down the side of his neck and came to rest in the hollow of his throat, against his pounding heartbeat . . . kissing him, tasting him.

Her impulse ignited the last bit of his restraint and his arms flew up to drag her hard against him. He lifted her chin and captured her mouth hungrily, wrenching from her a small, pleasure-filled groan. And her arms lapped around his neck as she leaned into him and gave herself up to his male strength.

Their mouths merged and slanted, each seeking and exploring the sleek inner contours of the other. Her head tilted and her body melted against his, molded by his engulfing heat and aching to absorb his tantalizing hardness, to have him fill that tightening hollow within her.

She felt herself slipping, surrendering . . . and tried desperately to hold back her reason while giving all of her response. He rolled back onto the wide shelf, carrying her on top of him, spreading her long, lithe body over him like a blanket while her unbound hair fell around his face like a curtain, closing out all other reality.

Deeper and deeper his kisses took her, with slow, swirling motions of his tongue . . . hard and devouring one instant, soft and toying the next. Then his hands began to move over her shoulders, down her armored back, and onto her taut buttocks . . . massaging, caressing. He cupped her buttocks and shifted her higher on him so that she felt the ridge of his flesh riding against her tingling womanflesh. The next instant, his hands slid down the backs of her thighs and pulled them to his sides, opening her inner softness, settling it against his hot, unyielding flesh-spear.

The shock of that new intimacy jolted her and she floundered, grappling for some foothold in reason. She wanted him . . . wanted this pleasure. It was so sweet, so close . . . But the conflict that had fermented in her heart these last days now boiled up inside her, searing and twice-potent for having been suppressed.

This pleasure was not without price . . . and the price was her honor, her courage, and her hard-won sense of worth. She had to remember; this burning in her heart, this fire in her veins would consume her—and him as well—if it were allowed to rage on.

He moved, thrusting slowly and gently against her tender center, devastating her senses and coaxing an answering motion in her hips. She arched and strained, uttering a deep, resonant sound that was half pleasure, half anguish.

He heard both the eagerness and the fear in her cry, but his passion-steeped wits were slow to understand their full meaning. He roused to take her face between his hands and gaze into her luminous eyes. "Aaren, love, don't be afraid . . . I won't hurt you . . . I'll never hurt you." He joined their mouths again, and his hands slid to the sides of her breastplate and began to work the leather ties free.

Afraid . . . don't be afraid—drummed in her heart. *Fight . . . you must fight*—echoed in her mind. The dissonance between them grew, becoming like a battle-roar in her head, in her very blood. And suddenly she could not bear it—the wanting, the fear, the division in her deepest, most vital longings.

She grabbed his hand and held it still as she pushed up onto her arm and stared down at him. Then with one swift, excruciating movement, she peeled her damp body from his and slid to the floor on her feet. Before he could draw a shocked breath to call her name, she had thrown the door back and darted outside. As she ran for the lodge, the pain in her innermost heart spilled out through her eyes. She felt her way through the door and wiped at tears to see to her sleeping shelf.

Both her furs and her blade were gone and she whirled, frantic. She spotted the furs on Jorund's shelf and turned toward the corner. There they were . . . a stark omen she now understood; her blade and Jorund's resting together, leaning against the wall, *waiting*. She snatched them up and ducked back outside.

Three strides brought her face to face with Jorund. He had run from the bathing house and now stood barring her way, bare-chested and trembling. His great arms were bulging, and his hands were clenched. The moisture and heat rolling from his huge body made it seem that he steamed in the cold air. And when he saw her standing there with a sword in each hand, his eyes went molten.

"What in Godfrey's Hell do you think you're doing?" he demanded. "Put those cursed things down!" She hesitated for one moment, then complied, tossing his sword at his feet and unsheathing her blade in a single practiced stroke, slinging the scabbard aside.

"I'm doing what I must. Do you want me, Jorund?" she demanded past the tears clogging her throat.

"Curse you, Aaren—you know that I do!" he roared, understanding now the strange tenor of desperation in her lovemaking. His whole frame began to quake.

"Then fight for me!" she cried. "I cannot surrender to you, Jorund, without it. I have lived too long as a warrior, I cannot just turn my back on the code I have spent my life learning and upholding. I could not face your father or your people ever again—I would have no place among them if I did not honor and defend my enchantment. It is as sacred to me as your way is to you." He roared a groan, shaking an impotent fist at the sky, then leveled a look of anguished fury on her.

"Don't do this to me, Aaren!"

"I wouldn't—if there were any other way," she shouted brokenly. "Don't you see? I cannot live without you anymore, Jorund. But neither can I live without honor." Tears streamed down her cheeks.

"*Nej*—I cannot fight you!" He stumbled closer, stopping just short of the blade at his feet, recoiling from it. "You know what happens to me when I fight. By the Merciful God"—he choked—"if we fight, I'll kill you!"

"*Nej*—you will not! I have the victory-luck from Odin himself. You will not harm me!"

"Dammit, Aaren—there is no such thing as *victory-luck*— and no Odin to grant it to you! Don't you see—Asgard and hammers and rainbows, it's all tales and twisted nonsense told to make men eager to kill and to die in some fat jarl's service."

How could she make him understand if he did not even believe— She seized a wisp of memory, something Brother Godfrey had said. Jorund believed in the White Christ and in that young god's curious weapon. She clasped the handle of her blade to her breast, her eyes shining. And she prayed she would get it right.

"Then if you do not believe in your people's gods, believe in your own. You will not harm me, Jorund. For your god's heart-weapon will steady your arm . . . and stay it, when need be."

He stared at her, his eyes burning, torment etched into every line of his face and frame. "What do you mean? What 'heart-weapon'?" And the pained longing he glimpsed in her glowing amber eyes cut him to the very quick.

"Love," she answered, her voice thick with feeling. "You do love me, Jorund . . . don't you?"

He felt as if someone had taken a war-hammer to his heart. His entire body contracted, straining against the swell of anguish in his chest. He could scarcely get his breath. She was standing there with tears streaming down her face, putting her life in his hands . . . trusting that his love for her would counter the madness that invaded his blood. After a long moment, he managed to thaw his frozen throat.

"I do," he said. "God knows, I do love you."

A radiant smile burst on her face, lighting her whole countenance. She wiped away the last of her tears . . . and raised her blade.

"Then fight me, Jorund." She took two steps back. "Pick up your blade . . . and let your White Christ shield your heart and mine with his Love."

He made a low, agonized groan and turned away. He stood with his broad back to her, trembling and choked with fear . . . hating her for forcing him to this . . . loving her for her courage and her boundless faith in him . . . in his love. He was roused beyond bearing; angry at fate, at his conniving old father, at himself . . .

He wheeled and knelt, stretching his big hand out . . . seizing the horn grip of his tarnished silver-handled blade. The metal sang as he drew it from its cradle. Then he pushed to his feet and kissed its cold, killing steel, lifting it skyward.

"I call on you, Merciful Christ," he ground out from the bottom of his soul, "to guide my arm. And if you spare her life . . . I swear, you will have mine in its place."

He turned to the love shining in her eyes, swung his wolf-blade in a great arc above his head—then brought it crashing down on her.

She met his blow with an upward cut of her blade and steel rang on blood-tempered steel. The shock radiated through her arms and jarred her heart to a raw, familiar cadence, spurring senses to battle alert. She wheeled her blade and returned the blow, watching his face, intent on the nuance of his paling eyes. Again the iron sang, each tone ringing free and clear before it thinned and faded on the cold mountain air. She leaped to the offensive and suddenly the meadow was filled with the strident clang of blade battle . . . the radiant sun and cold, naked trees the only witnesses to the song of triumph or of tragedy unfolding.

She braced and lunged, swinging, and caught his blade-tip as he jolted aside. With another lunge and swing, she caught the back side of his blade and knocked it upward . . . a bit too easily. Her mind raced as she pressed the attack and watched him falling back into the meadow, parrying her blows only in defense . . . returning none of them. He was holding back; she could see the strain of containment in his face and almost felt the power trapped and bulging in his massive arms. She recognized his strategy: wear her down and move in late, to take her with as little force as necessary. Her first impulse was anger that he would demean her blade-skill so. But reason soon tempered pride; it was his way of protecting them both. She was torn between accepting his restraint and coaxing him to give himself fully to the fight—to face his inner beast and conquer it, even as he conquered her.

"Do not be afraid to strike me, Jorund!" she called out, planting her feet and swinging from the waist, ripping her blade forcefully up the edge of his, producing a grating sound. "I am a warrior—I can defend myself!" Again, she lunged, swinging broadly and rolling the edge of the arc back upon itself—reversing to immediately engage his blade again. And again he met and deflected her well-aimed cut without launching his own attack.

The old motions, the feel of the blade in his grip, the sound of blades meeting . . . it was all so chillingly familiar, so cursedly easy to slide back into. Jorund felt the old heat trickling into his blood and fastened his eyes on Aaren's face, willing himself to see her, to never let her eyes leave his sight. Aaren, his own voice chanted in his head, *this is Aaren . . . my Aaren.*

She could feel the battle-heat rising closer to his surface; there was an extra tremor of force in his blade as he met her blows. The familiar battle-burn was beginning in her lungs and spreading into her blood as well. Digging her heels into the dried grasses, she coiled and released her shoulders and sliced a singing arc through the air, landing a blow near his sword hilt, visibly jarring his arms.

"Do not fear it, Jorund. You give it power over you," she called, charging in again and again. "Look at me!" She grasped for something to make his mind reach past the present battle. "Think of the future . . . of the wine you promised me . . . I will drink that wine, Jorund. And think of the soft furs . . . and long nights by the fire . . . of the pleasures you have promised me . . . of children we will make . . ."

"Aaren," he gritted out, desperate to hold on to her words, which were slowly being drowned out by the roar of his own blood in his head. He felt his control slipping and returned her swing, down-cutting savagely so that he grounded their blades for a moment.

They stood with sword points crossed, panting, hot-eyed. Sweat glistened on his bronzed shoulders and trickled down his corded neck, his light hair glowed golden in the sunlight, and his body heat reached for her the way his weapon would not. Anguish rose into his eyes—and she knew he was on the verge of retreating from both the fight and her. Her arms trembled, her legs suffered a surge of weakness as raw, searing need for him slammed through her frame. She couldn't let him stop—she would lose him!

"If you want me, Borgerson, I am yours. Come and take me," she declared with all the smoldering sexual heat she could summon. Then she ripped her blade aloft and brought it crashing down on him.

He reacted instinctively, jerking his blade up to meet her blow. The shock of the hit and the blast of heat from her unshielded desires seared his senses. His perception fragmented and he suddenly saw her as parts instead of a whole—smooth, powerful arms lashing . . . legs coiled, then exploding like white-hot embers . . . shoulders and body flexing, supple as a mountain cat's . . . long hair whipping about her like living flame. And her face . . . exotic, heat-polished, filled with a startling blend of battle-lust and female heat. Passion roared through him, pushing his response to the very limits of his control.

He battled on two fronts: against her blade and against his own violently erupting passions. The conflict raging inside him slowed his reflexes for one fraction of an instant . . . long enough for the tip of her blade to dart in. He wrenched his shoulders back, but it caught the edge of his upper arm, laying a gash across it.

Stinging pain lashed through him, narrowing his consciousness further, and the red running toward his elbow suddenly exploded in his vision, consuming his whole awareness. The battle-beast straining inside him broke free and with a great, pained roar he raised his blade and charged her full out.

Aaren had no time to register the horror of her act or concern for the wound she had dealt him. His massive blade came crashing down on hers a heartbeat later, dragging her braced arms and sword down with it. She scarcely had time to pull away before he aimed a sidelong slash at her, narrowly missing her thigh. Her whole consciousness sprang to reflexive action and quickened battle-timing . . . propelling her to the very edge of that stark boundary between life and death. Her senses now raced, anticipating as much as perceiving, and her lithe, powerful frame braced to receive blows, then again to deal them out. Soon her arms ached and her back muscles burned from the pounding, unrelenting force and the constant whirling, jarring motions needed to withstand it.

For the first time in her experience, Aaren faced an opponent her equal. His size lent massive force to his blows, and again and again she felt her sword rattle in her grip as his mighty blade connected with its edge and all but ripped it from her hands. But for all his size and strength, he still moved like a great hunting cat: legs crouching, then erupting; shoulders flexing gracefully; arms striking like a seasoned whip. He was both beautiful and terrifying . . . and he was bent on sinking his blade into her flesh. It took every bit of agility she possessed to escape his savage cuts and all her strength to deal him countering blows.

She gritted her teeth as he battered her back into the trees. Gradually, defensively, her senses pared away all excess stimulation and constricted around the stark essentials of him. She began to see only the movement of his eyes, the angles of his body, and the whirling arcs of his blade.

They fought on into the early afternoon, going on raw nerve, senses dulled to all but the other's presence and the struggle being waged between them. She sensed more than saw his tiring, as the pounding force of his blows slackened and the pace of his assault slowed. But his reserves of energy were greater than hers and as she struggled to mount one last offensive—trying again to wrench his blade from his grip—her strength began to fail. Her responses slowed dangerously as he drove her back through the forest.

Her lungs were raw, her heart felt as if it would burst from her chest, and an ominous leaden feeling was creeping down her limbs. She tried to rally, feeling for the first time the brush of death's cold breath upon her face. But even mortal danger could not pull strength from limbs long spent. Her agile feet began to falter, leaving her more and more vulnerable. With her power ebbing and her reserves gone, she sensed the end was near and in her deepest heart she called to the White Christ . . . begging that presence . . . entreating without words.

Dodging a wide slash of his blade, she stumbled back and her heel caught on an exposed root. She caught her balance but dropped her blade-tip, missing her defensive mark. His sword surged in as she twisted to recover—and it sliced into her. She fell with a cry and came to rest, motionless, on the soft blanket of leaves.

Jorund stood quaking in the silence, hardly seeing, barely able to feel his own limbs. His chest was heaving, the battle-roar in his head was deafening . . . but the sense that she was gone penetrated his pain-filled consciousness.

Aaren . . . gone. All through the fight he had felt her vital presence with him; now she was gone. Slowly his perceptions began to right and broaden. And as the blood pounding in his head drained and he looked for her, his eyes fell on her crumpled form. He froze.

The seeping red on her tunic burst like a lightning bolt through his mind. Blood—she was wounded! Merciful Christ—he had wounded her—or killed her! *"Nej!"* Anguish boiled up from deep in his soul and escaped on a chilling, feral cry—a wounded sound that echoed through the forest.

"Curse you, Odin!" he shouted hoarsely, his face twisted in agony. "It's you that killed her—you and all the bloody gods of Asgard!" And he lifted the sword in his hand and whirled in a spiral of fury, flinging it with all his might into the trees, where it bit deep into a sapling.

He stumbled to Aaren and fell on his knees beside her, trembling, touching her face, her arm . . . peeling her stiff fingers from the grip of her sword. With the last of his strength, he gathered her up into his arms and lifted her, pressing his cheek against hers. He staggered back toward the lodge, seeing nothing but her drained face, feeling burned and hollow.

By the time he reached the meadow, he had reclaimed enough of his reason to examine her and realize that she was still breathing and appeared to be wounded in the shoulder or chest. As he crossed the clearing he began to run with her, thinking frantically ahead, recalling what he had to do.

Banging through the door with his shoulder, he carried her straight to his furs. He tore the tunic away from her chest and relief poured over him as he dabbed the blood away. She bore a cut along the top of her shoulder, from her throat to the top of her arm. It was not deep, he discovered, but, like his wolf-wounds, it was alarmingly bloody.

His fingers were cramped and swollen, clumsy as he worked the laces of her breastplate. Still, he managed to remove her armor gently and lifted her sodden tunic from her. He bathed the wound carefully and bound it, sickened at the sight of the fierce red gash in her fair skin . . . by the realization that he'd caused it. A fraction more, a slight stumble or a twist on her part, and his blade would have sliced straight into her heart. He lowered himself onto the shelf beside her, cradling her protectively against his chest, recalling the way she spoke of Love shielding their hearts. And with his last bit of strength, he whispered to his new master.

"My heart aches to thank you, White Christ, for shielding and sparing her life. I owe you more than one unworthy soul. So I swear to you, on my beloved's heart, that I will never raise a blade against another man . . . not as long as I draw breath."

And in the quiet of the little summer lodge, he laid his cheek against her head and slept.

Some time later, Aaren roused to find herself in Jorund's *shieling*, in Jorund's furs, and in Jorund's arms. She turned her head toward the throbbing pain in her shoulder and glimpsed the makeshift binding and the traces of red on the ragged strips of linen. Lifting her hand, she traced the thick muscles of the arm which lay across her, following them upward to a linen binding. They were both alive, she thought wonderingly, and they would mend. An exhausted smile flickered over her features as her eyes closed and she joined him in rest.

Chapter Sixteen

It was past nightfall of the next day when Aaren awoke fully, to firelight, a dull-throbbing shoulder, and a howling stomach. She lay quietly in the furs, reclaiming her senses and assessing her condition. Just what did it feel like . . . this "defeat?" Moving her feet, hands, and knees, she determined that her body seemed whole and still moved properly—albeit with some soreness. Her inner condition was a bit more difficult to assess. She could detect no great difference in herself . . .

The smell of food that filled the lodge registered in her senses. She abandoned her musings to push back the furs, lever herself up on her good arm, and look around. Jorund was sitting by the hearth, staring into the dancing flames. Her movement caused him to look up and she smiled at him as she rolled stiffly from the sleeping shelf.

"Are you well enough?" he demanded, bolting up and hurrying to steady her.

"I am fine," she said, wincing as she straightened and ran a hand down her neck with a grimace. "Except for my shoulder." She stretched gently and felt a twinge of discomfort in her wound and an ache rolling down her spine. "And my back . . . and my arms . . . and my head . . . and my legs. Even my buttocks ache. By the gods, I feel awful." The look she raised to him was so absurdly pitiful that it positively begged a smile. She got a small one.

"Then you must go straight back to the furs." He gave her an authoritative nudge.

"*Nej*, I'll never get rid of the aches if I don't move about." She wobbled around him and moved stiffly to the hearth to discover what was releasing such tantalizing smells. "And I'm half starved. What is all this?" She peered into the stone crock and breathed deeply of the rising vapors, closing her eyes to savor the aroma. "Apples. I think I was just dreaming of apples! Where did you get them?"

"Helga knows I like them. She packed a few at the bottom of the grain."

She sniffed again. "And pork . . . wonderful, salty pork . . ." She turned on him with a bone-melting smile. "Feed me, Borgerson. It is the least one warrior can do for another who is wounded."

He managed a stiff smile at her jest, then did just that . . . fed her. She attacked the bowl of salt-cured pork and cooked apples he handed her, and groaned appreciatively, complimenting his hearth-skill. When she finished, she sat back with a sigh and let the heat seep into her bones while she licked her fingers with sated leisure and sipped a horn of ale.

Quiet descended and after a few moments she glanced up and found him staring at her across the fire with an odd look. She was puzzled at first, then followed his gaze to her own ripped tunic, which hung entirely open from her wounded shoulder, revealing much of one bare breast. As quickly as the impulse to cover herself bloomed, it was countered by a shocking new thought: he had earned the right to look . . . and to touch, if he wanted. *And so*, she realized, *had she*.

She had been defeated—her enchantment was satisfied! There was nothing to stop their mating now. She sat in stunned silence, letting the idea wind through her thoughts, where it stirred the coals of old curiosities and ignited new ones. What would it be like to make love, as Jorund called it . . . freely and openly? The very thought sent a tingling through her skin and drew the tips of her breasts taut. Her eyes widened and her gaze slid straight to his.

He had hungrily watched her every movement, his fears for her recovery subsiding more with each small evidence of her resilience. As he absorbed the darting of her tongue and the way she sucked the tip of each finger, he felt a familiar drawing in his loins. And when she slid her gaze from her breast straight into his eyes, he felt a spontaneous wave of heat rushing through his blood.

That instinctively lusty reaction appalled him and he buried his nose in his dwindling bowl of food. After a few moments, he glanced at her from the corner of his eye and found that she was still staring at him.

"You defeated me, Jorund," she said quietly. There was a deep undercurrent of feeling in her voice.

"I wounded you, Aaren," he corrected, with a darkening scowl. He set his bowl aside and picked up a piece of wood to nudge the stone crock away from the coals.

"So you did," she said, discerning the reason for his pensive mood. He felt a burden of guilt for having injured her. She tried to lighten it. "But not before I wounded you." He reacted as if her blade had just bitten him again.

"Dammit, Aaren—no more of this warrior nonsense!" He pushed up from the hearth, shifted his weight irritably, and ran his hands through his hair. "I could have broken your shoulder or hacked your arm off—or worse."

"But you didn't break my bones, Jorund." She flashed a beaming smile and spoke those all-important words: "You broke my enchantment instead."

"Enchantment?" He stiffened, reacting to that one word, not to the suggestion embedded in it. "I don't want to hear another word about that wretched curse. It's caused nothing but—" He bit off the rest of what he was about to say and turned away, struggling to contain himself. A moment later he announced, "I'm going to bathe," and seized a glowing brand from the fire, starting for the door. He turned back briefly before striding out into the frozen night. "And you . . . Get yourself into those furs and rest."

The cold draft from the slamming door and the impact of his abrupt withdrawal struck her in the same moment. She sat, stunned. What was the matter with him? Surely he understood what ending her enchantment meant. They could be together . . . they could . . .

She shivered and wrapped her arms around her waist, wriggling closer to the coals. His reaction to their fight went deeper than she realized. His dread fear of raging out of control and hurting her had made fighting her an ordeal for him. And to have wounded her, then tended her and worried over her, had deepened his remorse.

It was too late to do anything about what had already happened, but she could certainly comfort him now. She cast a speculative look toward the door and her face lit as she remembered his parting order. *Get yourself into those furs.* She eyed the warm, soft pallet, recalling his earlier promise . . . something about her bare buttocks and his warm, silky furs.

And for once, she obeyed.

By the time Jorund returned to the lodge, the coals were dying and Aaren was half asleep. She roused at the sight of him, sliding to the far side of the furs to make room for him beside her. Her heart was pounding, and she felt jittery and shivery inside. She held her breath in anticipation, admiring his handsome frame and his easy, graceful movements in the dim light. He stirred the coals and put more wood on the fire . . . then sat down on the stone ledge, leaned back against the wall, and folded his arms over his chest. She frowned. After a pride-battle with herself, she finally pushed up on one arm and spoke.

"Aren't you coming to sleep?" Her voice startled him and he jerked straight, locating her in the furs.

"*Nej*, I have slept enough." His voice was ragged. "Go to sleep."

He sat back, re-folded his arms, and stared at the fire. His troubled mood sent an intense heart-longing through her.

Years ago, in their mountain home, she had held her little sisters in her arms and stroked their hair to comfort them. She recalled that day in the meadow with the other children; it had worked for them, too. But Jorund was a grown man, a warrior, and she wasn't sure if a woman should do that to a man . . . if Jorund would allow her to do it. She sank back into the furs, grateful that the darkness hid her confusion and the mist forming in her eyes. Comforting was women's work. If only she were more of a woman, he had once said to her. Now she said it to herself.

In the quiet darkness, that longing to love and comfort became a wish and the wish became a powerful force moving within her heart. And the walls that had contained and shielded her softer self came crumbling down before it. What good was her strength without her softness? What

good were the hard virtues of power and honor . . . without
the softer gifts of wisdom and compassion to guide them?

She had struggled valiantly to safeguard her inner softness, the woman-heart of her, against the harshness of the
world and the role into which she had been thrust. Now it
rose up against that well-meaning restraint, refusing to be
suppressed any longer . . . demanding a rightful share of her
heart and mind, whatever the consequences . . . demanding
she use her vaunted warrior's courage in the service of her
heart . . . to risk being tender. Jorund needed her softness.
He needed her to be a woman tonight.

"By the Norns . . . I cannot sleep either," she said thickly,
throwing the furs back and sliding to the floor. "Not with
you making so much noise." He looked up in surprise, then
frowned.

"I did not make a sound," he protested, sitting straighter,
uncrossing his arms. Then he noticed the moisture in her
eyes and froze.

"But you did," she declared, pinning him with her gaze.
"I could hear your heart-groanings all the way across the
lodge. You are sitting there feeling miserable for fighting
and giving me a nick with your blade. You cannot deny
it." The mist in her eyes became deep, glittering prisms of
liquid.

"Aaren . . . I don't want . . . to . . ." He floundered, staring at her glowing face.

"Don't want to what? Think of it? Speak of it? Neither
do I." Her voice softened to match her gaze. "I will bury
it, Jorund . . . if you will."

For a long, tense moment neither spoke. She stepped
closer, her movements supple and womanly.

"Will you, Jorund? Will you accept that I hold nothing
against you . . . and then hold nothing against yourself?"
Her heart ached at the way he, who had forgiven *her* so
many times, had so much difficulty forgiving himself.

"I swore to myself—I even promised you—that I would
never hurt you," he said. "Then I fought and the madness
came on me . . ."

"It was not much hurt, Jorund," she said, reaching the
edge of the hearth beside him. "No more than I dealt you

and less than the pain you have dealt yourself since. A little discomfort is a small price to pay for honor and duty, and for the pleasure yet to come." She summoned the courage to place her hands on his shoulders and caress them. A shiver went through him. "Do not make your heart pay *wergeld* for a slaying which never happened."

"Do you honestly not recall what it was like?" His voice and countenance were pained. "I might have killed you . . . I might have lost you forever . . ."

"I remember it all. But I especially remember that as we fought I was never afraid. Not even when the battle-fury came upon you. You see, I trusted your heart-weapon, your *love*, to protect me. And it did." She swallowed hard and slid her arms around his neck, pulling him closer, hoping he would accept the comfort of her embrace. Then she risked all, pouring her melted heart from her eyes into his.

"Now . . . trust the love in my heart to comfort and heal the hurt in you. For I do love you, Jorund. With everything in me." And she held her breath.

"Aaren—" Jorund's arms flew around her waist and he buried his face against her breast, hugging her with all his might. "Aaren, oh, Aaren . . ."

Then he looked up at her and grinned. "You love me!" Bounding up with her in his arms, he whirled her around before he remembered her injury and stopped instantly, setting her back on her feet. "Are you all right? Did I hurt anything?" She shook her head, then squeezed her eyes shut, dislodging the tears down her face. They stood in the flame-glow, holding each other, letting their love fill the silence as it filled their hearts.

"Say it again," he demanded in a thick voice against her hair.

"What part?" she said, laughing, guessing what he wanted and feeling suddenly buoyant and victorious.

"Say it," he commanded, squeezing her waist and lifting his face to her, his eyes shining. "Say it again . . . then kiss me."

"Are those the terms of my surrender? Heavy tribute, I say."

"Sweet tribute," he countered, and she could not argue. "Say it again."

"I love you," she said softly.

He closed his eyes, savoring those words, letting them wash through his body and soul. When his eyes reopened, a new light burned in their depths. She wiped the wetness from her face and grinned, too.

"Now kiss me," he demanded in a rougher, deeper tone. Those stark, male vibrations set the tips of her breasts tingling. A new tension was suddenly rising between them . . . a hot, sweet excitement. His hands slid down the curves of her hips, claiming them and all the treasures enclosed within their bounds.

"I doubt you made such demands of the other warriors you've defeated," she said, feeling a delicious liquid heat invading her body wherever he touched her.

"None of them had lips like yours, or breasts like yours." He nuzzled her. "Kiss me."

"But we haven't finished discussing the terms of surrender," she insisted, raising her chin. She liked the huskiness of his voice, the thick, sensual undertone of his command, and the excitement it stirred in her blood. "I have a few demands of my own."

"Demands?"

"My shoulder," she said, lifting her arm and grimacing as dramatically as possible. "You can clearly see . . . I will be unable to tend the hearth for quite a while." A mischievous glow entered her expression as she conjured additional possibilities. "And no hunting or trapping or skinning. No carrying water. And chopping wood is much too difficult . . . I may not be able to swing an axe until spring. That means you will have to do the hunting and cooking and tanning and fire making . . ."

"Anything else, my greedy little captive?" He pulled her closer, staring at her mouth, anticipating the pleasures of sealing her surrender with something vastly more pleasurable than a hand-clasp.

"A bath," she said, slipping from his hands and eluding his attempt to retrieve her. She darted for the door and he sprang after her, slamming the half-opened door shut and trapping her against it with an arm on either side of her.

"You demand a bath?" he said, lowering his head, crowding her with his heat. "At this hour?" She nodded, sweeping him with a long, sensual challenge of a look.

"I'm not the least bit sleepy, Jorund. And I demand that you come along. To help."

She ducked under his arm. He followed her out and up the slope to the bathing hut.

Moments later, she perched on the edge of the wide wooden shelf, watching as Jorund stoked the oven until the rocks heated and the bathing house grew warm. When he got to his feet and turned, she reached out with one long leg and kicked the door shut. There was a wry, tempting curl at one corner of her mouth, and her eyes glowed like liquid amber.

"I need more of your help. I need you to remove my garments." Her requirement, issued with a smile and carried on a husky purr, was a pure invitation to pleasure.

"You can start with my boots," she said, arching one long leg onto the low shelf and waving her knee ever so slightly—and suggestively—from side to side.

He ambled forward, watching that knee, then glancing at the luminous, dark centers of her eyes. She was playing a game, he understood, kneeling by her upraised leg and working the laces of her boot. And he loved games . . . especially ones he was fated to win. As he worked, his eyes traveled up the shapely arch of her braced leg, lingered on the tantalizing wrinkles in the deerskin at the other end of that leg. His skin heated as he slowly peeled back the worn leather of her buskin and slipped it from her foot.

"My leggings, too," she coaxed, flexing her foot sinuously in his grip.

The small bathing chamber filled with a tension as palpable as the light haze of smoke produced by the fire. She could both see and feel the effect she was having on him; his big, square fingers trembled as they made contact with her skin and a sheen of moisture appeared on his face. The tips of her breasts and her woman's core tightened, responding to his arousal and to her own newfound sensual power. Over and over his words had invaded her body, and now she experimented with words of her own, discovering how it felt to compel such longing in another.

"What is it about my legs that you find pleasing, Jorund?" She raised her bare legs one at a time, turning them to offer him a critical view of each side. "Their length? Their shape? Their hardness? Or is it just the thought of having them wrapped around your body that appeals to you?"

Ohhh, she had struck a spark with that one, she realized, as a flame flared in the depths of his eyes. A trill of response raced through her shoulders.

"You said . . . you could teach my arms and legs sweeter duties . . ." His lips parted and his chest rose and fell harder. She leaned back on her arms, luxuriating in the pull of wanting between them. "Now my breeches."

He slid closer, still kneeling beside the shelf, a willing participant in her exploration of sensual power. His hands trembled as he untied her breeches and peeled them down over her sleek, curvy buttocks. She lifted her bottom slowly to let them pass and sat up, bent her naked legs, then slid them over the edge of the bench, on either side of his big, heated body.

"Now my tunic. Take it off." She followed his burning gaze to her thighs, which were spread erotically before him, pale skin framing a dark wedge of shadows pointing to the liquid heat smoldering at the base of her belly. He grasped the ripped shoulder of her garment and eased it over her injured arm and her head.

She sat before him, naked except for her wound dressing. His eyes became hot, simmering pools, his tunic clung to his damp body, and she could feel his tension through her knees, against his sides. But still he made no move to claim her.

"My breasts . . . you said you like how soft they are," she whispered, sliding her fingers across one full, rounded globe, cupping it briefly and lifting, as if offering it to him. She released it to rub her fingertips over the tightly contracted tip. "But part of them isn't soft just now. Do you like their hard parts as well?"

Her sultry eyes allowed no evasion, demanded an answer. His hands rose and hovered. When they closed hotly over her breasts, a wild shower of sensation cascaded through her body and she gasped.

"I love both their soft swell and their hard tips, Long-legs," he whispered thickly, dipping his head to kiss one taut nipple, then to swirl it with his tongue. He suckled that peak, then paused, watching her sleek body undulate helplessly with pleasure and longing. "Such breasts. Like the rest of you . . . so hard . . . so soft."

"Oh, Jorund," she said, feeling rivulets of liquid fire running along her nerves. Somewhere in the play of words and desires he had usurped her game and turned it against her. Her head dropped back and she arched into his hands, her whole body aching for his touch, for the half-remembered weight and feel of him. Unable to bear the yearning much longer, she lifted her arms, sank her fingers into his silky hair, and pulled him nose to nose with her.

"The enchantment is broken," she said forcefully. "But you must wield your blade against me one more time, Warrior-heart." When his muscles stiffened, she reminded him with a triumphant smile: "To make good your vow to mate Odin's she-wolf."

The challenge rang in his very blood. He grinned and slid his arms around her, reeling her hard against his body, devouring her lush mouth with his eyes as he savored the anticipation of tasting it.

"I know which blade you want, She-wolf. Be warned— from this day on, it is the only one I will ever wield against you. Now, wrap your long, dangerous legs around me . . . and prepare to reap the rewards of defeat."

Moving them back onto the bench, he spread himself over her body like a great bear skin. She wrapped her legs around his, welcoming him into the cradle of her thighs, and she laughed, knowing the victory was all hers.

"Now," she said huskily. *"I surrender."*

He plunged into her kiss, demanding and claiming her softer recesses, then gentling to explore and relish the territory he had conquered. Their kisses gradually lightened and became a varied feast of sensation—playful toying one instant, deep stirring penetration the next. Heat rose precipitously between and around them and he pushed up, sliding onto his knees between her legs. When she made a groan of disappointment, he laughed.

"I'm roasting in these clothes. And I want to feel my bare skin against yours."

But when his tunic and boots and breeches were shed, and he knelt between her legs again, he did not move immediately to fill her outstretched arms. Instead, he surveyed her body with exquisite leisure, running his eyes up her parted legs, then up her flat belly and curving waist to the full, dark-tipped mounds of her breasts.

She lay in a tangle of burnished hair, blushed with heat, dark-eyed with desire. Her lips were parted and reddened from his attention, and her body was covered with a light sheen of moisture that made her glow golden in the dim light. She was passion incarnate . . . the lush, receptive goddess of a warrior's dreams.

"I want to learn you, Long-legs. Every part of you. I want to know you with every part of me." His fingers started at her ankles, tracing her form, reaching beneath the sleek exterior for the firm muscles beneath—massaging, caressing, stimulating every bit of her he could reach. And his mouth followed where his hands led. He tongued and kissed the curves of her calves, the bends of her knees, and the silky skin of her inner thighs. She started when she realized where he was headed and tried to prevent him, but he simply laughed and nuzzled the soft furring of her woman's mound, then continued up her belly, her waist, to her breasts.

He held his body away from hers on his massive arms, braced above her like a great, devouring beast. But his mouth was achingly gentle over her nipples and his sucklings set her writhing softly, erotically beneath him.

When she could bear it no more, she wrapped her arms around his shoulders and pulled him down on top of her. "Now, Jorund," she murmured, feeling the throbbing heat of his great flesh-spear against her woman's mound. She braced and held her breath, but his shaft merely parted her folds and thrust gently along her moist inner channel. She gasped and pressed against him, meeting each stroke with a motion of her own. And with each perfectly aimed thrust, she felt a frisson of pleasure radiating outward, from the very heart of her.

"Now, Jorund," she said with a groan, arching and straining to rub harder against him. But each time she deepened the contact between them, he eased back by the same amount, maintaining that gentle but relentless friction against the core of her sensation. She began to tremble, grew desperate for the weight and force of him against her, for the filling of the hollow ache inside her.

"I want the lightning . . . make the lightning in me," she entreated.

"Soon enough, greedy wench," he whispered maddeningly into her ear. "Enjoy this first part . . . it is better if you are prepared."

Prepared. He was preparing her . . . for a pleasure storm . . . for the rending to follow. She could feel her body responding, could feel the liquid heat swirling, coiling in her womanflesh. A small, lingering anxiety in her melted. She knew what it was to prepare for fighting . . . and now Jorund prepared her for loving. . . .

She gave herself over to it. It was oddly familiar, this driving, mounting tension that reduced all sensation to broad strokes. Suddenly her whole consciousness focused on a pale halo of hair, a lush mouth, a great, warm weight molding her body, a wild thudding in her veins, and fluid, rhythmic surges of pleasure lapping through her loins. The pace quickened and she felt her blood-heat rising, felt the gathering in her loins . . . she was suddenly launched into a fire storm of pleasure.

She felt herself expanding and contracting at the same time, as she shuddered through searing blasts of pleasure. Then she felt him pause and draw back . . . and enter her. The sensations of fullness, of parting and opening, were overwhelming. Her untried flesh yielded slowly before his invading force. Over and over he withdrew partway and thrust again, each time deepening his conquest of her until they lay completely joined.

"Did I hurt you?" he murmured softly into her ear. She could not speak, but shook her head. "There is more, Longlegs. Much more."

With her gaze captive in his, he began to move inside her, watching the shifting lights in the depths of her eyes as he filled her loins with his throbbing heat and poured a new tension in her blood. She arched and clung to his shoulders, feeling his shimmering eyes penetrating her soul as he penetrated her body.

Each long, luxuriant stroke lifted her again along a sleek, tightening spiral of sensation which exploded abruptly, flinging her into a wild, soaring arc through brilliant, uncharted realms of pleasure. She felt him stiffen and shudder, then clasp her fiercely against him as he poured his passion into her receptive depths and launched into those enchanted realms with her. Suddenly they were one . . . joined in light and warmth . . . known and knowing . . . giving and given, without reservation.

Together they settled back into the smoky warmth of the little bathing hut, lying side by side, their bodies wet from the steamy heat and their eyes glowing like the hearth's cooling embers. She traced the thick mounds of his chest, lingering over his taut male nipples, and marveled that the shape of his body was so very like her own, and yet so different. Beside her, he was thinking much the same thing, until his eyes fell on the binding on her left shoulder and he touched it gently.

"Your shoulder," he said softly. "Is it all right? I forgot about it."

"It's fine, Jorund," she said, rubbing the furrow from his brow with her fingertips. "All of me is fine. It is wonderful . . . your loving. It was well worth fighting for." The light in his eyes flickered and she seized his chin and pressed her nose against his. "Promise me you will wield your pleasure-blade against me again." Then her fierce expression softened to a frown and she bit the inside of her bottom lip. "We can do it again, can't we?" The brazen sound of her question made her pull back, but he caught her before she moved far.

"Eager for another taste of defeat, are you?" He laughed softly, then saw the genuine embarrassment in her face and realized that it was the maiden in her, not the warrior, who asked. His tone gentled. "We can do it again, any time you want . . . as long as you give me a few minutes to rest between requests." He glanced down his body, drawing her eyes too.

His flesh-spear was softer, but still swollen, and she glanced up quickly, flushing a deeper red. Moments ago she had yielded up all her body's secrets to him . . . and now she felt unaccountably shy. "I don't mean to . . . it's just that I've never . . ."

"Done it before?"

"Everyone knows I've never gone to the furs with a man before," she said, dismissing that as cause for chagrin. She studied the warmth in his eyes and was drawn to trust it. "I meant . . . I've never had anyone to ask about such things." She reddened more, feeling that revelation was somehow more personal than anything relating to her body. "I . . . I have never lived around women, except for my little sisters. And they know even less about such things than I do." Her voice was small and she could not meet his eyes just then.

A tender smile lighted his face and he pulled her close, sheltering her in the curve of his body.

"Ask me your questions, Aaren. I can teach you."

Her eyes burned for a moment. Then she did ask . . . about the ways of men with women, about the times for loving and the words that speak of loving. He answered each question in his quiet, authoritative way, easing her embarrassment with warm smiles and tender touches. Women, she learned, thought and spoke of mating in terms of its benefits or its outcome . . . as fur-warming and pleasuring or baby-making and cradle-filling. Men, on the other hand, spoke of mating in terms they knew best: strength and conquest . . . a wrestle in the furs, the sheathing of flesh-blades, fur-sport, or hard riding. There were no set times for loving, except as a woman's body required, and most loving was done quietly in the sweet darkness of a woman's furs . . . at a woman's invitation.

Then came a silence and he could feel a question working its way up out of her depths.

"Did I do everything right . . . just now?" she whispered. He might have laughed if the anxiety in her face hadn't been so real. She needed to know if he had found her truly pleasurable. How very womanly of her, he thought, smiling softly.

"You did everything wonderfully well, Long-legs. You were perfect." He ran a finger up the side of her breast, then nuzzled her nipple and continued up her chest to kiss her neck and ear. "In truth—I have never enjoyed a loving more." Her relief was so visible that it tugged at his heart.

"I'm afraid I have a lot to learn to become a woman."

She was so serious that he pushed up onto one elbow and stared at her in the dimness. Was it possible that she still didn't understand?

"What is wrong?" She tensed with alarm and he caressed her cheek reassuringly.

"Aaren, you don't have to *learn* to be a woman or to *become* one, at all. You are a woman already . . . in every way. Being a woman isn't a matter of knowing certain things, or doing certain things. Your woman's body *makes* you a woman, and your passion, your brave spirit, your tender heart and compassion . . . make you a beautiful, strong, and desirable woman. What more could a woman be?"

She turned his words over and over in her mind, trying to find a way to make them fit within the maze of her inner thoughts and feelings. "Are you sure? Jorund, I do things no other woman does. I blade-fight . . . and I like it. And I like hunting and fishing and wrestling . . ."

"Many women hunt," he insisted. "It's just that they do it with falcons while you do it with a bow or a spear. And women fight, too. They just use different weapons: their tongues, their claws, and sometimes their silence. And wrestling . . . you really like to wrestle?"

"I do." She sat up, nervously watching his surprise. He thought for a moment, then raised his brows and nodded.

"I suppose most of the women I've known wrestle in some way. It's just that they confine it to their furs. Which—if I have anything to say about it—is exactly what you will do, Long-legs." He chuckled at her frown and ran a distracting finger up the underside of her breast and around her nipple, wringing an eloquent shiver from her. "And any time you want a match, I'll be more than pleased to provide it for you."

"You!" She blushed and a smile bloomed briefly on her face, then faded. He could see from her expression that she wasn't convinced and realized that she was struggling to reconcile new thoughts of herself as a woman with the long-held ideas of herself as a warrior.

Another of her many puzzles was suddenly solved in his mind. There were not two hearts within her breast, there was only one . . . and it was divided. She was part warrior and part woman. And the sum of her parts was something strange and wonderful, a marvel to experience and to enjoy. As he lay back and watched her exquisitely carved features and vibrant eyes, he had to wonder if perhaps there wasn't something a little god-kissed in the makings of such a being, after all.

"Jorund?" Her voice brought him back from his musings. She was lying on her side, propped on her elbow and running her toes up and down his shins. "I know now why they call you Heart-balm." His ears reddened as he reached for her and drew her onto his chest. "You know so many ways to soothe a troubled heart. With your words . . . your smiles . . . your hands . . . your loving." She ran her fingers back through his hair and suddenly thought of the women's other names for him.

"And they call you Silk-hair. And Slow-hand." She cast a rueful glance toward his male parts. "It occurs to me that it may not be just your hands they refer to. . . ." He laughed and pulled her down so that their mouths were almost touching.

"Greedy wench—then I must set the record straight. They do mean my hands . . . and the slow way I make pleasure with them."

"And Gentle-rider . . . I begin to suspect that has little to do with horses."

He ran a hand down her side, brushing the edge of her breast, then in a blink rolled her onto her back and slid on top of her. "But I am good with horses," he protested. "Always firm but gentle in the saddle."

"And Honey-hunter . . . they don't call you that because you help rob bees." She could feel the heat from his blushing as he tried to divert her by nuzzling her ear and nibbling her neck. But she was curious now and refused to let him drown her wits in pleasure quite yet. "But Flesh-skald . . . that one puzzles me."

He stilled with his mouth by her ear, and cleared his throat as if embarrassed to speak it. "They tease that my fingers write magical runes beneath a woman's skin . . . and the runes turn to poetry and songs in her heart."

She pushed on his shoulders, forcing him up so that she could see his face. In the dimness, her eyes were luminous and filled with new wonder.

"It is most certainly true, Jorund," she said tenderly. "For you surely make magic beneath my skin . . . and fill my heart with songs." Through the sweet silence she became aware of every aspect of his body as it lay along hers . . . so hard and yet so gentle, just like the rest of him. A fierce wave of longing crushed through her chest and eddied downward into her loins. He was a man of a thousand names . . . and every one of them meant pleasure.

She raised his hand on hers and kissed his fingertips, one by one.

"Make a new song for me, Jorund . . . now."

He smiled and lowered his lips to hers.

A light snow fell that very night and they awakened to a pristine white world that seemed created just for the two of them. That day and for the several days that followed, they slept and ate and loved according to their desires, which recognized no bounds except those which the impulse of a loving heart imposed. The work of daily living was divided in an equally haphazard way; each simply did what they hoped would make the other pleased or comfortable. Thus, Aaren tended the hearth and repaired her garments and even carried water—when Jorund let her. And Jorund spent more than an hour untangling Aaren's hair and combing it . . . which led to a long, salty bout of loving on the floor before the blazing hearth. Together they gathered branches for firewood, tended the horses and rode into the next valley, and dropped a hook into the stream for a bit of fish . . . which she cleaned and he cooked.

By the fire each night they sat and talked . . . trading stories and speaking of Jorund's village and his travels, and of Aaren's mountain life and education. She revealed to him the rigors Serrick had required of her in training: the unceasing running, the stacking and unstacking of boulders to strengthen her back and arms, and the intense testing periods in which Serrick demanded that she be ever ready to fight and challenged her without warning. And Jorund shared his knowledge of faraway places and related to her his understanding of the White Christ and told stories of his kinsmen and the village folk. In those precious exchanges, they drew closer in both love and understanding.

When they returned, half frozen, from a ride one afternoon, Aaren reluctantly donned her padded breastplate once more, for the added warmth it provided, and took it upon herself to fashion warmer garments for the two of them. Jorund's fleece jerkin had been ruined in his wolf-fight, and the only readily available materials were the sleeping furs and woolen blankets. She planned carefully and managed to make two large tunics from one blanket, intending to line them with marten skins from the thick sleeping pallet.

Planning and stitching clothing were not among her natural skills, she discovered; needlework was harder than it looked and tedious in the extreme. But the thought that Jorund would wear the garment kept her at it.

She liked doing personal things for him: mending his tunic, making a special pine bark tea when he took a sneezing fit, and wiping him down when he bathed. Best of all, she loved combing his hair as he sat by the fire of an evening. A Norseman's hair was his pride, and Jorund had more reason than most to be proud of his long, flaxen locks. And it did not take long for her to learn that the combing of hair—whether hers or his—was a certain prelude to pleasure.

Once or twice, she did feel a twinge of concern over her enjoyment of the womanly feelings blossoming in her, the most unnerving of which was the pleasure she took in the size and strength of Jorund's big body. He made her feel small beside him, which ordinarily would not have been a pleasant thing for her at all. But when she was next to Jorund, she positively loved the feeling.

She found herself watching him move about the lodge, recalling the way he looked without his garments . . . the way his flat belly tightened, the way his chest muscles bulged as he held his naked body above hers, and the way his buttocks, thighs, and well-muscled calves flexed as he walked and stooped before the fire or lifted armloads of wood.

"Did you know . . . there is a rip in your tunic," she said one afternoon as she sat watching him across the fire.

He looked up from his seat on the hearth, where he was weaving a snare, and frowned, transferring his gaze to the front of his garment. "Where? I don't see it."

"It's in the back," she said. "Take it off and I'll mend it." She set aside the tunic she was stitching but retained her needle and knife. He shrugged and did as he was bade, then stood to hand it to her. She took it from him with a long, raking glance down his body. "And your breeches . . . Jorund, you must be more careful. You've cut the leg." He scowled again.

"Where?" He ran his eyes over his legs and—sure enough—there was a small cut in the woolen. "Oh, it's nothing. When I was carving your comb, my knife slipped."

"Well, while I'm mending . . . take them off and I'll stitch them, too," she insisted, clutching his tunic to her breast. He started to say something, then thought better of it and shrugged, removing his sandal-boots, leggings, and breeches, and handing the latter to her. As he stood before the fire, naked and waiting, she feasted on the sight of his wide shoulders, heavily muscled chest, and the taper of his ridged ribs and narrow waist. Swallowing hard, she continued on down his hips and taut, rounded buttocks, to his powerful thighs . . . and the maleflesh that nested in a soft golden haze.

Her face heated and her lips grew sensitive as she stared at him . . . her inner hollow tightened with longing and expectation.

"What are you doing?" Jorund's voice was soft and thick, and there was a knowing gleam in his eye. He came to stand in front of her, his legs spread and his body radiating sensual heat.

"I am . . . ummm . . ." She faltered and her cheeks flushed. His eyes said that he knew she hadn't wanted his clothes just for mending. And that he didn't mind. "I am looking at you," she confessed, meeting his heating gaze. The flame spreading through her loins flared up into her eyes as well. "And making honey."

He laughed, a deep, entrancing rumble. Reaching for his clothes in her hands, he tossed them aside. Then he pulled her up into his arms and carried her straight to the furs.

Jorund watched her adjusting to her new role as a woman, his woman, with abject fascination. He had always loved watching her body; now it became an obsession for him. He took pure sensory pleasure in every stride she made, in the casual flexing of her thighs, the taut movements of her buttocks, and the graceful, catlike roll of her feet. And he measured her with his eyes . . . laying permanent claim to every part of her magnificent frame. Around her he didn't feel quite so oversized and overpowered, which, he realized for the first time, he had sometimes felt around other women.

It was in just such an admiring mood that he sat on a log at the edge of the meadow, watching her on a stump nearby. They had ventured outdoors to take advantage of the bright light of the midday sun for a bit of fine handwork, and their faces were now cold-blushed and their fingers clumsy.

Her nearness distracted him. He savored the tense rise of her shoulders, the dent her frown made between her eyes, and the erotic, pink roundness of her tongue as it crept out to lave her lips. As his admiration grew, so did his desire, and he couldn't help but make a bid for her attention.

"Have I told you today how lovely you look?" When she nodded and continued on with her work, he put down his knife and chuckled. "What a sight you make—just like a little girl learning her stitches." Still, she gave him only a glance. "If only Freeholder could see my she-wolf now . . ."

Her head snapped up and her eyes focused intently on him.

"So gentle, so womanly. I doubt anyone in the village would recognize you."

A genuine trill of panic raced through her heart. Would they not know her? Was she so changed? The combination of *Freeholder* and *she-wolf* in the same breath suddenly brought to mind the warrior's ugly comments about tamed she-wolves and lost teeth. Her spine straightened and her dozing warrior-pride roused instantly. Feral instincts sprang into play.

"Ohhh. So you think you've tamed Odin's She-wolf, do you?" She emptied her hands and stood up, fastening a look of quiet ferocity on him. "Think again, Wolf-tamer."

She moved closer, her features smoothing with determination and her eyes taking on a dangerous, wolflike glow. The sight of her moving toward him with such intensity sent a quick frisson of excitement down his spine. He thrust to his feet and took a step back. Still she came, moving with hypnotic grace . . . her hair whipping around her shoulders, her feet caressing the ground. He took another step back, then another. He'd never seen her quite like this. She was stalking him!

Then he realized he *had* seen her like this . . . when he watched her fight in front of the women's house and then again in the long hall. There was that same air of danger about her that had tantalized him the first time he'd set eyes on her. Only now that sensual menace was trained on him. . . . Every fierce male instinct he possessed was suddenly hurtling into his blood, setting his heart pounding and his body heating.

By the time he could tear his gaze from her, he was all the way across the meadow, near the slope leading to the lodge. In the instant it took him to cast a look around, then behind him as he started back up the grassy rise, she launched herself at him, swept one foot from beneath him, and pounced, knocking him down.

The shock of his fall allowed her to seize his arms and pin them to the sides of his head while she straddled his stomach. Recovering his breath and vision, he struggled for a moment until he realized, with some shock, that she did indeed have him pinned. And when he looked up into her fierce amber eyes and wicked little smile, he felt his blood ignite in his veins.

"You now have a wolf at your throat, Borgerson," she said in a half growl, sliding back on his stomach just enough to lower her face to his. She arched her body deliberately, rubbing feminine-heat against him and watching the jolt of desire that her movement caused in his eyes. "Beg for mercy . . . and she may not eat you."

"And if I don't?" he demanded, his voice a bit choked. By the Norns—he'd never been at a woman's mercy before in his life! And he'd certainly never had a woman use physical force against him in a sexual way. His loins were on fire!

"Then face the consequences," she said, tightening her thighs against his sides and wringing a moan of pleasure from him.

"I've never been eaten by a wolf before," he said thickly, his gaze filling with the smoke of internal fires. "Is it terrible?"

"You're about to find out," she said in a husky, sexual purr that strummed his very nerves. Then she slid lower on him and bent her head to nuzzle open the tie placket of his tunic and bare his neck. And she bit him. Slowly, softly . . . with exquisite restraint . . . her teeth raked his skin. His whole body convulsed with pleasure beneath her.

She paused and released his hands, drawing back to search his face. His skin was bronzed, his eyes burned, and his lips were hot.

"Do it again," he said from deep in his chest.

The vibrations rumbled up through her thighs, magnified by her own desires. After a long moment, she suddenly pushed to her feet and stood astride him, looking down at his sprawled body. Then she stepped over him and climbed slowly up the slope, while watching him over her shoulder.

He was up on his knees in a flash, staring hungrily after her. The angle of her chin and the sinuous movement of her hips made it clear the game would continue . . . but that the rules were about to change. "Wait!" he called out, and she halted.

"One bite?" he demanded with a growl. "That's all I get? One wretched bite?"

She turned back halfway and raked him with a look that all but shredded his garments.

"If you want more, Borgerson . . . you'll have to work for it."

Her challenge struck him right between his male pride and passion. He shot to his feet, and with his next heartbeat he was charging up the slope. She gave a triumphant laugh and bolted up the path ahead of him.

"I'll get you, She-wolf!" he called, racing after her. She darted toward the cabin door, then feinted at the last moment and went running farther up the slope toward the horse shed.

"And what will you do with me if you catch me?" she called out, ducking between the horses and scaring them so that they reared. When Jorund arrived, the nervous animals kept him at bay long enough for her to skitter along the stone trough and out the other side. In a flash, she was racing at breakneck speed down the slope again . . . and he had to untangle himself from the horses to follow.

"I'll have you at my mercy, She-wolf!" he roared. "And I'll make you into a wolf-skin to warm my bones at night!"

She laughed as she dodged and ran like the wind ahead of him, crisscrossing the meadow and snaking in and out of the trees. Her long legs stretched out powerfully when she needed to cover open ground, then danced effortlessly through mazes of downed branches and underbrush when she flew through the woods. He charged after her in a wild rush, cutting corners wherever he could and using brute strength to plow through the underbrush instead of darting over it. Their mad chase slowed as she darted back across the meadow and up the slope, then ended abruptly when she ducked into the lodge and slammed and barred the door behind her.

"Aaren!" Jorund pounced to a stop before the door, panting and burning with unspent heat. "Open up!" When there was no answer, he set his fist to the planks. "I'm coming to get you, She-wolf!"

The door trembled under his mighty blows, but the bar held and after a while all went silent. Aaren crept to the door with her hand over her thudding heart, quieting it so she could listen. There was no sound. She scowled, thinking that he wouldn't have given up so easily.

Timber groaned against wooden timber at the top of one wall, and the roof beams suddenly creaked. A scraping noise across the roof made her look up and her jaw went slack as Jorund's boots plunged through the smoke hole at the peak of the roof. With a twist of his body he lowered himself through the opening and dropped onto the cooled hearth, raising a cloud of ashes.

"Oh, you—" She scrambled for the door.

"Prepare to surrender," he ordered as he pounced down from the hearth and bounded across the lodge to slam the bar back in place. She dashed back across the chamber and stood with her chin high and her eyes defiant.

"If you taunt a she-wolf, you're likely to get bitten," she warned, suffering a wild shiver of excitement at the raw hunger in his face.

"Is that a threat or a promise?"

She could tell a move was imminent in the twitches of his muscles, and when he lunged for her, she raced for the door again. But he had read her intentions in the barely perceptible flicker of her eyes and had her in his arms before she reached the door. She braced and shoved, to no avail, then tried twisting her body around and down . . . slipping out of his arms. But he slid down with her, maintaining his grip, and she quickly found herself toppled and lying on the hard-packed floor with him atop her.

She twisted and bowed her back, arched and rolled her body, using every wrestling move Serrick had taught her to try to throw him off or to escape. But he was massively strong and—worse—knew exactly how to counter her moves. Using his legs for leverage and his full weight to advantage, he trapped her again and again, corralling her legs with his and finally pinning her on her back.

"What are you going to do with me, Borgerson? Skin me or tame me?" she challenged, panting softly, her eyes bright with excitement.

"Tame you . . . first," he said hoarsely, catching his breath. Then he captured her mouth in a wild, searing ravishment of a kiss that left them both air starved and reeling. When that kiss ended, another sweeter one took its place . . . then another, deeper and more pleasurable still. His towering heat melted her resistance and her body softened beneath his. When he pushed up on his elbows above her, she realized that her arms had somehow wound themselves around his ribs.

"Now, I skin you." He sat up, astride her, and proceeded to strip her garments, flinging them aside in his eagerness to claim the treasures they concealed. Scooping her up, he carried her to the great pallet of furs on the sleeping shelf and deposited her in the middle of them.

She wriggled sinuously against the silver fox pelts, luxuriating in their silky slide against her bare buttocks and seeking their delicate rasp against her sensitive nipples. She bowed and arched with a feline awareness of every part of her long, exquisitely muscled body. Then she pushed up onto her hands and knees, and turned her tawny, golden eyes on him, looking exactly like her fierce namesake.

"I'm waiting, Wolf-tamer."

Within heartbeats, Jorund's garments lay on the floor and she had pulled him into the furs with her, stretching her long, soft-skinned body over his like a big, sleek pelt. She teased his lips with hers and slid her mouth down his chin, then down his neck. His flesh was so firm, so warm, with a slightly salty taste. When she fastened her teeth gently on the side of his neck, he jerked reflexively and groaned one word: "More."

Lavishing long, sinuous licks and soft, voluptuous bites on his neck and shoulders, she began to work her way down his chest, then his belly. Over and over she raked him gently with her teeth, nipping then releasing him. He shuddered and twitched and arched in a sublime agony of arousal. He was slowly being consumed . . . mind, body, and self-control. With each kiss, each slow, erotic flick of her tongue, each hot, delicious bite, he could feel the hungry beast in him prowling and clawing his insides, coming closer and closer to the surface.

When she reached his maleflesh and caressed him, he opened his eyes and raised his head . . . and saw her face rubbing against his shaft . . . saw her kiss-swollen lips parting . . . coming nearer . . . The sensual beast in him tore free of its constraints, and he reached for her and dragged her beneath him, plunging his tongue into her soft, pleasurable mouth and sinking his hands into the wild torrent of her hair. Through the blood-heat in his senses, he felt her surprise and then her powerful response rising swiftly.

She suddenly writhed and arched beneath him, challenging his control, testing his mastery of her with every bit of her formidable strength. The physical contest between them fired his senses in ways he hadn't realized were possible. Every nerve and sinew in his body vibrated with the strain of containing her. It was like riding a lightning bolt down from the sky . . . or trying to kiss a tigress . . . or mate a she-wolf.

The primal, surging rhythm of their blood permeated their bodies, slowing their responses and gradually blending them. Their wild straining ceased and their bodies began to move in concert, thigh to thigh . . . breast to breast . . . his hardness against her softness. Her arms now wrapped around his shoulders and her body sought his. She lifted his face between her hands and looked into his white-hot eyes.

"Now, Jorund."

With one heart-stopping thrust, he joined their bodies, and for a moment, neither had possession of their senses. Slowly, that earthy and vital connection between them brought them back to reality, and they began to move together, arching and undulating, heated flesh surging against heated flesh. Their fever mounted, even as their motions slowed. The tension drained from their limbs to coil tightly in their loins. With each stroke, each caress, the delicious strain mounted like volatile vapor in their blood, until just one heated spark escaped and sent a blinding explosion of pleasure through her . . . igniting him as well.

Together they peaked and soared . . . like flame spread upon the searing winds of pleasure. And for a time neither could see or feel or hear . . . could only be.

The pace of Aaren's heart slowly returned to normal. When he called her name, she had to fight an overwhelming lethargy in order to turn onto her side facing him.

"Are you all right? I never meant to be so—" He choked off the rest, frantic with the thought that he might have hurt her. He sat up partway and examined her both visually and with his hands, starting with the half-healed cut on her shoulder and working his way gently down her body.

"More than all right," she murmured, rippling under his touch. A pleasure-filled smile curled the ends of her mouth. "I feel . . . wonderful."

He had to admit; she looked wonderful. Her skin glowed in the dim light and she had a languorous, sated look, like a cat gorged with fresh cream. Her obvious good health reassured him and the tension finally flowed from his exhausted frame.

"I think I just met the *he-wolf* in you, Borgerson," she teased, her eyes half closed. "And I think I like him." With that, she let her eyes drift shut and was instantly asleep, leaving him staring at her in complete bewilderment.

He had never, not in his entire manly life, unleashed the full force of his passion-fury on a woman before. Mindful of his size and strength, he had always held back when taking his release, always considered the woman's smaller, more fragile frame. But just now, he'd been roused enough to erupt through his long-practiced restraint and plunge into Aaren like some wild animal. Like the he-wolf she had just named him.

He'd never imagined lovemaking could be like that . . . so furious, so wild and thrilling. And he understood instantly that it would only be so with Aaren. She matched him passion for passion, strength for strength, absorbing all of his intensity and returning it in kind. She not only withstood his overpowering strength, she wanted it, sought it. She was indeed the mate to his body and his soul.

And with his body at perfect rest for the first time in his life, he smiled and drifted into sleep with her.

She awakened some time later to find him watching her. She smiled, intrigued by the glow in his eyes. "What are you doing?"

"Watching you. You wrestle very well indeed. I don't know when I've enjoyed a bout more."

Her eyes danced and she gasped quietly as she felt his hands sliding up her belly and over the tips of her breasts, caressing and rousing them.

"There is only one thing that could have made it better . . ." he murmured, kissing his way down her shoulder to one of those hard-tipped mounds.

"And what was that?" she asked, closing her eyes and groaning as he sent lazy spirals of pleasure wending through her. She heard a perfectly wicked chuckle.

"A pot of grease."

Chapter Seventeen

The following days deepened the bond between Aaren and Jorund. They came together again and again, as strong, vibrant lovers, as playful children, and as quiet, deep-seeking souls. The intangible connection Aaren had always felt between them deepened and broadened to include every waking hour and every possible task, from the delicious intimacy of lovemaking and the fun of bathing, to the mundane chores of daily living. It was as if she were fated to be here with him . . . and he with her. And for the first time since she had left her mountain home, she felt a peace and belonging that reached all the way into her bones.

"Close your eyes." Jorund's voice surprised Aaren as she knelt before the hearth, coaxing the coals to share their flame with the small branches she was adding as she prepared to make some roasted fish and flatbread. She turned halfway.

"No, don't turn around! I have a gift for you and you'll spoil it if you look," he said with tantalizing excitement.

She dutifully closed her eyes and sat back on her heels, feeling a cold blast of air from the door and listening to the sound of his movements. A moment later something soft brushed her cheek. It wasn't his hand, she thought, frowning and concentrating harder on that brief sensation.

"Now hold your hands out . . . close together."

When she extended her cupped hands he laid something soft and warm . . . and *wriggling* in them. Her eyes flew open and there was a small gray and black forest cat baby, all head and ears and eyes, not more than three or four weeks old. Her jaw dropped.

"A little forest cat!" The creature mewed and wobbled, sinking its needlelike claws into her wrists to steady itself as she held it up and peered into its big eyes. "Its eyes are just opened. And those ears . . ." She drew it close and rubbed one of its seemingly oversized ears with her nose. "It's a little heart-stealer! Where did you find it?"

"I came across a wrecked den while I was hunting. A badger or wolverine probably got the mother. Alone in the forest, it would line a marten's belly by nightfall. So I thought you might like it."

"What a little mouse you are . . . look at you," she said to it as she sat down with her back to the fire and began to inspect and play with the little beast, quarreling over its sharp claws, crooning over its fuzzy ears and tail. "We'll have to fatten you up, little beast. How about a nice piece of fish?" She retrieved a small piece of fish from the hearth behind her and let the cat baby eat it from her fingers.

"Whoa—that was my meal!" Jorund said, laughing as he removed his outer tunic and sat down beside her. But his protest was belied by the warm light in his face. He was utterly charmed by the girlish pleasure she took in his gift.

"I had a tame forest cat once before. A long time ago." Her eyes shone and her cheeks turned rosy. "Father Serrick brought it back to me from a hunt. I fed it goat's milk and let it sleep with me in my fleece. It followed me everywhere until . . ."

"Until?" he prompted.

She winced. "It wandered too far from me while I was picking berries with Miri and Marta, and a fox got it." The sadness, the longing in her face touched him. "I heard it cry and ran to help. I had just begun my training as a warrior . . . and I picked up my small blade and chased and chased it. But it was too late for my little cat." The feelings she had known then lived again in her face, and he slid close and put his arm around her and rubbed her shoulder. "I found that old fox later and killed it."

"Females are at their most dangerous when defending their young," he mused, scratching the little cat's ear with a finger. Then he teased to lighten her mood. "What a ferocious mother you will be."

"A mother?" She stopped dead still and looked at him. "Me?"

His smile was irresistible as he leaned close to whisper in her ear and send a hand sliding down her belly. "You might even now bear a cub, She-wolf. Why do you think the women often call loving by the name of 'cradle-filling'?"

She sat up straight, setting the kit on the floor beside her, and clasped a hand over his on her belly. "But, Jorund, I don't know anything about being a mother." She turned wide, frightened eyes on him. "I . . . I never even had a mother myself."

Jorund felt a shiver run through his shoulders. "But of course you did, your mother was—"

"A beautiful raven-haired Valkyr," she repeated, as if she'd said it a thousand times. Her voice dropped to a hush. "She left us not long after she set me upon Father Serrick's knee. I never saw her. I do not even know her true name. Then Father Serrick found Leone and brought her back to us. She was so beautiful, so kind and good. But when Miri and Marta had two summers, Fair Leone began to pine for her home in Asgard . . . and to waste away. When he finally let her go, Father Serrick wept and wept. I had six or seven summers by then, and I missed her, too. After that we did not even see the few women who sometimes came with the trappers into the mountains."

He watched the emotions in her face as she spoke and imagined her as she must have been as a little girl . . . dark, fiery curls and huge golden eyes . . . running barefoot in a meadow . . . then wiping tears away . . . grieving for a little cat . . . wishing for a mother.

"Do you know, I had no mother either," he said wonderingly, lifting her chin to look into her eyes. "My birth-mother died before I was weaned. The women of the village took me in. They nursed and fed and taught me and cared for me. After a while, I began to think of them all as my mother." His laugh was a bit pained. "I spent much time with them, and they kept my hands too busy for mischief and my ears filled with their talk. You had no mother . . . well, I had many . . . often too many."

Aaren returned his poignant smile, then suddenly thought of the village children and their reaction to her. Her smile died.

"But what if . . ." In the last fortnight she had learned to trust him. There was no one else in the whole world to whom she could reveal her deepest fears and longings. She took one more step into that trust. "What if my child is . . . frightened of me? All of the rest of the village children are."

As her face paled and her eyes grew rimmed with moisture, he recalled the devastating blend of hurt and longing on her face that afternoon in the bee meadow . . . when the children scurried back to their mothers' arms. An odd pricking began at the corners of his eyes and he pulled her against him, wrapping her securely with his arms.

"They will love you, Aaren. All your children will love and revere and adore you . . . I can promise you. Babes take in their mother's love with their mother's milk, and they cannot help but return it. It is the way of things." He saw the stifled hope in her eyes and sighed, trying to think of a way to convince her. Then it came to him.

"Like your sisters . . . they love you, Aaren."

"But I'm not their mother. I just took care of them when they were small . . . tended their ills and helped them learn to walk . . . and milked the goats so they would have something to grow on . . . and made sure they wore their fleeces in winter . . ."

He took her face between his hands and smiled into her glistening eyes. "What more could a mother have done for them, Aaren?"

His words found a target in the very center of her heart. For a long moment she sat, stunned, seeing her care of her sisters in a very different light. She had not been just "sister" to them, but "mother" as well, without even knowing it. She had fulfilled a woman's role for almost as long as she could remember. And somehow that realization freed her from the doubts that had plagued her about whether she could truly live as a woman. In one way, she already had! She slid her arms around his ribs and buried her face in his shoulder.

"Why is it you, a man, know so much about being a woman . . . and I, a woman, know so little?" she said, sniffing back tears.

"I don't know. The way I was raised by women, among women, I suppose," he said, laying his cheek against the top of her head.

"Your many mothers . . . it was from them that you got your woman's heart," she said, raising her face to him and running her fingertips over his lips. She saw him with different eyes now, understanding that the woman-heart in him had nothing to do with cowardice or valor. It had to do with the way he looked at things and the way he conducted himself, sharing the depths of his strength and his passion . . . lending them to others. "It's true, you do have a woman's heart in many ways. You value many of the things women hold dear . . . like children and harvests and peace-weaving. And you know and can do many of the things a woman must know and do."

"I did not always," he said quietly. "I was eager to be a warrior . . . to redden my first spear. Now, my life's path has brought me back to the things of my early years." He looked at the sadness-tinged wonder in her eyes and suddenly wanted to fulfill every longing of her heart.

The little cat had wandered away and now mewed from the corner near the door, sounding lost. Aaren slid from Jorund's arms long enough to rescue it, then came back to settle in his embrace and gave him a lavish kiss that he would have pursued if the little beast caught between them hadn't started to yowl. She pulled away, then laughed at his disgusted look.

"We're hungry, Cat and I. And I'm afraid you'll have to roast the fish." She lifted the ball of fur with an impish grin. "Well . . . I have my hands full."

That next afternoon, Jorund persuaded Aaren to leave her new pet asleep in the lodge for a while and accompany him on a hike to collect sweet root and birch limbs suitable for arrow-making. They had ranged far from the lodge, along the banks of the stream, and were returning when they reached a small clearing and sat down to rest.

Jorund looked up at the lowering sky and took stock of the moisture-laden wind.

"Snow." A white breath-plume rose from his mouth as he pronounced his conclusion. "And plenty of it. It's good we have lots of meat and a sizeable stack of wood . . . we'll need them."

She nodded, reading in his face that he had reached the same discomforting conclusion she had. "We should probably have started back for the village already," she said with a sigh, rubbing her hands together and breathing on them to warm them. "My sisters are probably frantic."

He got to his feet and rolled his shoulders. "I wonder how many wagers Borger has made on my neck."

"On your neck?"

"He doesn't have much faith in my willingness to use a blade. He's been badgering me to take up a sword again for the last three years. And he finally found the perfect persuasion."

"He did?" She looked at him in surprise. "What?"

"You." He chuckled at her puzzled expression. "Surely you know that was why he decreed that only I could challenge you with a blade. He could see I wanted you and counted on you being either stubborn enough or enchanted enough to make me take a blade to you."

She shifted the bundle in her arms and halted, staring at him, then she chuckled, too. "That was it? Truly?" When he nodded and continued along, she hurried after him. "I thought it was because he was testing me . . . my honor and my willingness to fight."

It was Jorund who paused now, searching her, seeing more clearly why she had considered fighting him such a matter of honor. "I suppose that might have been part of it. But it is not the first time he has tried to force me to fight. He has decreed that whoever will succeed him on the high seat must fight him for it. He will not acknowledge me as heir unless I take the seat by force. The old boar . . . he knows how badly I want the high seat and is determined to use my own desires against me."

"But why won't you fight him, Jorund?" she asked. "It would be only one fight . . . and you would make a wonderful jarl." Her wholehearted support brought a smile to his face.

"I want the high seat . . . but I want the fighting to stop even more. As long as anyone living in the village can remember, our people have been fighting jarl Vermud's and jarl Thorvald's and especially jarl Gunnar's people. But some of the old ones, now dead, told of a time when our peoples were part of the same large clan. We once married and traded and prospered together . . . now we war and prey on each other like rogue wolves. There must be another way to live and to rule a clan . . . besides with a sword."

"But, Jorund, a clan must defend itself. Why just recently, jarl Gunnar tried to steal—"

"Gunnar was not stealing . . . at least he hadn't yet, when Borger rode to the attack," Jorund protested. "Borger has never tried to live peaceably. If he has no cause to fight, he will make one. He came back from his voyage early this season with the battle-itch still strong in his blood. And when the herdsmen brought word of a dispute over the ear-notches of some of the sheep brought down from the high country, he bellowed like a gored ox and mounted a raid to reclaim his property."

"Well . . . it is important that a jarl assert his property rights," she said, pausing, scowling. Jorund halted beside her and searched her doubtful look.

"Less than a score of sheep . . . and a small planting of grain. Is that worth risking and possibly squandering three-score lives to redeem?"

She drew a huge breath and let it out in a disgusted huff. "I suppose not. Not when you lay it out side by side like that."

They walked on in silence until they came to another small clearing. Jorund slowed and looked around him, his senses roused by something. Aaren slowed as well, searching the trees for a sign of what had alerted him.

"What is it?" she whispered.

"Do you not recall this place?" he asked, turning to her. The confused look on her face said she did not. "It is where we exchanged last blows . . . where you were wounded." He dropped his bundle of limbs and strode across the clearing, looking for something on the ground. When he stopped, she emptied her arms and joined him . . . and gasped.

There, half hidden by leaves, lay her sword, Singer. She snatched it up and wiped away the dirt and leaves with her cold fingers. Some of the spots stayed . . . they were rust. Fully five different emotions flickered through her face as she stroked the tarnished silver handle and clasped it to her breast. But foremost in her reeling heart was anguish at the thought that in the days since their battle she had not missed her sword . . . or even thought of it. Her precious weapon, which had been like an extension of her very arm . . . she had lost and forgotten it. She raised a troubled gaze to Jorund.

"Father Serrick traded Leone's fine silver beads and two seasons' bounty of furs for this blade. I lived with it, slept with it, defended myself from animals and plunged into blade-fights with it. . . . How could I have not even thought of it?"

He struggled to respond to her distress, but could offer only one comfort. "Perhaps because you found something more precious to you?"

His thought settled in her mind like a warm, soothing presence and she recognized the truth in it. But she still felt a keen sense of loss, a displacing of something precious and familiar in the core of her. Her throat was constricted and her word-well seemed completely dry.

Only another warrior could have understood her sense of loss in the passage she was making in that moment. And only Jorund was both warrior enough and woman-heart enough to make that passage with her. From this time on, the woman, more than the warrior in her, would direct her course along her life's path. It was a passage ordained for her . . . inevitable, but painful all the same. He put his arms around her and held her, sheltering her with his warmth, lending her his certainty.

When she looked up and nodded, he understood she was ready to go on, and he picked up her bundle as well as his, balancing one under each of his big arms. He indicated their direction with a nod, sensing that she did not need words at this moment, and she struck off ahead of him.

A short way into the trees, she stopped dead, her eyes widening.

"Aaren, what is it?" But his gaze struck the handle of his own sword in the same instant the words left his mouth. He stood, dumbstruck, staring at the blade, which was embedded in the trunk of a birch sapling. A dim memory flooded back, dragging with it a feeling . . . pain.

"Jorund, your sword! How could it have . . . ?" The turbulence in his face when she turned to him made her realize it had to do with their fight.

"I flung it away after you were wounded," he confessed. "I saw you lying there . . . covered with blood." The depth of the blade's bite into the tree was a chilling measure of the fury with which he had hurled it and of a pain that had approached madness in him. Moved beyond bearing, she hurried to the tree to seize the handle and draw out his sword.

"*Nej*, Aaren, leave it!" he called out, halting her just as she grasped it.

She turned with her hands on it, astonished by both the words and the vehemence with which they were spoken. "But your blade, Jorund—"

"Leave it, Aaren. I will not need it."

"But, Jorund, your heart may change. You cannot just leave it here."

"My heart will not change," he declared, his voice thick as he turned his face from the sight of it. There was a lump in his throat, and he had to strain to speak around it. "I have made a vow to the White Christ that I will never raise a blade to another man as long as I live. And I will not be tempted to break that vow if I have no sword to raise."

The horror of it slammed through her. "A vow. But Jorund . . . a vow is sacred . . . you cannot take it back!" Her hands fell, empty, to her sides.

"I do not intend to take it back. Ever." As he said it, his eyes were pained and leaden.

Not to fight . . . not to wield a blade ever again . . . it was his choice alone to make, she realized. And she understood too well his reasons, his fear of slaughtering others, his sense of guilt for having fought and wounded her. Still, she could not accept that a warrior could willingly lay down his weapon, the fierce companion of his struggles, and turn his back on the bond of pride and honor that adversity had wrought between them.

"It is just as well, Aaren," he said in a constricted voice. "Someone must be the first to say enough to the killing. There must be a way to forge peace among our clans . . . and I will now have to find it." The finality in his voice and manner sent a chill through her shoulders.

"Jorund, you speak of peace and an end to killing, but what of the other jarls and clans? They do not share your god or your vision . . . most of your own clansmen do not even share it. And until such a time as all lay down their blades, we must be ready to defend ourselves and our people. The surest way to ward off an attack is to be strong . . . to make others fear your might."

"As long as all carry swords, then swords will always be wielded," he said, trembling. "It must stop somewhere." The full impact of his vow was borne in on him as he confronted the pained disbelief in Aaren's eyes.

"I am trying to understand, Jorund. . . . I do understand your loathing for the reddening of spears. But sometimes swords must be wielded, victory must be won. Some things are worth fighting for . . . to secure or to defend. Surely you can see that." She clutched her own blade to her chest as she came to him. "Jorund . . . you had to fight for me, for our love." But even as she said it, she knew that it was the tumult that fighting and wounding her had stirred in him which had caused that grim and difficult vow. And she felt great remorse that she had forced him to do something so painful for him that he would make such a drastic vow.

His gaze flew back to the handle of the blade which had shielded him on near and distant shores . . . had been his companion, his livelihood, his honor, and ultimately, his shame. He clenched his teeth and his eyes reddened.

The decision of whether or not to rescue his blade was almost physically painful for him. Only another warrior, one who knew the value, the honor, and the piece of his spirit that resided in a warrior's battle-blade, could have understood the magnitude of the decision Jorund was making in that moment. And only Aaren, who loved him, could have shared that pain so keenly with him.

He wheeled and moved off quickly through the trees, his decision made. Aaren blinked to clear the blur of tears in her eyes and followed him.

"And what of the high seat, Jorund?" she whispered. "What of your people?"

It was quiet that evening in the lodge. There was a new tension between them as they went about tending the horses, stringing a rope line from the lodge to the nearby shed, and preparing an evening meal. After they had eaten and laid in a store of water and dry wood and meat for the snow that was already beginning to fall, there came a long silence as they sat before the fire. Each eyed the sleeping shelf and contemplated meeting the other in the furs.

"I . . . I will go to bathe," Jorund announced, rising. "If the snow is deep, it may drift in and block the door. It may be a while before we can get out." He grabbed up his warm tunic and glanced at Aaren, who nodded and focused her interest on feeding the cat.

Later, she banked the fire and transferred the dozing cat baby to a nest of hay lined with a marten pelt. More than once she went to the door, intending to join Jorund in the bathing house and dispel the tension between them. But each time she halted and drew back, thinking that he needed time to sort out his thoughts. So did she. It was well into the night hours when she donned her warm tunic to make her final trip for the night down the slope into the woods.

Instead of going straight into the trees nearest the cabin, she climbed up the slope toward the bathing house and stood for a moment, studying the smoky glow from the hole in the roof. She wanted to bang on the door, to tell Jorund she understood his decision never to fight again . . . except that she still hadn't fully accepted it.

All evening she had come back again and again to the uncertainty it cast over their future. Without a weapon, how could Jorund ever hope to take the high seat? How could he expect to lead his people without ever wielding a blade? And what would his decision mean to their place in the village and to their future children?

Sending a cold hand beneath her fur-lined tunic to her belly, she drew a long, troubled breath. Then she turned aside and climbed around the slope and into the trees beyond the bathing house for her nightly duties. She had finished and was just starting back to the lodge when a movement in the undergrowth nearby startled her. She froze, her mind racing from one possibility to another as she slowly turned.

Against the snow-whitened ground, despite the dimness, she glimpsed a dark, crouching blur of movement. An animal—large, but not deer or elk sized—she determined as she began to run for all she was worth, back through the trees and around the slope. She could hear its panting as it gained on her, and she knew instantly: it was a wolf.

"Jorund!" she called out, racing for the nearest shelter—the bathing house. "Jorund—wolf—*wolf!*"

The door was flung open and he burst outside in a billow of steam, his body taut. He spotted her just as she called his name again, and without hesitation he bolted around the hillside, straight for her. But when he reached for her hand and turned to run back to the bathing house, his bare foot slipped on a loose rock and slid from beneath him. He scrambled on the rocky slope as he went down, and shoved Aaren ahead of him.

"Go—go on!" he yelled. The next instant the wolf sprang through the air and pounced on him, pinning him on his back and barking wildly.

"Jorund!" Aaren screamed, stumbling to a halt and reversing to rush back and help him. For a heart-stopping moment she saw it all in stark relief: Jorund's big, naked body sprawled on the snow-dusted slope, the dark, bowed shape of the wolf atop him. As she reached them, she sensed something odd happening . . . and it slowed her frantic response. Jorund wasn't struggling and the beast wasn't growling or twisting! She charged in and seized the beast's fur, and it yiped and clawed before lunging from her grip, terrified.

"Aaren—look!" Jorund's voice penetrated her confusion. "It's Rika!"

It was some time later that Jorund and Rika poked their heads through the lodge door and located Aaren kneeling before a fire she had stoked so high the flames almost singed the roof beams. She turned a dark glare on the pair of them, then gave them a shoulder and continued feeding the blaze. Jorund bent near Rika's head and whispered, "I think I'd better go in first."

"Aaren," he said coaxingly, slipping through the door and closing it partway behind him. He didn't see Rika's ears perk up . . . or her nose thrust into the opening, quivering with excitement. "I know you are angry. But when you think about it . . . it was enough to make the Devil himself laugh . . . Rika cowering, you chasing her . . ."

She cast a very narrow look at him.

"And the way your feet slipped and your arms kept flailing—" His mouth began to quiver again and he had to stop and get control of himself. "I'm sorry I laughed so hard." He felt the door banging at his back as Rika tried to squeeze her way in, and he shoved against it with his shoulders to prevent her from entering. "Aaren," he said, leaning forward, "how is your hip?"

But just as the sincerity in his voice melted Aaren's resistance and she turned, Rika lunged at the door and knocked him forward, bounding in. She charged to the middle of the floor with her nose up, sniffing, her wolf eyes bright and her ears standing on end. Then before Jorund could grab her, she lunged straight for Aaren, who toppled straight over onto the floor and choked out a sound that was half scream, half growl. Rika leaped over her and was suddenly upon her intended prey at the corner of the hearth.

The cat baby arched and hissed at Rika's great nose and countered the expected attack with its claws. Rika yelped and scrambled back, shaking her head—just long enough for the little cat to dart away.

"My cat!" Aaren shouted as Rika went diving beneath the bed shelf after it. And Jorund dove after the wolf.

There was pure chaos for several minutes: the little cat darting like a blur from pillar to post, Rika barking and blundering after it, and Aaren chasing Rika—intent on doing her in. Jorund didn't know who to grab first. In pure desperation, he grabbed Aaren by the waist and hauled her off Rika. An instant later, he released her to dive after Rika, who had just reached the little cat. He managed to grab a furry tail . . . which jerked and twisted from his grasp . . . while he was trying to shield it from Aaren's righteous anger.

When the panicked cat finally found footing in the logs, climbed the wall, and raced up into the roof beams, Rika leaped and barked below, which allowed Jorund to seize her by the neck and haul her outside into the snow. When he returned, Aaren was trying to coax the cat down. He rescued the little beast and placed it in her arms.

"I will not lose this little cat." Aaren laid down an ultimatum: "Rika has to go." But it was the tears in her eyes that worked on Jorund.

He looked a little sick as he dragged himself outside. Aaren could hear him scolding, then talking . . . and after a while the door opened and two noses appeared in the opening.

"Now, before you get angry . . . at least give her a chance," Jorund entreated. And before she could object, the door swung open and the two of them entered.

"Jorund—are you daft?" Aaren thrust to her feet and lifted the cat baby above her shoulders, bracing for the attack. None came. Rika's eyes shone as she looked at Aaren and the kitten, but at Jorund's hand motion, she sat down beside him. Aaren knew instantly what was afoot.

"*Nej.* Jorund, I won't allow it!"

"Just listen, Aaren. Rika has been around forest cats before. She was raised with one and I don't think she meant it any harm. She was just taken by surprise and got . . . a bit excited." He moved forward, one step and then another, and Rika moved with him, dutifully sitting by his feet each time. "Will you trust me with the little beast . . . I won't let any harm come to it, I promise."

She finally handed over her pet, but her clouded eyes said it was a measure of her trust in him . . . not any belief in his wretched wolf. She stiffened and held her breath as Jorund lowered the cat for Rika to sniff. But, despite a panicky swipe or two of the cat's sharp claws at her nose, Rika remained merely fascinated . . . her tail sweeping the floor behind her. Then came the real test, when Jorund placed the cat baby on the floor and held it, while Rika sniffed and nudged it, then hopped aside and whined, as if eager to play.

"There . . . no harm done," Jorund said, bringing the little cat back to Aaren's lap. "The worst she would do is tire it out . . . playing. The snow will keep us both inside for a while, and we can keep watch. Now, can she stay, Long-legs?"

Aaren looked between him and Rika, who lay exactly where he had ordered her to stay . . . in the corner near the door. He apparently knew the secret of making Rika obey . . . just as he knew how to make her want to cooperate, in spite of her better judgment. Those bluer-than-summer-sky eyes, that bold, mischief-filled mouth . . . how could she resist? She nodded, and got up to settle the kitten in its nest for the night.

When she turned back, Jorund had settled onto the hearth and was motioning to Rika. The wolf crept over to lay her head on his lap for a stroking. Aaren sighed, watching them, knowing exactly how it felt to yearn for the touch of Jorund's hand. Both of them, it seemed, would do anything for him.

The full impact of that realization struck her. What an extraordinary man he was. He fought with stunning power and courage, tamed she-wolves with his bare hands, and held fast his convictions even in the face of great opposition . . . even temptation. There was such largeness of spirit, such depth of strength, such intensity of honor in him. Then it came to her: if any mortal man could lead a Viking clan with only his bare hands, that man was Jorund Borgerson.

Her eyes misting and her heart soaring, she went to Jorund and sank onto her knees beside him. He sat straighter, looking at her moist eyes and laughing mouth with alarm.

"What is wrong, Aaren?"

"Nothing, Jorund. Everything is right . . . perfectly right." All evening she'd been searching for a way to make peace with his decision and dissolve the tension between them.

And insight had come bounding in on four boisterous legs. It was an omen, she was sure.

"I believe you can do it. You can take the high seat somehow and lead your people into a better life-way. I don't know how . . . I only know there must be a way . . . and that you will find it, without wielding a blade." When he blinked, then grinned, she laughed and threw her arms around him.

"A man who tames two she-wolves with only his bare hands can surely handle a few fat old jarls the same way," she declared. He slid his arms around her and began to laugh, too.

Then he ordered one she-wolf to the corner . . . and carried the other to his furs.

Jorund paused in the doorway and gave one last look around the lodge. The storage box, the sleeping shelf, the hearth; all was tidy, swept clean of everything but memories. He ducked back out into a sunlight so brilliant on the snow that it hurt his eyes, and pulled his fur hood up around his head. When he mounted his horse and looked at Aaren, she wore a pensive expression.

"You don't want to leave either, do you?" she asked.

He shook his head and glanced around the white-garbed meadow and the ice-rimmed trees that sparkled in the sun. "But we cannot stay the winter. We don't have enough food . . . and people and duties await us."

She cast a last look around the little meadow, recalling with a heart-pang her first glimpse of it . . . and the anger and dread she had felt. Much had changed in the month and more they had spent here. She reached out a hand to Jorund and he squeezed it briefly before calling to Rika and setting off into the woods toward home.

Chapter Eighteen

For the last fortnight, things had been either monstrously dull or blessedly peaceful in Borger's village—depending on one's point of view. The coastal traders had come and gone, most of the harvest work was completed, the skalds and itinerant craftsmen had journeyed on to warmer climes, and the additional month Old Gunnar had claimed to raise the ransom was not yet past. There hadn't been a blade-fight or a domestic brawl in weeks, and the next batch of feast-draught hadn't finished brewing—so there wasn't enough ale for a prolonged drinking rout to liven things up. Borger was at his wit's end with all this peace. But the women and the common folk, while not all happy, were at least content with the lack of excitement.

Into the quiet and drowsing village, one cold, sunny afternoon, rode two fur-swathed figures on horseback accompanied by a great, rangy wolf. Two young boys spotted them first, on the edge of the stone-walled home-fields, and went running ahead of them, announcing their presence. The village folk poured out into the paths to ogle the shaggy strangers and were stunned to recognize them. From one to another, the word spread like wildfire, and the young boys went running to the smithy, the granary, and the women's house with news that Jorund and the battle-maiden had returned.

By the time Aaren and Jorund reached the commons, they had collected quite a following of folk, who waved and called greetings and scrutinized their odd garments. Jorund smiled as he answered their questions about the game and the snow-cover in the mountains, while Aaren searched the crowd for Miri and Marta. She spotted them and swung her leg over the horse to dismount.

"Aaren—it is you!" Miri cried, throwing herself into Aaren's outstretched arms.

"We were so worried!" Marta declared, wrapping both her sisters in a tight hug. For a long moment they embraced, then Marta pulled back and ran frantic hands down Aaren's face and shoulders. "Are you all right? Nothing hurt—nothing missing?"

"I am fine, Marta . . . and so is Jorund," she said, wiping tears from her sisters' faces. Jorund came around the horses just then and put his arm around Aaren, drawing her tight against his side. When she blushed and made no move to rebuff him, her sisters' eyes widened and a murmur of surprise raced through the crowd.

Rika nosed into their midst, prancing and sniffing, demanding her share of attention. "In fact, we're all fine . . . Rika, too." Aaren laughed, giving the wolf a fond petting, until a mewing came from a cloth bag hanging from her saddle. Aaren pulled out a large gray and black ball of fur, announcing: "And look who we've brought with us. My little pet . . . Jorund found him for me in the mountains. You'll have to help me think of a name." Miri took the cat baby from Aaren and laughed and cuddled it, while Aaren sought Jorund's arm again.

At that moment, Borger sat huddled on a stool before his sleeping closet in the hall, his shoulders wrapped in a length of linen. His countenance was glowering as he submitted to the twice-yearly trimming of his hair and beard. At the sound of the great doors banging open and an explosion of voices, he bashed his beleaguered bondsman aside to charge out to his high seat, demanding to know what was afoot.

"Jorund . . . and the battle-maiden!" Hrolf the Elder called out over his shoulder. "They're back!"

"What?" Borger started at the news. "Both of them?" He tore the linen from his neck and flung it aside, barreling toward the door. But he was quickly met by a stream of his own men who were hurrying back into the hall before a crowd of villagers. He fell back toward his seat, turned, and planted himself before his great chair with his feet spread and his fists at his waist.

Jorund and Aaren removed their makeshift wolf-skin cloaks as they entered the hall and entrusted them to Miri and Marta. Then they strode toward the center of the hall, where Borger awaited them. They halted halfway between hearth and high seat, as if caught and held by the shaft of hazy sunlight coming through the smoke hole. Borger's gaze slid over them, assessing their bulky fur-lined garments and the way they stood shoulder to shoulder before him.

"So, First-born," Borger's voice boomed out across the hall, "you have returned!"

"I have," Jorund answered resoundingly.

Borger's eyes narrowed as he scrutinized his son, noting the determined glint in his eye and the power that emanated from him. There had been a change in Jorund . . . but to what extent and to what end? He cast a calculating look at the warriors and villagers who crowded eagerly around both them and the high seat in a circle.

"When last you left this hall, you vowed not to return unless you had defeated and mated yon battle-maid. Now I ask you—did you fulfill that vow?"

All held their breaths as Jorund flicked a look at Aaren, then raised his chin.

"I did."

A clamor broke out: laughter, cheers, muttering, and one or two desultory calls for proof. Borger snorted a laugh at the spark he witnessed when Jorund's eyes struck Aaren's. He stepped down from his seat onto the hard-packed floor, scratching his belly and striding back and forth, savoring his moment of drama. Then he jerked to a halt before Aaren.

"Is it true? On your honor as a warrior . . . did he take his blade to you and defeat you in honest battle?"

"He did," she answered, without hesitation.

"Ho, ho! And did he also mate you, as he vowed to do, Valkyr's daughter?" Borger grinned, sending a speculative gaze over her, as if searching for some lingering trace of either the violence or the pleasure.

Aaren's face heated, but she had expected a public airing of the matter; her enchantment and Jorund's rash vow had both made an issue of her maiden state.

"He did that also," she declared, with a dart of her eyes toward Jorund's broadening grin.

Laughter, raucous shouts of congratulations, and inevitable questions of whether the pleasure had been worth the fight, filled the hall. Borger's lusty expectation deepened as he eyed the stunning pair and the subtle, speaking looks they exchanged. There could be no doubt that something momentous had occurred to bring about such a reckoned air between them. How perfectly foul of the gods to deprive him of the pleasure of witnessing their fight with his own two eyes . . . when it was exactly the sort of excitement he'd been pining for! He stumped back up to his high seat and threw himself into it, his crafty mind searching for a way to still wring a bit of pleasurable commotion from the situation.

"You have never been known to speak falsely, First-born," he declared, stroking his brushy beard. "But neither have you been known to fight, in recent years. What proof have you that you *fought* her, as well as won her?" Contention arose in the onlookers; some agreeing with the jarl, and some declaring that proof was no concern of theirs—since it was Odin's and Freya's enchantment to begin with.

Proof? Aaren and Jorund stared at each other. Neither had given a moment's thought to the possibility that some proof might be required. Aaren shot a narrow look at the lusty old boar who sat in judgment on their lives and realized there was but one proof . . . and that she must provide it. She strode forward, then she turned to face both Borger and the villagers, her eyes bright with indignation.

"You demand proof? You insulting pack of hounds. Jorund's word is his bond . . . as sure as death and the jarl's wretched taxes." She raised a furious finger. "But once—this once—I will grant you proof." Grabbing the neck of her tunic at the edge of the cut she had mended, she gave it a hard jerk, ripping the stitching apart. When her shoulder lay bare, she turned into the sunlight, proudly displaying the long, dull red line along her shoulder bone . . . pivoting slowly, so that all could see it. "There is the mark of the blow Jorund dealt me."

Miri and Marta gasped, the women frowned or covered their drooping mouths, and the warriors all murmured and nodded excitedly. Borger's eyes widened on what was obviously a fresh scar . . . a blade wound, there was no doubt. There was but one way the fierce fighting-wench could have received such a cut, all realized. Jorund had dealt it to her . . . and with a blade. And their collective shock deepened when she turned to face Jorund and burst into a beaming smile.

"By Thor's Arse-thunder—he did it!" Borger roared, jubilant. "He took a blade to her and defeated her!"

When Jorund extended his arms and Aaren walked straight into them, the hall erupted in a wild commotion of voices and stomping feet and lusty wolf howls. Jorund Borgerson had indeed tamed Odin's She-wolf! And if any further proof of *that* was needed, they provided it instantly . . . in a very lavish and very public kiss.

Good words and good wishes bombarded them from all sides as they stood together, faces flushed, eyes shining. After a few hectic moments of celebration, Borger raised his hands to speak.

"Well done, First-born!" he declared. Then he turned a crafty eye on Aaren. "And as for you, Serricksdotter . . . is it the taste of defeat you relish so, or the taste of the victor?"

Amidst laughter, she raised her chin and declared, "The victor, of course."

Borger turned to Jorund in a boisterous, expansive mood. "What will you have, First-born, as your reward?" he demanded. "Name it . . . and it is yours."

As Jorund contemplated Borger's offer, his eyes flickered briefly to the high seat and back, then settled on Aaren's glowing face. "I'll have Aaren Serricksdotter to wife. This very night . . ." He paused and stared into her eyes as he finished it: "And in the Christian way."

Aaren stood, stunned, and the crowd quieted abruptly, in equal shock. To take a wife in the Christian way meant Jorund was declaring himself a believer. As a Christian he would have one wife and pleasure only one woman in days to come . . . the impact of which was momentarily lost on

Aaren and appallingly clear to the other women of the village.

"W-what?" Borger sputtered.

"Y-you!" Aaren stammered. "You said nothing to me of marriage—much less of this Christian kind." She thrust back out of his arms and glowered at him.

"Well, I'm saying something about it now," he said with a grin, advancing on her.

"How dare you lay claim to me as if I were some battle-prize!" she declared hotly, stumbling back a step for each one he advanced.

"What man in this village would you have over me? Or what man in the whole rest of the world, for that matter?" He paused, insisting she answer. "Which man, Aaren?" When she would not, he answered for her. "*None.* And whose furs do you intend to share ... whose children do you wish to bear?" His voice lowered as he answered for her again. "*Mine.*" He grabbed her wrists, overcoming her resistance, then captured her eyes as well. "And who do you want to love and companion and pleasure you for the rest of your life?" A wickedly irresistible grin spread over his mouth. "*Me.*"

He hauled both of her hands up and laid a kiss on each of her tightly balled fists. "So, you want to be my wife ... to share my property, to share my furs, to share my life. Now the only question you have left to answer, Long-legs, is whether you also wish to *share* me with other women. Do you?" The heat shimmering deep in his eyes ignited every feral and possessive urge in her nature.

"*Nej!*" She managed to answer that one for herself, and he smiled.

"Then quit being stubborn, She-wolf, and speak the Christian vows with me. Pledge yourself to me alone ... as I pledge myself to you." He released her wrists to wrap his iron-thewed arms around her and pull her against his body. "And then let us get on with the pleasuring and cradle-filling."

And he covered her mouth with his. At first touch, she strained against him, but somehow could not quite bring herself to break that luscious liquid contact between them.

And the longer that searing oral caress endured, the more her resistance melted. Soon she stilled in his arms, warmed and pliant, and her body slowly molded to his. When he finally lifted his head and looked down into her eyes, she could see nothing but his glowing, half-focused features. He had just tamed and claimed her publicly . . . and she didn't even care.

"What say you, She-wolf?" he murmured. It was suddenly quiet enough in the hall to hear their hearts' wild beating.

"I say . . . I'll wed you, Wolf-tamer. Any way you say." And she brazenly pulled his mouth back down to hers to seal her acceptance with a blistering kiss.

A wild celebration erupted all around them; Borger bellowing for Helga to break out their richest mead and most costly Frankish wine, Miri and Marta hurrying to hug their sister, and Garth and Erik and a number of the other young warriors crowding around to congratulate Jorund.

The warriors pried Jorund away from Aaren and carried him off to the smithy for a horn of ale and a thorough inquisition on the details of the battle and its aftermath. Aaren suddenly found herself surrounded by women . . . Helga, Inga, old Sith, and Bedria, and her little sisters. Helga ran a judgmental eye over Aaren's ripped tunic, worn boots, and scuffed breastplate and shook her head.

"Well, we cannot let you marry Jorund," she said with a mischievous twinkle—adding belatedly, "looking like that, Serricksdotter. You must bathe and clothe yourself as befits our next jarl's wife." She looked to the others, who voiced full agreement. "And I know exactly where to go for the goods to clothe her . . . Jorund's trunk!" Her eyes lighted and the others chuckled. They bustled her along before them to the rear of the hall and Jorund's sleeping closet.

Aaren hadn't honestly given any thought to where Jorund had spent his nights, or what possessions he might own. His "closet" was actually a generous alcove, set off from the main hall by a heavy curtain. The floor was wooden logs, split and embedded into the dirt to make a warm, level flooring. Along one wall was a wide wooden platform and along the opposite wall were a fancifully carved wooden bench and a great iron-bound trunk. Lining the three wooden walls were colorful woven hangings that dazzled Aaren with their vivid colors and wondrous pictures of life in far realms. These were some of the things Jorund had spoken of, she realized . . . "tapestries."

"That's from Byzantium." Helga came to stand by her. Then she opened a hinged lid on the sleeping platform and drew out several large rolls of furs. "Jorund went there as a young lad with Borger. And the others are Frankish. Those Franks—they surely know how to dye and weave." She managed a tentative smile. "It is yours now, Serricksdotter. All this"—she waved a hand toward the massive trunk and the bright fabrics and garments the others were pulling from it—"and our Jorund, too." Then she sobered and sought Aaren's eyes. "Be good to our Jorund. He has . . . needed someone." And she gave Aaren's arm a small pat, then hurried over to join the others in pulling Jorund's treasures from his trunk.

Bright woven silks, yellow as buttercups and red as sunset, blue like morning sky and purple like oncoming night, spilled forth . . . followed by fabrics with rich, cut pile, and cloth from the Eastway with real silver and gold woven into glittering patterns. Next they drew forth silver drinking bowls inlaid with beautiful stones, gold neck and arm rings, green glass and amber and silver beads, brooches as beautiful and delicate as hoarfrost. Then came clothing already stitched and ivory combs and silver needles and tiny silver bells for stitching to garments. It was all wondrous to behold.

They brought water and insisted on helping her bathe, chatting merrily about the goings-on in the village during Aaren's and Jorund's absence. Taking charge of the beautiful combs, they groomed her hair, recounting suggestive tales of their own weddings and various husbands. In between, they held up one length of fabric after another, remarking on the colors and how they complimented her skin or her eyes.

Aaren twitched and fidgeted and cast doleful looks at Miri and Marta when the others weren't looking. But for all her discomfort, she realized it was important to have the goodwill of these women, among whom she would make her life as a woman. And she sensed that with their tentative smiles and touches they were doing their best to welcome her into their midst.

Old Sith held up a great swath of sky-blue silk and teased Miri: "Perhaps she'll be lettin' ye use it soon . . . fer yer own weddin' to Garth." Miri blushed furiously when Sith lowered her voice and leaned toward Aaren to advise: "Get her wedded quick. That boy's been makin' our lives a misery . . . makin' us keep our eyes on her day an' night."

Bedria laughed and elbowed Marta. "And don't forget little Marta and our Brun. Garth says that the jarl listens favorably to talk of a match. Brun has great forge-skill and Borger is anxious to find him a pleasing bride."

Aaren watched Miri's obvious pleasure and Marta's ill-hidden discomfort, and meant to reassure them that they would have some say in their own marriage. But then, pale, timid Inga came to sit by Aaren on the bench and smiled up at her, saying, "It will be good to have a mistress in the hall again. Too long, Borger has let the hall run down . . . let his warriors wallow about and do and speak as they please."

"That be truth," Sith declared, jamming her thick, boney hands on her wide hips. "Time once was, there were linen cloths on the tables on feast days. There was minstrels and jugglers in the hall, as well as these contests of blade-throwing and wrestling. And many winters ago, we even danced . . . and the women sat in the hall with their spinning sometimes."

"And children came, too," Bedria put in. "You can see that we are welcome again, Serricksdotter. You can clean out the hall and plan good feasts and order the linen . . . and oversee the weaving . . . and speak for us before the jarl and in the assembly as the hall's mistress is permitted to do." The others nodded eager agreement.

"We make fine cloth and the best mead," Inga continued, "and could trade prosperously, if someone besides jarl Borger did the bargaining. The only things he values are sword-blades and spear and arrow-tips, and he bargains accordingly. He receives far too little for our wool and the sweet nectar of our bees."

"I tried . . . when I was his wife," Helga said softly. "But he is a hard man, and I was not strong enough to counter him." She lowered her eyes. "Borger respects nothing more than a blade, Serricksdotter. Because you wield a mighty blade, he will heed you when you speak as a woman . . ."

Aaren listened to their importuning with widening eyes and a tightening throat. They were looking to her as the new mistress of the hall . . . for leadership and support for their concerns. But she was barely a woman herself—and knew virtually nothing of women's matters!

She endured as much as she could and suddenly thrust to her feet and asked if she might be alone for a while. Then, seeing their distress at her request, she behaved in a perfectly womanly fashion without realizing it: she made a show of pressing her temples and vowed she had an ache in her head.

They exchanged relieved smiles, pronouncing her illness a result of the excitement. Helga promised to send her a bowl of wine and they bade her lie down to rest before the festivities started. Miri and Marta lingered after the others were gone to give her hugs and assure themselves she was well.

"Do you truly wish to wed Jorund?" Marta asked warily, searching her strained expression. Aaren's tension melted visibly and she nodded.

"I wish to live with him, to share my days and nights with him," she confessed. "I have come to love him, Marta. He is a good man and a strong man."

"Then I will be happy for you." Marta smiled bittersweetly and hugged her once more.

Miri admired Aaren's new garb and her eyes shone. "His woman-magic must be powerful indeed . . . to have turned you from a warrior into a woman in so short a time." She leaned close to release the question torturing her tongue. "What is it like . . . going to the furs with a man?"

"It is very pleasant indeed . . . with Jorund," Aaren said distractedly, her thoughts refusing to travel further than Miri's prior remark: " . . . *turned you from a warrior into a woman* . . ." She scowled, dropping her eyes and clasping her hands tightly together.

"You must be tired from your long journey. We'll go and let you rest." Marta smiled and squeezed her hands. "It is good to have you back, Aaren. We have missed you." With that, she bundled Miri out the curtained opening to join Helga and the others in preparing the evening's feast.

Jorund found her there some time later, standing in the middle of his sleeping closet, looking like a goddess he had seen in an abandoned temple in Byzantium years ago. She was clothed in a gold-trimmed tunic and draped in a rich kirtle of sunflower-gold silk which hung from two gold turtle brooches on her shoulders. The silk bared much of her sleek arms and caressed and emphasized her natural curves. Her long hair flowed around her shoulders like a dark, exotic river, and her skin glowed with warmth in the lowering daylight. But her eyes . . . they looked huge and luminous, and she regarded him as a rabbit caught in a snare regards the hunter.

"You look beautiful, Long-legs." He smiled reassuringly and held out a drinking bowl. "Helga pressed this into my hands with orders to ferry it to you and see that you drink it all." When she didn't take it, he took her hand, drawing her onto the sleeping shelf, where piles of elegant stitched pelts had been unrolled. He sat down beside her and settled the bowl in her hands. Then he took her face in his hands and rubbed her flushed cheeks with his thumbs.

"It's wine, Aaren. I recall promising you a taste. Go on . . . you'll like it." When she made no move to try it, he lifted her chin and peered into her downcast eyes. "What is wrong?"

She wanted to tell him; she believed he was the only one who would ever understand. But she felt a terrible knot twisting higher and tighter in her middle . . . so high and tight that it cut off her words. He sensed she needed help and tipped the bowl to her lips, directing her to drink. The liquid was sweet, with a tingling after-heat and lovely fruity vapors that lingered in her head. She could feel it spreading warmth through her frozen throat.

"Tell me what troubles you, Aaren."

"The women were here." When he scowled, she quickly assured him: "Oh, they were good to me . . . they helped me find these garments. They're beautiful, Jorund. I've never seen such things." She looked down and stroked the soft folds of the silk which flowed over her lap, delaying, sorting her words.

"And?" he prompted.

She looked up with her emotions working in her face and blurted out: "Jorund, I'm barely used to being a woman. I don't know how to be a *wife* . . . much less the mistress of a hall. They asked about linens for the tables . . . and jugglers and dancing . . . and speaking before the jarl and the assembly. They expect me to set the hall in order . . . and help them sell their wool and mead and oversee their weaving-craft. Jorund, I don't think—"

"That's it—*don't think*, Aaren. Drink first. Finish the wine." He tilted it up and made sure she drained every drop. Then he set the bowl aside and pulled her into his arms, enjoying the feel of her sleek body in his precious silks. "Do you know, I have had dreams of you wrapped in this very silk. My treasures . . . and my woman in them."

"Jorund . . ." Anxiety simmered in her face. "I don't know who I am just now. Everyone else—even Miri and Marta—seems to think I'm a woman. But I don't feel like a woman. And yet I don't feel quite like a warrior anymore, either—at least not as I used to be. Then what am I? A woman still? A warrior?"

She was overwhelmed by it all, he realized, and he sought to reassure her.

"You are a flame, Aaren." He wrapped her securely against him, lending her his certainty as a harbor against her fears. "A beautiful red-gold flame that warms me, and lights my days and nights . . . refines my heart-longings like precious metal . . . burns the dross from my soul. This village has never known anything like you before, and they never will again. You are *Aaren*, beautiful warrior and strong woman. Your strength is your strength, and it comes from the same well within you, whether you wield it as woman or as warrior. Be mistress of the hall, if you want . . . help where you see fit . . . share what you can of your strength and heart. All I ask is that you join your life to mine and stay beside me."

He set her back and his beautiful blue eyes were smoky with desire as he slid his hands down her body, caressing her breasts, her waist, and the curves of her hips through that soft fabric. And he spun his last words around her senses like precious Persian silk.

"The woman and the warrior are both part of your flame. Burn brightly, my warrior's heart . . . and warm me."

Burn brightly. Jorund loved her. *Beautiful warrior . . . strong woman.* She would always be part woman and part warrior, different from the other women. And he wanted both. She felt as if a dark husk had suddenly slid from her heart, freeing her. Her blood quickened in her veins and she laughed and sprang up from the pallet, twirling around and around in eddies of pure joy. "It's true . . . I am *me* . . . the *same* me!" She swayed and he lurched up to catch her. But she thrust him back an arm's length with a teasing scowl. "I'll wear breeches sometimes, I warn you!"

"I do like the sight of your long legs." He grinned, dragging his gaze down her.

"And I'll ride out with the warriors to hunt. And I'll drink with the warriors in the hall."

"As long as you don't take it into your head to sleep with them in the hall as well," he said, laughing. She was behaving a little wine-happy and he savored watching her spirits rising again. Then she paused for a heart-stealing moment, her gratitude and love shining in her face. Then he noted a subtle shift in the lights of her eyes.

"But, Jorund, I don't know about wearing these kirtles." She looked down at herself, running her hands over her breasts. "I am accustomed to sturdy breeches and a good, hard breastplate . . . I feel all naked underneath." She raised her head and swept him with a long, flirtatious look as she swayed closer. "Don't I feel naked underneath?" She nudged his hand with her hip and he laughed and picked her up, bearing her back onto the furs.

She sighed, luxuriating in the width of his shoulders and the weight of him against her breasts as he rolled her onto her back. His free hand gathered up her new kirtle and slid beneath, across the bare skin of her thigh and up the crest of her hip.

"Ummm, you feel wonderful underneath," he whispered into her ear as he nuzzled and kissed her.

She shifted slightly, twisting so that his hand slid onto her woman's mound and her hip rubbed seductively against his hardening flesh. When he raised his head to look at her, her eyes twinkled.

"You can make me feel even better."

That night, in front of the great hearth and the entire village, Jorund and Aaren spoke the vows of binding, pledging their love and support to each other with the words Brother Gregory suggested. Borger interrupted twice, demanding to know if that "till death" part was strictly necessary, and later, demanding to know what sort of magic Godfrey was dispensing with all the hand-waving and sign-making he was doing.

"I am entreating the Master's blessings," Godfrey answered tersely, turning back to the nuptial pair.

"Well, I already gave them my blessing," Borger declared. "Now get on with it."

Godfrey turned to the high seat with a longsuffering look. "I meant our *heavenly* Master's blessings." He poked a pudgy finger skyward. Borger scowled as a wave of titters went through the hall.

"Well, while you're at it tell him to send a whole quiverful of sons." He turned a surly look around the hall at the numerous faces resembling his own. "A jarl cannot have too many sons."

Godfrey bristled, but, not wishing to anger the jarl any more than necessary, did as he was bade. Promises given, arm rings exchanged, property bestowed, and a quiverful of sons dutifully requested . . . they were declared husband and wife. Jorund and Aaren knelt while the teary-eyed priest blessed their union in the name of his god and his god's son, and some other, ghostly, party. Then it was over and Jorund seized Aaren, whirled her around in his arms, and kissed her senseless.

Miri and Marta were standing by with a silver bowl of wine for Aaren and Jorund to drink . . . and when they had downed it all, a great shout went up from the people and the feasting began. The newly wedded pair wobbled to the table at the right hand of the high seat, which was spread with a linen cloth and draped with fresh-cut pine boughs.

They ate and talked and jested with Garth and Erik and Miri and Marta, who had been relieved of their serving duties in honor of their sister's celebration. When their meal was finished, they enjoyed the various contests of leg-wrestling, hand-walking, and knife-throwing. When the full wrestling began, Helga appeared with a number of women bearing harps, drums, and pan pipes, and after a shaky start, music floated out over the chaotic merriment. Borger glowered at his old-wife, but Helga stood her ground. After a while, even Borger was grudgingly smacking his thigh in time with the music . . . between calling out dire threats and lucrative rewards to those who wrestled on the floor before him.

The strong drink quickly took its toll on heads used to weaker ales . . . including Aaren's. She leaned into Jorund with a mead-warmed smile and a wicked twinkle in her eye.

"Perhaps *we* should agree to wrestle a match." Her voice lowered to a provocative purr. "We could show everyone that special hold . . . where you pin me on my back . . . and wedge yourself tightly between my thighs . . ."

Sexual lightning shot along his nerves and struck his loins, igniting his desires. He shoved up from the table and pulled Aaren to her feet. Before she had time to ask what he intended, he made it clear to all . . . by stooping and hauling her onto his shoulder, then striding for his sleeping closet.

All watched in lusty fascination as he paused to snag the grease bucket in one hand and carried his laughing, protesting bride straight to his furs.

When they were gone, Miri felt Garth's eyes hot upon her and blushed, rising to carry a stack of bowls back to the small hearth. She did not see him follow her, thus was surprised when he caught her in the stone passage between the hall and the hearth and pulled her out the side door into the night. Pressing her against the wall, he trapped her small moan with a hungry kiss. She wound her arms about him, absorbing his heady passion until she grew dizzy and her knees lost their strength.

He pulled her sagging form against him and slid his hands possessively up and down her back . . . then onto her buttocks. Cupping his hands, he lifted her against his swollen desire and groaned, rubbing his aching ridge against her ardently. She shivered and her tongue darted into his mouth, exploring her new power to excite him and to revel in the pleasures of her woman's body. They kissed and caressed and rubbed against each other until the wanting was unbearable.

"By the gods, you are the sweetest thing I have ever tasted," he said hoarsely. He set her on her feet, groaning as her softness slid against his hardened flesh. Running quaking hands up her sides and beneath her kirtle, he cupped her lush breasts and teased their hard tips through her soft linen tunic. She shivered against his hands. "Now, Miri. The enchantment is broken and I cannot wait any longer."

"But Garth . . . the jarl's ban. He has not yet lifted it," she said, covering his hands with hers to still them and lifting her passion-darkened eyes to him.

"He will. It is only a matter of days, hours. He never says me *nej*. And he has not once objected to my claiming you." He smiled fiercely and kissed her. But this time there was no responsiveness in her mouth.

"But, Garth . . ." She swallowed hard. "Aaren fought hard to defend our honor. Would I be worthy of that honor if I defied the jarl's decree to go to the furs with you before he releases me? I want to take pride in being your woman. Can you understand?"

"Honor? But what has honor got to—" He glimpsed reproach in her dented brow.

"Please, Garth. Can we not wait a day or two more?"

He expelled a deep, shuddering breath. Honor. For some reason when she said it, he felt a sinking in his stomach. Before Miri, he'd never counted *honor* a consideration in dealing with women and pleasure. But it had become a matter of honor with him never to hurt Miri, or even disappoint her. As much as he wanted her body, he'd come to recognize, he also wanted her admiration, her tenderness, and the sweet outpourings of her heart. He thought for a moment of the little house he had started to build at the edge of the village, with its handsome upraised hearth and its cozy sleeping closet. It could be finished soon. He had planned it for her and her children. He felt the passion-heat in him subsiding.

"Very well, then. Tomorrow . . . I will speak to my father tomorrow. And if he doesn't release you," he declared with a fierce grin, pressing his forehead to hers, "I'll steal you. I swear I will. And I'll pay fines for you. I have silver of my own." She laughed softly and stroked his face, then offered him her mouth for a long, sweet kiss.

The torches in the long hall were sputtering their last, deepening the shadows over those sleeping on straw-strewn benches around the hearth and walls. Marta slipped through the door, as she so often did late at night, and paused, making sure no one was awake to see her. She hurried to Leif's corner, sank onto her knees beside him, and slid into his embrace.

There was an unusual intensity in the way she held him, and when he set her back to search her face, he saw that she wore a desperate, poignant smile.

"Did you see her? Did you hear?" she whispered. "Jorund fought Aaren and he won. And this evening—"

"They were wedded," he supplied, nodding. "I saw. Jorund is a fair man . . . one of the few in Borger's hall. And it is rumored, even in my village, that he has much woman-luck and word-skill." He smiled wryly. "Your sister will enjoy that, I suppose."

"She is very pleased to be his wife. And very pleased to have upheld—" She bit off the rest, looking down, and slumped to sit back on her heels. When he coaxed her chin up, her eyes were moist. "The enchantment is broken, Leif."

"Surely a cause for rejoicing, my little Marta. Not for tears." He wiped her cheek with his fingertips. "You are free now." The words struck a quiver in his heart and he looked down at his manacled hands. She was free . . . and he was not. He sat back on his heels as well.

"Little enough cause for joy, Leif. It means the jarl is also free to give me to a warrior as wife. And I have heard that he plans"—she could scarcely get the words past the constriction in her throat—"to give me to Brun Cinder-hand."

Leif's eyes closed. There came a fierce, crushing sensation in his chest as he thought of Marta in another man's furs, another man's arms. Worse . . . he knew there would be nothing he could do to stop it. Even if he weren't a captive and had all the silver in the world, old Red Beard would probably still deny his request for her out of hatred for his father, Gunnar.

"Leif," she said with tears in her voice, "I don't want Brun. I don't want any man . . ." When he opened his eyes to look at her, she added, "Except you."

"Marta, I cannot bear to see you cry." He took her hand and led her over to the wall. He sat down and leaned against it, drawing her onto his lap and wrapping her tightly in his arms. "I want you, Little Morsel, down to the very marrow of my bones. And if I were free, I would find a way to have you."

Tears rolled down her cheeks as she rested against his hard warmth. "If you were free . . . would you ask for me? Would you try to wed me?"

"I would," he said thickly. "I would take you to my village . . . to my father's hall. You would like my father's hall, Little One. It is not so large as Borger's, but it is very handsome, with many carvings and half-wooden floors and snug sleeping closets." An odd tenor of home-longing crept into his voice. "I have my own chamber, and my younger brothers and sisters sleep in three others, and there is the one for my father and mother." He paused, wondering if he would ever see it again.

"Would you take me in the Christian way?" she asked, looking up at him.

"You women . . . you will share everything with each other but a man." He chuckled, but briefly, then sobered. "Yea, I would forsake others to have you to wife, little Marta. You are beyond precious to me."

"And you to me," she said, stroking his chin. "I cannot bear to think that someday you might meet Aaren on a battlefield," she whispered. "And you might wound her . . . or she might wound you . . ."

Leif stared at her, glimpsing the cruel effects of the long-standing feud on her brave but tender heart. She loved her sister and she loved him. Yet, once he was ransomed, there was a good chance that he and the battle-maiden would indeed meet on a battlefield. With awful insight, he realized that for the first time in his life he dreaded meeting an enemy . . . and that it had nothing at all to do with cowardice.

"Why does there have to be so much fighting? Why can we not make peace . . . and live and trade and marry together?"

"There will never be peace as long as Red Beard is jarl here," Leif said thickly. "He is a greedy and treacherous old boar with an unholy thirst for the dew of wounds."

Marta's eyes closed and she clasped him desperately, sealing away those bleak thoughts of the future to treasure the present with him.

"I almost forgot . . ." She sat up and fished around in her kirtle for a small leather pouch. She pulled out a small, flat tablet weaving, made with rich blue yarns interwoven with finer, golden strands. Pressing it into his hands, she murmured, "I brought you this. I made it myself." The tenderness in his handsome features as he stroked it made her heart contract. She would never feel that touch on her body, would never know the sweetness of his loving. "The gold is my hair. I made it for you to remember me . . ." Tears spilled down her cheeks.

"I . . . I would never forget you, Marta. Not in a thousand lifetimes."

"Oh, Leif!" She threw her arms about his neck. "Take me . . . here . . . now," she whispered. And before he could speak, she pressed her lips to his and leaned her soft young body against his stark leanness.

He had no power to resist, returning her kiss deeply, softly . . . losing all awareness of time and place as he explored her shape through her clothes. But even as his passion for her rose and he thought desperately of ways they could conceal themselves and protect her from discovery . . . he knew he could not take her there, on his captive's pallet, with shackles on his limbs. She deserved better. The conflict between his care for her and his desires boiled up hot and potent in him.

He dragged his mouth from hers and set her back, his expression dark and turbulent. "*Nej*, Marta. I cannot do that to you," he said in a whisper so filled with anguish that it might have come from her own heart. She sat on his lap, trying so hard to be brave. It was too much for his beleaguered heart to bear. He pulled her to him again, and as she clamped her arms around his waist, he pressed his cheek against the top of her head.

"There has to be a way, Marta. And I swear I'll find it. The ransom is due soon . . . any day. Hold on . . . delay . . . kick and scream . . . hide, if you must. You must not let them force you to marry before I can come for you." He crushed her tightly to him. "Promise me."

"I promise you, Leif. I promise."

And in their kiss mingled the sweet taste of love and the bitterness of tears.

Chapter Nineteen

Aren awakened early the next morning with Jorund's head on her shoulder and her arms around him. For a long time, she lay perfectly still, holding him, watching him. It was a particularly womanly pleasure, watching over the sleep of another . . . tenderly guarding him from wakefulness and thus from all the harms that lurked in wakeful hours. In dreams all was safe . . . all was possible . . . wealth beyond measure, joy without end, and pleasure without limit . . . even peace in the hearts of men.

In those quiet moments, she understood that it was her destiny to be at his side, guarding his dreams . . . including the one of making a better life-way for his people. She had always thought of her strength in warrior's terms: as a god-gift ordained for fighting. Now she saw, as Jorund apparently had, that her strength had other dimensions; it would continue to shape her life and the lives of those around her. Including Jorund's.

When she could not lie still a moment longer, she gently rolled Jorund onto his side and slid from the furs, gasping silently at the impact of the cold air on her naked body. She sorted through the pile of silk and linen on the floor and held up her new garments, trying to recall how the *ells* of fabric wrapped and pinned.

"Don't bother putting it on again," came Jorund's sleep-weighted voice from behind her. Her heart skipped at the sight of him leaning on one elbow, looking irresistibly tousled and newly wakened . . . his eyes filled with morning hunger. "Come back to the furs, Long-legs." He dragged a ravenous look down her naked side. "Come feed the he-wolf in me."

The raw desire in his words raked her like silky claws,

setting her most intimate nerves vibrating, bringing her unexpectedly to the taut edge of arousal. Yesterday and again last night, he had been a generous and tender lover . . . the Breath-stealer, the Slow-hand, the Gentle-rider. But this morning, sated with gentler pleasures, he was hungry for more volatile ones . . . the kind to satisfy the Stallion-back, the Blade-wielder, the He-wolf. This morning he didn't ask, he demanded. She clasped the silk to her bare body and leveled a defiant look on him.

"And if I don't?"

"It is not wise to ignore a hungry wolf."

"Is it not?"

"Have you not heard it said . . . hungry wolves take big bites?" He sat up slowly, bracing on a thickly muscled arm. An aura of latent but explosive power saturated every line of his body, each nuance of his movement.

Big bites. The words sent a frisson of excitement through her, setting the tips of her breasts drawing tight. He liked being wolf-bit. Would she? And just what would it take to make him use his fangs on her?

She wetted her lips and turned, giving him her back and peering at him over her shoulder. He loved the sight and the feel of her buttocks, her long legs, and the curve of her back, she knew. Now she displayed them for him, spreading her legs, swaying her hips slowly from side to side, then stooping as if to pick up something that had fallen . . . and rising, ever so slowly so that her thighs and calves flexed, her buttocks tightened, and her spine curved.

She felt more than heard his movement as he sprang. A rush of exquisite heat engulfed her just before his arms did, and she came to exultant life as his great arms lashed around her. He hoisted her off her feet and dragged her—writhing and squirming—to the pallet, toppling with her into the still warm marten, fox, and sable. With lightning quickness, he pinned her on her back, and his naked body bore down on hers with elemental force.

Only her legs were free and she unleashed their sleek, sensuous power as he focused his weight against her belly. She raised them on either side of his hips and lifted him with her body, again and again, rolling, trying to dislodge him.

Her thrusts grew wilder and more provocative, a seething parody of mating that challenged him to counter with his fierce male strength, to tame and take her if he could.

"Where is this he-wolf . . . who takes such big bites?" she growled softly, flexing her shoulders, grinding her breasts against him. She could feel the beast straining in him, watched it clawing at the backs of his eyes, roaring to be free. And she sunk her nails into his wide, hard back. "I want him. Set him free."

With a terrible groan, he gripped her tightly . . . then drove his flesh-blade into her hot, receptive sheath with one stroke. She lay still, breathless, trembling with shock waves of pleasure. Heat billowed in her lungs, in her heart, in her head. Then she sought his mouth hungrily, kissing, sucking, raking his lips with her teeth . . . coaxing him.

He responded in kind and soon his kisses and licks gave way to voluptuous suckling and delicious rakes with his teeth. She arched and shuddered and he paused, staring at her with eyes like white-hot brands.

"Are my bites too big?" It came out on a growl and it took a moment for it to right in her mind. Her ravenous he-wolf was asking if she wished to be consumed a bit more gently. There was something delicious in the irony of it, but she had no time to explore that sweet paradox in him, only to enjoy it and to cling to the pleasurable fury in him that was driving her to the limits of her own passions. She had breath for only one word.

"Nej."

He laughed raggedly and plunged into her kisses and into her woman's body, plying his pleasure-blade with devastating skill and power to overcome her exquisitely sensual resistance . . . winning her cooperation bit by bit. Then at last they moved together, straining, writhing, melding their bodies the way they had already joined their souls. And when her senses were finally stuffed full in that wild feast of pleasure and she erupted in his arms, her response ignited an explosion in him that rocked him to the very bottom of his soul.

It was some time before they parted and lay side by side, bodies moist and glowing, spent. She began to laugh and he turned to her with a light frown.

"What is it?"

She smiled and ran her hand up his chest and across his mouth. " 'Are my bites too big,' you said." Her eyes were liquid and warm, shimmering with love. "That is some soft-hearted beast in you, Borgerson . . . to be so concerned about the comfort of his victim."

He looked a little shocked. "I . . . I said that?"

"You did." She pushed up onto her elbow and leaned over him, giving his love-bruised lips a brush with hers. Then she settled her chin on her palm, letting her love rise into her gaze. "You must not be afraid to use your strength with me, Jorund. Why do you think the Norns sent you such a strong wife? You needed someone to match your strength . . . or perhaps someone to free it."

Jorund stilled, feeling her words washing through him, releasing a warm tide of insight. Freeing his strength. It was true. For these last three years, an essential part of his nature had been imprisoned and denied . . . the raw physical strength and the intensity that were interwoven with the very maleness of him . . . It was as though he had gradually built a shell around his stronger impulses, fearing them . . . forbidding them.

With each touch, each look, each fiery exchange between them, Aaren's strength had called to his, awakened it, sustained it . . . even as he had called to the woman-softness in her, roused and nourished it. Each time he saw the love in her eyes, each time he felt the power of her marvelous body moving against his, each time she pushed his control to its limit and beyond . . . he had reclaimed a bit of himself.

Despite the exhaustion in his body, he suddenly felt like running and jumping and even flying . . . anything that could express the joy he felt at his returning life. He rolled from the furs and scooped her up into his arms and swung her around and around in an exuberant demonstration of raw power.

"Jorund!" she cried breathlessly, her eyes sparkling as she was caught up in the release of his pleasure.

"I don't know why the Norns gifted me with you, my

beautiful she-wolf," he said with a laugh. "But I will be forever grateful that they did."

Word came, late that morning, that jarl Gunnar had collected the silver for his son's ransom and the news spread through the hall with the speed and impact of a bolt of lightning. Borger roared up and down the hall, shouting orders that reverberated mercilessly in heads still mead-sick from the night's revelry.

"Couldn't have come at a better time!" he bellowed. Lumbering to the planking tables nearest the high seat, he snatched up a sleeping head by its thick brown hair. "Hrolf?" He cocked his head to peer at the face, then grunted disappointment and dropped it back onto the table to seize the one beside it. "Hrolf?" Another miss, and he dropped it too. "Where in Hel's sway is Hrolf? Hrolf!"

"Here, jarl!" Hrolf came hurrying in from the cook-hearth with his mouth and hands full of warm flatbread.

"I will need a dozen men to take to the exchange . . . Garth, Erik, you and your son . . . Get some buckets of water and roust these deep-gulpers. Then see to the horses and provisions." As Hrolf went about rousing the men, Borger strolled back through the hall and stood looking down at Leif Gunnarson.

"The old goat collected the silver I demanded. It seems you will go back to your people, after all." When Leif's eyes narrowed, but he made no other response, Borger laughed and stroked his beard. "You're a better whelp than your old woman of a father deserves, Gunnar's son. And to think: but for a coin to buy your mother's favor . . . you might have been mine."

Leif jerked forward furiously and Borger lurched back a step, then laughed raucously and strolled out the doors.

"You will pay for the pain you have caused, old man . . . I swear it," Leif gritted out, sinking back onto his ragged pallet, his eyes flinty. "Your blood will redden my blade ere long."

Most of the villagers and all of Borger's head-sore *hird* gathered outside the long hall that afternoon as Borger's ransom force assembled. The warrior's iron-banded helmets, finely honed spear-tips, and iron shield bosses glinted darkly in the sun, and their horses pranced as if eager to be gone.

Leif Gunnarson was brought outside and Brun Cinderhand struck the irons from his hands and feet. Leif straightened to his full height for the first time in weeks and turned a look of utter loathing on Brun, then on Borger. As his hands were re-tied with rope, he looked up to find Marta standing at the edge of the crowd, her face pale and her eyes pained. He watched her as they led him to a horse and forced him up on it. Then he turned his head and sat arrow straight in the saddle, his face grim.

Garth, who was among the warriors selected for the mission to collect the ransom, sought out Miri, standing by Marta at the front of the crowd. Before the whole assembly of warriors and villagers, he removed his helm.

"I have not yet spoken to the jarl, little Miri. There has been no time," he announced boldly. Then he pulled her straight into his arms and placed a lush, possessive kiss on her upturned mouth.

A murmur of shock spread through the crowd. All other warriors who had entertained thoughts of bidding for Miri's future had their hopes dashed utterly when Borger merely threw back his head and laughed at Garth's coltish heat. Garth's bold action had just won the jarl's tacit approval, as he had hoped it would, and his grin at Miri afterward said it was only a matter of time before they would sleep in each other's arms.

Borger mounted his great Norman-bred stallion, accepted his helm from his bondsman, and bellowed for Bedria, the Brewer. When she hurried forward, he gave her orders, his voice booming with confidence.

"Hurry your best mead and ale along, Bee-woman. Make them ready three days hence, for my return and a great celebration of my new riches!" Cheers and shouted luck-wishes filled the commons as he gave his mount the spur and led his men and their captive out of the village, along the lake path.

Jorund and Aaren stood by, watching as Borger and

his men departed, then turned to each other with warm, speaking looks.

"It will be over soon," she said quietly, slipping her hand into his.

"Let us hope so," he answered with a half smile. Then he turned to another topic. "I should go see about that foaling in the stables and check the roof on the granary. Then I need to see Brun in the smithy, and I promised Garth I would look over the house he is building. Do you mind?" She shook her head, understanding his need for action to dispel the tension in him. He gave her a kiss, which drew curious looks, then gave her hip a pat of promise as he strode off.

Aaren re-entered the warm hall with Miri and Marta and stopped dead as the heat-ripened smell of the place assaulted her nose and lungs. She grimaced at the stench, looking to Miri and Marta with alarm.

"Foul, I know," Marta said, glancing at the empty corner where Leif had spent nearly two months of captivity. Her voice was small and tight as she fought to keep back tears. "The jarl's men are . . . not a cleanly lot."

Aaren's mind was so set on the disgusting sight and smell that she failed to catch the emotion in Marta's voice. The tables were still littered with bowls and bones, the straw on the benches around the walls was damp and soured, and the floor was puddled in places. Over the unpleasant odors of moldy straw, stale mead, and damp earth floated the acrid smell of sickness, from the unlucky revelers who had drunk more mead than their stomachs could hold. Aaren picked her way through the mess, her nose curling.

Nearly as disgusting as the smell was the sight of grizzled male forms sprawled over the benches and tables, sunk into near oblivion. "Even crows and cowbirds know better than to foul their own nests," Aaren said, eliciting a one-eyed glare from a nearby table . . . for having the temerity to invade their domain.

Their domain? she thought, scanning the disheveled benches and the stagnant floor, the smelly torches and greasy hearth. This was *her* home now, too . . . the place where she slept and ate . . . where she would bear and rear her children. She made straight for her sleeping closet, Miri and Marta close on her heels. Minutes later, she returned, garbed once more in her warrior's breeches, tunic, and breastplate, and ducked down the stone passageway into the small hearth.

"Come with me," she ordered the thrall women who were peeling cabbages and onions. She turned to Kara and Gudrun. "We'll need brooms, buckets, and brushes . . . where can we find them?"

When they arrived in the hall, Aaren set the women to emptying the benches of straw and scrubbing them down with vinegar water. But they hadn't gotten far when a major obstacle presented itself . . . in the form of a large, surly warrior who refused to be dislodged from his seat. Aaren watched the thralls, Olga and Una, shrinking from the fellow's ugly temper, and she strode over to take charge. She politely asked him to carry his carcass elsewhere, and when he gave her a defiant snarl, she lifted the other end of the heavy bench he was seated on and dumped him into a foul-smelling puddle. There was an outcry from the others and a number rose to their feet, glaring threateningly at her.

"We intend to clean this filthy bog of a hall," she said evenly, meeting each pair of eyes, one after another. "And if you expect to eat here this night, I suggest you go clean yourselves . . . sweat out the ale-poisons and make yourselves clean and presentable."

They stared at one another in hot indignation, but none of them was of a mind or of a condition to truly oppose her. They had seen her blade-work firsthand. Glowering and red-faced, they shuffled out, abandoning their hall to the she-wolf and her minions.

As the last warrior quit the door, Helga, Kara, Gudrun, and old Sith arrived and stood gaping at the sight of Aaren, garbed in breastplate and breeches and wielding a broom instead of a blade. Aaren paused, seeing their shock, and shifted uneasily on her feet, wondering what they would think. But when Helga's surprise melted into a pleased look, she squared her shoulders and plunged forward into her new life.

"If you would take a broom or a bucket, Helga, Kara, Sith . . . There is plenty of work for all."

By nightfall the great hearth was cleaned of grease and

ashes, the planking tables had been scrubbed and oiled, and fresh straw had been spread on the benches and the few remaining damp spots on the floor. New torches burned brightly in the post brackets, and pine boughs and fragrant juniper were draped around the hall to counter any lingering odors.

Borger's warriors slowly trickled back in, sniffing the air and muttering amongst themselves as they re-entered what some now irritably referred to as *the she-wolf's lair*. Most had heeded Aaren's advice and taken themselves to the bathing house for a good, restoring sweat, and a number of them had changed their tunics and groomed their hair and beards. But there were a few who had chosen to spend their time in the forest, hunting . . . and had returned empty-handed, with mud-caked feet and sullen tempers. They stomped into the hall and threw themselves onto benches conspicuously near the high seat . . . and planted their begrimed boots in the middle of the clean tables.

Aaren emerged from Jorund's sleeping closet, freshly garbed in womanly attire once more, eager to greet Jorund in the newly cleaned hall. When she rounded the high seat, she spotted two warriors with their backs braced against the roof posts and their filthy boots fouling the table planks. She halted and her eyes traveled over those offending feet, up those slouching bodies to the grizzled faces of Hakon Freeholder and Thorkel the Ever-ready. She considered her course carefully. Then she walked straight to the table where the Freeholder's foul boots held sway.

"I must ask that you take your boots down, Hakon Freeholder," she said. He gave an ugly smirk, sat up partway, and flung a wad of spit to the floor—precariously close to the lovely silk of her kirtle. Behind her the women gasped and she saw men thrusting to their feet and edging closer.

As he just sat, smugly defying her order, her eyes narrowed slightly and flickered to her right. Without warning, she snatched a great dagger from the belt of the warrior at her side and stood turning it over in her hands. "You will take your feet down, Freeholder," she said with unnerving calm. "The women have spent hours this day purging the filth from this hall. You should honor their labor, for it is meant to see to your comfort." Then her tawny eyes settled on his. "Shall I remove your boots for you?"

The tension thickened, and women and warriors alike exchanged looks of consternation. Proud Aaren Serricksdotter, the she-wolf . . . removing the Freeholder's filthy boots?

In the blink of an eye, she raised that long dagger and plunged it into the table top—straight through the side of Freeholder's boot. Hakon shot up with his eyes bulging, then reddening as he realized she'd pinned his foot to the table . . . without breaking his skin.

"Now, if I continue removing your boot in this manner . . . there will be precious little of it left to wear, Freeholder," she said above the gasps and exclamations. "Perhaps you would prefer to do it yourself." After a long moment, she pulled the dagger from the planking. It was another breathless moment before the Freeholder dragged his feet from the table, his face crimson. He shoved to his feet and Thorkel rose also . . . with his hand on his dagger.

Aaren met his furious look head-on and plunged the blade straight back into the table plank. "You are seasoned and valiant warriors, Hakon Freeholder and Thorkel Ever-ready. I salute that strength in you. In any fight I would be proud to have you at my back and would be honored to defend yours. But from now on, in this hall, you must be more than a fierce fighter—you must be a man of honor and bearing." She drew a womanly cloak around the hard core of her voice, shielding but not disguising its strength. "I believe you can be that, as well."

The Freeholder scowled and opened his mouth to speak, but shut it as he glimpsed the scowling women and gawking warriors standing around. He turned on his heel and strode out, and Thorkel joined him.

A while later Jorund entered to find the hall clean and green-scented and bustling with activity. He had already heard of Aaren's confrontation with Hakon and Thorkel . . . and of the subsequent rules she had established for cleanliness and conduct in the hall. He caught her in his arms and drew her behind the high seat to kiss her breathless.

"You've been busy," he murmured, nuzzling her temple.

She pushed back in his arms, searching his face.

"My stomach churned at the smell, Jorund. I had to do something—this is our hall, too, our home," she protested. Then she saw the grin lurking at the corners of his mouth and eyes and relaxed.

"Yea, but . . . no spitting, no blade-fighting, no blood-letting, no pissing . . . what's a man got left?" he said with mock outrage.

"A sweet-smelling place to sleep," she said tartly, arching her body into him. "A warm, tasty meal . . . the companion-ship of his fellows . . . and a pair of soft thighs that part willingly. Isn't that worth a bit of restraint?" He slid his hands down her back and clasped her buttocks, pulling her tightly against his rousing hardness.

"Ummm. I'm not sure. Refresh my memory about the 'thighs that part willingly.' "

Her squeal as he carried her back into his closet was heard all over the hall.

That night the hall was crowded with women and war-riors and village men . . . and a number of children. Aaren and Jorund sat close together at their table, watching the women making music and the warriors telling tales of bat-tles past, each a little grander than the last. Aaren listened for a while, then rose·from the bench and disappeared for a few moments.

When she returned she carried a great wolf-skin in her arms and led her two sisters . . . each of whom carried another large wolf pelt. They spread the skins over the edge of the wooden platform and high seat, and Aaren called for the children to come forward. She held her breath and waited, seeking out the little ones with her gaze. They stared at their mothers, then at each other, hanging back. Then she caught a glimpse of Helga's boy, standing nearby with a wary but fascinated look on his face. With all the courage of a warrior facing her first battle, she steeled herself and engaged his eyes . . . and smiled.

A small miracle was worked in his expression as he melted to the offer of warmth in her face. He edged closer, then took a tentative step, then another. She sat down and patted the edge of the platform beside her and when he settled there with a shy grin, the other children began to come forward, too. Aaren flushed with pleasure and looked up to find Jorund watching her with shining eyes.

Then, seated among the children at the feet of Borger's great, empty chair, she began to spin a tale of a foot-chase through a forest . . . of three wolves and one man . . . of a great fight and a great victory.

The warriors and women drew closer and closer, listening, watching her eyes glowing brightly as she portrayed the stalking wolves, the heroic warrior, and the furious battle. Her arms spread wide, her hands flew—claws one instant, a dagger the next—and her body writhed expressively as she related the events. Her face filled with passion, then pleasure, then pride as her tale climaxed.

"And do you know who that great warrior was?" she asked the children. With their mouths agape and their eyes as big as goose eggs, they shook their shaggy heads. She looked up to find Jorund standing nearby, in the ring of adults surrounding the children.

"It was him." She pointed to Jorund. "Jorund Borgerson is the wolf-slayer of my tale. These three great skins are the proof. And if you ask kindly . . . perhaps he will show you the marks the wolves left on his hands."

Not a breath was expelled as all eyes turned on Jorund. He stood, red-faced, both awed and embarrassed by her glowing portrayal of his deed. She had made a veritable tapestry of the truth . . . delicately spun and masterfully woven . . . brilliantly colored with love.

"Can we see, Big Brother?" Helga's boy asked in the hush. "Your hands?"

Jorund met Aaren's glowing eyes, filled with conflicting urges to shake her and embrace her. He hadn't sought deed-fame in fighting those wolves—he had sought only to protect her, his eyes said.

Take the tale and the honor it brings you, as my gift of gratitude, her eyes responded.

He stretched out his hands and the children flocked to him with oohs and squeals of excitement. And when the children were done and were dragged away by their equally wide-eyed mothers, the warriors crowded in to inspect the great pelts and to clasp his wrists and congratulate him on his great deed.

The music resumed and the evening floated by as Aaren and Jorund resumed their seats, holding hands and exchanging private smiles as they presided over the merriment in the hall.

Aaren's wolf-tale was told and re-told throughout the next day—sometimes faithfully, sometimes with bigger, bolder strokes—until every man, woman, and child in the village had heard it. Everywhere he went, Jorund was congratulated and heralded for his courage and fighting prowess. He realized with amazement that the story had worked a change toward him in the eyes of his clansmen. He was torn between savoring their renewed regard for him and despairing of it—since it was based on the very thing he wished to lead them away from: fighting.

But, in truth, the wolf-slaying was only partly responsible for his new esteem. Among the folk of Borger's hall and village, there was but one byname used with "Jorund" now, and that was "Wolf-tamer." And the wolf they referred to him taming was none other than Odin's She-wolf, Aaren. They had seen her fierceness, watched her struggle to uphold her honor, and witnessed her courage in the face of great odds . . . and they respected her. Now, as they watched the way she honored Jorund, they transferred their respect for her to him, as well.

To claim a heart so fierce and proud was truly an achievement, they realized. And Jorund, it seemed, had found a way to gentle the she-wolf without diminishing her remarkable strength. She was still very much the warrior-heart . . . only now she was much more: a strikingly beautiful woman, a calming presence in the hall, a devoted wife, a tantalizing blend of power and grace. And in taming the she-wolf, Jorund had apparently found a piece of himself that had been lost . . . his warrior's strength, his will to fight. The wolf-slaying was witness to that.

Each word, each kiss, each quiet exchange made with their eyes told eloquently of the regard each held for the other, and of the passion they bore like glowing embers in their breasts. Between them was a bond of such depth and intensity that all wagged their heads in wonder, tantalized by thoughts of what had passed between them up in the mountains. With traded nods and whispers, they recalled Aaren's first volatile days among them . . . and the warriors speculated on the methods Jorund had employed in claiming her warrior's heart.

Godfrey laughed when he heard the men's talk in the smithy. "I told you how he did it, and your thick ears would not listen," he said. "No mystery and no magic . . . just kindness, pure and simple." As an afterthought he added with a twinkle in his eye, "And perhaps kisses had some part. Kindness and kisses . . . the surest way to conquer a woman's heart."

As Godfrey carried the basket of hearth-irons Brun had repaired back to the hall, the warriors watched him go, musing on his words and on the great relish Aaren Serricksdotter had displayed for those deep and shocking mouth-meetings with Jorund. They had been oddly stirring to witness. How much more rousing would they be for those who participated? They recalled Garth's adoption of Jorund's pleasure-habit, and its effect on pretty little Miri.

And kindness; if Jorund was any example, that wasn't so hard to manage. Carrying a basket or a pail of water . . . smiling and listening to a woman's prattle . . . offering a word of praise for a tasty bit of hearth-work. Their faces heated and their eyes narrowed to hide the glint of calculation as they each found excuses to hurry off toward the hall and the granary, the dairy and the small hearth.

By dusk there was a veritable epidemic of kindness abroad in Borger's village. Oleg Forkbeard was seen carrying pails of whey from the dairy out to the pigs for salty-tongued Sith. Young Svein helped plump Una, the hearth thrall, with her fish-cleaning and water-hauling, and thick-fisted Brun dropped everything to help Marta carry two bales of wool from the barn to the women's house for spinning. All over the village men could be seen in the company of women, carrying and lifting and holding and assisting . . . and, more importantly, talking and listening. A line formed mid-afternoon before the freeman woodcarver's hut, and that fellow's trade in combs, carved picks, and needle boxes was remarkably brisk for the balance of the day.

The sharing of tasks and the awkward words of appreciation soon led to exchanges of smiles and jests—and by nightfall, occasional touches of hand and body. With each bit of kindness and each bit of warmth that responded to it, a new possibility was glimpsed, a new way of being together was explored. By the time the torches sputtered in the hall, a still different kind of exploration had begun . . . of the pleasures of kissing. And by morning there were a number of fur burns on knees and elbows, and quite a number of smiles in the houses and huts of Borger's village.

The second day of Borger's absence proved every bit as remarkable. Noteworthy in the morning's events was the reappearance of Thorkel and Hakon Freeholder in the hall . . . freshly bathed and garbed in clean tunics and boots. They scrutinized the jesting and teasing and the frequent physical exchanges between warriors and women, and demanded to know what had happened while they were out fishing. Brun took them discreetly aside and horrified them with the truth.

But as they lurked around the village and home-fields, they too were influenced. By dusk, the lusty and pragmatic Freeholder had begun to pay rough but kindly court to the plump, rosy-cheeked Gudrun. And, feeling Hakon's defection keenly, Thorkel reluctantly began to try to smile at the frisky little Alys.

By the morning of the third day, Hakon swaggered into the hall and stood with his thumbs tucked in his belt and a satisfied look on his face. When Aaren appeared, he nodded solemnly to her and took a seat at a table with his feet stowed properly on the floor. In moments, he was served by a very bright eyed Gudrun. He smiled and gave her a playful but possessive pat on the buttocks.

Aaren and Jorund watched the burgeoning kindness in the village with nothing short of wonder. "I never imagined anything like it," she said, shaking her head as she sank down beside Jorund on a bench outside the stables that afternoon. "Did you see the Freeholder? Smiled, he did.

And that sour Thorkel . . . I saw him repairing an ox harness just now and he was whistling. Whistling!"

Jorund laughed and pulled her into his arms for a warm kiss in the frosty air.

"You're probably to blame. It's all this love you inspire . . . we cannot hold it all in our heart-wells and it overfills and spills out onto others." He laughed as she shivered and snuggled against him, using their public embrace to cover the private wanderings of her fingers across his belly and below.

He jolted as she touched him, and again, an instant later, as a voice broke in on them.

"Jorund!" Helga's boy stood before them with his cheeks red and his chest heaving from a run. "There's a rider come. My mother said to get you."

"I'll be along shortly, Little Brother. Run and tell your mother for me." The boy jerked a nod and ran off, leaving Jorund to groan softly and writhe pleasantly under Aaren's questing fingers. "Not yet, my hungry she-wolf." He snatched up her hand, giving it a kiss. "Somewhere more private." He pulled her up with him and took a deep breath, adjusting his tunic. "Come—I'll race you back to my closet." He leaned close to her ear and whispered hotly, "The last one there has to undress the other . . . *with her teeth*."

He bolted into a run, Aaren at his heels. Through the village they raced, laughing, cutting corners, dodging villagers, and drawing hounds and children into motion with them. They rounded the women's house and raced across the common toward the hall . . .

And they jerked to a dead halt.

Standing before the doors of the hall was a knot of women and warriors . . . and a horse that was so lathered and winded it looked ready to collapse. As the group parted, Jorund saw that on the ground beside the horse was Hrolf the Younger . . . blood on his face and covering half his tunic.

The sense of it exploded in Jorund's head as he ran forward, and he knew what he would hear before a word was spoken.

"The jarl at the exchange . . . it was a trap . . . attacked in numbers," Hrolf rasped out as Jorund crouched beside him to check his wounds. "Harald killed . . . the jarl hurt bad . . . near dead. Several wounded . . . I came for help."

"Is Gunnar riding to attack the village?" Jorund demanded urgently. When Hrolf gritted this teeth and shook his head, Jorund cursed softly and sent Helga's boy for a blanket with which to carry the injured warrior into the hall. "Where are Borger and the rest?"

"Where bog meets the forest . . . and just across th' river . . . in trees . . ."

"A strong half day's ride," Jorund said, nodding. "You've done well, Hrolf. Save your strength now. It is a clean shoulder wound—Dagmar and Helga will see you mend." He pushed to his feet and turned to Hakon and Thorkel, who stood glowering nearby. "Take a dozen villagers . . . even younger lads will do . . . and set them out along the river and the lake and the forest paths as watchers. Gunnar may yet decide to strike here, if he knows how badly Borger is wounded."

He stalked aside, running his hands through his hair, then squaring his shoulders. "Curse the old fool—he brought it upon himself—upon us all!" He turned back and found Aaren standing taut, watching him. Her eyes were bright and fierce with anger . . . and expectation. He did not disappoint her.

"Aaren, you will keep half the men here in the village and make them and the village battle-ready. Brun keeps our store of weapons in the smithy. I'll take the rest and ride out to get Borger and the others," he ordered. She nodded curtly.

When he looked up, Hakon and Thorkel were still standing flatfooted, watching between him and Aaren . . . as if evaluating the pair of them . . . and his orders. He leveled a fierce scowl at them, and roared, "Go!"

They took off at a dead run.

Chapter Twenty

J orund led nearly a score of armed men through the gray, skeletal forests, riding as quickly and defensively as possible. Borger's and Gunnar's villages were separated by a two-day ride and Borger had craftily demanded a meeting site that was closer to his village than Gunnar's . . . at a series of cliffs, well known to him and strategically defensible. Once again, facing an adversary, Borger's cunning had served him well. The casualties from the surprise attack would have been much higher if they had been on level ground and had had to watch their backs as well as their flanks. When it was clear they would be defeated, Borger had used his only route of escape—through a crag in the cliffs into the forest. Now Jorund could only hope that Gunnar and his men would not linger in territory so far from home to press the cause of revenge even further.

When they reached the river and forded the shallows, they were greeted by Garth, who had rallied the less injured men and set up a defense for their small camp. Jorund found Borger lying on the ground, covered with the men's winter fleeces. The old jarl had taken two deep wounds, one in his shoulder and another in his side, but he was awake— and in unspeakable agony. When Jorund knelt beside him, he managed to raise a hand and grip Jorund's arm with desperate force. A flame in his gray eyes flared at the sight of his son, and his mouth worked silently. The pain-filled combination of pleading gaze and soundless speech worked on Jorund the way no words or exhortations could. "Do not strain," Jorund said hoarsely.

The effort taxed Borger's already depleted strength and he surrendered to the mercy of oblivion. When Jorund tucked his father's arm beneath the fleeces and rose, he found Garth beside him, staring at him with clouded eyes.

"He would not let himself sleep until you came. He said you would come," Garth said thickly. "I was not so sure."

Jorund's jaw flexed and his hands curled into fists as he resisted the pain Garth's words inflicted on him. The warrior-pride he had believed long buried flared and crackled at his brother's lack of faith in him. He glanced around at the faces of warriors he had journeyed with, fought with, and shed blood with. It had been three years since he had sailed with them, and in that time they had forgotten the strength that had carried a number of them from the battlefield, forgotten the honor that would not allow a comrade to be abandoned on a foreign shore—even when the jarl ordered it so. And then he realized that, for a while, he had forgotten it too.

"I am here, Brother," Jorund declared. "And that is what matters." He looked around the camp, breathing in the smoky green-wood fire, the tang of leather and oiled steel on the air, and the scents of blood and damp earth . . . and suddenly it was as if he had never left. This was a warrior's world. This sacrifice. He looked up into the eyes that studied him, the eyes that questioned him, and the eyes that welcomed him back. This kinship.

For a moment, he could not speak. Then he turned away to order the horses unloaded, and several of Borger's warriors hurried to obey.

The food, blankets, wound-bindings, and extra horses Jorund's party had brought were put to quick use. Of the wounded, only Borger was too injured to ride; a pallet of blankets was stretched between two horses to carry him back to the village. Jorund ordered the others onto horses and told the men he had brought with him to spread out and form a retreating wedge behind and around them, to guard their rear against further attack. Even as he did so, he realized it was the first time they had used that tactic on their home-soil in many years.

He led them as swiftly as they could travel, through a damp forest, beneath a glowering sky. It was dark when they approached the village, but Hakon's sentries spotted them and relayed word of their coming. Aaren, Helga, and the other women waited in torchlight outside the hall doors as they rode up. Aaren flew to hold Jorund's horse as he dismounted, and she caught his hand in a brief grasp before he moved back through the horses with the warriors and distraught women. Together they helped the wounded down and sent them into the hall for tending.

Helga spotted the blankets strung between the horses and ran to them with a cry, calling for someone to bring a torch. She covered her mouth to keep back a sob at the sight of Borger's ruddy face, now gray and bloodless beneath his great beard. "Hurry—we must get him inside!"

Jorund and Garth and some of the villagers carried the wounded jarl into the hall . . . then, at Helga's insistence, into his sleeping closet. She had water and wound-bindings prepared, and with Garth's and Jorund's help she stripped her old-husband and began the task of staunching the bleeding. But try as she might, his wounds would not cease their grim weeping. In desperation, she called for Jorund and Garth and asked their help to sear the wound.

Aaren had never seen such a wound. She sat on one of Borger's arms as they laid the red-glowing blade into his side and shoulder. But for her stern warrior's training and her experience slaughtering animals, she might have lost either her stomach or her senses.

As quickly as it happened, it was over, and soon Helga announced with tearful relief that the burning had stopped the bleeding. She packed his wounds with moss and covered them, then sent everyone out to wait for word while she sat with Borger alone.

In the hall, benches had been drawn near the hearth and spread with straw and fleeces to make pallets for the injured, who were tended by their women and by old Sith, who was knowledgeable of wounds. Brother Godfrey moved among them bringing words of comfort, offering healing blessings, and lending his strength to those whose hearts were bleak.

A grave mood settled on the hall as the warriors filled their stomachs and drank the new ale that had been intended for celebration. There was no talk of the glory of Valhalla, of the great honor of the fighting or the dying . . . only of the attack and the wounded and the long-standing blood feud which had blazed to life again between the two peoples.

The hall slowly filled with villagers made nervous by the rising howl of the night wind and seeking both news of the jarl and reassurance. The uncertainty that the warriors and clan had lived with for the last three years had become a dreaded reality: their jarl was seriously wounded, perhaps dying, and there was no designated heir. Hard on all their minds were thoughts of who would succeed him. Again and again their eyes sought Jorund and were comforted to see him moving about the hall, checking on the injured and speaking with the warriors about what had occurred.

"It was a well-planned treachery." Garth recounted the events, at Jorund's request, calling on first one warrior, then another to assist with their recollections. "We were to have twelve men, as they were . . . and at first twelve was all we saw. Then as they hauled the trunk of silver up the slope and we released Leif, a score more warriors broke out of the trees. We had set Harald out as a watcher—they must have found him and killed him first. Then they came in fast . . . circling the cliffs and attacking our flanks . . ."

"When they charged, Leif himself snatched up a sword from one of his men and took after Borger, cuttin' an' slashin'. None of us would have escaped alive if the jarl hadn't known the pass through the crag in the cliffs," Erik vowed in a choked voice. "He blocked the mouth of the crag himself to give us time."

"When we went back later to get him," Hrolf declared tightly, "he was half dead."

"That he is . . . half dead," Helga said, standing beside the wooden step of the high seat. The men shoved to their feet at the sight of her. She answered the unspoken question in their eyes. "The end is far from certain . . . it may be days before we will know if he lives. But if he lives, he will never fight again. He will not be the jarl you knew."

Dark muttering swept the hall. For a warrior-jarl like Borger, not fighting would be worse than death itself. A muffled wail went up from some of the older women, and a rumble of discontent raced through the seasoned warriors. The young warriors—stirred by Garth's reckless talk—began to demand they mount a raid on jarl Gunnar's village in retaliation.

Aaren stood up from the bench near the hearth and caught Jorund's gaze in hers. The conflict of a thousand tortured hours, the anguish of inner strife, the questions a man must answer in his deepest soul . . . the time for those was past. Jorund's people—her people now, too—needed a leader. Jorund no longer had to blade-fight for the high seat; he had only to mount one step . . . and take it.

She moved slowly toward him through the confusion, searching the tumult in his face, knowing the depth of his honor and of his desire to lead his people. Then she stood before him, calling forth his strength with the belief in him that shone in her eyes.

"It is yours, Jorund," she said in a whisper, turning her gaze to the high seat, which loomed eerily empty beside them. "You were fated for this. Your people need you."

She slipped her hand into his, joining her strength to his, and he smiled, feeling her warmth, her certainty all through him. It was true. A new sense of his own power, a new belief in his destiny surged through him. He clasped her hand tighter and moved toward the wooden step and the great carved chair upon it. A deepening hush fell over the hall as he mounted the platform and pulled Aaren onto it beside him. Together they faced the sober countenances of the warriors and his kinsmen.

"Hear me!" he called out. "By right of birth . . . by right of might, and by right of years . . . I claim this seat and all powers attendant." The clamor of voices and shuffling feet rose as the warriors and folk crowded closer to the high seat, staring at Jorund's imposing form and the way it was enlarged by Aaren's tall, powerful frame beside it. The pair stood shoulder to shoulder, their faces strong, their eyes glowing, and the common folk grew wide-eyed with wonder.

"You?" Garth pushed through the stand of warriors, his countenance dark as a thunderhead. "The jarl has not yet named you to the high seat. He would not name you until you fought him—"

"The old jarl is gravely injured—next to death—and can no longer state his wishes," Jorund declared. "There is no time for talk of what might have been, or even of what was. There is only now. And *now* there are wounded in this hall and dead to mourn . . . and perhaps a village to defend." He looked out over the faces of the villagers among whom he had grown to manhood. In some he saw doubt, in some anger . . . but in others he saw trust and hope.

"Defend? Do you intend that we just sit here, licking our wounds? We must strike back . . . mount a raid while Gunnar believes we are injured and in retreat!" Garth said hotly, pushing forward. "We must draw blood for blood—"

"When you draw blood for blood, you must also *shed* blood for blood!" Jorund thundered, his features suddenly fierce with a depth of passion none had seen in him in years. "How many more widows would you make, Garth, to salve your stinging pride?"

"I say we arm ourselves and ride on Gunnar's village at daybreak!" Garth shouted back, gathering nods and cries of support from the young warriors gathered around him. But Jorund saw the indecision in the faces of the more experienced warriors and knew he had to give them a compelling reason to delay—believing that time would dull their anger and blunt their desire for vengeance.

"Then you say wrong!" Jorund's voice rang out. "A raid launched now would flounder . . . in snow. Did you not see the sky—feel the wind heavy on your face as we rode back to the village? By midday tomorrow we will have snow to our knees. And when the land groans under a burden of snow, the North Wind will hear and will ride down out of his lair to exact cruel tribute. There will be no forage, no fuel, no warmth to be found. Those caught out in the fields will freeze."

Confirmation of his prediction came from an unexpected source. Old Sith shoved forward. "Jorund speaks well. All Autumn Month I have seen the signs of early storms. And tonight the evening clouds swirled wild and low . . . like the dust raised by the Wild Hunt." The fire in her eyes called forth old images, old tales, old beliefs.

"Listen! The wild steeds approach, even now!" Her gnarled finger thrust skyward and in the settling hush, all heard the moan of the night wind across the smoke hole. Eyes widened and faces grew blank with alarm. Odin was believed to lead the other gods of Asgard in a great and terrible hunt each autumn . . . riding his eight-hoofed steed over the countryside, stirring storms and discord, trampling all in his path.

For once Jorund was grateful for his people's lingering belief in Odin's fierce and capricious ways. "It is fool-hardy to feed warriors and horses to the Land Waster," he declared. "We will bide here . . . allow the wounded to heal and the snow to melt. By the spring thaw we will be ready for whatever befalls."

"The spring thaw?" Garth snorted. "That is months away, Jorund! Perhaps it is not the snow and cold you fear . . . but the battle!"

It was finally said . . . that which hovered below the surface of their thoughts. In recent years, Jorund had made no secret of his loathing for blood-letting and his people could not help but wonder how he would lead them when they needed to make war.

He had to reassure them . . . while concealing the disquiet in his own soul as to his future course. He felt Aaren's hand tighten on his. He glanced down at her other hand on his flexed arm, then at her speaking look. *Trust your courage and your strength, Jorund*, those amber eyes said, *for I trust them*. Her faith in him renewed his determination, and he turned back to Garth.

"I fear no battle, Garth Borgerson," Jorund said, raising his hands and curling them into fists. "It is true, I loathe fighting and killing. But I challenge you"—he addressed the whole assembly—"there is not one among you who truly wishes to lose forever the companionship of a friend, a wife, a husband, or a child. *Not one*." When there was not one voice raised to refute him, he turned back to Garth. "For all your talk of Valhalla and the glory of battle, which would you rather take to your breast . . . a shaft of cold iron"—he thrust a finger toward Miri, who stood at the side of the platform—"or yon maid's warm and willing flesh?"

The question bit deep into Garth's pride and the distress in Miri's luminous eyes made his face flame. He scowled and looked to the other young warriors, who shared his anger and confusion.

"Yea, I loathe fighting. But I have fought when need be," Jorund continued, "I have truly fought." He opened and lifted his scarred hands and all but those who had ridden on that ill-fated ransom mission knew the significance of that gesture. Eyes began to glow, heads to nod.

"And I say now is not the time to fight," Jorund declared. "We will heal and mend and prepare. And when the time is right, I will decide how to best settle our grievance against Gunnar Haraldson."

Palpable relief went through the hall on a wave of muttering, and Garth drew back a step, studying Jorund's powerful presence and the agreement he had just wrung from his clansmen. Under the prodding stares of his comrades, he jerked a bitter nod and strode out.

The villagers drifted back to their houses and huts, feeling vastly relieved that Jorund was in charge, and that the battle-maiden stood at his side. Miri and Marta flew to hug Aaren, and Brother Godfrey, his fleshy face beaming, came to clasp Jorund's hands. As Jorund returned the round priest's hand-clasp and bearish hug, he muttered, "If you know a prayer for snow, my friend, say it. And if you don't . . . you'd better make one up . . . quickly."

Whether it was the prayers or not, Jorund could not say. But by the following midday, the already frozen ground was covered with a mantle of white, and great, wet feathers of snow continued drifting down at an astonishing rate. Jorund's bold prediction had come true and most of the people took it as a sign of his wisdom and an affirmation of his leadership. With the snow-blanket, peace fell over the village as well. The folk rested and went about their daily chores and at night kept watch in the hall for their old jarl, who was reported to be passing through the worst crisis.

On the morning of the third day, Helga emerged from Borger's closet with tears streaming down her care-worn face. "He calls for you," she said with a sob, seizing Jorund's arm and pulling him into a run through the hall. Jorund found his father weak, but awake and lucid.

"You . . . you must take the high seat," Borger said in a tortured rasp, groping for Jorund's hand. Jorund felt a squeezing in this throat and a peculiar hollowness in his chest as he stared down at the pale face and burning eyes.

"I have already claimed it," he answered truthfully, not knowing whether it would anger or reassure the old man to hear it. "The high seat is mine."

"Then you got your way, First-born. Took it without a fight." A smile, which on a healthier man would have seemed crafty, curled Borger's parched lips. He raised his grip along Jorund's iron-thewed arm. "Well enough. But you will have to fight to keep it. And I will be there, First-born . . . to see you fight."

"Hush, you old fool," Helga chided, dabbing at her eyes with the rim of her kirtle and inserting herself between them to tuck Borger's hands back beneath the furs. "You with your talk of fighting. You might have been killed—and already you're eager to see blood shed again."

Borger winced and cast a pleading look at Jorund. "If you have any mercy in you, find me another to tend my wounds. She'll make me into a puling babe . . . or a mouth-foaming madman."

Jorund laughed at the old bear's predicament. "If that be true, old man, then I believe I'll leave you closeted with Helga's kindnesses a while longer. For either would be something of an improvement." And he ducked out the curtain.

It was not long before the hall was filled with villagers and warriors and with the news that Borger had affirmed Jorund's succession to the high seat. The warriors of Borger's *hird* seemed reassured that the old jarl had given his blessing to the new and they settled back, assuming their winter tasks, to await the thaw.

That very night, as the North Wind ravaged the countryside, mead-foaming horns were being raised in old Gunnar's long hall to celebrate the rule of a new jarl . . . Leif Gunnarson. For three days after his rescue, Leif had eaten well and slept soundly in furs he had never expected to use again . . . letting time and nourishment restore his strength. Then he sat with his father and his father's chief warriors, detailing his experiences in Borger's hall and relating what he had observed of Borger's village and standing force of warriors and armament.

"They are well manned and stoutly armed," Gunnar had said, shaking his head. "And they will be watching for a raid." He pushed up from his great, carved chair and beckoned his wife to help him stand . . . something he had not allowed publicly before now. "Such is a task for a young jarl . . . for a man of sinew and might. I am no longer that man. From this day on," he said hoarsely, meeting the eyes of his loyal warriors and captains one after another, "you will follow my son and heir, Leif, into battle."

With that, he stepped down from the high seat and waved Leif to his feet. He stretched out his hands, clasping Leif's wrists in a strength-blessing. Stunned silence reigned; never before in the history of their clan had a living jarl vacated the high seat for his son. But as their old jarl walked painfully back to his sleeping closet, all sensed a poignant rightness to it. When a jarl could no longer fight, it was said, he could no longer lead. Then a round of shouts went up from Gunnar's warriors and, one by one, starting with the chief among them, they made their way forward to pledge fealty to their new jarl.

Now, well into the night and into the ale-feast of celebration, Leif sat upon the high seat, surveying his hall and the gaiety of his people. The high seat was what he had set his heart upon, what he had prepared for his entire life. He would now lead his people . . . and one of his first acts would be to lead them into battle. That thought weighed heavy on his heart and it took only a small turn of his thoughts to know the reason why . . . to see her face in his mind and feel her phantom softness against him.

One of the captains posed the question on all their minds. "Well, Leif, what will be your first stroke as jarl?"

All knew that the first act of a new jarl from the high seat carried much significance and bore a portent for the coming years of his rule. All expected that a raid on Borger's village would be uppermost in his mind. Thus, they puzzled at the slow smile spreading over his face and were thoroughly surprised by his words.

"My first stroke from the high seat?" He rubbed his chin as if savoring his thoughts. "I believe . . . I will *take* me a bride."

For the next several days, all went well in Jorund's village. Jorund was accepted as jarl, the wounded began to mend, the snow stopped just short of the knees, and the Sky-Traveler reappeared to push the clouds back to the snarling North Wind's lair. But at night, in the rare privacy of their sleeping closet, in the warmth of their shared furs, Aaren knew all was not right with Jorund. His loving bore the stamp of his inner turmoil, by turns tender to the point of hesitation, then volatile to the brink of sensual rage. And when the pleasure was done, he lay awake for long periods, holding her and staring into the darkness. She finally understood what it was he searched the darkness for: the path of the future.

"Do not torture yourself with it, Jorund." She finally spoke in that quiet, comforting darkness. "When the time comes, you will make the right choice. You will do what must be done." There came a long silence. But she knew he had heard her and she waited.

"If you see so well into the future, then tell me also what I will do," he said thickly. "For I swear to you, I am not yet sure myself."

"What is it you want, Jorund?" she demanded, searching his features in the dimness. "Serrick taught me to make and hold an image in my mind . . . of armor, of victory, of something I wanted. Think of what it is you would have. You cannot reach for something until you know what it is you wish to grasp." He turned his head to look at her.

"Peace with the other clans. An end to the feuds and fighting and killing, so that we may build and trade and prosper."

"Peace. You cannot grasp that by yourself, Jorund. Peace takes two. As with us . . . there could be no peace between us until both of us wanted it." She paused and scowled, unsure where that thought should lead. But Jorund seized and carried it further, suddenly seeing in their intimate battle elements similar to those present in the larger conflict between clans.

"And how did I make you want peace with me, Aaren? What changed your heart?" he demanded, pushing up onto his elbow to face her. He could see the flash of her teeth in the darkness as she grinned.

"Your words. You spin wondrous silken webs with your words." She lifted her fingers to his lips. "And your touches. No one had ever touched me as you did . . . or wanted me as you did. And finally your strength. I did not see it at first, for I was taught to see strength in men as force of might and skill with arms. But I believe now that there are other ways to be strong. You are strong, Jorund Borgerson, on the inside as well as on the outside . . . your great body, your wide-reaching mind, and your deep-seeking spirit. I had to find your strength to respect you . . . and to respect you before I could find peace with you."

"Words . . ." he said, pondering all she had said, thinking of how it might fit the larger conflict as well. "It began with talk, then." He grinned and pressed a kiss in the palm of her hand. His spirits were on the rise again. "There is time before the thaw. Time to talk. Time to let words begin to work an understanding." He pulled her against him and pressed his lips to her temple. "It is a place to start . . . something to reach for . . . a meeting . . . to talk."

As his spirits rose, his passions soared with them, and in a single, deft move, he rolled onto his back and pulled her atop his chest. "Ah, She-wolf . . . you are a wise and wily one. Truly, I am honored to be a prisoner in your lair."

"A prisoner?" she said, smiling, relieved to hear the playful tone in his voice once again. "You are hardly . . ." She stopped as she recognized the sensual vibrato in his voice. Then she seized his wrists and slid her bare body over his to sit astride his belly. "I believe I owe you, Wolf-tamer, for the time I spent as your prisoner."

"And what revenge will you take on me, She-wolf?" he said, sucking in a breath as she began to move. Above him her rounded breasts jiggled and swayed, their dark tips hardened by the chilled air, and against him her honeyed heat rubbed and writhed, blazing a searing trail of sensation down his belly.

"You kept me cold and naked in your lair," she purred. "I intend to keep you hot and naked in mine."

The next day, as yet another snow fell, Jorund called the assembly of warriors and prominent villagers together before his high seat and laid forth his plan to send an emissary to Gunnar Haraldson. He braced as he finished, expecting a storm of protest, and was not disappointed.

"Talk?" someone from the back shouted. "I say we make 'em scream for mercy!"

"Talk?" Garth bellowed in a voice reminiscent of his father. "They rob and bleed us and you would have us *talk*?" And behind his complaint there welled a fist-shaking, finger-jabbing clamor of agreement.

"They wouldn't have attacked if Borger hadn't been so eager to bleed them . . . of both blood and silver," Jorund answered, boldly engaging one pair of eyes after another among the warriors, pouring the oil of new reasoning on the troubled waters of their thinking. "Ask yourselves: what would you have done if it was your son held captive, your last mark of silver demanded to free him? I say Borger would have done the same to Gunnar . . . and more so."

"That be truth!" old Oleg Forkbeard cried, thumping his knee. "Borger wouldn't rest 'til he carved the blood-eagle on old Gunnar's back . . . if it was Jorund held for ransom."

"That be truth, old warrior," Hakon Freeholder declared, rising. "The old jarl—he knew how to answer force." He raised a brawny fist and shook it. "With greater force!"

There was more commotion around the assembly as Jorund's attempt to get them to think of more than one side faltered. He tried again.

"Who among you would not defend his home, his flocks, his harvest? Perhaps Gunnar believed that was what he was doing when Borger attacked on the first raid. It could be he wishes peace as well. I want to end this feud before there is more killing."

"We'll end it," Freeholder proclaimed. "When the last son of Gunnar goes to ninth Hel!"

"It seems to me you don't mind killing, Brother Jarl," Garth snarled, just loud enough for a number of others to hear, "as long as your opponent has four legs."

Jorund's fists clenched as he confronted the surly Freeholder and his backers, then swung his gaze to an equally hostile Garth and his comrades. He had tried talking with them, tried reasoning, and they were too stubborn or too stupid to see. All they understood was force. . . . Well, then— by Godfrey's Hell—he would give them *force*. He took a deep breath and stalked toward them, his eyes narrowing, his shoulders swelling.

"I have tried to reason with you, but you stop your ears and harden your hearts. So be it," he declared, his voice deepening to a raw, angry scrape. "I need no counsel or blessing from you. I am jarl here and if I wish to send someone to talk to Gunnar and his son Leif, I shall!" He raked a challenging stare through the ranks of his warriors. "I need but two warriors to carry my words . . . two men of courage willing to risk much . . . to gain much for all our clan."

"It'll be ridin' to a useless slaughter," Garth proclaimed sullenly, crossing his arms and glaring at Jorund. "No warrior of any sense will go."

"Someone of courage will," Jorund decreed. "Who?" He searched the faces of his men, looking for that spark of belief, or that trace of loyalty which would yield to persuasion. One by one they lowered their eyes or turned their faces away, squirming under the challenge he had laid upon them.

"I . . . I will go. I will speak to jarl Gunnar for you."

Shock rippled through the hall and eyes widened on the source of that clear, feminine voice. Marta Serricksdotter stood at the edge of the high seat, clutching a fur wrap to her breast. Her face was pale and her clear blue eyes were wide and utterly sincere.

"I am not afraid to go, Jorund. I will carry your words . . . and speak of peace."

With the first stunned moment past, a gasp, a stammer, and a choked laugh of surprise were heard, but quickly died. She came to Jorund, squaring her shoulders under the weight of their collective disbelief. It took every bit of her courage and her hidden love for Leif to speak out so in public. This was her chance . . . her *one* chance. She managed a tentative smile at Jorund, then turned her earnest eyes on the others.

"Who will go with me?" Her words dealt them all a stunning blow.

"Marta . . ." Jorund smiled wanly at her, then shook his head and made a gesture of exasperation. "I cannot send you, Little Sister."

"I am not afraid, Jorund," she responded, wincing at the way the men glowered at her. She did not mean to shame them . . . only to find a way to be with Leif and to stop the feuding. Her voice dropped to an urgent whisper. "Send me."

A shocked hush fell on the assembly. A mere girl was making cowardly fools of them!

"I will go with her," Aaren said, shoving to her feet and hurrying to put her arm around Marta. "I believe in your desire for peace, Jorund." She turned a fiery look on her fellow warriors. "Perhaps it does take a woman's heart to yearn for peace. But most certainly it takes a warrior's courage to seek it out." This time even Jorund was dumbstruck . . . and scrambling for a way to deny them.

"Nej," came a seasoned male voice from the side, "you must not go, Fair Warrior. You are needed here with the jarl. And you, Little Maid . . . your heart is bold, but it is a warrior's task." It was Hrolf the Elder who spoke. He stepped forward and turned to search the hall for another. When he found the face he sought with an inquiring look, he received a nod in response. "You have two now. My son and I will go."

"But Young Hrolf was injured." Jorund shot a look through the assembly to the young warrior who stood with his arm still in a sling. Young Hrolf promptly removed his arm and showed it to be hale enough to travel.

"You have your peace-speakers, jarl," Hrolf said solemnly. "Now grant us a boon in payment for our hard task." Jorund jerked a nod, admitting his petition. "While we are gone, sharpen your spears, swords, and axes. Strengthen your shields and prepare well for the fight . . . if we should fail."

Jorund searched Hrolf's leathered face, understanding the warrior's message. So it was. Speak of peace and prepare for battle. It was the price of his vision. He looked around him at the proud and stubborn faces of his warriors and kinsmen. Without their cooperation, there would never be real peace. He would have to give them this, to let them have their weapon-strength, and to pray their preparations would prove unnecessary.

"So be it," Jorund declared. "Hrolf will go to speak. And we will prepare ourselves for battle . . . if the talking fails."

The next day, Jorund sent a rider carrying a colored arrow to all the outlying farms, alerting the freeholders to their defenses and summoning them to armed duty at the first major thaw. After much consultation with Jorund, Hrolf and his son set off for the farmstead of a prosperous farmer, nestled in the oft-disputed borderlands between Borger's and Gunnar's holdings. From there they would send word to Gunnar's village of their mission and await reply; admittance or refusal. The entire village turned out in the fresh snow to bid them farewell and a new blessing that had nothing to do with the gods of Asgard: peace-luck.

After all the others, even the Hrolfs' wives, had returned to the warmth of the hall, Aaren and Jorund stood together in the pristine cold, watching the two figures growing more distant. It was the launching of a dream. With a sigh, Aaren threaded her fingers through his and strode with him to the smithy . . . to prepare weapons for battle.

The night was moonless and the trees loomed black and spidery at the edges of the village. Great patches of night-blue shadows veiled all movement, cloaked all presence from the few dozing watchers still posted along the routes to the village. The snow-blanket cushioned the sounds of feet and hooves, and only the occasional creak of harness and the motion of limbs against leather bore witness to the ominous gathering in the trees along the eastern edge of the village, between the dwellings and the silent lake.

Stealthily, a dark tide of human forms flowed along the edge of the houses surrounding the commons, wrapping past the smithy, extending like an uncoiling serpent to loop the granary . . . then gliding through the snow-laden huts . . . inching toward the women's house. An arm flashed as a signal, and a well-tended coal ignited a torch, which lighted another, then another. A ring of fierce yellow flames soon circled the granary, and with another signal the serpent struck, sinking those searing yellow fangs into the low-hanging roof.

Soon the cedar roof was burning and the thrall who slept on a pallet inside awakened to the flames and came tumbling out the door—straight into the invaders' hands. They allowed no sound as they dragged him away and silenced him.

"Fire!" One of the night-watchers by the shore spotted the flames and came running toward the village, banging on doors and calling out the alarm. This time, the invaders let him run and call and bang. Soon the hall itself was being alerted with cries of "The granary—fire!"

A horde of invaders burst through the unbarred door of the women's house with weapons drawn and torches raised. They pulled the shocked women from their pallets and muffled their screams. Snarling threats and shoving them back against the walls and down on the floor, they groped the women's frantic, writhing bodies with coarse pleasure. Then the raiders' attention focused on two of the thrashing, protesting forms, and they seized them, stuffed cloths into their mouths, and wrapped them in blankets snatched from nearby pallets. With ugly laughter and talk of taking their rewards in their captives' flesh, they slung the two over their shoulders and carried them out into the frigid night.

At the same moment, the doors of the smithy were breached and the thralls who slept there were knocked asunder. Brun tried valiantly to prevent them from gaining access to the armory, blocking the door with his thick body and flailing fists—for, ironically, he seldom wielded a blade and thus never kept one near at hand. The attackers soon overpowered him and bashed him senseless, and poured into the armory to seize newly struck blades and spears and set flame to the new wooden shields stored in the smithy's open shed. Then with their arms full of weapons, they raced for the nearby trees. And in the burgeoning confusion of fire and shouting and running, they were not even noticed.

Fire! Aaren and Jorund sprang up in their furs at the first shout in the hall and in a heartbeat were frantically donning their garments. Jorund only bothered with breeches and boots before racing out into the hall and seizing the sentry to rattle the news from him.

"F-fire—the granary's afire!" the man gasped. It might have meant a hundred things . . . Around Jorund, warriors were lurching from the benches to their feet, instantly awake and reaching for their blades.

"Garth!" Jorund shouted, and his younger brother appeared at his shoulder in a bare tunic, his boots half laced. "Take a dozen men through the village—find out what's happening. The rest of you—follow me!"

As they ran across the commons, the door to the women's house swung open and old Sith and Inga and Gudrun staggered forth, crying. But their shock and anguish was caught up in the general panic of the fire, and not even Aaren, running past in her breeches and boots, Jorund's tunic in her hands, could hear more than fire-fright in their calls and did not stop to listen. When flames were spotted on the roof of the smithy as well, the entire village was galvanized. Panic erupted and Jorund and Aaren and the Freeholder and Garth had to seize control and shake people to make them listen and obey.

"Buckets and pails and bowls—bring all you have!" Jorund shouted at one after another.

"Keep the children back—bring spades and shovels, rakes—blankets—anything to beat out the flames!" Aaren yelled, running for the smithy and seizing a pole from a corral fence to pry stacks of burning wood away from the walls.

They worked in shifts in the freezing cold, wetting blankets and braving the thick smoke to beat at the flames and pour buckets and pails of snow on them. The entire village, from the youngest child and lowliest thrall to the mightiest warrior and jarl, labored heroically to save the granary and the forge. The plentiful snow proved a blessing. Cold and wet, more accessible than water would have been, it gradually turned the tide as they scooped it up and threw it onto the flames. The fire at the smithy was beaten without heavy loss to the enclosed structures, the harness storage and armory. It was mostly the open shed over the great hearth and bellows that suffered.

But the fire in the granary was hotter and fiercer. The dusty grain itself had caught fire. Then the burning roof timbers collapsed on the interior, and all they could do was pour snow on the smoldering wreck and watch with heat-singed faces and frozen hands as much of their bountiful harvest turned into cinders and smoke.

As the frantic pace eased, someone spotted the granary clerk in a nearby snowbank, bleeding from a belly wound. The sight of blood on snow, in the light of early dawn, was a grisly shock to senses already reeling. Even as they called for help to carry the fellow, Aaren was discovering the half-smothered forms of Brun Cinder-hand and his helpers outside the armory door. She called for help to carry them to safety—then glimpsed the nearly empty armory and realized the blood on Brun's battered head was from a beating, not from the fire.

"Jorund!" She went running to find him, searching through the sooty, exhausted villagers who stood like crumpled stalks around the smoking granary. She found him standing before the blackened doors, his back rigid, his face scorched and glowering.

"It's ruined. A whole year's harvest . . . most of a year's grain," he said bitterly, as if still trying to comprehend it. He looked around at the devastation in the faces of his people. "They worked so hard . . . even the children." They had come together, had struggled side by side to snatch their harvest from the jaws of the Cold Reaper—only to see it go up in flames. In their faces he could already see fears for the winter ahead; there would be much hunger in the village before spring.

"Jorund . . ." She touched his gritty arm. "It was an attack," she choked out, scarcely able to speak as the cold air seared her smoke-weakened lungs. "Brun and his helpers—they were beaten. Someone broke into the armory and stole most of the weapons—" The news produced such a look of loathing in him that she shivered.

"Gunnar," he said hoarsely. "He came back to finish his treachery." A searing pain slashed through his consciousness. While he had talked peace and tried to convince his people to set aside old hatreds and lay down their arms, Gunnar and Leif had been talking of war and spurring their warriors to a raiding frenzy.

He shifted his gaze back to the smoldering wreck of the granary. It was a perfect lesson in the destructiveness of the fighting and bloodshed . . . but one that could only incite his people to new hatreds and deepen their desire to fight. Then the crowd that had gathered around him murmured and parted to admit four men carrying a body. He stared down at the limp form of the thrall man who had tended the grain . . . stained with garish, jarring crimson. And inside he felt something cold and brutal inside him beginning to loosen . . . to uncoil . . . and he tensed furiously, trying to fight it, clinging to reason.

Aaren looked up, her face filled with horror. "Jorund, something must be done."

He wiped his eyes with both hands, as if trying to clear away that hideous red from his vision. "I have a treasury," he ground out, looking into the faces of his people. "I will buy grain." But even as he said it, he knew that finding surplus grain amongst the clans would be difficult. "No one will starve!"

"That is not what I meant. Jorund, this cannot go unredressed," Aaren declared, drilling her meaning into his eyes with quiet force. His breath came harder and faster as he looked around him at the anger and expectation in the others' faces. They believed it, and now his Aaren believed it, too.

A commotion at the edge of the crowd disrupted that painful exchange. Oleg Forkbeard jostled people aside and ushered a weeping, wild-eyed Sith forward to Jorund. Between sobs, the old dairywoman choked out: "They come for . . . the women. An' took—" A shuddering gasp choked off the rest. Aaren wheeled to face Sith and felt a tremor of panic for the first time that night as the old woman's anguished eyes turned on her.

"Who?" she demanded, rushing to the old woman and seizing her shoulders. "Who did they take?"

"M-Miri and Marta . . . our little Miri and Marta!" Sith gasped out.

The news hit Aaren like a blow to the gut. She was unable to take a breath. Her senses contracted massively . . . she could scarcely hear Gudrun's tearful voice saying: "They broke in on us—snatchin' and grabbin' and shovin' us— sayin' old Gunnar would have the lot of us for flesh-sport. Then they spotted Miri's and Marta's yellow hair and took them . . . bound them up in blankets and carried 'em off . . . laughin' about how they would . . . would . . ." The shock and pain in Aaren's face stopped her from finishing it. But Aaren knew—they all knew—what fate the raiders had planned for her sisters.

"Nej! Nej!" she wailed, making fists and stiffening against the pain erupting in the middle of her belly and slamming upward through her chest. "Not my Marta—my little Miri— *not them!*" She ran for the women's house.

"Aaren—" Jorund grabbed her, but she wrested from his grip and kept going.

He bolted after her, as did half the village. They raced to the women's house and he charged in after her to find her standing, staring at their empty pallets. She began furiously stripping the furs and blankets and straw from the bench, dragging them onto the floor piece by piece, as if searching for some shred of their presence. Anguish mounted in her.

"Nej—they cannot be gone—taken—" When there was nothing left to fling away, she stood heaving for breath, holding in sobs as she stared at the bare wooden benches. Suddenly their faces rose up inside her, as they had been that first night in the village . . . pale, frightened . . . filled with trust in her ability to protect them. But she *hadn't* been there to protect them . . . she had been lying safe in Jorund's arms in the hall. And they had been terrorized and abducted. Even now they might be lying beaten . . . or raped . . . or both.

Torn between anguish and rage, she fought Jorund's arms as they tried to encircle her. She dug in with her heels and managed to drag both of them out the door before Jorund finally halted her and seized both her wrists.

"Aaren—look at me! Dammit, look!" He jerked her arms and called to her until the sense of who was calling to her penetrated her reeling thoughts. The anguish in her face pierced him to the core. His pain equalled hers . . . was spawned by the same grief. His Aaren and her little sisters . . . he hadn't protected them, or the rest of the village . . . and it was a warrior's duty, *his* duty, to protect.

"Gunnar's men took Miri and Marta," she said with a groan.

"Aaren, we'll get them back. Aaren—" He banded her with his arms and pulled her tight against him. She fought at first, struggling against his comfort even as she struggled against her pain. But slowly, as he talked to her and his warmth seeped through her shoulders, she began to still in his arms.

Then she reached for the one thing in her life that meant as much to her as what had just been stolen. Her arms wrapped frantically around him, and she buried her face in his shoulder as the dam of her emotions broke. He lifted her and carried her through the crowd to the hall and straight to their closet.

His head was spinning, his whole world suddenly turned upside down. As he sat holding Aaren, overwhelming waves of loss broke over him . . . the harvest, his people's safety, Miri and Marta . . . and his dream. Peace. He had wanted it so much . . . believed in it so strongly, and had convinced Aaren to believe too.

Now, other beliefs, other values—long suppressed— roiled up in him, hot and potent. *A warrior's duty . . . might makes right . . . fear no man . . . protect your hall, your people, and your land.* Those beliefs were as much a part of him as his desire for peace.

Inside him was still the warrior, and the warrior was not the same as the beast. *Don't be afraid of your strength*, Aaren had said. *I had to find your strength to respect you . . . to make peace with you.* Now he understood . . .

he needed the warrior part of him and the courage and determination it lent him. Aaren and his people needed it.

And his enemies needed to respect it.

More than a score of horses thundered down the forest paths, their hooves churning the ground, sending mud and snow flying. Dawn was an hour behind them, but their riders had driven them relentlessly onward, bearing the raid-spoils of Borger's village well beyond the reach of immediate retaliation. It was only when they reached the first river and crossed it that the leader slowed and raised a massive hand to halt them. He pulled the blanket-wrapped body lying across his knees into a sitting position on the saddle before him. And before the hard, eager stares of his warriors, he peeled back the blanket to bare a fair, tousled head and a pair of soft shoulders.

Marta could scarcely see or hear—her lungs burned and her whole body felt pummeled from being carried across a horse for an hour. Her first thought was to struggle—her second was that the voice that laughed, the arms that cradled her, seemed oddly familiar. And her third thought, as she stared up into a helmeted visage and slowly recognized Leif's beaming grin and glowing eyes, was that she was dead and this was Brother Godfrey's "Heaven."

"No need to fight, Little Morsel," Leif said warmly, subduing the last of her squirming by pulling her tightly against him. "I don't intend to eat you up right here."

"Leif! It is you!" she cried, and she flung both arms around his neck with such force that he barely kept his balance in the saddle. Around them rose a number of husky male laughs and a whistle or two. When she released him and pulled back, her cheeks were rosy and her eyes were jewel bright.

"You came," she said, glancing at the rough, armor-clad warriors around them, then returning her gaze to him. She smiled and lowered her lashes, embarrassed by the depths of her eagerness and pleasure.

"I promised," he said.

"She is indeed a beauty, Leif," a warrior in a mail shirt and helmet said from the horse beside them. "And she seems pleased to see your ugly hide. Is the other one as pretty as she?"

As the warrior spoke, Leif turned his mount so they could see the horse where Miri rode. The warrior who held her had just peeled the blanket from her head and they saw her gasp for breath and stare blearily at her surroundings. And when the sight of a dozen leering male grins turned on her registered in her mind, she sucked in air and screamed with all her might.

Chapter Twenty-One

Jorund had to act. He strode through his long hall, shouting orders at the sooty, grieving villagers who had collected there seeking reassurance from their new jarl. He seized the shipwright by the shoulders, giving the dazed fellow a shake which made him come to life. "Go for a sail hoist and rope . . . take your men and lift and drag the burned roof beams from the granary." When the fellow took off at a run, he turned to a group of village craftsmen and charged them: "You, you, and you . . . get shovels and be ready to dig through the rubble to salvage what you can of the grain beneath." He had still other duties for the chief women: "And Helga, Sith, Bedria—organize the women with baskets, anything that will hold grain, and carry what is saved to the main barn."

The other villagers and a number of his men scrambled out the hall's main doors after him, and he turned to his warriors. "Thorkel—did they take any horses? Where are Brun and his helpers? How bad are their wounds? Oleg, Svein—gather up all the blades, spears, and shields in the village—see how many weapons we have—" With each question he laid hands on a warrior's shoulders, then gave him a turn and a shove, sending him off to find the answer.

As Jorund came to life beneath the pall of gray smoke that hung over the village, the folk saw their jarl in motion, clearly in control, and they came to life, too. Villagers came running with the reassuring news that no houses or huts had been stormed or torched, and no other women were missing. It was not much comfort, but it appeared that the granary and smithy and Miri and Marta Serricksdotter were the only victims of the raid.

But the storm of activity that surrounded Jorund could not drown out the voices echoing in his head and heart. *This cannot go unredressed. Some things are worth fighting for. Until all lay down their swords, we must defend ourselves.* It was true, both the warrior and the peace-weaver in him knew: peace could never be bought at the cost of his people's safety.

Just then, Garth, Erik, and Hakon shoved into his vision like a grim wedge of trouble. They pushed aside the villagers and planted themselves directly before Jorund, their swords drawn and their faces swollen with anger.

"The village is secure. We rode about and posted watchers . . . none of the raiders lingered," Garth declared bitterly. "They got what they came for and fled." He paused and lifted his chin to a challenging angle. "We wait for battle orders, jarl." He raised and brandished his drawn blade. "Or do you still think to *talk* to our enemies . . . while they rip the food from our mouths and steal our women from their pallets? That is my woman, my bride they've taken!" He spat on the ground. "There's what I think of your peace, Brother. Peace and mercy are for the weak . . . and tonight's raid has proved it!"

"Listen to yourself, Garth!" Aaren's smoke-coarsened voice broke in on them before Jorund had time to respond. She shoved quickly through the villagers and halted a few paces away, facing both Jorund and Garth. Her jaw was set with pained determination and she wore her breastplate.

"Peace and mercy are gifts . . . *treasures*." Her words were spoken with such intensity that they crackled on the air. "So precious that they are often bought with a great and terrible price. I grieve their loss as much as I grieve for my sisters." She stalked closer, her eyes blazing, her body vibrating with tension. "Are you so filled with pride or hatred that you cannot begin to understand that?"

Her fiery words and the grief evident in her face caused Garth to lower his chin and move back stiffly. Then she turned to Jorund, her heart wringing inside her breast.

"And do you see it, Jorund? The price that must be paid?"

She moved closer to him, trapping his burning gaze in hers, knowing his desire to lead his people without leading them into battle . . . and knowing now, as he must, that battle was inevitable.

"I see it," he said in deep, emotion-filled tones. He saw more clearly than anyone the price that must be paid. And he saw that he must be the one to pay it.

"It is no longer a fine, high-minded ideal or a belief to be argued, Jorund. It is my sisters," she said hoarsely. "They have taken my family."

"We will get Miri and Marta back, Aaren. I swear to you." Jorund met her desperate plea with grave determination.

"Then do you lead the raid to rescue them, Jorund?" Garth demanded.

"Will you lead us in the fight, jarl?" Hakon asked.

"Yea, I will lead you," Jorund's voice rumbled forth, deep and pained, his eyes glowing like coals, his body quivering as he stalked forward. "I will fight with you . . . fight for you." It was true, the warrior in him vowed fiercely; he would fight with all his heart, with all his might to return Aaren's sisters and to protect his people.

"Garth—take Erik and two others to the stables, prepare the horses," Jorund ordered. "We will take every man we can mount and arm." As Garth burst into action, Jorund searched the commons beyond the others' heads. "Where are Oleg and young Svein? I sent them to search the village for blades—And Helga—we need provisions—"

"*Nej*—you'll not need Helga," Aaren said, taking hold of his arm. "I'll see to that."

He nodded. "We will need sleeping rolls and warm cloaks and linen binding." When she jerked a nod and bolted for the storehouse, he turned to the others. "The rest of you fetch your armor, weapons, and shields. All men with arms . . . assemble on the commons when you are ready."

Shortly the entire village was charged with the activity and tension of preparation. The warriors donned helmets and mail or leather breastplates, sharpened and oiled their blades, then ran to the stables and byres to saddle their horses and tie on their sleeping rolls. Aaren led a number of the women to the storehouse and began packing cloth bags with provisions and filling all the ale skins they could locate. Between the frantic pace of trying to salvage the grain and preparing to ride after Gunnar and his men, nearly every person in the village was pressed into service, even the children.

Confusion mounted alarmingly in Jorund's soul. He would lead them . . . but how long would they follow when they realized he carried no weapon into battle? How long could he hold the high seat bare-handed? Old Borger's words came back to haunt him: *you will have to fight to keep it.*

And yet he had made a vow to the White Christ. To pick up a blade now would be to turn his back on the faith he had come to see as the way of truth . . . the way of the future for his people. But if he clung to his vow and honored it, he might lose everything . . . his wife, his people, his dream . . . his whole life. And more of his clansmen would die senseless battle-deaths. How could abandoning his people in their need and watching them march off to kill or be killed serve his new Lord's will?

There had to be some way, some answer. And there was only one person who could help him find it . . . one person who loved both his Lord and his people as much as Jorund did. He looked up and spotted Helga's boy hurrying toward the granary with a water bucket in his hands. He called to the lad and grasped his young shoulders.

"Fetch Godfrey for me . . . tell him to meet me down by the fishing boats . . . quickly!"

Godfrey came running down the snow-drifted path with his cassock hitched up around his knees and his beefy, heat-scorched face glowing like a beacon in the gray, wintery air. As he bounded from one of Jorund's huge footprints to another, he spotted Jorund by the prow of one of the large fishing boats and headed straight for him. As he halted, puffing, and stomped the snow from his feet, Jorund turned to him with a face so bleak it was painful to witness.

The priest's shoulders rounded. "My friend, you must not punish yourself for what has happened. This raid . . . the burning . . . you could not have stopped them. You must think of where to go from here. Only you can bring your people to peace in the days ahead."

"I tried to uphold peace and reason . . . to prevent more fighting. But it was too late. There had already been too much conflict to avoid more. Then Gunnar burned our grain . . . and stole Miri and Marta . . ." The muscles in his face worked as he struggled for self-control. He turned on Godfrey with dark anguished eyes.

"My people don't need a peace-weaver now, Godfrey. They need a leader. They need a *warrior*." He flung a finger toward the village. "Even now they prepare to ride into battle."

Godfrey despaired, looking heavenward and making a sign upon his breast and again on his lips . . . asking his Lord to make his words come out right.

"Then there is only one man who can lead them . . . one man strong enough, determined enough . . . who loves them enough to pay the price required to lead them through these present battles and into peace. Jorund, that man is *you*. You are indeed both a peace-weaver and a warrior. And this day your people need both. There is no other with your strength and understanding. Can you not see? The task is yours, my friend. Your great size and power, your warm and generous heart . . . you were made for it from the beginning. And all that has happened has prepared you for it.

"You must go with Aaren and the others and lead them," the priest urged. "If you go, you may find some way to halt or reduce the fighting . . . and if you do not go, they will flounder and many will die needlessly."

"But . . . I don't know if I *can* lead them," Jorund said desperately. "Not into battle . . . and if not there, then perhaps not anywhere." He halted, scarcely able to say it. "They will not—cannot—follow a leader without a weapon."

"A leader without . . . ?" Godfrey scowled.

"Godfrey . . . I have taken a vow to the Christ that I will never again raise a blade to another man." He watched Godfrey's eyes widen and his jaw go slack.

"A vow? But Jorund . . . such a vow is sacred . . ."

"As is my warrior's vow to defend my people . . . and my vow to love and protect my wife," Jorund said hoarsely. "But how can I defend and protect and lead my people without a weapon? What am I to do, Godfrey? Which vow do I break?"

"Ohhh—" Godfrey groaned, seeing the full scope of Jorund's dilemma. "This is the very reason our Lord dislikes vows and swearing about things. They almost always cause more ill than good."

Godfrey squeezed his eyes shut and began praying feverishly for inspiration. A *weapon* . . . he knew little of weapons. But he knew the hearts of men, and he knew that if Jorund picked up a blade again and fought, breaking his pledge to his new Lord, his heart would never be quite the same. And if Jorund's splendid heart was lost, then peace and love and his people's burgeoning faith in the White Christ would have no champion in Jorund's clan . . . and no chance to succeed among his people. A weapon . . . Jorund needed a weapon.

Suddenly the memory of Aaren's voice came to him . . . asking what sort of weapon his god wielded. His eyes flew wide. And what had been his answer? His heart began to hammer wildly in his breast as his thoughts raced. Could it be?

"But, my friend, you do have a weapon." There was such emotion, such portent in Godfrey's voice that Jorund's heart paused, as if telling him to listen.

"What weapon is that?" Jorund said, tensing, his eyes burning into Godfrey.

"The same weapon our Lord had when he battled the powers of death and darkness—a most powerful weapon— a weapon of the heart. Jorund, you have *Love*."

Godfrey watched the words lodge in Jorund and saw his massive fists clench and his jaw tighten. He hurried on, desperate to convince him.

"Our Lord was not a man of riches or power. He had no warriors, no long ships, no rank. Nor did he carry a blade. But he carried a powerful weapon within him . . . and he wielded it without fear. And when they took his life and thought they had defeated him . . . he made his greatest triumph. For he gave his life willingly for the good of others . . . his one life, sacrificed for many . . . so that he could share his heart-weapon, his Love, with other hearts."

The priest paused, his throat tight, his heart afire, and he grasped Jorund's big fists. "You have that heart-weapon in you, Jorund. Your love for your wife and for your people is all you need. You are given great size and strength . . . you have much power in these hands. Go and wield that power for them . . . and let our Lord's love strengthen your heart and bring you victory."

The storm raging in Jorund's soul set his whole frame quaking. Godfrey watched, clinging to Jorund's fists, praying that his words would find fertile soil in Jorund's heart. He could not have known that of all the words he might have chosen, those were the perfect ones to seize and move Jorund . . . for they were almost the very ones Aaren had used before their fight up on the mountain.

"Your god's heart-weapon will steady your arm . . . " she had said. *"Let your White Christ shield your heart and mine with his Love"* And the Christ had shielded them both . . . even when the battle-madness came upon him. How had she known?

A heart-weapon; he turned it over and over in his mind, wondering at it. It was a fitting armament for a man who was both warrior and peace-weaver. How could Godfrey have known what she said to him? *Someone to match your strength . . . someone to free it. A man who tames she-wolves with his bare hands can surely handle fat old jarls the same way. One life for many. A sacrifice. The price to pay for peace.* He heard Aaren's voice again in his mind and heart, speaking those words and more, joining with Godfrey's voice. . . .

The spirit-storm in him began to pass. He had to fight . . . bare-handed . . . and trust for the victory. Fight . . . with all the love he possessed. The turbulent waters of his soul began to calm. A strength, a sense of purpose slowly permeated his tension-wracked body. It was a warm tide of surety, a certainty he could not explain.

With stunning clarity, he suddenly understood what he had to do. He closed his eyes and relaxed his fists and his rigidly held shoulders. With a great breath, he accepted it wholly, embraced it, letting its warmth curl through him. A moment later, he seized Godfrey's shoulders with a bittersweet smile.

"A heart-weapon. Yea . . . I have that, my friend. And now I know how it must be used. Now . . . go to my closet and get my cloak and warm tunic off the pegs, and bring them to the stable. Hurry!"

Godfrey's eyes glistened as he clasped Jorund's big arms and gave him a beaming smile. Then he turned and ran as fast as his thick little legs would carry him toward the hall.

Jorund strode back into the village to find that the charred ruins of the granary roof beams had been removed and the process of digging through the rubble to salvage the unburned grain was well under way. He went from there to the stables, where he spotted Aaren among the warriors packing and preparing their mounts. The sight of her in her warrior's garb, her hair braided, her wrists banded with leather, and her body encased in leather armor, caused his stride to falter.

She was a warrior, he told himself. But he still had to fight a consuming urge to seize her and haul her back to the hall and tie her up to keep her from riding into battle. He smiled bitterly at the realization that she would probably be insulted and outraged by his protective impulses toward her. If she had set her head on fighting—he had learned too well—there was little he could do to stop her.

Aaren turned into his gaze as he approached and his eyes fell on the sword strapped against her left shoulder. He halted not far from her, his attention fixed on her blade, his fists curling as his face became a shield around his thoughts.

But Aaren knew what turmoil lay behind his flinty mask . . . the conflict within his deepest soul, the dread of battle and of seeing his people slain, the sorrow for a broken vow and a dying dream. She pulled her sword from its cradle and carried it to him . . . offering him her love and pride with her eyes, as she offered him the hilt of her precious blade.

He stood searching her face and made no move to take it from her.

"Jorund, take it," she said, her throat tightening as she thrust the hilt closer to him.

Around them several warriors paused, watching the odd exchange. They frowned and glanced at each other.

"It is your weapon, Aaren," he said, staring at the silver pommel, the graceful, blue-streaked blade. "You will need it."

Aaren felt a small trickle of panic and turned to young Svein, snatching his blade from its cradle and offering it to Jorund instead. "Svein will find another," she insisted, and when she gave him a scowl, young Svein jerked a nod and hurried off to take a blade from one of the unmounted men who would stay behind.

When Jorund took the blade from her, her knees almost buckled with relief.

Jorund led his mount to the commons where the rest of the men were already assembling. He separated out those with weapons but no horses, and set a captain over them, charging them with defending the village. He spent a few moments checking provisions and laying orders with Helga, then donned the fur-lined tunic Aaren had made for him in the mountains.

His heart was pounding as he mounted his horse so that he could be seen and speak to his band of more than two-score mounted warriors.

"We will ride fast and hard . . . to catch up with Gunnar's force before they reach his village. Our best chance to get Miri and Marta back is to catch them while they are still in the open." He took a deep breath and gave the final order: "Say your farewells . . . and mount up."

As the last of the warriors disappeared down the path leading along the frozen shore of the lake, Borger burst from the doors of the hall, bellowing like a gored ox. Clad only in a tunic and breeches, and barefooted, he lurched along by leaning on a wooden staff with one arm . . .

alternately fending off Helga and holding his injured side with the other.

"Why didn't you say something, Woman?" he roared, battling Helga for possession of his own arm. "My first-born leads his first raid . . . and you hold word of it from me?"

"I feared you would fly into a fury and do yourself damage," Helga argued. "And now just look at you. Turn back to the hall, you old fool . . . or at least put on your boots." She brandished the footgear she held in her hands, but he batted it aside with a growl.

"I have to see him leading them!" he insisted, craning his neck as he hobbled after them, searching through the trees for a glimpse of Jorund. "I swore I'd see him fight!"

"Godfrey!" Helga called and beckoned to the priest across the commons. "Come help me get him back to his pallet before he pulls something loose and bleeds again!"

"By Odin's Aching Arse—I've missed him!" Borger bashed a fist against the air and winced as the movement sent pain shooting through his shoulder and back. Then he fixed his sight on Godfrey hurrying toward them.

When Godfrey started to take Borger's arm to help, the old jarl grabbed him by the front of the cassock and hauled him nose to nose with a red-eyed request.

"You—Holy-worm—I've a *good deed* for you to do."

Godfrey's eyes widened by the same measure as Borger's narrowed.

"I'm going to the fight," the old bear growled. "And you're going to take me!"

For almost two days they had ridden hard; eating on the move, taking snow for water, stopping only when the horses were spent, then remounting before either men or beasts had quite recovered. The tracks of the mounted force they followed had grown steadily sharper and clearer as they gradually closed the distance between them and the raiding party. Garth argued every time they stopped, insisting they were wasting precious time, despite the fact that their horses showed dangerous signs of fatigue. Jorund

grew short-tempered with Garth's surly harangue and finally sent him and Erik ahead as fore-riders, to search out how
far ahead the raiding party was. With the irritant of Garth's
impatience gone, the men were better able to endure.

It was all so familiar: the tension he wore like a second
skin, the long silences where the creak of saddle leather
and the thud of hooves provided counterpart to the beating
of his own heart, the quick speaking looks between men,
the constant and exhausting search of the terrain for signs
of movement. It was as if he had experienced it all just
yesterday.

Then he caught a glimpse of Aaren riding beside him, her
cheeks wind-blushed and her body taut with readiness, and
he was reminded of all the ways this was not like the old
raids. The warriors looked to him as leader, now. It was his
orders, his experience they counted on to see them through.
And his wife rode beside him . . . on a mission to reclaim
that which had been stolen, not to plunder or steal from
others.

When they encountered increasingly frequent farmsteads,
a clear indication that they were closing in on Gunnar's
stronghold, Jorund passed word to his warriors to be prepared to attack or to defend themselves at any time. Aaren
and the others gritted their teeth against the cold and fatigue,
donned their helmets, and shifted their blades to their front
shoulders instead of their backs. Only Jorund left his head
uncovered . . . and his light hair, shining and waving as he
rode at their head, became their banner.

All rode in readiness, but it was still something of a shock
when Garth and Erik came charging down the path toward
them, shouting that they'd spotted the raiding party—not
far ahead. Their relentless riding had bought them precious
time. Now they had to catch the party in the open, before
they reached Gunnar's fortified village, or all their frantic
effort was in vain.

Blades rang as they cleared sheaths, and the horses danced
nervously as men jerked their feet from the stirrups to prepare for a quick dismount, and tightened their knee-grip to
compensate. Jorund left his borrowed blade in its sheath,
but untied his great iron-clad shield and slid it onto his arm,

glancing at Aaren. It would be her first taste of battle, he thought. There was time only for a quick, speaking look of reassurance as she adjusted her borrowed helmet and rolled her tense shoulders. She flashed back a small, determined smile and he grinned. Giving his mount the spur, he jolted into motion with a cry of: *"She-wolf!"*

"Serricksdotters!" the men echoed as they bolted down the path after him.

Cold wind whipped the horses' manes, snow and mud flew from the churning hooves, and blood roared in the warriors' heads as they raced forward to do battle. Patches of light and dark blurred by trees, overhanging limbs, snow, and wind-swept bare ground careened wildly through their senses. The frantic race toward battle fired their blood, and from deep in a nameless warrior's belly, a savage cry was born. It was picked up by the others—until they roared, and rode, and thought as one. Aaren was suddenly one with them, her fierce anger blending with theirs . . . their savage cry becoming hers, torn from her soul, filled with her pain.

Suddenly they glimpsed open ground ahead—grain fields—and knew they were close to the village. Just before they broke from the trees, a hailstorm of arrows rained down on them from the barren treetops, sending them ducking and scrambling for their shields—and two of their number toppling from their mounts. But there was no attack from the side or front, and Jorund called out for them to ride and spurred his horse to lead them on.

The surprise attack had cost them precious moments. Old Gunnar's lead was widening as they broke from the trees, and far ahead they glimpsed the regular lines of rooftops and the smoke-plumes of hearths. Both the raiding party and the village were in full view now. The raiders were fewer in number, but riding fast and with safety in sight. There was no time to scan the raiders for Miri and Marta; there were suddenly tumbled stone walls and boulders hidden beneath the snow to dodge. Ahead, they recognized the mounded earthen fortifications at the edge of the village . . . the protective barrier Jorund had warned they must not let their enemy reach.

As they bore down fiercely on the raiders, the majority of Gunnar's force suddenly broke off and reversed direction, charging straight for them with weapons drawn and battle-cries borning. At some common and instinctive moment, Jorund, Aaren, and the others began reining up and bounding to the ground, abandoning their mounts even as their enemies did—to charge into battle on foot. Cries of "Odin!" and "Valhalla!" mingled with "She-wolf!" and "Serricksdotters!" . . . ringing across the frozen fields. And abruptly, the battle was joined.

There was no time to think or prepare. Aaren bore straight in on Gunnar's men, using her shield to deflect blows as she banged and slashed with her weapon. Again and again she wielded her blade, feeling its savage vibrations up her arm, jarring her nerves, her vision, testing her concentration. All around her there were shouts and noise and confusion. The ring of clashing blades, the thudding smack of steel on wood, and the fierce cries of battle-spirit and of pain filled her head. Again and again she heard male screams and caught glimpses of wrenching, recoiling motion and falling . . . not knowing if it was her kinsmen or her enemies who fell. Her opponents kept slashing and snarling, bearing doggedly down on her . . . their faces filled with battle-fire and hate. And slowly, mercifully, her perceptions narrowed.

Eyes disappeared into the recesses of iron and leather helms, and whole men were reduced to composites of line and density and force. Stark blade angles, arcs, raw vectors of shoulder motion were all that remained . . . twisting, hacking, thrusting were her only responses . . . until her blade finally bit bone. Her opponent fell with a cry and it took a moment for her to see clearly . . . blood . . . a shoulder. . . . Another form, another blade loomed up and she took a savage hit on her shield and wheeled to fight again.

Jorund had landed on his feet with only his great shield in his hands. As his first attacker charged, he used the shield with his massive shoulder behind it as a ram, jarring his opponent back. Then he lifted his shield and swung it so that the iron-banded edge became a weapon of itself. Again and again he swung and bashed, dodging blades and then charging and swinging with all his considerable might . . .

surprising his opponents with his odd way of fighting and sending them sprawling.

A cry for retreat rang out and Gunnar's warriors responded instantly, drawing back, then wheeling and racing for the earthen wall around the village with all the speed they could muster. It ended as abruptly as it had begun.

Garth screamed for them to give chase, waving the others on after him. But the few who followed turned back when it was clear Gunnar's men would make the wall and safety. A few shocked breaths later, a roar went up from the others . . . a venting of the battle-steam left boiling through their blood and of their frustration at not preventing Gunnar's raiders from reaching home. When their shouting died around them . . . Jorund's ragged voice came through the surflike rush of blood in their ears.

"Find your fellows—" It was an order to count casualties. When the answer came—several wounded, none slain— Jorund's head dropped back and his eyes closed briefly. He took charge once again. "Catch your mounts and carry the wounded into those trees." He pointed to a stand of woods which lay across the snow-packed grain fields from the village. "We'll make camp there!"

While Jorund saw to the posting of guards, the setting up of camp, and the erection of sailcloth shelters for the night, Aaren saw to the wounded, packing dried moss and herbs into some wounds and binding others with strips of linen. Jorund's warriors knew well the routine of foraging for fuel and making camp in hostile territory: each man was responsible for contributing wood to the fires, for raising some shelter against the cold, and for preparing food. They set about the tasks Jorund assigned without delay.

Above them, Night stole the Sky-Traveler's colored blanket, hiding it in her soft, dark cloak. And soon the smoky campfires provided the only light in the forest, flickering strangely around the white-barked birches and barren beeches. As the work of making camp was finished, the men collected around the fires, their voices subdued, their bodies heavy with fatigue. Their eyes drifted to Aaren as she did her best to comfort a wounded warrior, then turned back to the fire and stood holding her hands out to warm them.

"Serricksdotter." The Freeholder's voice startled her and she looked up to find he had risen from his seat and was stepping closer . . . his right hand outstretched. She looked at it, then at the nods and half smiles on the other faces turned her way. She extended her hand and clasped his wrist even as he took hers . . . in the manner of one warrior welcoming another. "From this day on, I will be honored to fight at your back, Fair Warrior," he said. He glanced at the others, speaking for them as well. "All of us will."

Jorund watched her nod tersely and manage a small, pained smile of gratitude. She turned to find her horse and retrieve her sleeping fleece, wrapping herself in it. But instead of rejoining the men at one of the fires, she strode to the edge of the trees and stood in the night-shadows, gazing toward the village.

There her sisters would pass the night. The raiders had taken no time along the way to either abuse or enjoy their captives. Now that they were in the village, she prayed that they would purge the battle-fire from their blood with other women this night. She dragged her mind from the terrible images of what might be happening to her sisters and let her eyes focus on the five or so crumpled forms left lying on the snowy ground.

It was her first experience of real battle . . . and it left a hard, metallic taste in her mouth, a smell of blood in her head, and a low ringing in her ears. There was no way to tell how many of Gunnar's men they had wounded . . . but by morning those left on that icy field would never rise again. And for what? Why had they been so eager to redden spears and gash shields . . . in the service of a jarl's pride? In battle, there had been a fleeting rush of excitement, a feeling of power, but there was also the sickening aftermath—the blood, the screams of the wounded, the hollow feeling inside.

Jorund came up behind her in the darkness and slipped his arms around her, pulling her against his chest and bending to her ear. "Are you all right?"

"You were right about the glory," she said softly, her eyes glistening as she pulled his arms tighter around her. "It is in living, not dying. In loving, not fighting." She was swept with a longing for him and turned in his arms to embrace him. Moments later, her gaze was drawn back to those dark, twisted forms, which seemed to be sinking into the earth as the cold and shadows deepened around them. Would she lie on that frozen field tomorrow, waiting for her raven-haired mother to finally claim her?

"Why has no one come to carry them into the village?" When he remained silent, she looked up into his shadowed features. "We cannot leave them there." She handed Jorund her fleece and turned back to the men warming themselves around a green-wood fire. "Come with me . . . we've wounded to fetch." When they saw her snatch up a blanket and start for the middle of the field, they called out to her that they had long since rescued all their wounded. "I'll not allow men to die needlessly," she declared.

"Those aren't men," young Svein shouted after her in earnest horror, "they're enemies!"

"They may be valuable to us alive . . . to ransom or trade," she shouted back, giving them a reason to show compassion. "Dead, they are valuable only to kites and eagles. Ask the jarl."

Jorund nodded, confirming her order as he watched her striding out onto that cold plain. It was the woman-softness in her that would not let even an enemy die cold and alone. She was intent on redeeming some of the destruction she had wrought with her blade.

Four were yet alive and Aaren helped carry them back to camp and tend their wounds. One of the wounds seemed oddly familiar . . . a deep shoulder wound that had cleaved a bone . . . though she did not understand why. Mercifully, she had little recollection of the throes of battle until later that night, when she settled into a fleece to sleep and saw it all again in dreams.

When the raiding party had reached the village, Leif had carried Marta into his long hall and set her on her feet by the glowing central hearth . . . in the midst of a noisy, curious crowd.

"Here she is. My bride," he announced in a booming voice, ripping the helm from his head and tossing it to a young lad to hold. Marta took a step back, closer to him, and stood straighter under their probing eyes, returning their scrutiny. A moment later Miri was carried in, wriggling and protesting, and Marta quickly embraced her distraught sister to reassure her.

"Two of 'em!" came a loud male voice. The crowd parted to admit a tall, gaunt and graying man leaning heavily on a wooden staff. As he came forward, staring hotly at Marta and Miri, a wolfish grin spread over his face. "By the gods, boy—you never were one to do things by halves!" He limped closer and inspected Marta boldly, surveying her cream-smooth skin, bright blue eyes, and curvy shape. He gave Miri a similar appraisal, which made her shrink and bury her head in Marta's shoulder. He laughed at the way Marta bristled and scowled at him, and he turned back to Leif. "Beauties, both. You mean to take both to wife?"

"*Nej*," Leif said with a chuckle at the spark that suggestion struck in Marta's eyes. "One will be enough, old man." He put his hand on Marta's shoulder. "This is the one I went back for. Her name is Marta Serricksdotter . . . her sister is called Miri." He glanced down at Marta's upturned face and explained: "This is my father, Gunnar Haraldson."

"Jarl." She looked back at Gunnar and nodded gravely.

"*Nej*." The old man sobered instantly. "I am no longer jarl. The one you will call husband is jarl here now."

Marta looked up at Leif in surprise, and he smiled and put his arm around her. "And this is my mother, Ida Eriksdotter." He directed her attention to a large, square-boned woman whose features were very like his own. Marta nodded respectfully and was relieved to see a softening in the woman's strong face as she gazed at her son's new wife. "She will help you meet the other women and learn the duties of the jarl's wife. She is also a fine midwife. . . ." He grinned at the blush that produced in her fair cheeks.

"Leif has spoken well of you," Ida said, coming closer. "I must thank you, Little One, for your kindness to him. You saved his life in Borger's hall . . . and you will find many here grateful for that."

"Enough of this—tell me of the raid!" Gunnar demanded, stalking closer. "How much damage did you do?"

"We burned the granary, took much of their store of weapons, and set their forge ablaze," Leif answered with a notable lack of enthusiasm.

"Is that all? You didn't fire the old cur's hall or stable or the houses?" Gunnar exclaimed.

"You burned the granary?" Marta started and looked up at Leif in disbelief.

"Well, at least you got the food stores." Gunnar comforted himself with the thought. "That means there will be plenty of hunger in old Red Beard's village by spring."

"Leif?" Marta said, searching him with wide, wounded eyes.

"It was necessary, Marta," he declared tightly, "to halt Borger's greed and blood-lust. Hungry men make poor warriors. And old Red Beard cannot lead his men against us if they are too weak to lift a blade."

"But it is not jarl Borger who leads our clan now, it is Jorund. And he is a man of peace," Marta said, setting Miri from her and turning to Leif. "He would not lead his men against you . . . he hates fighting."

Leif stared at her, searching her eyes for truth and finding it in their clear depths. It supported both his care for her and his own perceptions. He had kept his mouth closed and his ears open during his captivity, watching and learning from what occurred in Borger's hall. He had heard Jorund's angry words on the night Aaren Serricksdotter engaged him in a *flyting* . . . and had listened to Borger's men both laughing and complaining about Jorund's peacable leanings.

"But Jorund or someone has led a force to our doors," he said.

"My sister, perhaps . . . or Garth Borgerson, to whom Miri was promised. Jorund wants peace with your people, Leif. Why else would he send two men to seek a meeting with you and speak to you of peace? I said I would come, but he said it was a warrior's task and sent Hrolf the Elder and his son instead."

"We received no such messenger," Leif said, scowling and glancing at Gunnar, who reddened and looked disgusted with her words.

"Get your head out from under the wench's kirtle, Leif. How can you believe such a tale?" Gunnar chided. "Look to my fate for wisdom in dealing with old Red Beard and his treacherous spawn." He thumped his damaged leg. "She could have been intended by Borger to soften you up—"

"Enough!" Leif declared with a cut of his hand. "I'll hear no more against my wife, old man." He paused and looked down at Marta, whose huge eyes were unclouded windows on a pained and truthful heart. And he spoke to Marta as well as to his family and clansmen. "I will speak to the men who fought at our rear, and learn what I can. If it is Jorund, I will see how badly he wants peace. He will prove himself . . . one way or another."

Daylight came too quickly and the camp roused slowly to a sense of expectation. Jorund sent out scouts to survey the village's defenses and set watchers up in the trees to report on movements inside the earthen wall. But the Sky-Traveler seemed to drag his heels as he crossed the sky-vault, making the morning seem unending as they waited for reports to trickle in. There was little to do but tend their mounts and weapons, worry about the captives they had come to rescue, and think of the battle that lay ahead.

Their situation was not promising, Jorund learned from his watchers at mid-day. The village was well fortified on all approaches except the lake shore. And there was a large force of warriors and villagers—perhaps four-score— in armed readiness just beyond the fortifications. Garth argued hotly for a night raid, like the one Gunnar had sprung on them. But without the element of surprise and not knowing where the captives were being held, their chances of success were small indeed. Jorund left his warriors and stood for a while, staring out across the snowy field, turning it over and over in his mind and feeling the time approaching.

Well into the afternoon, he strode through camp, rousing the men, and with some relief they donned their arms and battle gear. Shortly, they were crossing the field toward Gunnar's wall, arrayed behind Jorund and Aaren in a stout wedge. Jorund called to Gunnar, knowing that the old jarl had watchers along that wall who would carry his words. He waited, then called again. On the third call, there came a rattling of swords and a thumping of shields from over the rise.

Aaren braced and unsheathed her blade, noticing for the first time that Jorund was not wearing or carrying a blade . . . only a shield. But the force of armed men that appeared on the wall pulled her thoughts from Jorund to the peril at hand.

A tall, broad-shouldered form appeared . . . richly garbed in silver-trimmed armor and crimson wool. His head was bare and they knew instantly it was Leif Gunnarson.

"I would speak with jarl Gunnar," Jorund declared in a booming voice.

"I am jarl here now," Leif answered. "You will speak only with me, Jorund Borgerson."

Jorund glanced at Aaren, scowling, fearing that Leif, with his fresh memories of Borger's brutal hospitality, might prove even more difficult to deal with than Gunnar.

"We have come for the women . . . the twin daughters of old Serrick," Jorund shouted. "Hand them over to us and we will leave in peace. There will be no more bloodshed."

There was a silence. Then Leif raised his deep voice.

"The women are taken in payment . . . for the pain and humiliation I suffered in your hall."

Aaren had no reason to hope, but still she strode forth and called out: "I am Aaren Serricksdotter . . . sister to the women you hold. You have no reason to trust me, Leif Gunnarson . . . but I speak truly when I say that even now your wounded lie in my camp, well tended. And I would know that my sisters are—" Her voice cracked and she paused to mend it. "That my sisters are alive . . . and not abused."

There was a long silence in which Leif seemed to study her and her proud stance . . . and the truth of her words. Then, miraculously, he gave her that which she asked.

"They are well, Valkyr's daughter. They sleep in my hall."

Aaren closed her eyes briefly, then pressed her luck once more. "I would see them with my own eyes, Leif Gunnarson." There was another long silence before Leif spoke again.

"They stay by choice, Valkyr's daughter. One will wed a warrior this very night. The other will wed soon."

Jorund heard Aaren's intake of breath and Garth's cursing behind him. His gut tightened. Leif Gunnarson lied. And all who knew Miri Serricksdotter knew it.

"I do not believe the young Serricksdotters stay or wed willingly," he shouted back to Leif. "I will not leave until I have them back!"

"You will not have them back," Leif declared, "until you sit upon the high seat in my hall!"

To sit upon that seat, Jorund understood, he would have to kill every man, woman, and child in the village. For such was the way of the Norse clans; each warrior and villager pledged his life to defend the jarl and the honor of his high seat. It amounted to a total declaration of war. Final. Implacable.

The talking had failed and there was no turning back. All that lay ahead was fighting and blood-letting between their peoples. And Jorund could not let it happen. He squared his shoulders and took a deep breath as Leif turned to go, calling to him one last time.

"Leif Gunnarson!" he roared from the bottom of his being. "I challenge you to fight."

Leif froze on the top of the wall and slowly turned back. "It appears we will indeed fight, Son of Borger. No doubt I will find you on the battlefield somewhere," came Leif's reply.

"You mistake me, Son of Gunnar. I mean just the two of us. We may save the blood of our kinsmen and end the strife between our clans . . . you and I. With a *holmgang*. I hereby challenge you."

Wild confusion broke out on both sides at his words. *Holmgang*. It was a kind of fight much fabled and often sung, but seldom witnessed in the clans. And with reason. It was a fight between two sworn enemies . . . to the death.

Jorund had issued a bold challenge to Leif Gunnarson's honor which could not be retracted . . . *or refused*. He was offering up his life for his people. And he was challenging Leif Gunnarson to do the same.

"Jorund . . . *nej*!" Aaren choked out, feeling as if she'd been dealt a blow to the chest. She made a step toward Jorund, but he put out a hand to halt her and she stopped, staring in horror at his proudly braced frame and glowing eyes.

"Hear and know my conditions, Leif Gunnarson, the terms of this challenge." Jorund raised his voice once more. "If you accept, one of us will certainly die. Your father and your people must swear that there will be no retribution for your death, ever . . . and my father and my people will swear the same. Our fight will end the fighting and bloodletting between our peoples. And your captives, my wife's sisters, will be set free . . . no matter what the outcome." He allowed a moment for his words to be examined, then demanded, "Do you accept?"

The air itself stilled, as if waiting for Leif's reply. But the bold and public nature of Jorund's challenge left no grounds for refusal. Leif had to accept or show cowardice, and dishonor both himself and his fighting men. When the reply came, all could hear the grit of anger in Leif's voice.

"I accept, Jorund Borgerson. The fight and your conditions . . . all but one. If you survive, the Serricksdotters will be freed. If I survive, they stay here and marry among my people. And there will be no recourse or retribution for that either."

There was another pause, while Jorund considered it.

"Done!" he shouted. Then there was only one thing left to settle. "I give you until sunset to put your hall in order and say your farewells, Gunnarson. Then I will meet you here, on this very spot. And we will finish the blood feud that should never have been started."

Chapter Twenty-Two

W hen Jorund turned to his men, he was met with shocked silence. They had never imagined he would do such a thing . . . and had no idea how to react to it. He seized Aaren's wrist and drew her along with him through their ranks, heading back to their camp to prepare for battle. Garth and the others slowly followed, casting bewildered, then increasingly irritable looks at one another. By the time they reached the middle of their camp, they had formed a firm opinion on what Jorund was about to do . . . and it was summed up in Garth's brash but honest blast.

"A *holmgang*? Have you gone thick-witted?" he shouted, stalking to the side, then back. "We came to fight, not sit on our hands and watch you! And—worse—you would hobble us so that if you lose we will have no recourse, no way to punish Leif or get Miri and Marta back!"

"If we fight . . . take up our weapons and our luck . . . at least we have a chance!" Hakon insisted, drawing a chorus of agreement from the others.

"The same chance I will have," Jorund countered. "To fight and to win freedom for Miri and Marta and an end to fighting between our peoples." He looked around him at their scowls and scarcely cloaked disapproval, and felt steam rising through his blood. They had always scorned his refusal to fight . . . and now that he was willing to fight, they were outraged!

"Listen to me, and mark what I say." He stalked toward them angrily. "I am jarl of this clan now and it is my word, my honor, my desires that will shape your future. My desire is for the safe return of my wife's sisters and for peace with Leif's clan . . . and it is my right to decide how they will be secured. It was Borger's way to shed blood; it is mine to spare it. It was Borger's way to bully and bash and threaten; it is mine to reason and talk and persuade. It was Borger's way to wield an axe . . . mine to fight bare-handed. If you have grown so accustomed to old Red Beard's ways that you cannot accept my way of being jarl, so be it. You are free to leave."

Never in all his life had he so resembled fractious, hard-nosed old Borger as in that moment. He trapped their gazes in his, one by one, and after each painful encounter a warrior dropped his gaze and shifted feet or fidgeted with his sword or spear. No one made a move toward the horses. Then he turned to Aaren and found her watching him with eyes filled with both pride and pain.

"But, Jorund, it is to the death," she said.

"Yea, it is to the death. Nothing less would end this blood feud." Jorund's voice grew husky as he glanced away from the painful sight of her to his men's faces. "I said I would fight for you. And I will. And whatever happens . . . you must uphold my honor and abide by the terms I have set for the fight. There will be no blood vengeance taken after the battle. Whatever happens, you will decamp and go home."

"Jorund—" Aaren's throat swelled with emotion, choking off her words. But the turmoil in her heart rose into her face, as plain to him as words . . . and twice as hard to bear. "I cannot bear it . . . to lose both you and my sisters."

"And I . . . I cannot leave Miri in Gunnar's village," Garth declared, looking agonized by the prospect.

They had begun to accept his decision and with it his unique leadership, Jorund realized, and despite the grave trial he faced, a tide of joyous relief began to swell in him.

"I don't believe it will be necessary for you to leave her, Brother," Jorund said. "Nor will you lose a husband, Wife." He shook his head at them . . . then his face took on a cagey, Borger-like grin.

"You see, I intend to *win*."

His words wound through them like a breath of warm spring. One by one, the warriors began to grin back at him, and shortly he and Aaren were engulfed in a boisterous crowd of jostling, cheering warriors.

After a while Jorund pried free and led Aaren out into the woods where he could spend a few moments alone with her. They found a quiet spot among venerable birches and she slid into his arms. He sank into the welcoming heat of her mouth again and let the joy of kissing her melt away his concerns. For the moment, there would be only her . . . only them . . . only love.

His wind-whipped hair, his soft tunic and the wide, hard chest beneath, his lightly stubbled chin . . . all that and more stormed her senses as he wrapped around her like a cloak. She drank him in, holding him fiercely, renewing the well-springs of her memories with the feel of his hard, sinewy frame, the smoky scent of his hair and cloak, the salty-sweet taste of his mouth. She grew breathless and her lungs ached, yet she would not end that sweet possession.

It was Jorund who finally ended their kiss . . . so that he could look at her . . . absorb every bit of her he could.

"I will do my best to get your sisters back for you, Long-legs." He held her face between his hands and stroked her cold, silky cheeks with his thumbs. "But if something should happen . . ." His voice snagged on those rough words and he had to pause and free it. "Safe-keep my dream. Uphold the peace . . . and see that my men obey it."

She put her fingers over his mouth and he seized them and kissed their tips, smiling. There was something more he had to say.

"You gave me back my strength, my warrior-heart, Aaren. And when I thought my dream was dead, you helped me see that it could still live. For that I will always be grateful." He kissed her tenderly and whispered, "I have loved you well, Long-legs. And that is enough."

She closed her eyes, feeling those words branding her very heart, then opened them again. They were filled with tears and fierce determination.

"Well, it is not enough for me, Jorund Borgerson. I want children . . . a whole quiverful of sons and a whole hearthful of daughters . . . and many seasons by your side and in your furs." She curled her fingers tightly into his hair and growled: "You'd better fight like Godfrey's Devil!"

* * *

Across the field of honor, in Leif's long hall, the new jarl of Gunnar's clan had also spent time with his warriors, listening, admonishing, and instructing them, and sought some privacy with his woman. He carried Marta to his sleeping closet and sat with her on his lap, caressing her body and holding her tears at bay with his hungry kisses. She pulled her mouth from his long enough to whisper, "Now, Leif. Take me now, before you go."

He set her back and looked into her luminous eyes, sorely tempted to do as she asked, for his need was roused. But Marta was yet a maid, and he had lived long enough as a man to realize that the physical spending of desire in so hurried and desperate a mating would scarcely be pleasurable. And he wanted nothing but sweet pleasure in these moments with her.

"*Nej*, Little One, there is not time," he answered. It was the agony of his soul that he had not pressed beyond both their fatigue to claim her during the night just past. But she had seemed so distraught and exhausted . . . and he had treasured just having her there, watching her sleep, never guessing what the morrow would bring. Now there was only time to touch and kiss and speak bravely of what would be.

"Please, Leif, give me some part of you," she said, entreating him with her hands . . . caressing his powerful chest, stroking his face, and sliding her fingers through his long, thick hair. He smiled despite the pain her touch inflicted on his heart.

"So I shall. I shall give you my vow." He stood up with her, carrying her out into the hall and bellowing to set the very roof beams rattling: "Get me that little holy-man—that Father Alfred! I want to take this little Christian to wife!"

Against the deepening red of the western sky-vault, Leif's men rose along the crest of the earth wall, beating on their wooden shields with their spears and swords, chanting as they came. Aaren felt her blood stand still in her veins . . . it was as though they crawled up out of the earth itself.

Aaren and Jorund joined hands, calling to Garth and the others that it was time, then moved out of the trees and across the field to meet the enemy. Jorund's warriors began a similar pounding on their shields as they started across the field. Drumming . . . chanting, louder and louder . . . lifting Jorund on their loyalty, invading his blood with their rhythm, supplanting the cold hand clutching at his stomach with the warmth and oneness of their sound and spirit.

A number of Leif's warriors carried torches tied to poles, and when they reached the field they quickly formed a glowing half-circle of light on the well-trodden snow. Jorund's warriors closed in to form the other half of the circle. Jarl Gunnar arrived to witness the fight, and Garth and the others stared at the gnarled shell of a man, once a feared and mighty warrior, who now leaned on a staff and a sturdy young warrior in order to walk.

Aaren's eyes darted beyond old Gunnar to another figure . . . a small, feminine shape topped with achingly familiar golden hair. She clutched Jorund's arm. "Marta." With her eyes fixed on her little sister, she took a deep breath and started across that frozen ground. Hostile and curious gazes buffeted her like blows as she approached their line, but she weathered them and soon stood three paces from Marta.

"Thank Jorund's God . . . you are well," Aaren said. For a moment, she studied Marta's face and form, her heart too full to say more. Then she realized that Marta stood by Leif Gunnarson . . . and that her small hand clasped his arm tightly. Her eyes fastened on that speaking gesture and when she managed to lift them, Marta's eyes were shimmering.

"Aaren . . . I took Christian vows with Leif a short while ago. I am his wife now and I will stay with him no matter . . ." She halted, unable to continue. Aaren looked from Marta to Leif, whose great size dwarfed her little sister, then back to Marta's hand on his arm. Leif had spoken the truth . . . one of her sisters had wanted to stay.

"Do you truly want him, Marta?" But even as she said it, she knew the answer, for Marta had always been strong-willed. Her heart could never have been taken by force . . .

even if her body had. And that slender hand resting of its own accord on his arm said that Leif Gunnarson owned her heart.

"I do." There were tears in Marta's voice. "I love him, Aaren . . . even as you love Jorund."

Aaren stiffened and took in a sharp breath to counter the constriction in her chest. For a moment she felt Marta's pain, shared it as only a sister-mother could. And she knew that from that moment on, whatever the outcome, she would carry Marta's hurt within her . . . doubling her heart's burden.

"Then pray to your White Christ, Marta, to help us all."

She turned and strode back to Jorund . . . her eyes glistening and her shoulders squared. She wanted to scream and rage and cry to the heavens . . . to all the gods, wherever they were . . . to stop this horrible fight. But somehow she continued her erect stride across the ring of warriors and resumed her place beside Jorund. As she stood holding his arm and waiting, she looked across that frozen circle toward her sister and saw that Marta looked her way as well.

Both knew: one of them would lose the man she loved this night.

She scarcely heard Leif's law-speaker calling for each side to affirm a vow against retaliation, or the roar from each side that answered him. The law-speaker then announced the rules of the contest and called the combatants into the center of the ring. Panic went through her as Jorund removed his cloak and placed it around her shoulders. He pulled her against him and kissed her long and hard. His kiss tasted of farewell. She seized his tunic and held him to her a moment longer, pouring her love for him into her eyes.

"Your God go with you, Jorund, and protect you." She touched his lips with her fingertips, then dragged them down his chin and throat to mold them against his chest. "You fight with two hearts . . . yours and mine."

"Then I have a mighty heart-weapon indeed," he said with a bittersweet smile.

And he was gone.

A leather thong was used to tether Jorund's and Leif's legs together, a pace apart. Jorund chose to remove his tunic, despite the cold; there would be that much less for Leif to grab or hold. After a moment's thought, Leif removed his and tossed it aside also. When they were offered daggers, Leif seized one. Jorund did not.

"You must take a blade, Borgerson. I will not have it said I slew a man unfairly matched," Leif declared.

"I need no blade to do what I must do, Gunnarson," Jorund replied, opening his massive hands. "These are my weapons."

"If you are so determined to die, then the fight will be so much the shorter," Leif said thickly.

Confusion raced around the circle of warriors and to the villagers beyond, as word spread that Jorund intended to fight bare-handed. Garth hurried to Aaren's side. "What is he doing? He cannot refuse a dagger!"

She shook her head, unable to speak. His vow . . . his cursed vow. She strode out into Jorund's line of sight, entreating his eye, pleading without words. He looked at her pained determination. *A mighty heart-weapon*; his last words echoed in her head. Now she truly understood. She drew back to the edge of the circle, dread settling heavy in her stomach.

"It is how he wishes it," she told Garth and Erik and the others. "He has taken a vow to the White Christ never to raise a blade to a man again. He will only fight bare-handed." She had no time to react to their horror. Her mind filled with the memory of the three wolves. At least that day he'd carried a dagger.

Jorund and Leif faced each other in the circle of light, eyes searching, bodies curling forward. Each shivered with both cold and tension and broadened his stance, flexing his thighs, lowering into a crouch.

They were magnificent to behold: massive, handsomely proportioned, deep of chest and wide of arm, ribs ridged tightly with muscle . . . corded, sinewed, and seasoned. They were uncannily matched, these sons of dreaded rivals; Jorund slightly taller, Leif the more heavily muscled. It was as if the Norns had decreed this fate for them . . . selected their god-gifts and woven their destinies to bring them to this moment.

"Fight!"

The order lashed through Jorund and Leif like the crack of a whip. They snapped forward and began to circle each other like great stalking beasts. Their huge shoulders rolled forward into thick yokes of muscle, flexed, straining . . . eager to unleash their power. A roar went up from the ring of warriors as Leif lunged in with his blade. Jorund dodged and gave a mighty jerk with his leg, upsetting Leif's balance as he recovered from the swing. Leif caught himself and wheeled, lunging again—this time dead on center.

Jorund jerked his knee up, knocking Leif's arm up enough to grab his wrist. Suddenly they were joined and locked, wrist to wrist, arms shooting above their heads, bodies snapped taut and straining. Together they staggered and grappled for footing in the packed snow, Leif trying to bring his knife slicing down, Jorund desperately resisting that downward thrust.

It was a deadly dance . . . two great bodies joined, circling, feet scrambling, sliding, and digging in again and again. They finally thrust apart and circled again . . . panting, eyes hot now, each having taken grim measure of the other. The shouts of the men joined with the blood pounding in their ears to blot out all distractions. Each focused on the other's face, reading in the nuances of eyes and the tensing of muscles the direction of intended movements.

Leif lunged and slashed, again and again, and each time Jorund dodged or met the blow with a foot or an arm. Twice more they locked and writhed and heaved. Twice more, their fierce straining gained them nothing but chilling sweat in the cold night air. Then, with a roar, Leif launched his whole body at Jorund with his blade flashing, laying a shallow cut along Jorund's ribs. The clamor from both bands of warriors was deafening.

Jorund felt the blade connect—a sharp, burning sensation around which his senses contracted. He glimpsed red as he whipped aside and that color now began to seep through everything in his vision. The knife—he had to get the knife away! Lowering his shoulder, he sprang at Leif with a bellow and knocked him onto his back—grappling with his powerful arms, squeezing and twisting Leif's wrist, trying to loosen his grip on the dagger.

Leif seized the ridge of Jorund's shoulder, digging his fingers in, squeezing like a pair of iron tongs. Pain shot into Jorund's head and down his arm, breaking his concentration, allowing Leif's knife to inch closer and closer. Jorund could see the sharp point coming toward him as the pain from Leif's hold curled through his head and around his brain . . . squeezing relentlessly.

Suddenly all he could see was eyes . . . filled with the primal rage from the bottom of another human soul . . . set to devour him and all that he was . . . all that he wanted. And the straining, clawing battle beast in him broke free with a snarl.

In conscious but unthinking fury, he thrust his arms wide . . . at the same instant he rammed his forehead into Leif's face. Leif groaned a strangled cry and for one stark instant his hold on Jorund and his blade thrust faltered. Jorund groped for the dagger with both hands and wrenched it from Leif's fist. He scrambled to his feet and just had time to locate the edge of the crowd—and fling it with all his might into a soaring arc above their heads—before Leif used the thong to jerk his foot and send him sprawling.

The dagger landed in the hard-packed snow in the darkness behind the ring of warriors—straight in the path of two approaching horses. The riders reined up, sensing something had just fallen in their darkened path. They frantically searched the torchlit ring of frenzied, shouting warriors for a clue to what was happening.

"Hear that?—a fight! I told you it was a fight!" Borger roared with both pain and impatience. "It's Jorund! Get me down off this beast—I have to see—"

Godfrey all but fell from his mount and groaned as he hurried his aching body along to help Borger down. Shortly they were pushing through the ring, Borger leaning mightily on Godfrey's stout shoulders. Borger's former warriors were startled by the sight of him and quickly parted to let him through. When he and Godfrey reached the open ring, both were galvanized by the sight of Jorund and Leif locked in mortal combat, Jorund bleeding from his side and Leif bleeding from his face.

Possessed by pure, elemental fury, they grappled on the snow-packed stubble . . . on their feet, then their knees, then their backs . . . each seizing the upper hand and surrendering it when the strain of maintaining control became too great. They twisted and levered each other's limbs and drove with their powerful legs, each attempting to roll the other beneath him—each relentlessly wearing the other down and recklessly spending his own reserves in doing so.

Driven by burning pain in his limbs, side, and lungs—Jorund managed an explosive twisting arch of his back, throwing Leif off for an instant, rolling to one side and gaining his feet. But as Jorund thrust up, Leif also scrambled for position . . . then plowed into Jorund's belly, smashing him to the ground near the edge of the circle. The back of his head smacked both the packed snow and a rock half hidden beneath it.

Suddenly Leif was on top of him, driving for his throat, and Jorund was momentarily too dazed to prevent him from reaching it. As Leif's powerful hands closed on his neck, Jorund managed to seize his wrists and counter the killing force of his weight as he bore down from above. But he could not counter both Leif's weight and the deadly gripping force of his hands.

Blood filled Jorund's head and drenched his vision as he strained and gasped for air, trying to rock their bodies and throw Leif to the side and loosen his grip. But carnal red—the dew of wounds, the stream of life—began to dam in his eyes, deadening his vision. Frantically, he kicked his feet and arched and strained against that choking hold, but still those viselike hands managed to squeeze tighter. His lungs felt ready to burst, his heart was wrenching wildly in his chest, and he felt darkness gnawing at the edges of his vision, consuming his consciousness.

As his sight constricted, the noise in his head seemed to recede into a dull wavelike roar. From somewhere, he heard Aaren's voice.

"Fight, Jorund! Fight back—for the love of God! You cannot quit—you have to live. Jorund—fight—fight for us!

Take my heart—" His own heart was air-starved, nearly spent; it convulsed fiercely in his breast. Once . . . twice. He hurt so. . . . It would be so easy to surrender and slip into the encroaching darkness, to let it all end.

You fight with two hearts . . . live . . . for the love of God.

Love was his only weapon. His strength. Those rumbling voices in his soul roused his heart-weapon to love's fiercest edge . . . slicing through the icy and seductive grip of darkness, forcing him to feel the warmth and life in Aaren's call. *Fight back!* And out of the depths of his soul came a mute cry of pain and longing . . . and love.

He summoned the very last of his strength, harnessing the wounded beast, yoking his heart-strength to it—blending the darkness and the light in him in the service of Life itself. And with an unutterable plea, he gave one last savage, heaving thrust.

Leif's pressure had eased as Jorund's struggles slowed and ceased. His fatigue and the numbed sense that it was over had dulled his reflexes. Jorund exploded beneath him, and he was knocked aside and rolled onto the snow. With a pained beast-roar that came from the very bowels of his being, Jorund kicked away, then staggered onto his knees, gasping and shuddering to take in air. A half-instant later, he lunged savagely, slammed Leif onto his back, and climbed atop him, quaking with battle-fury. Hoarse animal growls issued from his damaged throat as his hands shot straight for Leif's neck.

He seized that corded column of muscle and blood and dug his fingers in . . . squeezing . . . focusing . . . using every bit of his body weight to counter Leif's frantic grip and thrashing. The beast ruled, insensate with rage, impervious to Leif's fists beating at his arms and ribs from below. Gradually Leif's resistance and wild writhing slowed, but Jorund relaxed none of the pressure.

Aaren had fallen to her knees at the edge of the circle and pleaded with him to live, to fight back. Now, as he arched over Leif, white-eyed with savagery, she began to realize that the power that had saved Jorund was part of the killing-beast in him. Set free, tasting both blood and triumph, it was bent on destroying Leif the same way it had almost been destroyed.

She saw Leif slacken beneath Jorund's grip and lurched to her feet, wild with fear. If Jorund killed him, even bare-handed, it would violate everything he believed in . . . destroy his dreams for peace. But she was there to guard his dreams, to tend his hopes, and to call to his strength. She seized Godfrey's shoulders.

"He's in trouble, Godfrey! Pray!" When Godfrey just stared at Jorund, she shook him. "Pray, damn you—pray and get your White Christ to help him!" Dragging his eyes from the sight of Jorund's battle-madness, Godfrey turned a look of mute horror on Aaren, then seemed to understand and fell to his knees.

"Jorund—stop!" Aaren called out to him across the ten feet that separated them. She took three steps into the ring, jerking away from the hands that tried to restrain her. "Jorund, if you don't stop you'll kill him! Jorund—let him go! You want peace, not killing. The fight is over!" She crept closer as she called to him, defying the unspoken rule of combat to approach them. "Jorund—think of the White Christ—of peace! Love your enemy—let him live!"

Even as Jorund's hands slackened around Leif's throat, another form hurtled from the edge of the crowd to stand across from Aaren. The crowd roared and, at the sight of Borger's hated form, some of Leif's warriors had to restrain others to keep them from charging out after him.

"Here, First-born! Finish him!" Borger threw his own dagger onto the snow, so that it slid and came to rest by Leif's head. "There will be no doubt you won . . . and you'll prove to all you're not a woman-heart! Kill him, First-born . . . it is your right!"

"*Nej!*" Aaren's fury uncoiled. She exploded at Borger, plowing him into the ring of warriors, then slamming him to the ground. When she dragged herself from his groaning form and ran back, Jorund had released Leif's throat and seized the knife, gripping it fiercely in his trembling hands. Hands clutched at her—whether her own men or Leif's, she could not say. She stopped and knelt where she was, watching through a blur of tears and knowing she could not intervene anymore. The choice was Jorund's.

Voices on both sides clamored for him to release Leif—
though a number on Borger's side screamed for him to
finish his enemy. For the first time Aaren closed her eyes
and prayed to the White Christ, wherever he was, to save
Jorund.

There was cold iron in his hand . . . a smooth horn
grip . . . his enemy beneath him, exposed and weakened. *It is
your right . . . kill him.* The old ethic. The old curse. Through
the blood pounding in his head Jorund had felt Aaren's presence and some small part of his consciousness had fastened
on it. Her voice, her words . . . he pulled them in like a
life-line. *Think of peace. Love your enemy—let him live!*

As Leif dragged in breaths and roused toward consciousness, Jorund felt the beast, sorely wounded, rising up in him
again, raging. Now that he was safe, was the beast to be
denied its reward? *Think of the White Christ.* His eyes slid
from Leif to the icy white snow by his head. Guided by raw
faith and the images Godfrey had planted in him, Jorund
groped by unfathomable instinct toward the white and the
sound of Aaren's voice . . . felt them calling him, drawing
him toward safety.

He closed his eyes and shuddered as a pervasive white
invaded him and drove the red fog from his head. Once
wounded, then triumphant, the beast now stilled and was
subdued. Its time was past. It crept back into the recesses
of his soul.

When Jorund opened his eyes again, he saw Leif staring
up at the blade poised above his face. The steeled dread in
his eyes filled Jorund's senses and for a brief moment, he
felt it too . . . the way he had felt as he lay beneath Leif and
the darkness closed in. It was the despair of losing all that
was and all that might have been. It was the same pain he
himself had felt. . . .

In that moment Jorund truly knew what it was to love
an enemy.

"You may have your life, Son of Gunnar, for a price,"
Jorund declared hoarsely, trembling with emotion. "And
the price is this: that you call me *Brother*." He paused,
panting for breath. "Say it! Tell them . . . all of them"—

he thrust the knife in his hand toward Leif's people—"that from this day on, I am your brother . . . the same as if we had the same sire and mother! Say it!" After a long moment, Leif's voice issued forth, raspy but understandable.

"He . . . is my brother."

"Louder," Jorund roared, "so both your miserable old father and my miserable old sire can hear!"

"Jorund is my brother . . . from this day on," Leif declared in a ragged voice.

"Now swear that you will give me a brother's loyalty and friendship—that you will never lead your people in battle against mine again!" When Leif paused and swallowed hard, Jorund insisted, "Swear it. Then I will swear the same!"

"I swear."

Jorund fastened his aching eyes on Leif's and said loud enough for all those assembled to hear: "I also vow never to raise my hand to you again, or to lead my people against yours as long as I live. I will be as your brother . . . and from this day on, I will call you *Friend*."

Jorund moved shakily on his knees and raised his own forearm, drawing the blade across it. Then he seized Leif's arm and cut it in the same fashion. "Thus is the old blood feud ended!" he declared. Before that great warring force, he joined their arms and sealed their vow with the mingling of blood . . . in the way of warriors.

A breathless, almost reverent silence fell over the warriors on both sides of the circle as Jorund shoved to his feet and staggered as he reached a hand down to help Leif rise. When they were both on their feet, Jorund swayed and grasped Leif's shoulders . . . bracing to stay upright. They stood staring at each other, warriors of unequalled strength and courage, bonded now in brotherhood.

Leif searched Jorund's glowing eyes, grappling for some understanding of what had just occurred between them.

Then abruptly Jorund threw his arms around Leif and embraced him. And after a moment of shock, Leif understood and clamped his arms bearishly around Jorund.

In that moment, mercy and peace took on new meaning for each warrior and villager present. Both had once been deigned the province of weakness. Now both had been demonstrated as an ultimate expression of strength.

Aaren raced to Jorund, pulling him from Leif, wrapping the shallow wound along his ribs with his tunic. She slipped her arms around his waist to support him and turned wet, shining eyes and warm, receptive lips to him.

It was a second life . . . a resurrection of love and spirit and hope within her, after each had been buried beneath the dread weight of final thoughts. Moments before, she had been filled with an awareness of death . . . now her body, her heart, her spirit were vibrant with life. Their kiss was a celebration of life and joy and love, compressed into the deep, passionate blending of mouths.

Marta reached Leif a moment later and threw her arms around his waist, laughing, tears running down her face. "Oh, Leif—it's done! And you're both alive!" She hugged him fiercely enough for him to groan. When she looked up, the dried blood on his face and chest made her frantic. She began gently wiping his face with his tunic. "Are you all right? Is anything broken?" Leif grabbed her hands and stilled them, pulling her back into his arms.

"I am fine, Little Wife." He grinned tiredly. "I have never been better."

Suddenly the whole ring of warriors contracted in on them, shouting and jostling. Godfrey burrowed in to hug Aaren and Marta and Jorund, and to offer a smile and a hand to Leif. Then Garth and Erik and Hakon and Thorkel crowded in to clasp Jorund's hand and clap his shoulder. Many of Leif's warriors did the same, and in the tight quarters there was shoving, scowling, and snarling as their scabbards and shoulders and tender warrior-pride collided with that of Jorund's men.

Jorund and Leif had to pause in their personal celebration to halt the shoving and pushing between their men. And when the few trouble-makers were separated, Jorund managed to turn to Leif.

"I can see we'll have more peace-making ahead."

Leif nodded with an exhausted smile. "You are welcome in my hall, Jorund Borgerson. We must drink long and well to seal such a pact. And my mother will see to your wound.

What say you, Brother? Will you stay this night under my roof?"

"I will be pleased to drink with you in your hall."

Leif and Jorund hung their arms on each other's shoulders and stumbled toward the long hall, pulling Aaren and Marta along with them. But the instant their backs were turned, the quarrelling began again; somebody in Leif's band shoved young Svein, and Hakon tripped the offender.

Aaren stopped dead in her tracks and anger blazed in her tawny eyes as she whirled and strode back, shoving and sorting and battering her way to the center of the disturbance.

"Hear me, you quarrelsome spawn of badgers!" she bellowed, freezing them all in their tracks. Her own warriors glimpsed the fire in her eyes and backed up a step or two.

Leif's men—seeing the others' reaction and taking in her appearance—put a few prudent paces between them as well. She raked a glowering look around their widening circle, then with a single smooth movement snatched Garth's sword from its scabbard and held it poised in one hand.

"There will be no more fighting this night—no more blades drawn—" she declared, raking them with her eyes. "Any who violate the peace will answer to me! And so you will not forget . . . take out your blades and drop them here, at my feet. *Now!*"

A defiant mutter rumbled through them, and she stalked from Erik to Garth to Hakon, staring hard into their eyes, scorching them with her gaze. "There will be ale for every unarmed man. And your blades will be here when you leave." When stern Hakon scowled and complied, the others soon followed. Then she turned her fierce style of persuasion on Leif's startled warriors. "Now you."

"You'd better do as she says," Hakon advised his surly counterparts. "She's a Valkyr's daughter . . . and she fights like a mother wolf!"

Soon, two piles of blade-weapons were growing at her feet and Leif turned to Jorund with an awed grin.

"No wonder you fight so fiercely, Borgerson. With her in your furs, you must have to wrestle for your life every night."

Jorund threw back his head and laughed. The release purged the last of the tension that had kept him going during the fight and after. When Aaren's peace was well-nigh established, she hurried to slip her arm around Jorund's waist and help him up the steep embankment. He sank to his knees halfway up the slope, and in a blink was lying prone . . . claimed by exhaustion.

Aaren and Leif fell to their knees to see to him and realized he was merely sleeping. Leif ordered him carried to the hall to recover, and when Leif shoved to his feet he felt a strange clanging in his head and darkness closing in on him. He staggered and reached for Marta . . . and was suddenly weighing her down, bearing her to the ground with him.

The two young jarls were lifted and carried to Leif's hall for tending, under Aaren's and Marta's watchful eyes. The ale-feast would be delayed . . . it was announced . . . until the guests of honor regained consciousness.

As the last of the warriors trailed the others up the earthen wall, headed for the center of the village, Borger spotted his longtime rival hobbling along between a staff and a young warrior. He hurried Godfrey, who was steadying him, and caught up with Gunnar at the base of the mound. The two crusty old bears stood eyeing each other critically.

"You look like meat for old Hel's dogs," Borger finally declared, scrutinizing Gunnar's whitening hair and hunched shoulders with a smirk.

"And you look like an old bear with the mange," Gunnar responded through eyes narrowed to slits on Borger's brushy beard.

"Gone lame, I see," Borger snapped. "No wonder you wouldn't get off your horse at the ransom exchange."

"Took a wound, I see," Gunnar snarled, watching with taunting pleasure the way Borger clutched his side. "And reduced to using a Christian for a crutch!"

Borger's face reddened; that stung. "Sneer all you want, you dried-up old crack of arse-thunder . . . but it's *my son* drinking victory ale in *your hall* this night!"

Chapter Twenty-Three

Gunnar's long hall was just as Leif had told Marta . . . smaller than Borger's, but handsome in the extreme. Each post and rafter was beautifully carved and polished, and the main floor was laid stone, covered with clean, sweet-smelling rushes. Colorful weavings and banners hung from the rafters and the hearth glowed warmly.

Jorund and Leif were carried to sleeping closets where Leif's mother, Ida, tended them and pronounced they had been felled by exhaustion, nothing worse. Gunnar repeated Leif's orders for an ale-feast to his wife and she set thralls scurrying to erect the planking tables, bring in additional benches, and fetch ale barrels from the storehouse. Jorund's men were grudgingly permitted to enter the hall, since they bore no weapons. But Gunnar's generosity stopped short of allowing Borger inside and, that being the case, a number of Jorund's men refused to enter as well. They deposited themselves outside the main doors to wait for their jarl and their host to awaken.

Aaren asked to see her other young sister and Leif's mother sent for her. Miri came running with her arms open wide. Aaren hugged her tightly, not speaking for a time, then thrust Miri back an arm's length to look at her.

"You're all right? Not hurt in any way?" she demanded, stroking Miri's face and flaxen hair.

"I am well . . . I was so frightened, Aaren." Tears glistened in her eyes.

"All is well now. Jorund and Leif have made peace and you are free. And . . ." She scanned her warriors on the far end of the hall, finding Garth absent. "There is another here who has made our lives miserable on your account," she said with a grin. "Wait here, I'll fetch him."

Garth was one of those who waited outside the hall with Borger, intent on preserving his quarrelsome old father's pride. But when Aaren appeared with news that Miri waited inside and was eager to see him, Garth gave Borger a wordless wince of apology and bolted into the hall like a randy young stag. He scooped her up and whirled her around and around, then set her feet on the floor and kissed her breathless.

"Wed me, Miri . . . now . . . this night!" he insisted, struggling for breath, too. "For I swear, I'll not release you until you agree." She met his demand with an upraised chin and a fiery glint in her eyes.

"I am not sure," she declared stubbornly, letting her crystal-rimmed eyes work their persuasive magic on him.

His eyes widened and he looked a bit indignant. "You're not still angry with me for what happened in the hall that day?"

"You did not speak up for me, Garth Borgerson," she said with a perfect blend of sweetness and petulance. "Jorund asked you plainly which you would rather take to your breast . . . a blade or me. And you didn't choose me."

"Well, I—I didn't choose a blade, either," Garth sputtered in his own defense. When she suddenly wrestled to break free, he pulled her against him. "I want you, Miri. you're the light of my heart. You know that."

"You say so now. But I think you would rather sleep with your blade than with me," Miri said, lowering her chin so that she peered up at him through her lashes. "And I think I would not like a husband who would rather fight than make pleasure."

"Well, you're wrong, Miri." When she squirmed again in his embrace, he declared hotly: "Silly wench—of course I would much rather make pleasure with you than blade-fight!" His words boomed out over sudden quiet in the hall and after a shocked moment, peals of laughter rang out, from walls to roof beams. Garth whipped around, crimson-faced, to find both his comrades and his former enemies enjoying keenly his frantic attempts to appease his reluctant bride.

"Wed me, Miri!" He clasped her against him with a determined scowl.

Miri blushed prettily and smiled, having gotten the declaration she wanted to soothe her feminine pride. "I'll wed you, Garth Borgerson . . . as soon as jarl Jorund will allow!"

Jorund and Leif slept for several hours, time enough for the wounded from Jorund's and Aaren's camp to be moved into the village and for food to be prepared . . . and for Leif's men to become more accustomed to sharing their hall with Jorund's. Ida, Leif's mother, wisely held back the ale, to prevent the usual conflicts that came with hard drinking in a hall. And to ensure order, Aaren made herself . . . and the blade she had borrowed from Garth . . . quite visible to all.

When commotion near the hall doors drew their attention, Aaren went flying with Garth and Leif's mother to quell it. Outside, she found the two Hrolfs—Elder and Younger—in the hard grip of some of Leif's men. And Leif's men were being confronted mightily by Borger and those of Jorund's men who had remained outside. Aaren inserted herself into the fray with her blade ready and shouted for all to halt and shut their mouths.

"Hrolf! And Hrolf!" she exclaimed, turning on them. "Where have you been?"

Hrolf the Elder stared at her, then at his comrades lolling about in front of their erstwhile enemy's hall, and could scarcely speak. "W-we . . . sent a message. And waited and waited. Then found that the farmer's son had forgot the words of the message we made him learn . . . and was hiding out in the trees." He reddened deeply. "So . . . we decided to ride straight in and bring the jarl's message ourselves." He stopped and stared at her. "What's going on here, Serricksdotter?"

Aaren smiled, then laughed at goodly Hrolf's confusion.

"Peace, Hrolf! It's peace!"

The ale-feast was in all respects a celebration of the promise of peace between Leif and Jorund. Leif took the high seat, installing Marta in the slightly smaller chair beside his, and assigned Jorund and Aaren seats of honor on his right hand. Over Gunnar's sullen objections, Leif permitted Borger in the hall for the celebration . . . though he declined to offer the old jarl a seat of honor. The two former jarls sat across the hall from each other, exchanging sullen, hateful looks. But most of the men ignored them, and soon the merriment engulfed their animosity.

The first ale was poured and the victory toasts and declarations of peace were made. Leif saluted Jorund's courage and strength; Jorund honored Leif's strength and courage. But it was Aaren's toast that quieted the hall and conveyed the true meaning of what had just taken place.

"There were two victors this night," she proposed, raising her horn high and scanning the ale-reddened faces around them. "It was Jorund and Leif who fought . . . but the true victors were Peace and Mercy. I drink to them." After a stunned moment, everyone else in the hall drank, too. And when the ale was finished, another cheer went up.

As food was brought around, Jorund's eyes settled on Marta, who nestled so happily at Leif's side, then on Leif, whose arm seldom left Marta's waist. Aaren saw him staring at them in confusion, and she leaned close to whisper. "Marta says they took Christian vows this evening . . . before the fight." When she backed up her words with an emphatic nod, Jorund's surprise slid into a wondering smile.

"So that is why you were so eager to come to Gunnar's village . . . to speak of peace," he called to Marta, flicking a meaningful glance at Leif. Marta blushed prettily and her eyes danced.

"I cannot deny I was eager to see Leif again. And, of course, I hoped I could convince him of your desire for peace." She turned a stern look on Jorund. "I told you I was not afraid . . . but you didn't think a mere maid could speak to big, fierce warriors. If you *had* sent me . . . there might have been peace much sooner."

"That bears truth," Leif said, pulling Marta up and onto his lap. "If you had sent *her*, you would still have your winter grain." The comment made them all sober, and Leif looked at Marta, then at Jorund. "We had a bountiful harvest, too, my friend. We will have extra grain. Your people need not go hungry this winter."

"That is well, Leif." Jorund nodded, thinking on it. "My people will learn that peace between our clans will benefit them." Then he looked a bit sheepish. "And I have learned that from now on, whenever I talk with an adversary, I shall choose the prettiest maid in the village to be one of my peace-speakers." Aaren elbowed him in the ribs and he winced and amended it: "Or . . . or perhaps the prettiest warrior . . ." And they laughed.

At Leif's nod, Jorund finally called for Godfrey and he hurried forward to offer the words of binding for Garth and Miri, and to bless their union. Aaren watched with tears in her eyes, holding both Jorund's and Marta's hands.

There were more rounds of toasts and good wishes to the newly wedded: Leif and Marta, and Garth and Miri. Leif watched Garth with his bride and began to chuckle at Garth's overheated face and quaking frame. He extended his old enemy a surprising bit of mercy.

"Yon sleeping closet . . . on the left . . ." He nodded the direction. "I doubt my brothers will be able to find their way to it tonight, with all the ale they will drink."

Garth groped for words. Finding none, he seized Leif's hand instead and gave it a fierce grip. Then he snatched Miri from her seat and ran back through the hall with her, to the first available set of furs.

After several increasingly rowdy toasts, a disturbance broke out at the far end of the hall and Leif leaned across the table to Jorund. "You're the peace-maker, Brother. You deal with it." A hot glint entered his eye. "I was just wedded this day, and I have better things to do this night."

With that he rose and lifted Marta into his arms, carrying her back to his closet.

Leif set Marta on her feet on the platform where his furs were unrolled and kissed her deeply, luxuriating in the warmth of her mouth, in the soft curves of her body. When he pulled back in the dimness, his eyes were thin rings of silver around dark wells of desire and he emitted a low, hungry rumble from deep in his chest. "Remove your garments, Little Morsel," he said, nuzzling her neck and throat. "My eyes are as hungry for you as my body is. And my clumsy hands might rip your pretty kirtle."

"Your hands are not clumsy, Leif," she said quietly, unpinning the brooches on her shoulders to let her wrapped kirtle fall.

"They are tonight, Marta . . . they tremble and shame me with their eagerness." He ran his hands over her, tracing her hard-tipped breasts and soft, curving hips through the thin linen tunic. "Now the rest . . . I want to see you." Tenuously, she obeyed, and when she stood before him, naked, her eyes huge and luminous in her heartlike face, he groaned and stripped off his own tunic and pulled her into his arms.

"Now, Little Maiden," he said with a hungry rasp in his voice, "we'll see just how *tasty* you truly are." He lifted her and bore her back into the furs, covering her with his broad, hard body and devouring her slowly, sensuously from head to toe. By the time he joined their bodies, he knew each of her enticing flavors . . . and murmured a description of them hotly in her ear as he brought her to her first full taste of woman-pleasure.

Afterward, as they rested happily together, she wriggled against his big body and dragged her fingers down the middle of his taut belly. "It was wonderful, Leif. Aaren said it was worth waiting for." When he grinned lazily at her, she kissed his chest . . . then frowned and licked her lips . . . then licked his chest with her tongue. And suddenly she had a hot gleam in her eye.

"There is something you should know about us Serricksdotters," she said, sliding her supple young body over his heavily muscled frame, exploring these new sensations of physical desire and excitation.

"And what is that?" he said, sucking in a sharp breath as she wriggled against his most sensitive parts.

"We demand a certain . . . equality . . . from our men."

"Equality?" Leif laughed softly, until he realized she was deadly serious.

"Yea, equality." She seized his head between her hands and made slow, tantalizing circuits of his lips with her tongue. "And right now, I want to see how tasty *you* are."

After a few moments of allowing her equal exploration of him, he writhed and groaned pleasurably.

"Equality . . . I believe I could grow to like this idea. . . ."

Out in the hall, Jorund and Aaren had managed to enforce the peace on both sets of proud and fractious warriors. The old jarls, however, were another story entirely. As the ale settled hard in their senses, Borger and Gunnar had migrated to opposite ends of the same table, and had begun snapping at each other like two lame old turtles. Jorund grew tired of listening to them and set Godfrey between them to make sure they did not resort to more than verbal combat.

Poor Godfrey was hard-pressed to keep them from coming to blows around him, and finally issued them both a stern lecture on brotherliness and forgiveness, and a few choice words on how "A soft word turneth away wrath." Then he had the temerity to point to Jorund and Leif— their own sons!—as examples of fortitude, brotherhood, and proper manly conduct. Cagey old Gunnar paused and drew back, evaluating the forceful priest and his surprising persuasiveness.

"So, Borger Fat-beard," he said scornfully. "You've gone soft and *Christian* . . . keeping a priest around."

Borger sputtered and growled and glowered . . . staring at his old rival, trying to think of some way to best him. Then his eyes fell on Godfrey and he remembered: that cheek-turning nonsense had apparently worked for Jorund . . . more than once. It couldn't hurt to give it a try.

"Yea, Old Gunnar," he said with a duplicitously holy expression. "I believe I may take up this Christian belief, after all. The women love it. And this Christ fellow helped my Jorund tame a fierce she-wolf and strengthened his arm to victory against Leif this very night." He scratched his beard with taunting thoughtfulness. "Yea . . . I have recently decided to take Christian vows with my Helga. And I believe I am developing a yen to be"—he rolled his eyes, as if searching for the word—"*baptized.*"

Godfrey strangled on his ale, Borger guessed from the jerking of his shoulders. But it was Gunnar's shock that

Borger vowed to remember to his dying day. He looked like he'd swallowed a hen's egg whole and got it stuck halfway down. He reddened and clutched his throat and began to flap his arms, then cast frantically about for his walking staff. Borger shook with unholy glee as he sat watching Gunnar run from the "Christian taint." It was only when he refocused on Godfrey's glowing, moisture-rimmed eyes that he began to realize he might have put it on a bit too thick.

"Wait until Helga hears!" Godfrey began to gyrate joyfully. "She will be so pleased!"

Night was beginning to gather the twinkling stars and tuck them into her cloak, making way for the coming of the Sky-Traveler, when Jorund and Aaren escaped from the hall for a while. He led her to the edge of the village and up onto the earthen wall, well away from the noisy celebration. Pulling her to him, he kissed her again and again, reveling in the vibrant sense of life that surrounded him whenever he slipped into her arms.

"Jorund, I have never been so proud in my life as I was of you this night," she said, drawing back in his arms, feeling full to bursting with love and happiness. "You proved you could lead your men without a blade. And when you gave Leif his life, you made both your warriors and Leif's see strength in a new way . . . the way you had made me see it. You showed them there must be great strength before there can be great mercy . . . and that even the strongest warriors sometimes need to feel another's compassion."

"Is that what I did, Long-legs?" Jorund smiled and kissed her temple. "Your faith in me is nothing short of amazing. It makes me want to live up to it . . . to fulfill your confidence in me. I hope you won't be disappointed if many of my warriors turn out to be very much the same as they were . . . convinced that might makes right. They still have a great deal to learn about strength and peace." He chuckled, a low, sweet rumble. "And I am beginning to think I do, too.

"I thought that once it was settled with Leif and Gunnar, it would be settled. But tonight I saw that there are Hakon and Thorkel and young Svein and Erik still to convince . . .

and probably Garth, too, as soon as he can take his mind from Miri. And for every querulous Hakon and doubting Thorkel in our camp, there is undoubtedly one in Leif's." He sighed. "I have a feeling my peace-making days have just begun."

She laughed softly and laid her head on his chest, relishing the warmth he radiated in the cold night air. "Well, you made a wonderful start. Because of you and your courage, Jorund Borgerson, Marta and Miri both have husbands they love . . . the women of both villages will have no more sons to mourn . . . and my babe will grow up knowing what a wise and wonderful father he has."

"Ummm," he murmured, kissing her ear, her neck, and nosing his way into the opening of her tunic. "You give me too much credit—" He froze, then thrust her back. "*Your* babe?" He set her back by the shoulders and looked her up and down. "What babe? Are you with child?"

"I—I don't . . . I just meant . . . when I have a babe . . . someday," she said, lowering her head.

"Aaren!" He gave her a gentle shake.

"I . . . well . . ." She swallowed hard and turned her face away when he ducked his head to peer into her eyes. "I told you . . . I don't know very much about these things." In the thin moonlight, he couldn't quite see the heat from her face, but he could feel it.

"It has something to do with your woman's time. That's how the women always know; it stops coming. When have you . . . since . . ." His grin grew even broader. "You haven't! Not since that time in my bathing hut!"

"Jorund!" she said, giving him a shove and trying to turn away. He reeled her back into his arms and pried up her chin. "That doesn't prove anything," she protested. "It wasn't that long ago."

"No," he conceded with a wicked grin. "But it's a wonderful start." Suddenly his heart was overflowing and he pulled Aaren close. "It's *all* a wonderful start! The peace . . . the high seat . . . our loving . . . your sisters' marriages . . . and now a babe." He kissed her well and long. "Perhaps I was wrong. Perhaps it did start with an enchantment."

In the cool red-streaked dawn, as they were returning to the hall, a small, bent figure in a tattered woolen cloak stepped out of the deep shadows near the hall doors . . . straight into their path. Jorund pulled Aaren to the side, to move around the old woman, but she tottered quickly and planted herself full in their path again.

"You're the one," the time-withered woman said with a trace of awe, trembling as she pointed a gnarled finger at Aaren. The cloak she was wearing drooped wider, and Aaren and Jorund glimpsed a number of odd amulets hanging around the old woman's neck. They slowed and Aaren glanced up at Jorund, who wore an expression as puzzled as hers. The old woman squinted faded eyes at Aaren, searching her face, her shoulders, her very body. "Are you the Wild Raven . . . come back to us?"

"Am I what?" Aaren asked, frowning at the old woman's odd manner. She had never seen a woman so old or so oddly garbed. When the woman made a circular sign in the air with her finger, Aaren's eyes widened. "Who are you?"

"I am an old one . . . a far-seeing woman . . ." The old crone crept closer, staring up at Aaren with a mixture of awe and dread. "Are you the Wild Raven, come back to our village?"

Aaren shook her head, puzzled and growing uneasy at the woman's strange manner. "What is this *Wild Raven* you think me to . . ." Then the impact of it struck her. *Raven*. The word filled her mind and drew all her awareness to focus on that dried husk of a woman.

"The old jarl's bondwoman . . . the one called Wild Raven. It has been many years, but you have the look of her . . . and the size of her." The old woman came still closer and reached out a hand to touch Aaren, looking as if she expected Aaren to disappear in a puff of smoke. "She was great and tall like you, with burnished hair like you. And your face . . . it is the same nose and mouth. But perhaps she would be older now . . . unless she was indeed taken to Valhalla."

At the mention of Valhalla, Aaren was desperate to hear more of this great woman who had borne her face and part of the only name she had for her mother. "I am not the one you seek," she said, "but you must come with me, old woman, and tell me of this Wild Raven."

They led the old woman indoors and found her a place by the still glowing hearth, in the now quiet hall, where most of the warriors were sleeping on benches and tables. They got the woman a cup of ale to wet her throat and settled on a bench before her. Her eyes had never left Aaren, and Jorund sensed that Aaren sought an answer to the riddle of her origin in this old crone's tale.

"Who are you, old woman?" Jorund asked, feeling Aaren's hand tight on his arm and seeing the tension in her face. "Are you a *volva*?"

"Nej." She shook her head, but there was a glint in her age-faded eyes. "I have not the secret wisdom . . . though I sometimes see things. I nursed the old jarl's wife, Ida, when she was a babe and was sent here from jarl Olaf's village with her when she came to wed Gunnar. It was then I saw her . . . the Wild Raven."

"She was here? In this village?" Aaren asked, sliding to the edge of the bench so that her knees touched the old woman's. Her heart was beating like a small, tight drum in her breast.

"Yea . . . Gunnar's old father, jarl Harald, stole her on his last raid Eastway. She was his bondwoman, and his heart and loins burned for her with a fire like that of the Black Dwarfs' forge. But her heart was already given to one in her homeland . . . she did not want old Harald. He garbed her in the finest cloth and set fine shoes upon her feet . . . haltered her neck and wrists with gold, but still she fought him each time he took her. He was a ruthless old bear of a man . . . he bragged of her fierceness and called her his Wild Raven."

"What happened to her?" Aaren said.

"She was carried off by Odin . . . to Valhalla."

Aaren sucked in a sharp breath and her face paled. She somehow knew, beyond all doubt, that the old woman was speaking of her mother. "How do you know she was carried off? Tell me . . . please!"

The old woman sipped her ale and wiped her shrunken mouth. "The harvests were bad . . . there was much hunger.

For two years it seemed the gods scowled on this village. The priests who came, the ones who served Odin, looked at the Wild Raven and declared that she was to blame. Odin wanted her for himself, they said . . . and he would withhold the rain and send hard freezes to kill the grain . . . until old Harald gave her up. Some of the women hated the Wild Raven, for Harald had cast out his old wives from his hall and placed her in their stead. Now they grew angry with Harald and roused their men to demand she be given to Odin to appease him. Harald resisted. But after another hard winter, he handed her over to the priests."

Jorund watched Aaren, felt the trembling of her hands and the bright pain of discovery in her eyes. He wanted to protect her against whatever these revelations might hold. But she had a right to know. He moved closer and put an arm around her waist, guessing what was to come.

"The priests carried her to the sacred grove in the mountains . . . and there they hanged her, along with others the runes had marked for sacrifice . . . as a gift to old Odin."

"They hanged her?" Aaren whispered, her face and heart filled with anguish at the path the Norns had chosen for the one who gave her birth. She was stolen from her home, held captive, and forced to endure another's lust for her . . . then finally hanged as a sacrifice to a jealous god at the demand of jealous women. The old woman nodded.

"They hanged her and the others at sunset, as was the custom. And they said Odin came and claimed her in the night . . . for when they went to cut the sacrifices in the morning, she was gone." The old crone paused again to drink of her ale with a quaking hand. "The priests said Odin was pleased . . . for the harvest the next year was so great that our bins overflowed. But Harald grieved sorely for her and grew so angry that he slew two of the priests. Soon after he was killed in battle and Gunnar became jarl."

Aaren sat a while in silence, her eyes glistening. "What was she like, this Wild Raven? Did you know her name?"

"Ahhh." The old woman wiped her faded eyes with a gnarled hand. "She was frightening at first, because of her size. But when old Harald was out of sight, she had a tender way about her. She saved me from a beating more than once. It was hard for her to learn our ways and our talk, but she spoke to me of her people once. They were rich and her father was a king, she said." The old woman examined Aaren's face. "You look much like her."

"I believe I am her daughter," Aaren said with a tightness that spoke of deep emotion. She turned to Jorund with tear-rimmed eyes. "I think I have found my mother. Father Serrick said he called my mother *Fair Raven*. And this Wild Raven was a fierce fighter . . . and I look like her. Then it must have been her plumage my father stole."

But even as she said it, the sound of it was odd in her ears. Somehow—after the testing of will and limb and heart in the fiery reality of living—talk of plumage and Valkyrs and enchantments seemed like tales spun by a fireside . . . less than real, less than true. The stormy passage her thoughts were making left its turbulence in her face.

Jorund smiled tenderly and ran his hands up her arms to hold her shoulders gently. "Or perhaps it was all of her he stole . . . from the grove where she was sacrificed. In the old days, when they hanged to Odin, the victims sometimes lived—" He halted, not wishing to burden her further with such images. "Aaren." He took her hands in his and turned her more fully to him.

"There is no Odin," he said quietly. "So Odin could not have stolen her. I believe the thief was your father . . . the Sword-stealer. Don't you see . . . he stole more than plumage, he stole the woman herself. And he took her with him and cared for her."

Whether he stole for her plumage first or not . . . Serrick had stolen his Fair Raven, of that there was no doubt. And in Aaren's heart, sorrow and joy mingled inseparably.

"And he loved her," she whispered, tears rolling down her face. "He was a strong and good man . . . he could be gentle. Perhaps she found some happiness with him."

A warm wash of feeling overwhelmed her and she sank into his arms and wept . . . for the mother she never knew . . . for Serrick's pain at losing her . . . for so much loss. Jorund pulled her head against his shoulder and let her cry. After a while, he looked up at the old woman, whose eyes were distant and watery.

"Did you know her birth name . . . this Wild Raven?" he asked quietly. The old crone frowned and wagged her head—then seemed to recall something. After a moment she answered as best she could.

"Anjika . . . or some such. Old Harald did not like it, so he called her the other."

"*Anjika*. You have done much good, old woman. Stay here and warm yourself, and I will see you are repaid richly for your tale," he said. Then he lifted Aaren and carried her to the sleeping closet Leif had offered them.

He set her on her feet by the wooden bench and turned to close the curtain, but she refused to let him go. He held her close and felt the life-hunger in the tightness of her arms around him. After a while, she sniffed and wiped her wet cheeks.

"My mother was a mortal woman . . . not a Valkyr," she whispered thickly. "A great and glorious woman, a fighter, a woman fit for a god . . . but not an immortal." She swallowed hard, her face filled with an odd blend of sadness and relief. "That makes me . . ."

"A *woman*," he declared, grinning. "A great and glorious woman, a fierce fighter, daughter of a captive king's daughter, and a woman fit for a god . . . but destined to be the cherished wife of a rich Norse jarl."

Aaren bit her lip as a smile spread beneath her tears. "Yea . . . I am a woman." She said it louder. "I am a woman." Then louder still, embracing it on a new level with each repetition. "A woman—I'm a *woman*!" She clasped his head between her hands and gave him a fierce, sultry look of determination. "And you know that that makes you?"

"A lucky man," he answered, pulling her against him, luxuriating in the softness of her breasts and the hardness of her thighs. "A proud man." He flexed and raked his rousing hardness against her woman-softness. "And just now . . . a very hungry man."

"Ummm," she said joyfully, pulling his head down to speak against his mouth. "Well said, Hungry Husband. Come, and I'll feed you."

They sank into the soft pallet of fleeces and furs, stripping clothes and kissing and caressing. Jorund handled her tenderly, stroking, marveling anew at the way she was made . . . at the way their bodies blended and moved as one . . . and at the way their very spirits seemed to meet and join in their loving. Aaren responded from the very depths of her soul . . . womanly, open, receptive . . . taking him in deeply, enfolding him with her softness and her strength. And together they rode crest after crest of passion, pushing to the very limits of sensation . . . then tumbling into bright, foaming waves of pleasure and release that drained slowly and left them joined in pleasant exhaustion.

They lay together for a while in warm, sweet silence. Then Aaren's brow knitted with a new thought and she raised onto her elbow and contemplated him with a question in her eyes, which finally made it to her tongue.

"Are you . . . disappointed to learn that I had a mortal mother?" she asked, with a hint of anxiety.

He laughed and pulled her on top of him. "Not in the least," he declared, his eyes glowing with mischief. "I never believed in your enchantment anyway. I always thought it much more likely that you had been suckled and raised by wolves."

"W-why . . . you!" She gave him a punch on the shoulder and he rolled, dumping her onto the floor with a thud. She squealed, scrambled up, and began to stalk him with her eyes burning and her hair a magnificent tangle around her naked shoulders. He narrowly escaped her pounce and the chase was on . . . albeit limited to the narrow confines of a sleeping closet. She caught him standing atop the furs and backed him against the wall. Then his massive arms caught her tight against him and his mouth captured hers, hotly, masterfully. Her wrestling slowly became a warm, sinuous movement against his body.

She was caught again . . . tamed again . . . loved again.

Standing up in the midst of the furs, he picked her up and began to swing her around and around . . . caught, himself, in the real and unending enchantment of his love for his remarkable she-wolf.

From that day on, Jorund Borgerson was known by a number of new names among the clans of the Norsemen:

Jorund Peace-bringer, Jorund Strong-hand, Jorund the Bare-fisted, and Jorund the Bold. But in the depths of the cold northern nights, as he lay in the she-wolf's lair, he was known as Jorund Wolf-tamer and Jorund Breath-stealer . . . and after a few months, when the little form in the birch cradle stirred, as Father Jorund.